MIDNIGHT
AT THE
CINEMA PALACE

A Novel

CHRISTOPHER TRADOWSKY

Simon & Schuster

NEW YORK   AMSTERDAM/ANTWERP   LONDON

TORONTO   SYDNEY/MELBOURNE   NEW DELHI

Simon & Schuster
1230 Avenue of the Americas
New York, NY 10020

This book is a work of fiction. Any references to historical events, real people, or real places are used fictitiously. Other names, characters, places, and events are products of the author's imagination, and any resemblance to actual events or places or persons, living or dead, is entirely coincidental.

First Simon & Schuster hardcover edition June 2025

SIMON & SCHUSTER and colophon are registered trademarks of Simon & Schuster, LLC

Simon & Schuster strongly believes in freedom of expression and stands against censorship in all its forms. For more information, visit BooksBelong.com.

For information about special discounts for bulk purchases, please contact Simon & Schuster Special Sales at 1-866-506-1949 or business@simonandschuster.com.

The Simon & Schuster Speakers Bureau can bring authors to your live event. For more information or to book an event, contact the Simon & Schuster Speakers Bureau at 1-866-248-3049 or visit our website at www.simonspeakers.com.

Interior design by Kathryn A. Kenney-Peterson

Manufactured in the United States of America

10   9   8   7   6   5   4   3   2   1

Library of Congress Cataloging-in-Publication Data is available.

ISBN 978-1-6680-5726-1
ISBN 978-1-6680-5728-5 (ebook)

For Kathryn and Sean

Midnight
at the
Cinema Palace

Amarcord

IT WAS HIS FAVORITE RECURRING dream, always returning unprompted, always startling and delighting, leaving him a little wistful as he woke. As long as he lived in the city, every few months, as the seasons slipped by unnoticed, Walter would dream of snow falling over San Francisco.

There were many versions of the dream, but most did not feel especially cold. In most versions the snow was sparse, decorative, filmic snow with giant, waxy flakes, its silence the silence of a soundstage. From a bright overcast sky, fat flakes would fall evenly, equitably, over the Sunset, the Mission, the little saddle ridge where his apartment perched between the Haight and the Castro. Each neighborhood would surrender its character to the slow erasure of its details, its peculiarities, its grime and delights alike. He could see snowflakes catching in the Victorian traceries, settling upon gables, climbing stoops, and drifting along doorsteps, clogging the painted lathework of the Queen Annes. He dreamed of snow falling over the gardens of succulents and into their green crevices, glancing off the orange spikes of the birds-of-paradise, dusting the gargantuan thistles that were artichokes in full bloom, crowned by bristles of primordial purple.

Sometimes the snow whisked down among the cypresses like a train of heavy lace; sometimes it floated amid the date palms, as light as poplar spores. Or it spiraled atomically, like the tiny particles in the snow globe dropped from the hand of the dying Kane. When it fell along the Tenderloin alleys, delicately as if sifted there, even the dumpsters appeared quaint, Dickensian. In one intensely beautiful dream, the snow arrived as hoarfrost. Freezing fog trundling in from Ocean Beach deposited ice crystals on every branch and spire, frosting the deco towers, the green pagodas and granite lions of Chinatown. For an instant the city was etched in glass.

Rarely did Walter dream of formidable snowfall, a Midwestern storm like the ones he knew as a kid. But in one dream the snow piled so high it stopped traffic, icing the inclines and pulling buses from their wires, sleet freezing the rails of the cable cars. Sedans hunched under mounded banks. It was a vision of spontaneous jubilation as the city took a snow day. Walter— who in waking life was afraid of heights and never dreamed of flying—rode giddily on a ski lift over downtown as he took in the scene. There was a snowball battle in Union Square, and people sledding down the streets on serving trays; a luge race launched from Grace Cathedral, sledders rocketing down Sacramento Street toward the bay. The hideous brutalist Embarcadero fountain had frozen over; couples skated across it like holiday shoppers. Then the dream warped into a nightmare, as some wretched souls began to freeze midstep or drown in slush, while manic revelries raged all around them.

Walter didn't particularly miss the winter, not in waking life—that is, his new California life—so he was puzzled at first by the dream's snow-blind nostalgia. Only once was it clear to him, lucidly, in the dream itself, what had provoked it. He was walking through an ancient cloud forest in the botanical gardens, where massive tree ferns loomed amid soft veils of fog. It was so foggy he might have been in a cloud on a mountaintop for all he knew. Bright flakes began to tear from the fog and land in the moss that lined the path. Before him was a green pond, edged by a stone ledge, upon which a fat peacock waddled in a circle, seeking footing. As the peacock turned toward him fanning its enormous tail, which shimmered and waved its ultramarine eyes, Walter was certain he was dreaming and said, "You can't fool me, bird, I know you," as if the bird might answer and contradict him. It was none other than the peacock from Fellini's *Amarcord*, caught on film in a stone square in a freak Italian snowstorm. He had seen the movie the evening before, and all night long Nino Rota's score feverishly invaded his sleep. Walter awoke that morning wondering not the usual confusions provoked by the dream (What month was it? What season? On what planet had he landed, and who did he know here?), but more technically, more mysteriously: *How on earth did Fellini get that shot?*

Cléo from 5 to 7

"YOU DIDN'T *FOLLOW ME HERE*?" Eliot asked.

"What are you talking about?" Walter laughed a little as he toweled behind his ears. "You mean, just now? Down the hallway?"

They had raced through the apartment, flat-footed and dripping from a post-sex shower, down the long hall to Eliot's room, careful to avoid his roommates. Walter sifted through a tide of gray sheets eddied at the foot of the futon. He fished his boxer briefs from the folds and pulled them on.

"I mean, of course you followed me here." Eliot was scowling with childish sternness. He was nude, standing in a square yard of afternoon sunlight, wringing his long brown hair with a blue towel until it began to curl at the ends. "I mean: *You didn't move here to be with me?*"

"No! Of course not!"

Walter knelt on the floor and searched for his shirt among the slacker flotsam littering Eliot's carpet: flip-flops, book stacks, a fan of utility bills, a Danish butter cookie tin of hash.

"All I was saying was I was inspired, I guess. When you came back to Oberlin last year, it was inspiring, the way you described San Francisco: the nightlife, the street fairs, *Halloween*. You said, *You can just be gay and not have to think about it.* You sold me on it, that's all."

"It's getting late." Eliot tossed his towel onto the bed. "I have to get ready to meet Richard. This was a mistake."

The sun cut across Eliot's back and butt as he stood before the dresser, roughly shuttling drawers in and out. Walter was cross. He tried not to admire Eliot's sunlit skin, his shoulders copiously freckled—kind of animalistic—or how his buttocks clenched as he raised both arms to pull a margarine-yellow T-shirt over his head.

His lover. In fact, *his first love.* It was funny, really, how none of that meant anything. How language could tarnish, becoming antique before your very eyes. Maybe some of his friends—granted, his friends were oddballs—referred to their lovers and first loves, but no one he knew ever *made love.* He and Eliot had certainly never *made love.*

They had met at Oberlin two years ago when Walter was nineteen and newly out, and Eliot was a senior. For three terms Walter had admired him from across a campus lush with prodigious maples and trucked-in sod. Eliot exuded a belated hippie coolness: volubly out and proud, he headed the Lambda Society and talked about politics and social justice easily, freewheelingly, as if he were kicking a hacky sack. A strict vegan, he lived in Harkness, the coolest dorm, a veggie co-op notorious for its coed showers. He'd brag about his dorm as a bastion of bookishness and free love, a cross between the Algonquin Round Table and a nonstop love-in. Somehow both a stoner and an overachiever, Eliot also edited the student lit mag. The night they got together, they had run into each other at a kegger at Zechiel House, when Eliot separated Walter from the herd to congratulate him: that spring the *Plum Creek Review* would publish a sonnet he'd submitted. Eliot praised his poem, saying it was "surprisingly intelligent—for a freshman."

"I'm a sophomore," Walter said. "We were in a lecture together last spring."

It didn't matter. Walter had spent too many years damming up his adolescent, then postadolescent, then young adult lust to care if Eliot was a snob. Eliot was handsome enough, odd looking in an appealing way, his easy smile his sexiest feature. His long hair accentuated his forehead, which was unusually high—or maybe it was that his eyes were set low in his head. And maybe it was his massive forehead, and a kind of anatomical literalism, that had given Eliot the idea he was brainier than anyone else. That night Walter had followed Eliot back to his single in Harkness, and they had an on-again, off-again, off-again, off-again, on-again dalliance for the remainder of the school year. It lasted several months, or two weeks, or probably less than twenty-four hours, depending on who was counting and how.

Words Walter had learned from Eliot that spring: *counterculture, enjambment, rimming, fuckbuddy*. Words Eliot learned from Walter: *MacGuffin, crossfade, hornswoggle, watercress*.

And now, San Francisco, and new lives for each of them. Yet *how new* were those lives if they were still captive to their grubby undergraduate urges? It disturbed Walter that two years later Eliot was more or less living in a replication of his dorm room. The view from the window had changed: no longer a banner of Ohioan greenness seen from on high, but a range of dusty, dusky philodendrons in a sluggish courtyard garden. The futon was new, as was the dresser, but the trappings were the same: the large batik mandala, the CD towers flanking frayed posters for Soft Cell and Indigo Girls, the Christmas lights lazily tacked near the ceiling, the bong and roach clips and Trojans, the pervasive smell of burnt sage barely masking the deeper redolence of pot.

Walter *hadn't* followed Eliot to San Francisco. He *hadn't* moved to be with him, though his behavior since arriving was making it hard for him to argue this to Eliot and to himself. He simply didn't know anybody else, so naturally Eliot was the first person he called, and naturally they met up, on a cozily gloomy Wednesday night in late June, at Blondie's on Valencia. Wedged in a back booth, they spent two hours catching up over a few rounds of bracing cheap gin and tonics that smelled like aftershave. Walter told Eliot it was his birthday, his twenty-second.

"Happy birthday!" Eliot said. A discreet burp, a lone hiccup. "Uh, was I supposed to remember that?"

"No reason you would," said Walter.

"Oh, you know what? I remember now that you're a Cancer. Like, a *total Cancer*, always shrinking back into your shell."

Walter half smiled and tried not to slump his head into his rib cage or do anything remotely molluscoid.

Eliot loudly vacuumed the ice in his highball with a straw. "Well, since it's your birthday, we should probably go back to my place and fuck, right?"

And that's how it started again, after a two-year hiatus, their *fuckbuddyship*, their "friendship" with "benefits." Which Walter knew from the jump start he was getting all wrong. He knew—or at least he thought he knew—*friends with benefits* was meant to combine the conviviality of friendship with all the freebie orgasms you could handle, not all the baggage of overfamiliarity with the added anxieties of sex.

"Richard's picking me up in an hour," said Eliot. He held his bong in one hand and dangled a belt from the other. He looked to be weighing whether he had time to get stoned before he finished dressing. "You can't be here. And by the way, when *you do* meet Richard, *we're not lovers*."

"We literally had sex five minutes ago."

"You know what I mean, Wally. Nothing's happening here. *We're not together*." With a regretful shrug Eliot placed the bong back where it lived on the dresser.

"*I know that*—believe me—don't you think I know that?"

Walter cringed, recalling the time two years before when he'd brought Eliot a bouquet of grocery store carnations, incompatible pinks, cheerfully crackling in their cellophane. Eliot laughed when he saw them, then freaked out, saying, *This is all moving way too fast*.

"Sometimes I wonder if you *do* know it. Earlier . . . you gave me a look."

"A look? What look? When?"

"Right after you came."

"*We're friends*, for fuck's sake," said Walter emphatically, like he'd read all the fine print in the contract. He perched shirtless on the side of the futon, despite Eliot's goading to move along. "It's not a big deal."

"Good," said Eliot, "because I'm finally getting somewhere with Richard, and I don't want to fuck this up. Which you should know. Because we're friends."

Walter nodded, sighing inwardly. He wondered why he'd put up with Eliot for so long and racked his brain for any motive other than desperation. Eliot did have a weird charisma: he was headstrong and blunt in a way that could be disarming, a style of bitchy charm venerated by so many gay guys. Soon after moving, Eliot had taken a job helming a blender at a juice bar in the Castro called the Banana Hammock in hopes of meeting as many boys as he could as quickly as possible. And it worked. Eliot had a ton of gay male friends, and there was no chance that Walter was the only one enjoying benefits.

Friendship can be kind of awful, he thought, and this one was quickly becoming a sort of penance. Eliot was an irrepressible oversharer. Some weeks back he had assumed they were close enough, and casual enough, that he started confiding in Walter about Richard, the postdoctoral fellow in comp lit at Stanford, to whom he had slipped his number with Richard's wheatgrass smoothie. "Older men are so hot, don't you think?" Eliot asked. "Mmm, and bald guys, too?" As his *friend*, Walter had been privy to the play-by-play of how Eliot had reeled in this distinguished older gentleman like a wild blue marlin on a steel line. The courtship began with a few starchy dates in nice restaurants with button-down shirts (Richard was a PhD, after all) and culminated, after an entire month, in a night of (to hear Eliot tell it) *total sexual abandon* in exotic, erotic Palo Alto.

"I was beginning to think he wasn't interested or that he was frigid or something," Eliot crowed in the recap. "Wrong on both counts."

Some morbid part of Walter wanted to stay put, half dressed, planted right there on the futon, until Richard rang the front bell. Then he could ask Richard himself about being a closet case all through college and most of grad school, and hear the details of how his marriage had exploded when he came out and how his poor wife—his high school sweetheart, no less—was devastated, *she never saw it coming.* How had it come to this? Why did Walter *know all this* about a stranger's failed marriage? Why did he know, among other things, that Richard loved gewürztraminer and bottoming? Why had it been necessary for him to learn that Richard had a big dick that curved to the right like a boomerang? (*I can definitely work with it, though!* Eliot laughed and reassured Walter.) And all this information was offered freely, without Walter having to pantomime the slightest sign of interest.

"Is something wrong?" Eliot asked, shuffling into a pair of checkered Vans. "Walleye, you're being a space cadet."

"Please don't call me Walleye," said Walter. He loathed the nickname, Eliot's coinage, which to his dismay a subset of his college friends picked up and ran with. And yet somehow he didn't mind it as much as *Wally*, the nickname he'd been trying his whole life to outrun.

A lone spider plant sat in a pot on the sill, blades spread, pressing the force field of sunlit glass, longing for the freedom of the garden. Suddenly Walter thought he understood which *look* he had given Eliot after he came.

"Why did you swallow this time?"

"What do you mean?"

"I warned you I was coming," said Walter. "I pulled away—and you swallowed anyway."

"Uh, I thought it was hot?" Eliot, fully dressed now, handed Walter his T-shirt and socks, which had migrated across the room with the bedding. "Plus you're negative, right? Anyway, I read somewhere recently that stomach acid kills the virus. It's not a big deal!"

Walter couldn't believe his ears. In college Eliot had been as vigilant about prophylactics as he was about veganism, expounding the miracles of latex condoms and dental dams to anyone in earshot. He'd told Walter once to quit flossing because it made oral sex less safe. If nothing else, Walter had Eliot to thank for his gingivitis.

"*As far as I know* I am negative. But you don't know how many guys I'm sleeping with."

"Uh, OK, how many guys are you sleeping with, Wally?" Eliot strolled off to hang the towels back up in the bathroom.

Walter dressed and hustled out the door in plenty of time to avoid running into hot, balding Professor Boomerang on the front stoop. Yet that was the moment, the golden hour, descending Eliot's stairs into an unusually clear, gratuitously warm summer evening in Bernal Heights, that he decided to call it quits with Eliot, or at least no more fucking around. Being casual was one thing, but all at once he realized that even the most casual relationship required, somewhere within its bright afternoon fug, some mote of trust. It wasn't because Eliot was sleeping with Richard or any of the Banana Hammock regulars; it was because Walter had *no idea* how many fuckbuddies Eliot might have, or what his real boundaries around sex were, or how they had morphed and migrated since college.

So he called off the sex. But friendship is sticky, insidiously so. And whatever else happened in his love life going forward, however much he would like to deny it, Eliot Chambliss would always have been his first.

Late that summer, Eliot pulled the one stunt that Walter almost couldn't forgive him for: he stood Walter up for a movie date.

Cléo from 5 to 7—considered Agnès Varda's masterpiece—was playing at the Roxie as part of a French New Wave film festival. It was rarely shown, and Walter was desperate to see it, and he'd invited Eliot over a week in advance. They'd agreed to meet at the theater at 9:10, twenty minutes before the screening. When he arrived at nine there was a line, so he got two tickets, then waited a half hour for Eliot to show. It began to rain; nattering drops stirred the leaves of the large ficus he stood under. People without umbrellas began to scurry; soon Sixteenth Street was slicked black, freshly reeking, streaming with white and red headlights, taillights. Walter waited another ten minutes until the previews were over, then went in by himself. He would have gone home if he hadn't wanted to see the film so badly. The only seats remaining were in the last two rows, which was OK in a way, since he didn't much care to be seen alone amid an audience of Friday-night couples high on French New Wave romance.

The film was so wonderful that Walter almost didn't care that he'd been stood up. In fact he could almost have forgotten about it entirely. He often preferred to see movies alone, free to love it or loathe it (or some amalgamation of loving and loathing) without worrying whether his companion might be dying of boredom. The genius of Varda's movie was that it seemed thrillingly loose, free-form, and candid—at times even haphazard—but it was all a trick. The entire film was choreographed—timed out to the minute, its themes resonant in nearly every frame. Like a portal punched through time into 1962 Paris, the camera stalks Cléo, a young, gorgeous aspiring pop singer, in the two hours leading up to a meeting with her doctor, who will give her the results of a cancer screening. To Walter, there was something so daring about the way Varda revealed the whole story in the first five minutes: a fortune teller reading Cléo's cards spills everything, including the fatal diagnosis. Yet the film was so agile, so light and delightful, even dance-like, that Walter wasn't prepared for how hard it hit him, simply because he knew how Cléo felt. He knew what it was to wait a week for a test result, potentially a terminal one; he knew how agonizing those last couple hours could be, when every hypochondriac impulse in you rises up at once. He knew—as she did—how to pretend to agree with friends that he was being dumb and overreacting. He thought of his friend Sarah, who had held his hand at the free clinic, the one time he and Eliot had had a brief scare (a broken condom), and Eliot couldn't go with him because he was playing ultimate Frisbee. The entire night before, he'd mouthed the foxhole prayers, and in answer a chorus of demons whispered, assuring him that, for whatever brief respite of joy sex had provided, he was now *totally fucked*. An antibody test is a death sentence, right up until the final moment of reprieve. As Cléo cries to her friend Angèle, *I might as well be dead already!*

Halfway through the film, Cléo is compelled by her songwriters to rehearse a new song, and in the middle of singing, her composure cracks when she realizes the lyrics they've written for her, cruelly, are about confronting mortality: you do it alone, in the end, totally alone, and all your worldly ties and all your youthful beauty won't save you. It wasn't a good song; it had a cheesy melody, pretentious lyrics, and flights of chords so melodramatic it was almost silly, so Walter was surprised to find himself sobbing along with Cléo, then laughing at himself—*How humiliating, surrounded by all these couples*—as he wiped his face with his coat sleeve and slumped in his chair, sliding down as far as he could go and still see the screen.

That night, Walter assumed he'd been stood up for Richard, but Eliot never admitted as much. The next afternoon there was a message on Walter's machine. In lieu of an apology it contained an unbelievable story about how Eliot had been riding the 47 Van Ness to the theater when the bus driver lost control and crashed into a telephone pole in the parking lot of Whiz Burgers. People were injured, and everyone was detained by the police for questioning. "It was scary, but I'm OK," Eliot's voice warbled on the little cassette.

Walter couldn't believe it: *Whiz Burgers?* It seemed so far-fetched—the bus would have had to cross all that oncoming traffic. But if it was a lie, at least it had the virtue of being elaborate: so ridiculous it could have been true, because who would make up such a thing? Well, Eliot Chambliss, it seemed. And maybe that was one of the perverse pleasures of friendship, that you never fully knew your friends, or at least not what they were capable of.

Breathless

WALTER USUALLY HAD AN HOUR off for lunch, which often seemed like too much time. The one superpower being a temp gave him was, apparently, invisibility. In the engineering firm where he'd been filing and refiling blueprints, there was a cubicle class to which he didn't even arise, having neither cubicle, nor computer, nor quote-of-the-day calendar, nor Kodachrome vacation collage pinned up in his periphery. He had a closet to manage, with a vertical stack of cubbies, a librarian's ladder on wheels, and a standing desk with a ledger. No windows, no daylight, no company. One clique from the office, all twentysomethings maybe a little older than him, slipped out every day a little before noon to grab sandwiches at the Boudin nearby. They never asked him along. Why would they? He'd be gone in a few weeks at most.

So Walter took the hour as an opportunity, a chance to explore downtown. It never occurred to him to pack a lunch; he'd already embraced a vision of himself as a terrible cook. Couldn't make so much as a half-decent sandwich. Currently, he was training himself to eat alone in public and be fine with it. Not an easy task; to him there was still something mortifying about dining alone: reading, or pretending to read—daydreaming, eyes down, ears cocked, eavesdropping—while the gears of commerce whirred around you. Whenever he sat alone for table service, he felt like there was bright yellow caution tape around him, a sign over his head announcing: "Approach with Caution: Not a Friend in the World."

Many venues in the financial district were ideal for dining solo and remaining unbothered: steam-propelled cafés with to-go focaccia sandwiches, sushi bars so efficient they ticked like Swiss clocks, the rare (and middling) downtown taqueria. Tucked away around Chinatown, railroad lunch counters offered piles of satiny chow mein and lukewarm dim sum. Inexhaustible worker bees raced in wing tips back to their desks with burritos or bento boxes, some with hauls for the whole office. Behind big glass windows, pinstriped executives still had two-martini lunches that climaxed in exquisite desserts: crème brûlée, acquisitions; tiramisu, mergers. As often as not, Walter would order a Polish Boy and a bag of Old Dutch chips from a cheerfully gruff hot dog vendor by Union Square.

It was a beautiful September day, and the weather had been so clear and warm for so many days on end that he had started to take the financial district sunshine—abundant, however tranched by the shade of towers—for granted. He was drifting down Powell Street toward Union Square when he happened by Sears Fine Food and thought he'd peek inside.

As he opened the door, he was greeted by the intoxicating smell of clarified butter seizing upon a short-order griddle. What's more: bacon fat, onions frying, the wonderful warmth of breakfast starches. A waitress flew by and, having sized him up as a solo diner, flapped her check pad toward the back wall and shouted, "Counter's clearing out. Grab a seat!" At the counter a family of four, parents with two gangly Scouts-aged boys seated between them, were gathering their coats and shopping bags to leave. Beyond them, Walter noticed, with an introvert's great relief, a seat at the far end was free and set up, and he rushed to claim it.

The waitress working the counter was well beyond retirement age, friendly but curt, her rock dove–gray hair gathered up in the back into an old-fashioned hairnet, snood-like. A grandmotherly roundness to her. She huffed along the counter and ended every exchange with "All right, dear." Ignoring the menu for a moment, Walter took in the schmaltzy splendor of this interior. It was his favorite kind of place: a time capsule of indeterminate age, untouched from an earlier era, but when? He could imagine his grandfather coming here on shore leave during World War II and it looking just the same. Same waitress, even, same plastic tag: "June." Everything was perfect, in a way, from the too-bright light of the fluorescent panels and the ceiling tiles glittering like spray-can snow, to the flecks of gold in the Formica. The upper half of the room was papered in thin sheets of cork, like wood paneling but brighter, a variegated yellow gold, like gingerbread or a perfectly cooked pancake. The place looked as delectable as it smelled. Behind the bar a long mirror doubled the space. Speakers in the ceiling were broadcasting some old Vegas Rat Packer. Dean Martin? Bobby Darin? How could he know, how did anyone tell the difference?

He ordered the house special, heralded on the menu: *eighteen silver-dollar Swedish pancakes*, which June assured him, *No, dear*, was not a crazy amount of food for a hungry young man like him. As soon as he ordered, he realized in a panic that he had broken his cardinal rule of eating alone: bring reading material. Nothing in his backpack but a Walkman and movie calendars he had already practically memorized. He scanned the room by the windows and the door. There were no racks or informal stacks of free weeklies. He was seated too far from the windows, and craned to see the sidewalk outside, and couldn't tell if there was a yellow newspaper box just outside, but he didn't have the change for it anyway. For the moment, the four seats beside him at the counter were still vacant. A relief, in a way—an alienating relief.

He'd been straining to see outside, where the sun was directly overhead and the pedestrians streamed by sun-drenched, and dazzling comets streaked the windows of the dark sedans sliding down Powell Street. When he relaxed back on his stool, his focus shifted and he finally noticed the person seated closest to him, halfway down the counter. She was engrossed in a paperback she held up like a prayer book. Her head tilted down as she ignored the restaurant's hubbub, and her long blond hair was pulled into a ponytail at the nape of her neck and tied with what looked like a small vermillion silk carnation. The light from the window produced a thin halo that flashed along her profile and her hair, but she read on, unaware. There was something captivating about her, which might have been nothing more than her divine indifference to her surroundings. Just below her book, her apparent lunch sat upon the counter: a cup of coffee and an untouched slice of lemon meringue pie, pristine, the plentiful meringue piled high and nearly touching the spine of her book, as she dipped and raised it in the rhythms of her reading. *Such suspense! Oh, what was she reading?* Trade paperback, slightly oversized, the back banded in cream and deep magenta—of course he couldn't read the back cover from this distance, but in his head he was running through a roster of recent bestsellers he'd read or half read, or seen on sale shelves, or noticed deployed as masks on MUNI cars. He couldn't tell what it was, and by now he was overtly staring and—*thank god*—his lunch arrived before he began leering. He asked to see the menu again, to have something to appear to be reading. His embarrassment cresting, he developed a scenario for himself. He pretended he was a food writer who needed to concentrate on the plate in front of him, making manifold mental notes.

The Swedish pancakes were not hard to concentrate on; in fact they were uncannily delicious. Fanned in a mandala on the large plate, sugar-dusted, they were thin as embossed paper, lacy and crispy on the edges and crepe-like in the middle . . . *and goddamn it if it wasn't going to bother him that he couldn't place that girl's paperback,* he was sure he knew *that book.* Still, the buttery aroma drew his nose back to his plate. He had doused the whole arrangement in heavy syrup before he noticed the gemlike berries in a jam left for him in a little flared steel cup. He was testing their tartness when he thought, *She's so . . . lovely,* and simultaneously realized that he had been so distracted by her profile, and her discreet aura, and her mysterious book that he had not really looked at her face—the long nose, full mouth with a worried lower lip, fair skin, and no cheekbones to speak of—and had missed the crucial point that she was not a woman at all but a young man, about his age or maybe a bit older, or perhaps younger, but what persuaded him that this lovely person was older was her—*or wait, his*—remarkable, self-possessed poise.

A twink! Walter thought without thinking, and immediately realized this was wrong. You wouldn't call this boy a twink any more than you'd call the young Catherine Deneuve a twink, or—*who was he thinking of?*—Jean Seberg in *Breathless*. There, he had it. *Breathless* was one of his all-time favorites, and in the particular way Jean Seberg was always described, this elegant young thing was a *gamine*, a girl-boy, not a scrappy, scuff-kneed tomboy but a *French tomboy*, a kind of ethereal urchin. By now he was stricken and rudely staring, as he rapidly took stock of those features often thought to delineate male from female—the just-broader-than-slim shoulders, the just-thicker-than-thin wrists, the subtle Adam's apple—but no single feature seemed to overcome an overwhelming, easy aspect of *utter loveliness*. Ashamed of his rudeness, Walter huddled over his plate again and was relieved when a young couple, comfortably in the middle of an argument, overtook the stools next to him, blocking his clear view of the boy. As he retreated to food critic mode, it occurred to him, resentfully, that no amount of cream could redeem the awful staleness of this diner coffee.

Irresistibly, his gaze was drawn once again down the length of the counter, where now he could see nothing of the gamine but a pair of pale blue-green jacket cuffs and long, elegant, beringed fingers. Having nearly finished the pie, the boy had tented the paperback face down on the counter in order to have a good go at the crust, allowing Walter a clear, foreshortened view of the cover. There was a large black-and-white photo of the author, a rather glamorous woman styled like a silent movie starlet, pursed lips and a tight braid atop her hairline like a crown. Walter didn't recognize her, but the author's name and the book's title boldly framed the photo. Someone named M. F. K. Fisher. The book was called *How to Cook a Wolf.*

And then time sped a bit; apparently reading recipes for wolf had spurred the svelte creature's appetite, for in a few swift minutes the lemon meringue was a memory, the coffee cup emptied, and bills were unrolled from a coin purse and smoothed with care upon the counter. In one motion, the gamine slipped off the stool, placed book and purse in a riding-hood-red satchel—arranged over the shoulder like a sash—and headed for the door. The boy's departure at once forced a little crazed fracture down the surface of Walter's ego as he thought, *I am definitely* not *the type to run from a restaurant and stalk someone down a crowded street.* And at the same time: *I must know who she is—or he is—or fuck if I care either way, let alone if I'm a stalker or not.* For the moment, his reason won out. He asked for his check, like a sane person, and then sat and waited for June to fetch the bill and then his change, eavesdropping as the couple next to him mercilessly griped about a mutual friend—rejoined by the forceful strains of Bobby Darin singing "Don't Rain on My Parade"—and thought, *I should be getting back to work*, all like a sensible, nonobsessive human person. Yet the second he'd laid down his tip he fled the diner like a madman, his lunch half eaten, and rushed down Powell Street in the direction in which he'd seen the boy disappear through the window.

At the closest intersection Walter slowed to a stop. The elusive creature had evaded him, though half his mind was trying to persuade the other half that he was not in pursuit at all, not tapping his foot for the light to change, but casually cruising about, strolling, taking it all in. What a radiant midday sky, and here was Union Square with its billboard-crested facades, fat omega-crowned palms, pigeons, tourist droves. Should he cross without motive toward Saks, or should he take an equally unmotivated route past the portal of the St. Francis Hotel? Something about the green, freshly flat-topped rows of boxwood hedges prompted him to take a knight's double jump across Post and Powell into the square itself, and make a beeline for the bronze wingless Victory, balanced barefoot on a ball on a pillar and aiming a trident toward the entrance of Macy's. His intuition was rewarded, for as a slow-moving tour group began to disperse from the Victory's base, Walter caught a glimpse of the bright red satchel flashing in the small of the boy's back and the dot of red carnation bound to the blond nape.

He approached quickly—not too quickly—and the gamine never looked back. For the first time Walter got a glimpse of the young man's full height, slender and not too tall, maybe about five-eight or five-nine. He was wearing a seafoam-colored linen jacket with a vent in the back, and black tapered capri pants that showed his white ankles, and what looked to be women's pointed black flats. The black pants and flats (even the bare ankles) were paired in a studied manner. *Very Audrey Hepburn*, Walter thought. Boyishly, his slim hips barely swayed as he walked. He darted across Geary Street at the tail end of the walk signal and left Walter watching from the opposite shore as traffic streamed by, but it was clear the gamine was not in a hurry to get where he was going. He sauntered and window-shopped a bit, then backtracked and headed toward the door of Macy's.

Waiting for the signal, Walter was trying to reason through the paradox of what might be a respectful distance at which to stalk someone. How to invade without being invasive? And anyway, wasn't he really only concerned with *appearing* invasive, with getting caught and called out? This he puzzled over as he crossed the street and wove his way through the patrons streaming from the doors of the department store. He was embarrassed by his compulsion to follow this stranger, yet the ambivalence he felt about his own motives somehow, to him, mitigated his behavior. He made way for a laughing band of women, laden with shopping booty and tight-knit as bridesmaids, and entered through the revolving door, only to find himself wandering lost among the blinding, space-age, plate glass brightness of the perfume and makeup counters.

What on earth was he doing here? After all, the boy wasn't his type at all—not in the least! Skinny, blond, femme, twinkish if not definitively a twink—*ah, hold on, there he was, talking to a woman at the Lancôme counter*— in isolation not one of these characteristics was a clear turnoff, yet none was a turn-on, either, he thought. He sidled toward a seemingly free-floating vitrine topped with men's cologne. *And furthermore*—he continued his internal symposium—though he often told himself he was attracted to the whole person and not mere features or fetishes, he had to admit that *this whole person* was certainly *not the whole person* for him. In short, he had no idea what the hell he was doing or what he wanted from this stranger, much less what he would say if the gamine were to turn to him and say *Boo*.

To reach the display, Walter walked directly past his mark and noticed two things: as he spoke to the Lancôme lady, the boy's voice was too soft to hear in the cavernous hall; and what he had thought was a carnation in his hair was no more than a crushed velvet scrunchie. Walter feigned interest in the scents and started picking favorites by the labels and the crystalline heft of the bottles—Gaultier, Dolce & Gabbana, 4711, which looked to him like a fancy airplane bottle of gin—when the gamine walked behind him, and Walter could see from the corner of his eye that he was heading toward the jewelry counters. He hung back and sampled some colognes, spraying them onto cardstock strips and placing them to his nose, sniffing, mostly unimpressed, but with the last one he sprayed too liberally and sniffed too deeply, and the scent of peppery rubbing alcohol grabbed him about the septum and yanked. He began to sneeze uncontrollably. His instinct was to duck and hide behind the vitrine, but he saw through his convulsions that any place around the glass island would leave him equally exposed to the room, so he ran, still sneezing so violently he thought he might sneeze his nozzle right off, away from the teeming activity of the showroom, toward the restrooms.

Minutes later, he emerged from the bathroom feeling calmer and saner, having splashed his face with tap water. He was not refreshed; face and spirits were equally dampened. He emerged with the dull hope that, for the time being, he had sneezed the idiocy out of his fool head. Even so, he made a surreptitious tour of the jewelry counters on his way to the far exit and felt relieved—and sort of chastened—when the gamine was nowhere to be seen. Not until he was back on the street trying to get his bearings did he realize he would be late for work, even if he ran—*served him right*. And it wasn't until he was huddled in his filing closet, between his ladder and his ledger, that he realized he was still ravenously hungry.

In the weeks that followed, he nearly managed to forget about the encounter. Still, he'd often head to Union Square at lunchtime if the weather was good.

He always enjoyed the stroll up Maiden Lane. He'd visit his Polish Boy vendor, the sea-green Victory with her trident, sometimes the Macy's perfume counters or the men's shop. And always with a little half-conscious frisson of nonexpectant expectancy.

In the first week after the encounter he would duck into bookshops to see if they had a copy of *How to Cook a Wolf*—not a blockbuster evidently, as he never came across a single copy—but late one evening at Aardvark Books on Church he found a copy of M. F. K. Fisher's *The Gastronomical Me*. He gobbled it up, then continued to carry it in his backpack on the off chance that some ludicrous rom-com scenario would fall into alignment, where he would find himself sitting across from the gamine on the N Judah, and he would pull out this well-worn volume, and setting eyes on it, the gamine would exclaim, *We must be friends at once!* He returned to Sears Fine Food twice that fall: the first time it was crowded out the door and he couldn't wait; the second he tried the lemon meringue pie and in the middle of it felt overwhelmed by how weirdly obsessive he could be, silently berating himself as he choked down the pie. Anyway, he never cared much for meringue—marshmallowy and oversweet—and the lemon curd was nothing he liked: gummy, grainy, and bitter.

The Conformist

WALTER WAS ONE OF TWO passengers on the last 24 of the night to the Castro. He sat near the back of the bus, and the lights inside were bright and the streets dark, so the bus became a rambling hall of warped, convulsing mirrors. His reflection in the sepia-tinted windows was smeared, oblong and bleary. His dark blond hair became a mulchy brown, and he could barely see his own eyes, deep-set and cast in shadow. His eyes were slate gray, but in the murky reflection they looked much darker, almost black, and completely opaque. A cool effect—a little devilish, he thought.

The bus lumbered, heaving up and down the cement slopes of the Outer Mission and Noe Valley. He was getting a little motion sick, but in truth, Walter loved the electric buses, he loved the long, gangly cricket antennae that sprang from their tails and reached to the wires, he loved how they sparked when attached or detached, or randomly sprayed sparks as the bus gamboled. One of his favorite city sounds was the ricochet of the cables overhead as they were stroked and rattled by buses from below. Most of all he loved that, although they ranged all over the city, there was no mistaking that they were essentially overgrown bumper cars. He couldn't believe the system worked—a great example, it now occurred to him, of a *beautifully inelegant* solution.

Good bad design, if there was such a thing. In his head he was arguing a bit with a young man he had just met named Jeff. It was a blind date set up by Richard, of all people, Eliot's newly official partner. (They were *partners*, not boyfriends, because Richard was beyond all that, apparently. According to Eliot, *PhDs don't have boyfriends*.) Jeff was getting a master's in computer science at Stanford, and what Eliot and Richard imagined Walter would have in common with the guy was anybody's guess. Who ever heard of such a thing—*a gay computer geek*? But he'd agreed, warily, to meet Jeff for margaritas that night on the back patio at El Rio.

The date went pretty OK, right up to the fumbled hybrid hug-shake goodbye. Their conversation was stilted at first, which seemed inevitable. Walter didn't care to talk about his temp job, and his heart sank when he realized Jeff's extensive geekery didn't extend to movies. Jeff yammered about Stanford a bit and his program. He was studying something called HCI, human-computer interaction. Walter was on the verge of dismissing him as one of those nocturnal, lab-dwelling comp sci dudes whose brains were filled with nothing but files of code glowing green like fireflies, when Jeff described himself as *essentially a designer* who was *obsessed with good design*. Then he made a fascinating assertion that every single problem that exists is in fact a design problem, that he thought every problem in the world could be solved by good design. Walter was skeptical but found himself wanting to believe when Jeff asserted that the best design is not only functional but *elegant*, and not simply elegant looking but—what was it?—*parsimonious*. (*Parsimonious?* What a word! How long could he remember it?) Which is to say, an *elegant solution*.

Meanwhile, for someone who said he was obsessed with design, Jeff wasn't overtly stylish. He was tall and thin, his brown hair trimmed in a clean, square cut. He was dressed nicely but kind of invisibly in black and gray. He wore glasses with big, overbearing frames like Buddy Holly's; the thick lenses made him look perpetually wide-eyed and even a little weepy.

By their second margarita, Walter was into Jeff's design theory, and what he liked about it was how widely applicable it was, even absurdly so, a top-down theory of everything. What did a haircut have in common with a bus

24   Christopher Tradowsky

route? A sea anemone with a spray nozzle, a space shuttle, a hydroplane, a house of parliament? Each was a design problem having found—or still seeking—an elegant solution. Naturally Walter had the urge to poke holes in the theory.

"Do you think of friendship as a design problem?" he asked. "Or, like, relationships? Human relationships aren't really a *design problem*, are they?"

"Well, they are, in a way," said Jeff, "and one that computers can actually help with—like, how do you efficiently meet people who share your interests? That's a design problem."

Walter nodded, a little fazed that he'd inadvertently brought up their present situation.

"Look at it this way," Jeff went on, "our friends encouraged us to meet; that's one solution to a problem: we're both new in town, we both need to meet people. But in ten years—maybe less, maybe five—meeting through friends will be obsolete, I think. And cruising and meeting in bars like this. Everyone will meet online."

"Online. Uh-huh." Walter bobbed his head, knowingly unknowingly.

"You know, through message boards and stuff, on the internet. It will mean many more choices—infinite chances to meet anyone you might click with—anyone from anywhere around the world!"

And while Jeff's eyes had gone evangelically bright, Walter felt a little let down. It seemed that, for all his talk about elegance—and maybe it was Walter's mistake for hearing *elegance* and thinking *beauty*—in the end Jeff's head was still crammed with radiant code, and his brainy solution to a very bodily problem was to replace bodies cruising bodies with code chasing code, ones and zeroes cruising ones and zeroes.

The bus scooted to the corner, slumped in the gutter, and emitted an enormous sigh as the doors wheezed open and released the only other passenger, a middle-aged woman who thanked the driver with weary familiarity. Now Walter would feel that slight guilt—like he was being pampered, chauffeured—akin to how he felt when he was alone in a movie theater and couldn't help but imagine the projectionist peevishly changing reels for him alone.

By now he really wished he had his Walkman. As a rule he never went anywhere without it, except on nights out, like this, when he wanted to travel light. Since he had no music and nothing to read, his mind drifted. At such unguarded moments he had to admit he'd really fucked himself over, in a way. Sure, making a pilgrimage to the gay mecca seemed fun, and escaping small-town Ohio—all this seemed necessary. But moving to a large city where he knew basically no one was more isolating than he could have possibly imagined. Sure, his college friend Sarah had fantasized aloud about moving, too, and half promised to join him when she graduated next year. But that was nine months away, and in the meantime, his loneliness was beginning to crush him, he could feel the weight of it like stones on his chest, like a medieval punishment for witches. He'd always thought he loved isolation, yet as much as he craved solitude, it turned out he was *terrible* at being alone.

It wasn't like he hadn't met *anyone*. Walter genuinely liked his roommate, Fiona, though he never felt quite hip enough for her. He also almost never saw her. She was forever out working odd hours, then partying all night and sleeping all day on her days off. Kelly, Fiona's best friend and partner in club-kid high jinks, was in fact the first person he'd met when he arrived. She had a memorable, somewhat impossible name: Kelly Calypso. It turned out she had named herself, not after Homer, but after a Suzanne Vega song. Kelly and Fiona shared a weird, quasi-spiritual bond that ravers seemed to emanate: a wide-eyed, utopian idea that dance music heals all ills, that on any given night a DJ *really can* save your life, that love is the answer, and that the doors to consciousness can be unlocked by many keys and combinations— including palmistry and star charts, but also pot and mushrooms and acid and even, when called for, a dash of methamphetamine.

Every Wednesday night Kelly Calypso gave tarot readings at Café Macondo, Walter's favorite café, under a small gold-framed sign that said "Fortunes by Ms. Calypso." And that's how he met her, one week after moving to

San Francisco. At first sight he found her very intimidating. She was in her late twenties and had a hippie gutter-punk vibe; she looked exactly like someone who'd spent their teens sleeping in Golden Gate Park and had the tall tales and battle scars to prove it. The night they met, she wore a halter top that showed off a panorama of braided tattoos—lilies, lotuses, swoops of kelp and koi, and knots of calligraphy—stretching over her shoulders from one wrist to the other. Meanwhile, she had the most astonishing hair he'd ever seen, loosely arranged atop her head in two spiky buns like cactus flowers. Black at the roots, half her hair was deep fuchsia and the other half safety orange. That night, she wore black lipstick. She was weird and witchy, scary beautiful, almost hard to look at.

Walter was pretty sure astrology was BS, but he was desperate for human interaction, so he paid seven dollars for the reading, which seemed steep but wound up being worth it for a full hour of lively conversation. The fortune didn't reveal much: Ms. Calypso divined that he was new in town, that he'd moved to SF to escape the Midwest, and that he was looking for love. All of which, he assumed, would have been clear to anyone getting a look at him from a distance of a hundred yards. At any rate, the description was a safe bet, as it seemed to apply to half the population of San Francisco. In another way, Kelly's reading was auspicious. In the course of conversation it came out that Walter was living in a (quite literally) lousy, vaguely horrifying residence hotel on South Van Ness and that he'd spent his afternoon circling want ads for roommates. As fate would have it, Kelly's best friend, Fiona, needed a roommate, and as soon as possible, since her bitch of an ex-girlfriend had left her high and dry, moving back to Hawaii to sleep on a secret squatters' beach and stiffing her for three months' rent.

The next evening, Walter took the 24 north on Divisadero in order to meet Fiona at the mysterious store that was Kelly's more regular place of work. The shop was one of those unprepossessing plate glass storefronts that you could walk by dozens of times and not realize it was meant to be a business. Walter never found out if it had a name; it had no signage and no posted hours. As far as he could figure out from a few successive visits, the store was open only when Kelly Calypso felt like coming to work. There seemed to be no owner—Kelly didn't own it, though she did make remarks about José keeping tabs on her. José, it turned out, was the name of the pearl-white, cherry-cheeked cockatiel that lived in a large cage in the window, beneath an arid hanging garden of tillandsias.

When he finally found the place, he discovered Kelly and Fiona inside chilling on a fussy, phony Louis XV couch, gilt shellwork and voided velveteen, sharing a cocktail from a large leather flask. Fiona had the same intimidating coolness that Kelly did, with her long, pin-straight carbon-black hair and a mouth so full it was almost perfectly round. She was as beautiful as Kelly, though less edgy, less scary. In part this had to be because she was so petite— the mythical size zero that fashion houses designed for but it seemed no woman actually was. The two greeted Walter exuberantly without getting up, invited him to look around, and went on gossiping. He examined the store as they chatted—the evening light was butterscotch-colored. The store smelled metaphysical, like an old apothecary. Though none of the items were priced, as far as he could tell, the store "sold" crystals and incense, a few essential oils, some beeswax candles, a vase or two. On one tabletop was a skeletal army of Day of the Dead figures, alone and in dioramas, and a colonnade of veladora candles with their polychrome saints. As the women talked, they wove bits of exclamatory Spanish through their speech. (*De puta madre* was a favorite phrase; later Walter would learn that Ms. Calypso was, in fact, formerly Ms. Ramirez.)

Hanging on one wall was a display of handmade shadow puppets, their intricate black silhouettes beautifully menacing. When he asked if he could see one, Kelly hopped up to help him.

"It's Indonesian," she said. "They look super fragile, but they're surprisingly sturdy." The figure was spindly but tough under the fingertips—it was leather, carefully punched and tooled. He couldn't tell if it was meant to be male or female; a curious, androgynous profile protruded from a headdress lacy as lichen. As she shared some of her favorite puppets, Walter learned that Kelly was a performer: a lifelong dancer, later an actress, but now she wanted to get into puppetry. By this point he was won over by Ms. Calypso, her whole life was a kind of gritty, improbable riot grrrl fairy tale.

That evening, for all her volubility, Fiona remained an enigma. She stretched her legs out on the kingly couch, wearing clunky black heels Walter would soon learn were something of a trademark. She asked only a few questions—where he was from, if he had work—before she warmed to him.

"Oh! What's your last name? I guess that's important," Fiona asked.

"Simmering."

"Huh. Like a pot?"

"Yeah—it's actually a town in Switzerland."

"How *cute*!" Fiona declared. "A big, blond Swiss Miss Thang! You should come live with me for sure. You can make me some fondue!"

Walter wasn't sure what she was calling cute exactly, and he had no idea how to make fondue, but that weekend he visited Fiona's place on Saturday morning and moved in Sunday afternoon. It was a small two-bedroom on Ashbury in "Ashbury Heights," a nano-neighborhood invented by Realtors to sound up-and-coming. The apartment was in a big old Edwardian mansion, once spacious, its floor plan now coarsely chopped up and repurposed, with former closets converted to kitchens and bedrooms. The apartment was small, featureless, and cream-colored, with a single selling point: from the living room window there was a sweet view out over Cole Valley, and you could open the window and climb over the sill onto a tiny, rickety roof deck, wedged between two gables. Often it was too cold, but on warmish nights it was the perfect place to drink wine and stare oceanward hoping for a glimpse of the park or the Richmond, buried under a felt of fog. At first, $400 a month seemed an awful lot, but he could just swing it, and the view was wonderful, and of course, Fiona was fabulous.

Too fabulous for Walter, maybe. Fiona and Kelly were always strutting off to some party and inviting him as an afterthought, their encouragement (*You should totally come!*) somehow both emphatic and lukewarm. He'd see Fiona at home (rarely), or visit Kelly at her mysterious store, or run into her on a Wednesday at Café Macondo. Week after week Fiona would promise she was going to take him out and show him how to actually have fun, but they never synced up, like workers on rotating shifts—he'd be getting ready for bed as she rose from her disco nap to go out; heading to work in the morning, he'd discover her on the stoop, groggily fiddling with the dead bolt.

Now the bus was heading north on Castro, and as it crossed Twenty-Fourth Street Walter stared down the main strip of Noe Valley shops. The street was empty and ghost-town still. Walter loved it at night when a streetlamp grew straight out of one of the many sidewalk laurels, and the lamp turned the thick leaves an uncanny, resinous yellow amber. He wondered if this should go on his list—the mental list he'd been compiling of quintessential urban experiences, his favorites (including long, lurching bus tours like this one—provided he remembered his Walkman) and his most dreaded (the worst: getting mugged at knifepoint outside his hotel, week two). Now, as the bus scudded downhill into the Castro, he was reminded of the ultimate urban experience, the most quintessential, for him the most joyous. More than anything, Walter loved seeing a great old movie in a great old movie palace, and the most spectacular palace he knew was the Castro Theatre, up ahead and approaching fast. In the outer pocket of the backpack he carried every day he kept the Castro's monthly movie schedule, folded together with those of the Roxie and the California Theatre in Berkeley, and the *Bay Guardian*'s capsule reviews.

That same week, amid a Bertolucci retrospective, he'd discovered a new favorite film. He was floored by *The Conformist*. Going into the movie blind, he was convinced in the first ten minutes (and particularly by the wide, sumptuous takes of ruthless fascist architecture) that it was a masterpiece. It was a beautifully saturated film noir, a wartime spy thriller, complete with an icy blond femme fatale who turns out (no surprise) to be the only character in the film with any empathy, insight, or sense. But beneath the noir trappings was a film about misplaced longing—queer longing at that. Marcello, the conformist of the title, is a closet case so desperate to be ordinary that he becomes a fascist footman. His fiancée and unwitting beard, a gorgeous, naive brunette named Giulia, herself seems to be too irrepressibly sensual to be entirely straight. Walter knew he was about as gay as they come, and yet the most erotic thing he had ever seen was the scene in a glassed-in Parisian dance hall—red-trimmed and gas-globed, straight out of Toulouse-Lautrec—when inscrutable blonde Anna entices Giulia to tango, and their dance is so charged that everyone watches them, stunned. The defiant gazes they trade, the sheath of Anna's champagne gown like a second skin, the pearls swaying at Giulia's neck with the silver clasp at the back, the bandonion tango, slightly ragged, a little feral . . . and, of course, the fluid, frenetic beauty of Italian, in which even a rebuke sounds like a seduction. It was almost unbearable. Walter wanted to live in that scene forever, although he didn't see how he would fit in that world and was pretty sure he couldn't take it. It was like one of those erotic dreams you wake from feeling only helpless—and relieved that such intensity of desire cannot be a feature of waking life, of daily life, even if the jolt of it haunts you all day afterward.

It was past midnight. He pulled the cord to clang the bell and stood at the rear exit, braced for a rough stop. He wanted to walk up the block, to do a little people watching, to admire the facade of the palace and remind himself what was playing over the coming weeks. He was surprised to find the blocky, brilliant "CASTRO" sign still beaming: tall aquamarine neon broadcasting through the fog, the wide marquee lit, the carousel bulbs beneath it aflame. Why was it still alight? If it was showing a midnight movie, the sign didn't say. But the marquee did confirm what he'd hoped: *The Conformist* was still playing, along with *The Sheltering Sky*, which he'd never seen. A good name, *The Sheltering Sky*, evocative, and if he liked it half as much as *The Conformist*, he'd be thrilled. Right then he planned his Sunday afternoon: if there were matinees, he'd do a double bill. He was as free as a young man could possibly be. And he was desperate to go back, to get one more glimpse, to be haunted once more by that phantom Parisian dance hall.

Gilda

WALTER AND FIONA MADE A deal. She would go with him to a late show of his *boring, old black-and-white film* at the Castro if he would go clubbing afterward with her. Fiona had planned her entire weekend around going out: after the movie they would meet Kelly Calypso at her mystery boutique, then start the night at the Kennel Club. They were *gonna get faded*, as Fiona put it. Here it was at last: the wild, long night out she had promised him. Walter thought that *Gilda*, with its jaw-dropping performance by Rita Hayworth, could be a gateway drug for someone like Fiona, who flatly declared she didn't care much for old movies and (tragically) hadn't seen any film noir at all. Fiona made no bones about her feelings for Walter. While she loved *a cute, shy gay boy*, she was pretty convinced this boy had *no clue how to have fun.*

They were going out and staying out, so they had to dress for the night, which in San Francisco meant strategic layers, sufficient but as few as possible, and which also meant sharing the bathroom mirror and stores of product as they primped. Fiona was blasting Black Box from the living room and leaning over the bathroom sink, applying eyeliner with the care of a miniaturist. Fiona was twenty-seven, five years older than Walter. She came from a large family and easily slipped into treating him with the warm disregard she had for her younger brothers.

"Yes or no?" asked Walter, posing in the bathroom door. He was modeling a black Jughead cap with crown points that he had found at Villains on

Haight. It fit tight to his skull and flattened out his hair underneath in such a way that if he wore it, he'd have to wear it all night. He was sporting a kind of club-kid uniform: white T, just-worn-in wide-leg jeans, thick black belt, and eye-catching electric-blue shoes—a color he loved and associated with the early '80s, MTV, Chess King—they were Doc Martens, also from Villains.

"Aaawww, you look *adorable*!" Fiona cried. "Just like Jimmy Reardon!"

"I look *nothing* like River Phoenix!" Walter protested. *Adorable* wasn't exactly what he was going for, either.

"Oh"—she dismissed him with a swish of her mascara brush—"all you tall white boys look the same to me anyway." He was about to toss the hat away when she laughed. "Aw, fuck off and wear the hat. You look hella cute!"

He smiled because *hella cute* at least sounded sexier than *adorable*. "I just don't want to look like a Castro clone."

"You couldn't," she assured him. "First of all, you'd need a mustache, and I'm not even sure you can grow one of those." Fiona was a master of the soothing insult, flattering and knocking him at once. Big-sisterly.

"Are we walking to the Castro?" He was getting excited for the night out with this inveterate party girl and her insane-seeming friends.

"Girl, no!" She pointed down to her black six-inch platform heels. "Have you seen these chanclas?"

They promenaded the Castro, looking for a place to grab dinner. It was fun strutting around with Fiona; she turned heads. High and mighty as she was in her clunky heels, she still barely rose past Walter's shoulder. She was wearing a hip-hugging black miniskirt, a net top that gave glimpses of her black bra, and this incredible vinyl jacket-thing in sparkling seafoam blue, with puffy leg-of-mutton sleeves that covered her shoulders and arms and nothing else. It looked like it could keep her afloat—like something Jane Austen might wear to a pool party in the year 2000. But it wasn't her attire alone that made all the queens mouth *Go guurl!* when they saw her. She was also kind of gorgeous. She was Filipina and had glossy black hair that she'd recently sacrificed to a severe pixie cut, shaved in the back. (She said she'd loved having long hair, but this haircut was *girl bait*.) She had dusted her cheekbones with bronzer, and her face glowed, her full lips candy-apple glossy and red. Walking through the Castro with her made Walter giddy. The queers were out in force, in jean shorts and muscle Ts filled out with the requisite biceps. It was early evening, but already gaggles of drunken boys and thumping house beats spilled forth onto the sidewalks from the bars. In one swift move, Fiona stepped over a drunken twink, who had collapsed, giggling convulsively, in front of Badlands, and rebuffed a canvasser, who asked if she wanted to talk about gays in the military. Walter hoped that some of her imperious raver glamour might spill over onto him.

They had gotten to the theater with plenty of time to spare before the film. It was already crowded, and they nabbed good seats in the center. The much-touted Mighty Wurlitzer organ, painted yellow blond, had risen to its full height, and a man in a tan seersucker blazer was ranging all over it, weaving its innumerable, enormous tones with the deftness of a spider. For the moment the organ music was rather soft and chiming, like a celeste.

Fiona went to see how long the line was for the ladies', and Walter sat dreamily taking the whole place in. In spite of the fact that the glass-paned doors of the entrance always reminded him of those in the church in his hometown, in stark contrast, whenever he approached the Castro Theatre his blood pressure went down. Wandering into the Castro was like entering a realm of aesthetic bliss, where even visions of horror and blood-soaked plots came couched in plush velour, and the gold-amber pavilion that enveloped them assured him he was safe within this untouchable, eccentric realm. In here, the last judgment could come and the whole world could end in a rain of hellfire, and you'd still walk out unsinged. Without a doubt, it was the world *outside* that could kill you.

Yet if he tried to figure out what *manner* of realm he'd been transported to, he couldn't quite put his finger on it. A Spanish baroque garden, he guessed, someplace where Valentino might hang out, in a silent 1920s celluloid dream of Spain. But it was the warm color spectrum of the palace that always got him: yellow Wurlitzer, gold curtains, garish gold leaf lavished on the columns and the heaps of plaster ornaments—through the decades you could hear the designer shouting, *More gold! Spare no expense!*

By this time the organist had flipped the switches to skate-rink mode and pulled out the stops for an impassioned version of "Is That All There Is?" Fiona had apparently fallen into an abyss, but for the moment Walter was blissed-out, because he truly loved everything about the movies, including the loud Saturday-night gab all around him, and he even loved, for the moment, the milling, threshing sound of popcorn crunching, because with enough people it became a soothing white noise, and he adored the permeating smell of counterfeit butter, so penetrating you carried it out on your clothes when you left.

He was looking over his shoulder, hoping to see Fiona returning from the restroom. Scanning the crowd, he fixated upon a couple who appeared arm in arm in the yellow incandescence of the doorway and began striding down the aisle, searching for open seats. At first he only noticed how well-dressed they were, overdressed really, but they had clearly dressed for the movie: He was in a dark suit with a plaid tie and pocket square, and carried a gray fedora in his hand. She wore a beautiful leopard-print jacket, on an evening when it was almost too warm for it. Getting a good look at her face, he realized that she was none other than the gamine from the diner he had almost, but definitely never quite, forgotten. The gamine wore her—*his*—hair in a blond curtain that swept down in carefully styled waves, concealing half his face. It was very chic but also, to Walter's eye, a spot-on, deliberate film reference to Veronica Lake, the icy blond femme fatale, predecessor to Jessica Rabbit.

Walter held his breath. He was now sure that the Jughead cap Fiona had encouraged him to wear was utterly ridiculous; he pulled it off and tried to muss up his hair in a way that he imagined might be appealing. Still, he stared at the couple, dying to know what kind of man would be glamorous enough to strut arm in arm with . . . Then he gathered, with a surprise he immediately berated himself for, that the nattily dressed man was almost certainly not a man at all but a woman, butch enough to be mistaken for a guy, but not enough to *pass*, which anyway didn't seem to be the point. Rather, with her tailored suit and her formal manner, she seemed, like her companion, to be alluding to the glamour of old Hollywood. They descended upon this screening of *Gilda* like two starlets at a Golden Age premiere.

Walter was now helplessly staring as the couple wended their way between seats several rows back. The gamine's companion had dark brown hair parted carefully on one side, its waves pressed down and sleeked with pomade. She was tallish, like the gamine. Getting a better look, he concluded that she was right on the edge between being handsome and funny looking. Her slick dark hair and dark eyes made her look like some dandified matinee crooner, her eyes bugged slightly, and she had a toothy, crooked grin. She reminded Walter a little of a very young Tim Curry. They were certainly a couple; there was no way they were on a first or second date. They simply seemed to *fit*, moving as one with the gracefulness of dance partners, even as they *pardon-me*'d their way down the row of the darkening theater. Walter turned again as the lights dimmed and the Wurlitzer reached its bouncing crescendo, wailing loud as sirens: *San Francisco, open your golden gate! You'll let nobody wait outside your door!* The organist flipped the switch to start his majestic descent, and as the curtains parted, Walter made a silent vow: he must meet these two, he had to know them and, if at all possible, to befriend them. Halfway through the second preview Fiona finally slipped back into her seat beside him. Walter waited breathlessly for Rita Hayworth to arise, like Venus, on her famous hair flip.

He was swept away by the movie but, nonetheless, found himself gauging Fiona's reactions, noticing when she laughed or seemed startled or even—once—yawned. A couple times she laughed at things he was sure weren't meant to be funny: Rita Hayworth, with debilitatingly long nails, badly faking it on the guitar; or Rita attempting to rhumba while hobbled by a sheath dress—*did her stylists hate her?* Whenever his idolatry was interrupted, Walter had to fight a strong urge to look back at the glam starlet couple and catch their reactions, see if they dared to laugh when the screen goddess fumbled. When it was over, the crowd rose, and at once the couple was lost in the press of bodies—probably exiting down the far aisle—and Walter sighed a little as he lost sight of them. But they stuck with him: over the rest of the night he would find himself wondering about this strange duo who seemed to have waltzed right out of an old champagne musical and onto the beautiful, gritty, eucalyptus-and-urine-scented streets of San Francisco. Out on the sidewalk, while he and Fiona waited for the 24, he spied them once more strolling hand in hand down Castro Street with easy, synchronous steps. Some part of him wanted to run after them—the leopard-print jacket, the cocked fedora—he thought they must have been the most stylish people he had ever seen. And yet, like a dog chasing a Bugatti, what would he do if he caught them? Bark in admiration? And anyway, he had made a promise to Fiona—the longtime promise of a long night out.

On the bus heading to the Western Addition, Fiona explained that it was still too early for the club, so they'd hang out for a while at Kelly's store, have a drink. It was always economical, Walter knew, to get at least a little drunk before the main event. Fiona forced him to put his Jughead cap back on, adjusting it for him. He was no longer into it—it felt silly. But it was either this or carry it around all night. She said the movie was *cool*, but she didn't gush about it the way he wanted her to. He had seen it only once before, in a dorm room on a VHS tape as fuzzy as the moon landing footage, so this time Rita Hayworth's towering silver-moonglow face was a revelation. He let himself fantasize aloud about a prequel, in which some of the mysteries of the inexplicable backstory would be answered, but then he was back to gushing about Rita herself.

"I loved it." Fiona laughed. "She was such a *bitch*!"

Walter wasn't sure what to say to this and giggled complacently.

"You said you studied this shit in college, huh?" she asked.

"Yeah, I was a film major."

"So, you know how to make movies, then?"

"I mean, no, I've never even touched a camera larger than a Super 8. I was studying history and criticism and stuff . . . and of course it was great because I watched a ton of classic movies."

At this Fiona stuck her tongue in her cheek, raised her eyebrows at him, and said, "Huh," in a way that concisely implied: *That degree plus $1.25 will get you a large coffee.*

"I don't really think she was a *bitch*," Walter said. "She's supposed to be this femme fatale—you know what that means—like, a dangerous woman. Drawing men into deadly situations and stuff. But really, she's totally trapped and controlled by these men, and has no power of her own, so the only power she has is to manipulate Johnny and Mundson. And anyway, Johnny's such a self-righteous jerk, the whole plot is really sadistic, if you think about it . . ." Walter went on, slipping unprompted into a little lecture—stolen almost verbatim from his favorite professor—about film noir and sadism, but as soon as he used the word *fetishism*, Fiona cut him short.

"Dude, I'm an Asian woman, and most guys think I'm ten years younger than I am. I used to dance at the Lusty Lady in fetish boots. You want to tell me about men's kinks?" She smiled with her lips very slightly parted, showing her teeth, like Gilda.

"Omigod," said Walter. "I'll shut up now."

"It's OK, honey. You just keep looking pretty."

Inside the mystery boutique they found Kelly Calypso on a stool behind the counter, an open bottle of pisco and a shot glass at her side. Acid jazz drubbed from a small boom box behind her, the cheap speakers blown, the bass notes purring. She showed them what she was working on: she'd been busy with an X-Acto, cutting black cardstock into a shadow puppet of an ectomorphic gent in a bowler hat, his thin limbs joined by knotted cord. In Kelly's hands the puppet was surprisingly expressive.

"That's total genius!" said Fiona. "I think you should charge a lot for that one—"

"Not for sale." Kelly poured a shot of pisco and slid it toward Fiona. "I'm making a few I want to use in a show eventually. I'm still experimenting for now."

"I brought you that chaser you wanted," said Fiona, setting down a six-pack of cold Zima they'd snagged at a bodega. She slugged the pisco shot.

"Thanks!" said Kelly. "But also, gross, right?" She poured a shot for Walter.

Fiona and Walter sat on the Louis XV couch sipping Zima, which tasted like beer with the flavor carefully removed. Fiona and Kelly dove right into gossiping about who was coming out that night. Their friends Julian and Marco planned to meet them at the club. Fiona was particularly excited about a new friend named Val, who had moved from New York last month and who, according to Fiona, was five entire syllables of *fi-i-i-i-ine*. Fiona described Val as *butch*, but Kelly disputed it, saying that *wearing a wifebeater and leather cap everywhere you went didn't make you butch*. As they chatted, Kelly Calypso set aside her puppet, scraps, and shears, and began searching through a woven handbag. She extracted a baggie of white clumps, which she turned out onto the glass counter and began carefully mincing with her X-Acto.

"This is taking way too long!" she said, pulling a credit card from a coin purse. With mindless expertise she divvied up the superfine powder and arranged it in parallel rows on the glass: two measures of a brilliant, crystalline musical staff. Watching her, Walter was on edge; the shop was closed and the door locked, yet anyone walking by on the street could easily see what they were up to. José the cockatiel, with black eyes like fermatas and a crest like a tilde, scrutinized their every move from his palatial cage in the window. Kelly and Fiona went first, sharing a short straw that Kelly kept in the cash box for such occasions. Walter tried to decline at first but relented once Fiona got on his case.

"Oh, live a little, for fuck's sake!" She beat him on both arms playfully—but he felt it. "I'm going to pull that stick out of your ass if it kills me!"

He had never done coke before—he always imagined it would be like the ultimate brain freeze from a slushy: the stupefying flash as crystals formed behind your eyes, the deadening shock to the brain. It was milder than he imagined—there was no rush to it—at first. He tasted something acrid and felt a little viscous trickle dripping down the back of his throat—a momentary head cold. As the girls went on chatting, he thought for a minute that his vision was crisper or the colors in the store brighter, and then he noticed that the acid jazz, which had sped up and amplified into diva house, kept modulating upward—upward and upward—yet the bass stayed heavy and the pitches never became shrill—like the paradoxical peppermint twists of a barbershop sign, spinning in place, static and rapid, at once still and somehow rising eternally upward . . .

And then it was three hours later at least. Walter found himself on the patio of the EndUp. It must have been three in the morning, maybe later. He wasn't entirely sure how he'd gotten there. It was still crowded, and he sat by himself at a high-top covered in abandoned cocktail glasses. He was seriously thinking of clearing it off so he could rest his head upon it, close his eyes. He was pretty drunk, but from where he sat he could see Fiona motoring across the dance floor in her chunky heels, spinning and drumming the air like the Energizer Bunny. She didn't look *remotely* ready to share a cab home. Walter had no idea how she still had energy, except, most likely, it was one of the tabs of ecstasy she'd offered him that he'd turned down.

This late/early in the wee hours the music changed and became dreamy and atmospheric: coming-down music. The thumping techno bass lines eased, and the soundscape welled with synthetic strings, fragments of melodies, and floods of fricative samples. Walter suddenly recognized a song he loved: a dreamy song that began with phony, but still lovely, birdcalls and the breathy voice of a soprano *la-la-la*-ing along with a spate of piano chords, rote chords, standard-issue for house music. She sang of green grass and blue skies, but the synths painted Astroturf and outer space. A careening helix of scales could only be—*what?*—the SOS of a distant satellite, orbiting Saturn at the speed of sound, dodging the debris in its rings.

Out on the dance floor, Walter noticed that one of Fiona's friends loved this song as well. He did a little excited back-kick when it started, and he closed his eyes for a minute in an ecstatic groove. His name was Julian. Walter had met him hours before at the Kennel Club, where it was too loud to talk, so they amiably shouted their names at each other. Walter was sure Julian was with another guy, another skinny, cute guy named Marco, but Marco had spun off somewhere on the journey to SoMa. Julian seemed perfectly happy to be alone, dancing by himself around a vacated corner of the dance floor. He, too, was wearing black heels—neither as high nor as clunky as Fiona's. He wore satin disco pants and a blue polyester shirt with a '20s-themed vignette printed on it—some flappers, men in tuxes, and a roadster—like a book cover for *The Great Gatsby*.

And damn, the boy could dance, he was so light on his feet that at times he seemed to be floating, like a funky Fred Astaire . . . like Prince. He had one move where he pranced backward, hands in the air, shaking his ass—it was dead sexy. Sweat plastered his hair to his scalp. He had a dark complexion and fine, dark eyes with thick, girlish lashes, but what tickled Walter the most was his Burt Reynolds mustache, which was ridiculous, of course, something so literal and silly, the big, blatant *thereness* of it. And somehow it managed to make everything else about the boy kind of delicate, in contrast. One of those fashion statements the whole point of which is to say, *I can pull this off*.

Sort of like his Jughead cap, in theory. By now he hated the thing. Pulling it off, he felt like he might have been wearing a dunce cap all night. Watching Julian dance so freely, Walter felt a little electricity spark in his calves. He wondered, *If I go dance with this boy, could I convince him to take me home? His home—my home—wherever, some soft, springy, starlit Astroturf somewhere?* He messed up his helmet hair as best he could and, leaving his cap behind on the bench, headed out for one last dance.

Vertigo

WALTER HAD BEEN TRYING TO avoid Eliot, not least because Eliot was at this point demonstratively in love with Richard, spending every weekend with him and referring to him, nauseatingly, as *the professor*. (Richard, to his credit, would remind Eliot that he was not yet a professor, merely a *distinguished fellow*.) On the bright side, thanks to Richard, Walter was surprised to find himself becoming friends with Jeff, the world's only (Walter assumed) gay computer geek. While working on his master's, Jeff had moved to the Richmond and had plenty of time to spend. It turned out Walter and Jeff saw eye to eye, sharing a wry cynicism about certain things, like the gay community, and academia, and their lovebird friends, Eliot and Richard.

Making friends with another young gay guy in his twenties was always cagey: it meant gauging something new and tentative amid a flood of hormones telling you that what you needed most at every moment was not boring, old understanding or (*yawn*) companionship, but sex: unplanned, uninhibited, find-the-nearest-bathroom, porn-scenario sex. It came as a relief to Walter to realize early on that he and Jeff would not be an item, that there was no spark to speak of. No fuel, no flint, nothing at all combustible, thank goodness. So it definitely was not their fault the time they met for lunch and the restaurant caught on fire.

It was a Wednesday, and Jeff had a job interview downtown that afternoon and agreed to meet Walter for a quick lunch at Tú Lan, the Vietnamese hole-in-the-wall on Sixth Street. It was noon, crowded, and there was no space for them in the railroad dining room, with its single counter and sparse tables on the opposite wall, so a server led them up a back stairway to a tiny, windowless room that must have been a converted storage space. Textured white plastic panels covered the walls, for easy sponge-cleaning, like in a bathroom or a morgue. They ordered the imperial rolls to start. They were Walter's favorite because they were basically all sausage, with little glints of glass noodles, wrapped and fried in an egg roll.

Jeff talked about his imminent interview at a design firm called Iconic; he wasn't nervous about it, though he was concerned about juggling full-time work while completing his master's. Walter griped that he was deathly bored at the engineering firm and was beginning to worry that this temp gig was settling into something more permanent . . . yet he wasn't sure how to move on or where to move on to. The topic turned again to design, as it always seemed to with Jeff. They circled back to a conversation where Jeff was trying to explain something called *skeuomorphism*, which Walter kept hearing as *skew-morphism*.

"No," said Jeff, "it doesn't have anything to do with being *skewed* at all. It's really very simple, the best example is the garbage can icon on a Macintosh."

"So, it means an icon, like, a *picture of something*? Is that all?"

"It's not simply that it looks like something familiar; it's that it operates in a familiar manner. It looks like a tool and acts like that tool. So, like, a garbage can acts like a garbage can: you throw something in it, and it disappears. Or a volume dial turns like a dial, a sliding toggle slides, that kind of thing."

"Uh-huh, OK," said Walter. "So why is this a big deal?"

"Oh, it's not, really, it's just a way to make a friendly interface, if things operate in the digital world in the same way they do in the analog one— although there's no reason why they should have to . . ."

The egg rolls came, fresh from the fryer—too hot to touch—and the server shot back down the staircase in a flash.

Walter was laughing nervously—a couple of things Jeff said had a jargony strangeness he didn't know how to interpret. What was an *interface*, exactly? He thought of that optical illusion: a vase formed from two faces in silhouette. And there was a *digital world*? That is, the *digital* amounted to a *world*? And somehow, by implication, the *real world* was *an analog* of this digital one? Programmers were strange.

"I still think you could call it *skew-morphism*," Walter wondered aloud. "I mean, any picture of something 3D is going to be skewed by definition, right?"

"Hum. Why do you say that?"

"Because it's *flat*."

"Well, that's the thing about skeuomorphism—it's more three-dimensional," said Jeff, reaching for an egg roll.

"But it's still flat."

"Yeah, sure. But, you know, flatness can have dimensions."

At that moment, the server reappeared and informed them with utter dispassion that the restaurant was on fire, and they would have to evacuate immediately. There was no screaming and no fire alarm, but a loud, astonished commotion came from the kitchen. As they filed down the stairs, they saw a logjam of customers, some panicking—dashing for their lives—even as others could not be budged from their half-eaten bowls of pho, indignant that they should be asked to leave. More than one party was at the register, harassing the cashier for a to-go order or change on their bill, while everyone else pushed toward the doorway. The restaurant was indeed on fire, the woks and the griddle were blazing, and black creosote-belching flames were licking their way up the steel backsplash toward the hood, which was overwhelmed with smoke. Pushing forward, the mob extruded through the door and dispersed. Most everyone was on the street before one of the cooks managed to unleash the fire extinguisher. Walter and Jeff were among the last out; no one was hurt. On the sidewalk, there was some coughing and cursing, and neither sight nor sound of a fire engine. Regulars stood shaking their heads, saying, "Not again!"

On top of everything, the service had been slow, and now there was no time to find another restaurant. "I'll walk you down as far as Stockton," said Jeff, and as they headed toward Market, he handed Walter a romaine leaf. Wrapped inside it was an entire, beautifully golden imperial roll. Jeff had rescued one for himself, too. "Damned if I was going to leave these behind," he said.

"Oh my god, thank you!" said Walter, a little tickled, a little touched. "You're, like, my new best friend."

"No big deal. And it was free!"

They talked for another block as they walked and ate, then promised to hang out again soon and parted ways. Walter followed a familiar path alone up Stockton Street, absentmindedly licking his fingers, trying in vain to rid them of the smell of fish sauce and fryer oil.

It was overcast but bright and pleasant. He had time, so he thought he'd stop by the café cart in front of the Macy's men's shop, the one with the bistro tables, and get some coffee and maybe something sweet. He loved sitting there, under the canted sandstone overhang, because spread wide on the sidewalk was a flower stand that reminded him of the one in *Vertigo* where Scottie bought Judy a white flower—*an orchid, was it?*—for her green sweater.

As he approached the coffee cart, he was startled by a familiar pattern: it was the leopard-print coat of the gamine. He recognized first the print, the dangling belt, the high collar, then the back of the neck: there the gamine stood, plain as day and stylish as anything, buying coffee. His back was to Walter, and his blond hair was worn up, not in a bun but in a swirl—*a Madeleine swirl*, the same *Vertigo* swirl into which Scottie fell, and not a hair out of place, either—it was too much for Walter; this impossibly glamorous creature was now channeling Kim Novak.

As Walter stood dumbfounded, the gamine turned swiftly toward the crosswalk and strode between the two Macy's facades that faced off— *interfaced*—across Stockton, disappearing behind the glass doors into the jewelry displays. Forgetting coffee, or work, or any other motive, Walter ran after him, into the maze of shining display cases where he'd lost him once before, feeling like a brazen lunatic, not even keeping a respectful distance. He slowed down, he reasoned with himself, then overcame his reason, hypnotized by the belt that swung at the boy's side. Through the jewelry counters he stalked this stately cat, and then up the escalator, and then a second escalator, all the time thinking, *What the fuck am I doing?*

Hopping off the escalator, the gamine, never once looking back, catwalked through towering shelves of plush bath towels and rows of curtain displays, into which Walter was ready to plunge if the young man ever glanced back. But he never did. He moved on, waving *Hi, Martina!* to a cashier almost hidden behind a tall white laminate desk. She was busy reading a receipt, and Walter was thankful that she didn't leap from behind the desk and try to help him. He followed the boy into a large back room, which was white as midwinter, a glacier at noon, each wall with white shelves reaching to the ceiling and packed with folded clouds of goose down duvets. Fat white pillows, shining in plastic, were stacked in clear Plexiglas kiosks placed around the room. By the time he had taken the room in, the gamine had disappeared. But there was only one place he could have gone. A pair of white doors with black windows were still swinging on their hinges beside a sign that said "Employees Only."

Walter stalled in this heaven of plastic-wrapped clouds for about thirty seconds, long enough to imagine he was thinking better of what he was about to do, and to be sure no one was watching him. As soon as the doors stopped swinging, he pushed through them. He was in a long, tall, dark gray hallway stretching off to his left and right. But while the right-hand path was very dark and packed to impassible with carts freighted with inventory, the hallway to his left was a bit more welcoming. Although cluttered with hand trucks and shelving, light pooled at intervals from dim bulbs suspended overhead, and farther down, a couple of open doors brightened the passage. Here and there, mannequins stood sentry in various states of undress and disassembly. Armless sentries, legless sentries, helpless torsos. Creepy, but harmless. Walter sneaked a few yards down this hallway, wondering if he'd lost his mind—what on earth did he think the best outcome of this scenario might be?

He had decided to turn back, when a young man appeared in the closest doorway and, seeing Walter, came rushing toward him, saying, "Ah!" He was short and very slim, about Walter's age. He had brass wire-rimmed glasses with small oval lenses. He was carrying a large white poster board under one arm.

"Can you draw a lobster?" asked the man, holding up a Magic Marker.

"Uh . . ." was all that Walter got out at first, and even as one large portion of his brain was crying *Retreat, retreat!*—the wheels in another part spun to action, reasoning through how to draw a lobster, where he'd seen lobsters: in tanks, on banks of crushed ice at seafood counters, on restaurant signs . . . He knew he could draw well enough, especially things with hard edges, things that were halfway to cartoons already, like lobsters.

"I think I can," said Walter, and they moved down the hall to where there was some decent light and a stray pedestal where they could stand and draw. "It's basically like a giant shrimp with claws, right?" This sounded reasonable to him as he was saying it, and as he started to draw, he theorized, "I think the trick is figuring out how many segments they have, in the tail, in the, uh, arms . . ." He improvised six sections for the tail proper and five fanned out at the end. The serrated claws were easiest to draw, vicious oven mitts. He fitted the cone-like head with a pair of beady insect eyes on stalks and swoopingly drew two switches for antennae. Anatomically it must have been all wrong, but for a spur-of-the-moment thing, he was happy with it.

"Hey, this is great!" said the man.

As Walter fretted that the lobster's tail was too long, another man arrived, shuffling from farther down the hallway. He was a middle-aged man with graying hair, nearly bald on top, a reddish goatee, a ticking shirt, and old-fashioned button-in suspenders that stretched over a large belly.

"What's going on?" asked the older man.

"It's for the Cape Cod theme Cindy wants for the basement. I couldn't figure out how to draw a lobster, so he helped me."

"Who is this?" the man scowled, pointing at Walter.

"He works in the basement—don't you work in the basement?"

"Um, no, *sorry*! I somehow got lost . . ." And then, in the middle of a mortifying display of verbal backpedaling, Walter found himself saying, "I was looking for your HR department. I'm looking to apply to . . . a job—I need a job."

"In the display department?" asked the older man, still scowling.

"Yes!" said Walter, without hesitation, as if it had been his plan all along.

"It's the right time to ask," the man said, looking a bit more amenable, "with the holidays coming up pretty quick. You'll need to talk to Cindy, though. Clark, could you take him down to the basement to find Cindy?"

"Sure thing," Clark said. "Follow me, and we'll show her your awesome lobster!" When Walter thanked him, he said, "You can really draw. Hopefully she won't give you *my* job."

Private Lives

WALTER STARTED AT MACY'S THE next week, working on displays in the basement. The temp agency needed almost no notice to let him off his assignment—all those weeks in that filing closet, and in the end he was still a widget, as replaceable as his Swatch's battery. Underground at Macy's, the cafeteria, prepared foods, and kitchenware departments were in the middle of being overhauled to look like a cozy shop-lined street in a New England seaboard town. Massachusetts or Maine, who knew? Customers apparently liked to feel that at any moment they might run into Jessica Fletcher while choosing a panini press. It was funny to him that he'd gone from arranging engineering blueprints in filing cubbies to arranging smoked almonds and pralines on the tops of wooden barrels, under foam-core cutouts of seagulls he had made. And he'd gotten a pay bump to boot. His manager, Cindy, was a perky suburbanite who commuted from Livermore and was a little too excited about her job. He got along with her fine, despite the fact that she'd made him redraw the seagulls: his first batch, she claimed, were too *mean looking* around the eyes and reminded her of Hitchcock's *The Birds*, which was exactly what he liked about them.

The department store was huge; considering the square footage of both buildings and all the employees, he figured it was larger than his hometown. For the most part he stayed in the basement and almost never went up to the fourth-floor storerooms where he'd seen the gamine disappear. So it happened that, after more than a week at the job, he'd never once run into him.

He thought the boy might have psychically sensed that he was coming and quit the very day he started. Or maybe he never worked there: maybe, randomly, he had been visiting a friend who worked in the storerooms. He tried to put the whole thing out of his mind. He'd had this weird impulse, in a frenzied moment, and it had pushed him into a new situation where he now felt more or less calm and happy. Maybe the gamine wasn't a person at all, he imagined, but a phantom, a symbol. Or not even a symbol: a catalyst. A way for him to move on along an unforeseen path. Fate was a lovely idea, he thought, but a trite thing to believe in. Maybe pralines were his fate.

Then, the weekend before Halloween, Walter had another encounter that felt fateful. He was wandering around the Castro, thinking of taking in a matinee—usually his first thought when he had a free afternoon. He was killing time in that singular way that's so delicious when you get to live in your favorite city, when even boredom can feel diverting and luxurious.

He came across a card store on Eighteenth east of Castro Street, a small shop with a mystifying name: Bob's Your Uncle. Jeff's birthday was coming up that week, he thought he'd look for a card for him. Nodding hello to the man behind the counter, he headed to the back of the store. The shop was long and narrow and pale mango yellow; it was one of those *fun* eclectic card shops. There were rainbows everywhere, of course: tissue-paper rainbows, rayon rainbows, wind socks, and key chains, and rainbow-casting prisms turning slowly in the window. While the front of the store was aerated with rainbows, the back was stuffy, the air heavy and honeyed, smelling of beeswax candles. Walter sifted through birthday cards, looking for something not horrendously corny. He didn't notice the salesmen changing shift—he heard a bit of conversation, then one man left, and the music changed abruptly from Bananarama to some very old, bluesy jazz—Bessie Smith or something. He heard the sound of typing and saw that a man was sitting in the window, his back to the store, clacking away on an electric typewriter.

Displayed on the back wall of the store was a series of tidy handmade cards, all in the same style, and the more Walter browsed through them the stranger they seemed. Each was on heavy, cream-colored rag. Each contained a quote by some famous person on the front, or the inside, or spread out between the two. Each card had a picture of, ostensibly, the author of the quotation, in a glossy photograph pasted on the front. It dawned on him that some of the quotations and some of the photographs seemed . . . *off*, some of them *really off.* There was a Noël Coward quote that didn't sound anything like Noël Coward, while a quote attributed to Golda Meir, which sounded like it could be her, was accompanied by a photograph of an elderly Ingrid Bergman. A card with a photo of Quentin Crisp (at least it looked like Quentin Crisp, or it might have been someone from the cast of *Are You Being Served?*) suggested that beneath his lavender rinse was a scatterbrain:

```
If you're not ambivalent, you're not paying
attention! Or maybe you're paying too much
attention to the wrong things. Or perhaps
to the correct things. How should I know?
It's all style anyway.
                          —Quentin Crisp
```

Though the cards were labeled "All Occasions," he couldn't think of a single occasion they'd be appropriate for. On the back of each card was typed: Beggar's Belief Editions. All at once, he noticed the common font and connected it to the mechanical *rat-a-tat* that was firing away at the other end of the store. Intrigued, he had questions for the proprietor, and so he gathered up several of the cards and headed for the counter. From hidden speakers a very old-sounding woman was singing a beautiful blues rendition of "Sweet Georgia Brown." At first the man didn't notice that Walter had laid some cards on the counter, he kept typing away with his back turned. His shoulders were compact; he was wearing a print shirt with tiny violet florets and a black-and-white houndstooth vest. Walter waved to catch his eye and the young man turned, and Walter saw his mistake at once.

It was the woman he had seen at the Castro Theatre with the gamine—the night he'd seen *Gilda* with Fiona. There was no mistaking her. She was quite tall, taller than Walter, at least at the moment—she must have been on a platform behind the high counter. Her wavy brown hair was parted and combed down, silky with pomade. She had big amber-hazel eyes that bulged a bit, and her smile as she greeted him was crooked and toothy, but appealing. As he thought when he'd first seen her, she was right on the line between handsome and goofy looking. She wore a woolen houndstooth bow tie, made from the same material as the vest. The whole effect was . . . *dashing* . . . *debonair*, in a way. All the words he could think of to describe her were masculine, in a nineteenth-century way. British, antique. It struck him: she was a *dandy*—something he'd read about and seen in movies but never encountered—what's more, a *female dandy*. But she was also younger than he'd realized—not a girl, but not that much older than him.

No gal made has got a shade on swee-eet Georgia Brown, crooned the old blues lady, backed by brass.

Walter stood there dumbly, at a loss for words. Though she had stepped away from it, the typewriter was still sputtering along, the carriage return clunking and the paper inching upward, and after a short pause, the typing rattled on without the typist.

"I think your typewriter's possessed," said Walter.

"Good god!" said the dandy, placing her palms at her temples. "This can't be happening!" She spun around, as if looking for some weapon to use to bash the poltergeist out of her typewriter. Then she dropped the act and reassured Walter: "Ah-ah, it's actually this ingenious new invention they call a *word processor*." She winked. "In effect, it remembers what I've typed and can type it again." She nodded as if to say, *It's true!*

"Brave new world!" said Walter.

There passed between them a rather awkward pause, decorated by blue notes and the erratic percussion of the daisy wheel.

"I love your shoes!" declared the dandy, leaning over the counter. "I love the color."

They both stared down at his electric-blue Doc Martens. "They're my favorite color," he said. "Amanda."

"I beg your pardon? That is *not* my name . . ."

"No, I mean—sorry—I painted my bookshelf this color. When I got the paint from Cliff's, Amanda was *the name of the color.*"

"I see. So they're not just any old blue shoes. They're *Amanda-blue shoes.*"

"Right," said Walter, feeling idiotic.

"Fabulous!" said the dandy. "Would you like to buy those cards?"

"This one . . . I think." He handed her the Quentin Crisp card. "I have *some questions* about the others."

"Trouble committing?"

"More like . . . trouble *believing*?" As he laid the cards on the counter, he noticed her orderly assembly line: the blank cards by the typewriter, the pile of trimmed black-and-white photographs, the uncapped glue stick. "I think . . . someone . . . whoever . . . might have mixed up some of these photographs. And also, some of the quotes seem . . . *wrong*? I guess."

"You don't say?" She wrinkled her nose the way a quality inspector might on a factory floor.

I'll tell you just why, interjected the blues singer, *you know I don't lie, not much now* . . .

"For example, I like this quote, but I can't believe Godard ever said this." Together they leaned over a card with a picture of a man in horn-rims and a trench coat, pouting despondently on a park bench. It read:

```
You can't kiss a movie. But you can kiss a
gaffer. You can kiss a grip, go for the best
boy! You can kiss an electrician, if you're
brave, or a stuntman, if you're quick,
or a starlet, if you're lucky. If you find
yourself kissing a screenwriter, watch out!
                              —Jean-Luc Godard
```

"Isn't it amazing? He sounds a lot queerer than anyone knew, doesn't he?" she said, in all seriousness.

"Suspiciously so . . ." Walter was stumped. He knew the quote couldn't be right, and yet there wasn't the slightest indication on her face that she was joking. She was either an idiot, or maybe insane, or else making fun of him on a heightened level he'd never experienced before.

"You do realize," said Walter, holding up the card, "that this is not a picture of Jean-Luc Godard."

"It's not? It certainly looks like him . . ."

"It's Gene Hackman in *The Conversation*."

"Really?" She picked up the card, examined it, and shrugged. "Never seen it."

"San Franciscans ought to recognize him—it's the best San Francisco movie from the seventies, I think . . ."

At this, the dandy's eyes bugged, possibly from offense, and she leaned forward with theatrical concern. "Is that so? Better than *What's Up, Doc?* You'd better watch what you say in this neighborhood, unless you want the Streisand Mafia to put a hit out on you."

Feeling scolded, Walter handed back the card. The dandy laughed gingerly.

"It's so funny you should bring it up," she said, "because the whole point of the Beggar's Belief product line is to highlight quotes that you can't quite believe the person said or, in some cases, that anyone ever said. So then, the fun comes in suspending your disbelief."

Walter gave her a look of thoroughly unsuspended disbelief, and rather than ringing him up and wishing him good afternoon, she declared, "You can be my guinea pig! Will you be my guinea pig?"

Before he could answer, she had taken several cards and laid them out on the counter before him.

"Now," she said, "which of these sayings seem most plausible, and which seem most implausible? If you want, you can arrange them on a scale."

He considered each card carefully: she had included the dubious Godard quote with the Noël Coward one and three others. Not wanting to insult her right off the bat, he chose one that seemed pretty reasonable. It featured a photo of an etching of a serious-looking eighteenth-century man, big hair like Beethoven's. It said:

```
A dinner which ends without cheese is like
a beautiful woman with only one eye.
              —Jean-Anthelme Brillat-Savarin
```

Walter read it aloud and laughed. "This one sounds right, I guess," he said.

"Words to live by!" declared the dandy.

Then Walter took a chance: "I've never read this guy myself, but I think M. F. K. Fisher writes about him somewhere? When she's writing about France?"

A look of unrestrained joy bloomed across the dandy's boyish face. "Gah!" she cried. "You know about M. F. K. Fisher?"

Walter nodded, thinking he was glad he wasn't carrying one of her books in his bag, as he might have pulled it out and really embarrassed himself. In the back of his head, he was calculating how long this conversation could go on before he'd have to admit, *By the way, I think you're dating a boy I've been stalking for over a month.*

"Doesn't everyone know about her?" he asked.

"*Doesn't everyone . . . ?* Listen to you. No, of course not! Only the very best people know about Mary Frances. She's like a shibboleth for awesomeness."

Walter tried to suppress a smile; he had no idea what a *shibboleth* was, but he loved the sound of it. Meanwhile the dandy was pressing him to go on with his analysis.

"Well, let's see . . . Who knows what Pythagoras might have looked like?" Walter said, picking up a card with a picture of a bearded man with blank eyes: a photo of a drawing of a marble bust. "It's a funny quote, but honestly, on what occasion would you give someone this card?" He handed it to her. The card said:

```
The consumption of beans is a crime
equivalent to eating both one's parents'
heads.
                              —Pythagoras
```

She read it and set it down. "Oh, it's sort of a catchall greeting. Anyway, I guarantee Pythagoras said that. It's his second most famous quote, right after *everything is numbers*, but nobody wants to be told *everything is numbers* on their birthday! Don't you think? Except for, maybe, an accountant. Don't look at me that way. He said it. I read it in a book!"

"Books don't lie."

"No, not to me. Or at least, not if you read them right." Her hazel eyes sparked. Tigereye agates.

"OK, I'm taking your word for it," said Walter. "Anyway, I'm not sure I can tell Noël Coward from Pythagoras, but I can't believe he ever said this." He held up the card that said:

```
I should like to cut off your head with a
meat-ax.
                              —Noël Coward
```

"Oh *really?*" said the dandy, with narrowed eyes and a slightly haughty edge to her voice. "He most definitely did, I can prove it."

"When would he have said that?"

"It's a line from *Private Lives*. The first act balcony scene."

"So, technically, *a character* said it—"

"Yes, in the most glorious comic fight!"

"I've never seen that one," said Walter. "I love *Brief Encounter*."

"I think my copy is sitting on top of my VCR at home, if you'd like me to take you there and prove it to you."

He paused, noting that this eccentric young woman had just invited him to her apartment. "Huh," he said. "*Cleaver* would have been funnier."

"What's that?"

"The word *cleaver* is funnier than the word *ax*, don't you think?" said Walter. "He should have written: *I ought to chop your head off with a cleaver.*"

The dandy thought about this for a few seconds. Holding the card before her, she looked back and forth between Noël Coward and Walter. "You know what? I think you're right. But I'm also positive you need the word *meat*. The word *meat* is always funny."

"Hysterical," said Walter.

"*I ought to chop your head off with a meat cleaver!*" She took a pen from the desk, and in a few swift strokes she edited the quote on the card. "That's better, don't you think? He's dead, so he won't mind if we change it. To be honest, we haven't sold many of these, so maybe a change of wording would help."

By this point, Walter could not figure out what to make of this strange, nerdy, funny, exuberant, overgrown tomboy. She was so totally peculiar; everything about her seemed anachronistic, from her fancy, costumey outfit, to her shiny Rudy Vallee hair, to the rapid-fire *His Girl Friday* way that she spoke, to her bizarre sense of humor that he was now starting to catch on to. He also sensed from subtle currents beneath their conversation, and the way she sized him up from behind the counter, that she was flirting with him, a little, and this threw him off entirely. As far as he could tell, a girl hadn't flirted with him in years, not since he came out sophomore year. Yet it didn't feel like flirting with a girl, exactly, or, for that matter, it didn't feel like any conversation he'd ever had. He expected that at any second she would remember herself, ring him up for the card, thank him, and send him on his way. Instead she stood there, smiling her off-kilter smile, waiting on him . . . for what? Something. Then he saw that there was one card left that they hadn't examined.

"OK, I'll grant you your Noël Coward," he said. "And maybe this *is* a picture of Virginia Woolf, I don't know. But I am absolutely, totally, one thousand percent sure that Virginia Woolf never said this." He pushed the card toward her on the counter.

```
Style is a simple matter; it is all rhythm.
Boony-chi ba-dooly-doon, ba-dooly-doon-chism.
                              —Virginia Woolf
```

"Oh, you mean the second part?" she asked. "No, that's supposed to be the bongos she was playing while she said it. It's, like, a transcription."

He hid his eyes with his hand and laughed. It was a frustrated, disbelieving laugh that rumbled away in his belly until it burst from him in giddy relief. "I think that is the most absurd thing I have *ever heard*," he said, unable to look her in the eye.

When he calmed down, he looked up and the dandy was staring at him, eyes wide, as though she'd had a brilliant realization.

"You're a *writer*!" she proclaimed, as if it were both a revelation and a benediction.

Walter felt accused. "What makes you say that?" he asked.

"Because you stood on this spot, right in front of me, and brazenly line edited Noël Coward! Do you think you're a better writer than Noël Coward? Or Virginia Woolf?"

Walter froze in place, called out. She had called him a *writer*. He was thinking of the army of posers he saw every afternoon, crowding every coffee shop. *Working on their novels*. *Working on their zines*. Hammering out their epic *slam poetry*, their *screenplays*. Did she peg him as one of them? And yet . . . and yet. They couldn't all be posers, could they? Statistically, out of sheer simians-with-typewriters numbers, some of them would end up being the next Jack Kerouac, harnessing dharma; the next Allen Ginsberg, learning to howl. Meanwhile, what had he ever written? Some crummy poems and stories from high school and college he was too embarrassed to show to anyone. He stood there silently berating himself at the speed of thought, while the dandy awaited his reply with waning anticipation, like a kid watching a sparkler burn down, when it finally occurred to him that the simple answer to her accusation was *yes*.

"Yes," he said.

"Yes?"

"Yes."

"Yes . . . you think you're a better writer than Virginia Woolf?!"

"Oh god, no! No! I mean, yes, I'm a *writer*. Guilty, OK? I just haven't figured out what kind. Or how. Or why. You know, minor details."

"Minor details, agreed. I'll tell you what," she continued in hushed excitement, "maybe you'd like to contribute to Beggar's Belief Editions, my own line of greeting cards. I can commission you!" She shuffled through her stack of photographs, then handed him a picture of a tight-lipped girl whose hair was concealed by a black felt bell. He examined the photograph but didn't say anything, so she went on: "I'm having a little trouble coming up with a Dorothy Parker quote."

"*Coming up with?*" asked Walter.

"You know, *a new one*, a funny one that no one's ever heard of, and also one that doesn't make you want to kill yourself would be nice, unlike that *hilarious* one about how you'd better shoot yourself in the head, because nooses don't work or something like that."

"What do you mean you'll *commission* me?"

"Well, let's see, if you're interested, of course, how about a trial period? You can pitch me a Dorothy Parker quote or two in exchange for a cup of coffee. And then, of course, there is the prestige of having your words immortalized on a greeting card! And after that . . . we can deliberate and see if you want to do more."

Something stopped him from saying no right away, even though this was something that, in the abstract, he wouldn't have considered doing; it wasn't anything he would've dreamed up. And yet, he now had the inane thought: *Would writing a Dorothy Parker quote be any harder than drawing a lobster? It couldn't be that hard.* They were standing in a bright little echo chamber of blues music, teeming with rainbows, the dandy awaiting his reply, when it dawned on him that whatever else this bizarrely charming tomboy wanted, she was trying to befriend him. And, at the moment, new friends topped the list of things he needed most.

"OK," he said, "OK, I'll try. I'll probably suck at it, so I'm not promising anything! But, when I've come up with one or two, how will I find you?"

The dandy pulled a wallet from her back pocket, fat with dozens of cards. She selected one from the bunch, examined it, and handed it to him.

CARY MENUHIN
PRODUCER AND PUBLISHER
BEGGAR'S BELIEF EDITIONS
SAN FRANCISCO

Her phone number was on the bottom. "I'm Cary, by the way," she said. "Like Cary Grant!"

"Exactly. I, too, hated my birth name . . ." She blinked. ". . . Archibald."

"Oh! OK." Walter laughed skeptically.

She held out her hand, and he shook it. Then, remembering her job, she rang up the card and slipped it in a small bag.

Walter paid and said, "Sorry—I don't have a business card!"

"That's OK. You can find me here most evenings, feel free to drop by! Or, otherwise, I mean sometimes, if I'm not here, I'm taking a break at Pasqua—across the street. Or in the morning I often hang out at Jumpin' Java on Noe."

Walter said he was sure he would see her soon, thanked her, and left. As he crossed the street and walked toward Cliff's Variety, he was thinking how strange people's social impulses are, really. She couldn't possibly have wanted him to come seek her out at a coffee shop some random morning, could she? How awkward would that be? She was certainly an *interesting* person. And what if they did become friends, and it turned out she really was dating the gamine? He began imagining a humiliating scenario in which he had to confess and explain to both of them that even though he'd been mildly obsessed with the gamine, it really wasn't in a *sexual way* or anything, nothing like that, so it wasn't *creepy at all*. At the most, he'd *taken a new job* in the hopes of meeting him. *Ha ha!* they would all laugh together. *What a perfectly normal thing to have done!*

He turned and walked into the most beautiful hardware store in the world, which was all done up for Halloween: giant cobwebs radioactive with purple black light, haunted William Castle sound effects, rubbery skeletons dangling, and funereal lawn ornaments everywhere, though nobody in San Francisco had a lawn. As he browsed the aisles seeking inspiration for a costume, he thought of something else embarrassing. When Cary had introduced herself, he wasn't at all sure that he'd told her his name. She was kind of an overwhelming person—she talked very fast. He wasn't sure. He stopped at the end of an aisle stocked with puzzles and toys. Bobbleheads bobbled to the baying of a werewolf. *Had he told her his name while they were shaking hands?* As he stared at a mannequin that was dolled up like the Invisible Man—wearing an embroidered smoking jacket, black aviators over a face concealed by bandages, and a fedora—he knew for sure that he hadn't.

Children of Paradise

WALTER AND JULIAN WERE STANDING under the marquee of the Castro. It was shortly after nine at night, but they were awash in warm light from the array of bulbs above them. Julian was smoking while leaning against a poster display advertising a lesbian vampire film series coming up next. Catherine Deneuve peered peevishly over his shoulder. They weren't saying much. It wasn't clear what either of them really wanted at the moment.

Julian broke the silence. "Yeah, I think I'm gonna go . . ." He'd just started his cigarette, so he didn't seem in a hurry.

Walter's heart sank. Julian was one of Fiona's best friends, but he was surprisingly hard to get hold of. Like Fiona, he was a party girl, a raver with a full dance card. They'd been playing a very sporadic game of phone tag ever since the morning they'd danced together at the EndUp. That morning they'd hopped in a cab on the way to Julian's and started making out in the back while the cab raced by the Brannan flower market setting up at sunrise—it was so lovely—until Julian remembered he had promised to meet some friends at Sparky's Diner and redirected the cab. Walter tagged along and was completely spent that morning and the whole next day. But he remembered vividly what a great kisser Julian was.

Walter had pretty much given up on him, when Julian called out of the blue, murmuring, *I'm free tomorrow*, over the phone, his soft voice a little gravelly. But Walter should have known better than to propose this for their first date. A three-and-a-half-hour black-and-white French art film? What the hell was he thinking? The movie was so long that it required an intermission, which is how they wound up standing outside the theater, getting "fresh air," and waiting for the second half. But Walter had wanted desperately to see *Les enfants du paradis*, and if he missed it this weekend who knew when he would get the chance again? Plus it was a romantic movie—that part was guaranteed—so he convinced himself it would make a good date movie.

"I kind of guessed you weren't into it."

Julian pressed his lips around the cigarette as he inhaled and fixed Walter with his sleepy brown eyes. "It's kinda not really . . . my thing," he said, a little chagrined. He looked down. "I guess I thought it was boring." Exhaling, Julian smiled at him in a sheepish, irresistible way that asked, *Forgive me?* The boy clearly knew he was cute, and up close—outside of a nightclub—his mustache was even more absurd, like a kid's idea of adult sophistication, while it was clear from his perfect complexion that he was not a day over twenty.

"That's OK," said Walter. "I guess it is pretty slow-paced—but you don't want to stay and see what happens?"

It was a hopeless thing to ask. The movie was a love story where a mime pines away for a prostitute, and people said things like, *I will wait as long as it takes for you to love me in the way I love you!* Wasn't Julian dying to know if the mime ever gets with the prostitute? Clearly not, because a half hour into the movie he had fallen asleep on Walter's shoulder and didn't budge for the next hour and a half. Walter didn't dare move, even as his shoulder fell asleep and tingled irritably. The truth was he was swept away by the movie: the magnificent sets, the costumes, the unrelenting *Frenchness* of it all. He loved the staginess of the whole thing, the acrobatics of the Funambules, framed within the soundstage of the Boulevard of Thieves, framed by the gilt proscenium of the Castro. He was in heaven. And heightening his nirvana was the weight and warmth of this handsome boy's head on his shoulder. He smelled sweet, too, like sandalwood. Walter was only sorry that they'd broken for intermission at all.

"What was wrong with that guy's teeth?" asked Julian.

"What do you mean?"

"The mime guy—Baptiste. His teeth were so gray! It was kind of gross." Julian laughed.

Walter shook his head and conjured a smile.

Julian finished smoking. "Look," he said, "maybe tonight wasn't the night for it. I gotta work tomorrow—I was up all night last night. Can we do something another time? Get a drink or something?" He dropped the cigarette and crushed it underfoot.

"Sorry," said Walter. "Yeah, sure! I'd love to get a drink."

They hugged, and he readied himself for a peck on the cheek goodbye, but Julian leaned in and kissed him for real, kissed him deeply. The kiss was a kind of promise, or maybe an apology *and* a promise. It was bursting with smoke but so toe-curling that Walter almost ran after Julian as he walked off toward the bus stop. But he didn't. As mute and obstinate as Baptiste, he wandered back into the theater, back to the Boulevard of Thieves.

The following Sunday, on Halloween, Walter and Jeff were tripping down the steep blocks of Seventeenth Street from Ashbury to the Castro, sharing sips of Maker's Mark from a large flask. The fog had come in at dusk and it was dark, and they made it about halfway down the hill before they realized how late they were to the party. Market Street was closed off at Castro and a stage had been set up there, and although it was still early, the crowd was already massive and the noise intense.

Jeff was dressed as someone from the starship *Enterprise*, but Walter didn't have the heart to tell him he'd chosen the most boring character. Who thought twice about Commander Riker? His maroon-and-black polyester leisure suit was the genuine article, purchased at a Trekkie convention, along with a silver-and-brass communicator badge, which looked like an arrow clicking on a dot, as if his chest were itself an interface. Jeff had tried to grow a beard to look more like Jonathan Frakes, but after a full month the beard was sparse, and at any rate, his thick glasses spoiled the illusion. He looked more like some nameless ensign, glassy-eyed and abandoned by the crew, whose anonymity—in the *Star Trek* plot template—would mark him as the first to die on an alien planet of painted plaster.

Walter couldn't judge—he knew his sailor costume wasn't particularly inspired. At first he wanted to be a very specific sailor: Brad Davis as Querelle in the Fassbinder film, an ultra-pretentious movie it seemed most people hated—even gay guys—and yet it was hotter than any porn he'd ever seen. The problem was that, as Querelle, Brad Davis was basically sex incarnate, strutting around a priapic pier where it was perpetually sunset, glazed in sweat, with his pecs bursting out of his tank top. Walter knew there was no way he could pull that off, not least because half the eroticism was in the movie's hothouse atmosphere. So he wound up being a generic sailor, buying a cap and an authentic wool outfit on Haight Street. He felt pretty cute, but in the end, had to admit he was probably about as sexy as the Cracker Jack sailor.

They were running so late already. Eliot and Richard had expected them at *eightish*.

"Too bad your communicator doesn't work," said Walter. "We could have Eliot beam us over to Café Flore!"

At Sixteenth and Divisadero, they stood looking down to where the Bagdad Café shone yellow in the distance, overflowing with people. A parade of pedestrians was marching into the middle of the street from every spur of the three-way intersection, the denizens of every neighborhood on the peninsula—and beyond—descending upon four blocks in the heart of the Castro.

"We'll never find them!" said Walter.

"Oh, it's not so bad," said Jeff. "I can still see some asphalt."

Even as he said this, they watched a phalanx of drunken ghouls crash into a police barricade, flattening a temporary fence and tumbling into the crowd.

"Should we have started earlier?" asked Jeff. "Eliot said no one would be here before eight."

As they marched down the block toward the café, to their left the Metro Bar, with its wraparound balcony, was pouring techno down into the street, an oppressive, trudging bass line, shrill synth chords, and a muscular male voice singing, *What is love? Baby, don't hurt me . . .*

"God, I fucking hate this song," said Jeff.

"But it's the music of our people!" Walter laughed.

"If I have to dance to *this*, I don't want to be part of the revolution."

It was crowded out the door at Café Flore, and every table was taken, inside and out, and there was no sign of Eliot, Richard, or anyone else they knew. The kitchen was open; dinner was served on the patio of the damned: demons with their vampire teeth and bloody, leprous limbs were piled upon benches under the faded wisteria, sitting in each other's laps, drinking cappuccinos and Lillets. They toured the café, then waited on the sidewalk sipping whisky, and Walter, ever the lightweight, felt it going to his head.

"Walleye!" yelled a soldier in a small platoon coming toward them on the sidewalk. The platoon was decked out in olive camouflage fatigues and combat boots, and yet their outfits were falling apart, and rainbows erupted from their seams: rainbow undershirts, socks, boxers, armbands; color-wheel bandannas around their necks. For a second Walter hadn't recognized Eliot, because his long hair was tucked up under a camo helmet.

"We're gays in the military!" Eliot gave Walter a hug and a direct, undodgeable kiss on the lips, then looked him up and down, and said, "So are you!"

"Yes, I was trying to make a political statement, for sure."

"Don't ask, don't tell, baby!" Eliot yelled, and laughed as he hugged Jeff.

As the platoon's commander, Eliot ordered the group to cede Café Flore at once and head up the block toward Café San Marcos; the balcony there would have the best view of the stage and the rest of the action. They waded into the wide intersection, a bay of boogeymen in a sea of shades, and it was clear the crowd had grown even thicker. A woman darted in front of them dressed as Lorena Bobbitt, her costume no more than a big, curly brown wig and half a silicon dildo she wagged in one hand, fresh fake blood on the cut. Stumbling behind her was a drag king John Wayne Bobbitt, smiling demonically, a bloody rubber scrotum bandaged to his crotch.

"She sacrificed a perfectly good dildo for that costume!" declared Richard.

"Ugh, there are so many bridge-and-tunnelers out tonight!" Eliot scolded the crowd around him. When Walter asked how he could tell, he said, "Obviously! They're the drunk heteros who didn't bother dressing up."

"What are you bitching about?" asked Jeff. "I've never seen so many people in drag!"

"All dress is drag," said Eliot.

"True enough, I guess . . ." Jeff rolled his eyes.

As they stirred through the witch's brew of the crowd, Walter began a quick taxonomy of costumes, which fell right away into three general categories: dead (or rather undead, including vampires, zombies, mummies, etc.), drag (scary, clownish, or glam, but otherwise plain, old cross-dressing), and sexy/slutty (mostly sexy sluts in uniform, and he included his lame gesture toward Brad Davis here). The categories could be crossed, so you had your sex-bomb drag queens with their sculpted foam curves under layers and layers of bronze hose; your pallid, goth zombie queens (definitely undead, definitely scary, definitely not sexy); and, most obviously, your sexy vampires; and then, of course, all three combined into one: your sexy/slutty undead drag queen/king vampires. Night of the Streetwalking Dead. Distracted by the bare chest and swirling salt-and-pepper pelt of a werewolf, Walter almost tripped over a pink-skirted, middle-aged man dressed as Jem. Jem was carrying a 40 in a brown paper bag and screaming for the Holograms to *wait up!*

As they soldiered on past the Market Street Gym, Walter caught his first glimpse of what would prove to be the most impressive costume of the night. A queen was promenading down the center of the street in full Elizabethan costume: a gigantic hoop skirt, monstrous inflated sleeves, a collar like a black pterodactyl wing that towered over the tiers of her hair and crown, and, trailing from her shoulders, a black-and-silver train, many yards long and raised above the pavement by four attendants, all in black Elizabethan garb. She came with her own soundtrack: one of her footmen carried a large boom box blasting Dead Can Dance's "Saltarello." In the mobbed street, people were pushing back and clearing a path while she frowned down her nose at them imperiously.

"Get her!" said Eliot.

"She's *fabulous!*" Richard gasped.

If this was Elizabeth I, Walter realized, she had arrived in San Francisco after an extensive tour *Beyond Thunderdome.* Her bustier and sleeves were not fancy jacquard but black plastic striped with duct tape, her high collar a ruined umbrella, the ruff around her neck an old carburetor filter. Her shimmering black dress and train were garbage bags and silver spray paint. The curls of her humongous wig enveloped not one but three crowns; two of them appeared to be large gears, the third a Bundt pan. Walter was so entranced by her that he almost lost track of his friends, who had marched onward.

It took them a full fifteen minutes to get up the stairs at Café San Marcos and another fifteen to fight their way to the bar and order drinks. Walter got Long Island iced teas for himself and Jeff; they came in pint glasses and were like three drinks in one. Economical. The bar was packed to the last square foot, so they stood slurping their drinks through tiny straws while they were elbowed and jammed from every possible angle.

"We're leaving!" shouted Eliot.

"We just got here!" said Walter.

"There's no room on the balcony—we might as well go back outside," said Eliot, pulling Richard back down the stairs with him.

By now the street was almost as packed as the bar had been. Walter had slammed his drink and was now drunk, and everything from then on was a blur of looming, menacing masks, distended by screams, bloated with laughter. Eliot, wanting another drink, determined they should troop over to Badlands, and the platoon fell in line. At least it was somewhat quieter outside. On a stage raised up above the Castro MUNI station, a counterfeit Eartha Kitt danced, in full Catwoman costume, motorcycle and all, lip-syncing to "C'est si bon." The crowd was raving, the inmates of Bedlam were let loose for the night, baring their bodies and their teeth, seducing, spooking, thrilling each other in kind.

Eartha was on a francophone kick, and the high accordion strains of "Je cherche un homme" echoed through the asylum. Walter recalled the carnival on the Boulevard of Thieves, for as they neared Castro the crush was so tight that their platoon was squeezed into single file, and he had to hold Jeff's hand to make sure he didn't lose the pack entirely. Everything looked like a set to him: the stage, of course, but also the painted facades of Castro Street, with Boschian revelers leaning, scrambling, nearly falling from the windows; the sky was a scrim, the low clouds stained a drab mauve and roiling with sulfur. It *was* the carnival of thieves, not bright and silvery, but dark and riotous with gruesome color, and instead of Pierrot they had a man dressed as Catwoman, and instead of acrobats they had zombies in jockstraps, and instead of blasts of confetti, fiends were throwing streamers of toilet paper over the electrified bus lines that crisscrossed above them, so that at any moment Walter expected the sky would catch fire.

They were being pulled along past Twin Peaks when the current got so rough that he could no longer keep his grip on Jeff's hand. He was last in the chain, and Jeff and the rest were swept along ahead of him. Above the riot he heard a fanfare of industrial music, and heavy metal guitars washed down upon them and drowned out Eartha Kitt. That was when, looking directly upward, he saw her again: floating ten feet in the air above them was the dark-matter Queen Elizabeth. She had scaled a pole and stood atop the metal bracket of the "Don't Walk" sign. She had lost her collar, and her long train, and her attendants, but she still had her music: her boom box was strapped to the traffic light with a bungee cord, blaring, *Sex on wheelz! Sex on wheelz!*

so loud the speakers were about to blow. She danced frantically, one hand clinging to the traffic pole, the other trying to manage her giant hoop skirt ballooning up around her. Below her, her subjects were screaming, beside themselves with adoration.

The swarm scooted Walter underneath the umbrella of her skirt; he could see directly up into the Thunderdome. Above the laces of her high leather boots, her gyrating, muscular thighs were bare and thick with black hair, and farther up he could see the only bit of color in her costume: a bright lipstick-red jockstrap. *Sex on wheelz! Sex on wheelz!* She shimmied and her black skirt shuddered around her. Walter's only thought was: *Poor thing, she must be freezing.*

The mob gasped as all at once the queen's boot slipped, and she lost her grip and went tumbling headfirst into the crowd, landing on a dozen people and taking half of them down with her, while the bungee cord snapped and launched the boom box after her, *Sex on wheelz!* rocketing toward the pavement. Something pummeled Walter hard on the forehead, he was knocked flat, and everything went black. For a while he couldn't move and he could barely see, but he could hear horrified screams: *"Somebody help!" "Call 911!" "He's badly hurt!"* He pulled himself up to his knees and opened his eyes—*ah*—it wasn't him they were screaming for. He saw the boom box shattered all around him on the asphalt and a tableau of stricken bodies like a bloody battle scene. Some bystanders had pushed back to make room; others rushed in to help. There were no paramedics, but a coven of the Sisters of Perpetual Indulgence, with their lofty black wimples, went immediately to work. Queen Elizabeth and at least two people who had fallen in her wake were wounded—maybe seriously.

"Don't move him! Don't move him!" cried the sisters.

"Are you OK?!" thundered a man's voice. The hand that reached out to him was covered with bejeweled rings.

"I think I'm OK," said Walter. His head throbbed. He grabbed the hand offered to him and, as he rose to his feet, saw that it was none other than the pope, in a white gown with scarlet slippers, a bloodred cross around his neck, and miles of gold trim on his cape and miter. He wore round, green-tinted glasses. Of course the Sisters of Perpetual Indulgence had their own pope.

"Bless you, my son." The pope made the sign of the cross, and Walter stumbled on down the block, in search of Commander William Riker.

Jeff and the rainbow platoon were nowhere to be found—they must have forged on to Badlands. Walter's tumble sobered him up a bit. For a few minutes everything was excessively clear—painfully clear—with all the noise and frantic carousing around him, while every few feet his body announced a new ache. His right knee was buckling strangely, and when he looked down, he saw that his wool pants were torn, his knee bruised. He was lucky the fabric was as heavy as it was, his scrapes might have been much worse. Ambling through the intersection and trying not to get plowed down again, he realized he was lightheaded—he needed something to lean upon as soon as possible. The first thing he came to was a newspaper box, surrounded by garbage, on the sidewalk outside the Elephant Walk. He rested there a moment, then realized that leaning wasn't enough. He was going down. He cleared some trash with his feet and slumped down to the sidewalk, resting his head on the vending machine, delirious.

People streamed by, and most took no notice of him: a drunk boy squatting on the sidewalk in the Castro was a common enough sight any weekday. He closed his eyes, and from the open door of the Elephant Walk he could hear an MC with a loud, effete voice conducting a costume contest, rated by raucous applause. He almost dozed—but was too uncomfortable and too nervous to nod off. Then he felt a shadow upon him and, looking up, saw the backlit outline of a man in a fedora and a trench coat. He must have emerged from the bar. At first he thought it was someone dressed as Philip Marlowe or, more likely, Dick Tracy. But then the man crouched down beside him and spoke in a concerned, alto voice.

"Jesus, are you OK?" The figure's eyes were shaded by the fedora's brim, but he knew that face. It was the dandy from the card store, Cary Menuhin.

In his wallet he still had her card and her picture of Dorothy Parker. She placed her palm on his forehead, as if taking his temperature, and asked several more times if he was OK. Her hand was soft.

"I was knocked down . . ." he managed. "I was hit on the head . . ."

"Is this blood real?" she asked. She reached into her coat and, pulling out a patterned handkerchief, pressed it along his hairline.

"I think so—it must be," he said, realizing how dumb that sounded, but also realizing, considering the context, that no one would necessarily stop and check on him if his brains were throbbing out of his skull.

"I can't leave you here—you're a mess. Can you walk?"

"Sure, I think so," he said, though he wasn't sure he could stand.

She mopped his brow some more, and the genuine worry on her face made him more worried for himself. "I live a couple blocks from here," she said. "Let me take you home and get you cleaned up, get you some water . . ."

"OK," said Walter, so disoriented and so touched by her concern that he might have teared up. He couldn't imagine what he looked like to her. "OK, thanks."

She steadied his arm as they walked slowly up the sidewalk. They passed Badlands and took a minute to peer inside, looking for Walter's friends, but the boys had either never made it or come and gone.

"My place is so close," said Cary. "It's a couple blocks up on Eureka."

They spoke very little as they strolled up the gentle incline toward Eureka Street. They were about the same height, and her stride easily matched his. It was such a relief as the hordes dissipated and the noise became a soft mad roar in the background.

"I'm so glad I was passing by just now," said Cary.

"I hope I'm not ruining your plans," he said. "I should head home—"

"I insist you come with me. There is nothing to ruin, I have no plans at all."

"You'll want to go back out—"

"We never go out on Halloween, god no! Like the true queens say, it's amateur night for the poor suckers with no imaginations—the ones who don't know how to have fun the other 364 days of the year. I was only out because I promised Robert we'd keep the store open as long as we could. And then, of course, we needed a drink."

They turned up Eureka; it was moodily lit by streetlights and an uneven patchwork of bright windows in the facades. They arrived at a cheerfully painted Victorian—every detail outlined by bright trim—with a sunken, potted garden in front, surrounded by a waist-high wrought-iron fence.

"Here we are!" said Cary, unlatching a little gate. "I told you it was close!"

She skirted a wide staircase leading to the first floor; it concealed beneath it the door to a garden apartment. The entrance was shaded by a laurel, and it was so dark he didn't know how she could see to unlock the door. But she managed it and led him through a tiny, dark vestibule into the dimness of a cozy living room. It was empty and lit by soft accent lights beside a large couch. Candles burned on a console. The walls were painted a rich burgundy.

Cary removed her hat and overcoat; underneath she was wearing an elegant vintage suit and a silk tie.

"Darling! Darling?" Her voice got deeper when it got louder. "I brought home a wounded sailor!" She raised her eyebrows at Walter while she hung her coat and hat on a hook. "I think he might be a *drunken sailor*, too. What shall we do with him?"

"Be right there!" came the reply from somewhere down the hallway.

"My partner. You'll *adore* him."

Apprehension swelled over Walter, and he realized he'd been pressing Cary's handkerchief to his head throughout their walk. Now he saw the beautiful paisley pattern, which matched her tie, was clotted with his blood. "Oh god," he said, "I'm so sorry—I ruined your nice handkerchief."

"It's a handkerchief," said Cary.

"Hello, darling!" came an unfamiliar voice. Walter looked up from the stained paisley, and there was the gamine, across the room, standing in the doorway. His long blond hair flowed down over one shoulder, and he was wearing an ankle-length bathrobe, plush and bright cherry red; it clashed with the burgundy walls. "Who's your friend?" he asked, his voice soft and a little raspy. Walter could feel his face flush red but was relieved that there wasn't a hint of recognition in the young man's eyes, as he desperately hoped that his eyes betrayed none.

At once Walter took in the bathrobe, the candles, a single bottle of wine set out on the console. "Oh god!" he said. "I'm definitely interrupting your plans!"

"Not at all!" said Cary. "We have no plans, do we, darling?"

"No plans." The gamine shook his head, smiling.

"This is my partner, Sasha," said Cary. "And, Sasha, this is . . . the *writer* I met last week . . . I mentioned him to you . . . this is *Amanda Blueshoes*!" She looked at Walter. "Nom de plume, I think."

"Amanda Blueshoes," echoed Sasha, as if it were a perfectly normal name for a young man to have. "Nice to meet you, Mr. Blueshoes."

"Oh god!" cried Walter.

"Sorry!" said Cary. "But honestly, you ought to know, those shoes are gaining you a reputation. You can't go gallivanting around the Castro all the time in electric-blue shoes and not expect people to talk!"

"But tonight his shoes aren't blue, are they?" Sasha approached Walter. He held his hand out, palm down like a lady at court, and Walter took it. "What's your real name?" he asked.

"Walter."

"Not Amanda."

"Not Amanda at all."

Double Indemnity

THE LIGHT WAS BETTER IN the kitchen. Walter sat at the table in the center of the small room, while Sasha went to see what they had in the way of bandages. Cary told him to stare at the ceiling lamp as she examined his hairline. A plate glass window over the sink reflected the room, behind it a darkly comforting jungly greenness. The kitchen was tidy and white with black trim—it looked like it had been painted recently, but otherwise hadn't been updated for decades. The wide enamel stove had two small ovens in it, side by side. It must have been there since the '40s—maybe the '20s. The only color in the room was a display of deep ruby glass plates and glasses on a shelf above the counter. It was exceedingly quiet—so quiet you could hear the wind catching fronds in the garden.

"What the hell happened to you?" asked Cary. "It looks like you were attacked!"

"I was, in a way," said Walter. "I was attacked by Queen Elizabeth the First—"

"*Really?* The old girl still has some fight in her!"

"She was a kind of *goth-industrial* Queen Elizabeth. I think she kicked me in the head with her steel-toed boot."

"Oof! Unbecoming of a queen!" said Cary.

Sasha returned with some gauze and things in a little caddy.

"There isn't really one big cut, but he's scraped up pretty badly."

"Let me see," said Sasha.

"You must need some water." Cary moved toward the sink.

Sasha stood over Walter with a warm damp cloth in one hand and used it to wash his forehead, which provoked in Walter a kind of mortified delight. How funny it was when you thought you knew what someone looked like, but it was a kind of caricature, and then you got a good look, and they turned out to be so different. Up close, Walter could see Sasha's eyes were an unusual bright olive-green color—he'd never seen eyes that shade. And Sasha's face was thinner than he'd imagined, and from this close he could see a little blond stubble; how demystifying to think that the gamine—to him a paragon of femininity—could grow a beard.

"We should use a little rubbing alcohol on this," Sasha said. "It's not bleeding much anymore, but there was plenty of grit in it. You'll be bruised for sure."

Cary placed a tall glass of ice water on the table before Walter. "We have wine, too," she said. There was a linen cloth on the table—scalloped edges printed with lemons and strawberries of equal size—it looked antique, '40s maybe, like the stove. Sasha tipped some rubbing alcohol onto a pad of gauze.

"This will probably sting," said Sasha. It did, but it was cool on his cuts and felt good. When he'd finished cleaning Walter's forehead, Sasha asked him to lift his hands and began gently swabbing the grit out of the scrapes on his palms. Sasha's fingernails were painted a glossy, milky jade. It was so intimate, with Sasha holding his hands, Walter couldn't wipe his eyes—only then did he realize he'd been crying. These two were being so kind, so indulgent; it hadn't occurred to him to excuse himself to the bathroom and wash his own face. Why were they being so warm to him, a total stranger? It seemed both extremely odd and perfectly natural at once. There was a presumptuousness about them—they were treating him like they'd been friends for many years.

"Are you hungry?! Who's hungry? I'm hungry!" said Cary. She'd traded her suit jacket for an apron, tie tucked under the bib, and was rolling up her sleeves.

"I'm hungry, darling!" said Sasha. He had just noticed the cuts on Walter's knee. "What a shame about this tear! It can be patched, though, I think . . ."

"Oh—I should probably get home," said Walter half-heartedly. "What time is it?"

"It's after nine thirty," Cary said, leaning into the fridge's white glare. "And we have . . . nothing. Eggs. Butter. Ketchup. Capers. Hmm."

Walter was stunned—all that Halloween helter-skelter somehow packed into a swift ninety-minute whirlwind. How was that possible?

"There are still those smoked sardines in the cupboard you bought god knows why and never ate," said Sasha.

"Those are the earthquake kit. Saving those for the big one. Never fear! I've got it! You open the wine, darling." With that Cary pulled a large ceramic bowl from a shelf and began cracking eggs and whisking them with milk.

"Red or white?" Sasha asked, and in the same breath, answered himself: "Oh, *red*—it's Halloween."

"You've been *so nice*," said Walter, knowing the polite thing would be to excuse himself, but Cary was busy leveling flour in a measuring cup with a knife, and Sasha was selecting ruby wineglasses from the shelf, and Walter began thinking it might be *more rude* for him to leave than to stay.

"What do you say, Dr. Stravinsky, is the patient well enough to be discharged?"

"He's stopped bleeding," said Sasha. "He's banged up, but I think he's OK. Worst-case scenario: he has a concussion, and halfway home he passes out on the sidewalk from head trauma." Walter couldn't tell if he was joking. In one hand Sasha held a gouge-like corkscrew, pointing the tip straight up like a nurse with a twisted needle.

"Excuse me," said Walter, "but what kind of doctor did you say you were?"

"Oh." Sasha smiled. "I'm a . . . big-animal vet."

"Megafauna!" cried Cary. "Anyway, we're not at all sure it's safe out there for you yet—the demons are still out in force. We couldn't risk you being jumped by Queen Elizabeth twice in one night, now could we?"

There was no more discussion of whether Walter would stay or go. Sasha poured wine, and Cary two-stepped around the kitchen. She unhooked a large crepe pan from where it hung over the stove and began making batches of crepes, swiftly flipping them with a large spatula, adjusting them in the pan by shaking it or with a quick little firewalk of the fingertips.

"Cary is a wonderful cook," said Sasha. "For years she was a sous-chef."

"Yeah—I had to quit because the chef was a monster—a tyrant. And the hours were miserable—forget about having any social life. I'm sorry we don't have much to fill the crepes with."

Cary served Walter first. He watched as she took two large crepes, perfectly round and speckled brown like planets, and, sprinkling each with brown sugar and a liberal squeeze of lemon, rolled them up and placed them before him, trailing sweet steam.

"*Mangia!*" said Cary.

Sasha raised his wineglass: "Eat."

It was one of those dead simple, elemental meals: sweet and sour, buttery and warm. Walter took a childish delight in feeling the sugar crystals dissolving in lemon on his tongue. It was delicious, and he said so, but he was too fazed to admit what he really thought, that it was one of the most delicious things he had ever eaten, and he'd have it every single day if he could. Then he went lightheaded at his own embarrassment when he remembered the first time he'd seen Sasha—he'd been eating pancakes then, too—but this was a coincidence he'd never be able to share without revealing himself as the crazy person he was. And yet, as they sat there eating, drinking plummy red wine and chatting away, something about it was so relaxed and unremarkable that it felt *inevitable*. Who was this strange pair, this dandyish woman and this lovely man; she who could magically conjure up crepes without a recipe, and he with his easy shape-shifting glamour, and both with their peculiar humor and their obvious delight in each other? He'd never met anyone like either of them.

"What is your real last name, Mr. Blueshoes?" asked Sasha.

"Don't tell me!" Cary cried. "I know!"

Sasha and Walter stared at Cary expectantly.

"It's *Neff*. Your name is *Walter Neff*."

Taken aback, Walter smiled zanily, despite himself. He could have kissed Cary. This was one of the most amazing things she could have said to him; more amazing, in a way, than if she'd guessed his actual name. But he maintained composure and said, "Actually, it's *Huff. Walter Huff*."

"You're *lying*!" said Cary, repressing a smile, slapping the table so the wineglasses jumped in place. "That is a brazen lie!"

Walter and Cary stared across the table at each other in silence. Something in their eyes regressed into a kindergarten scuffle, a staring contest—each pinned the other with a scrutinizing gaze, making a visible effort not to laugh.

"What's happening?" asked Sasha. "Could someone please explain what's happening?"

"Walter *Neff* is the name of Fred MacMurray's character in *Double Indemnity*," said Cary.

"I know that, darling, I'm not a complete moron."

"And Walter *Huff* is the original name of the character, from the James M. Cain novel."

"Ah, I get it," said Sasha. "Our guest just *out-noired* you."

"Can you imagine? The *nerve* of some people. And after we've been so welcoming."

The three then dove deep into a conversation about film noir that made Walter dizzy—or maybe it was the wine or the recent blow to his head. Cary and Walter discussed *Double Indemnity*, comparing the film with the novel,

agreeing fundamentally that while the book's plot was much more elaborate, none of the best dialogue from the movie could be found therein. They
then moved on to favorites: *Double Indemnity* was Cary's—Barbara Stanwyck deciding it—and it was probably Walter's favorite, too, although it
was torture to choose just one; and Sasha's all-time favorite was *Gilda*. They
moved through categories: best plots, most melodramatic, most absurd (a
large category taking a long time), and biggest MacGuffin (*The Maltese Falcon*, of course—no contest). Their favorite femme fatales naturally coincided
with their favorite films—no surprise there. Then, of course, there were the
shrewdest gumshoes and most dastardly villains, which is how Walter got
around to confessing that he had been a film major and that he'd written
a senior thesis on the not-so-subtle queerness of Clifton Webb's evil closet
case, Waldo Lydecker, in *Laura*.

They digressed into a subcategory of bad, but still classic, performances,
including very bad accents—Orson Welles's hilarious Irish accent in *The
Lady from Shanghai*—and was Marlene Dietrich supposed to be *Mexican* in
Touch of Evil? While they were in the heat of discussion, a very elegant Per-
sian cat with long smoke-gray hair came padding into the kitchen. Noise-
lessly, it leapt up onto the counter beside the sink and began to lick the syrupy
traces off the plates Cary had stacked there. Sasha had just voiced the inde-
fensible opinion that Gloria Swanson was too hammy in *Sunset Boulevard* and
that the whole movie was overrated, and Cary and Walter were reeling from
this shocking betrayal. Ignoring them, Sasha pulled the cat off the counter
and arranged it upon his shoulder like a stole, a big question mark formed by
a curl of smoke.

"This is Mona Lisa," said Sasha.

"She's beautiful," said Walter.

"She's so like the lady with the mystic smile," sang Cary, who then, without
a beat, introduced a new line of discussion: best locations and the best use of
different cities. Then she broached the crucial question of which films made
the best use of San Francisco. For Cary the contenders were *The Maltese*

Falcon and *The Lady from Shanghai*, with a consolation prize going to *Woman on the Run*, a movie Walter had never seen.

"I do think San Francisco is the ultimate film noir city," said Cary.

"I agree," Walter replied, "although most people would say it's LA, don't you think?"

"LA does have a flimsiness and a phoniness that makes it great for film noir, sure. And New York has a grimy bleakness that San Francisco can't rival. But San Francisco . . ."

Sasha watched Cary expectantly while she searched for the right words, as Mona Lisa unhooked from his shoulder and pooled in his lap.

". . . San Francisco is *silver*," said Cary. "Whenever I go to LA I feel like I'm seeing all the horrific suburban tackiness they try so hard to crop out of the movies in order to convince you that LA is an actual city and a nice place to live. And New York is great to visit, but it's a cesspool, it's vile and filthy and so expensive you're practically being pickpocketed every minute you're there. And most movies that take place there are now filmed in Toronto—and they have to import trash to make it look like New York—I read that somewhere. But San Francisco is a *silver city*. The palette is just right, it's ice blue and pewter and gunmetal gray and blue sunshine and brilliant fog. It's moody and glorious! And everywhere you turn there's a perfect spot for a lovers' tryst or a shady deal of some sort. It's the perfect backdrop for any-thing. I *always feel* like I'm in the movies here."

Walter and Sasha couldn't argue with this fine thesis. But in the end there wasn't time—it had gotten late. Somehow it was already past midnight, and they'd polished off a couple bottles of merlot. Cary was not tired in the least. She proposed firing up the VCR and watching *Double Indemnity* right then and there. Sasha looked content but very sleepy. Halfway through their con-versation he had excused himself to remove his contacts and returned wear-ing thick glasses with oval lenses that greatly scaled back his fey glamour, even as they magnified his green eyes. He was now a beautiful nerd, the most beautiful nerd Walter had ever seen.

"I hate to break up the party," said Sasha, "but I'm afraid I have to work in the morning."

"Me too," said Walter, with a rush of anxiety. He had been happy to avoid the topic all night.

"Oh! Where do you work?" asked Cary.

Walter hesitated. "I work at Macy's." He coughed. "In the display department." He said it as flatly as he could manage.

Sasha looked at him incredulously, as if he hadn't heard right. He then turned and gave Cary the same look. Walter felt his heart sinking, like he was on the verge of confessing everything and releasing a sleazy pall over what had been up till then an innocent and charming evening.

"I thought you did!" said Cary. "Or I thought you *might*. I mean, don't freak out, but this week I was browsing in the basement after meeting Sasha for lunch, and I thought I saw you leaning into a display case arranging a cornucopia full of pretzels and mustards and things. I mean, I wasn't sure it was you, but I recognized those blue shoes! Well, then, you must have met Sasha before. He also works at Macy's."

"In the display department," said Sasha, continuing to look incredulous. He and Cary traded a series of inscrutable glances—somewhere between knowing and deeply confused. They both turned to him.

"That's amazing!" said Walter. "What are the odds?" He said it and, as he said it, felt ridiculous in his very soul. He tried hard to disguise his embarrassment, but he was no actor. He knew he must be utterly unconvincing, and to make matters worse, the only thing he could think of was Miss Piggy, the time she was stranded by a highway at night needing a ride, and a perfect Miss Piggy–sized motorcycle fell off a truck and landed in front of her, and she squealed, *What an unbelievable coincidence!*

Pennies from Heaven

THE NEXT DAY IT WAS November. That week, Walter learned how it was possible that he'd worked at Macy's for over two weeks without running into Sasha once: the culprit was Gavin. Gavin was the balding man in suspenders and ticking who had scowled at him the afternoon he'd strayed into the display department and applied for a job. Walter thought Gavin looked kind of sweet, actually, with his ruddy goatee, like the picture of Burl Ives on a record he'd had as a kid, but in fact he was sour and persnickety, with the brittle arrogance of a petty dictator.

Sasha had the misfortune of being Gavin's assistant, and for most of the holiday season and especially the weeks leading up to it, he kept Sasha chained to an industrial sewing machine in a hermetic fluorescent workroom in the deepest reaches of the fourth-floor storage. Walter, who had been working in the basement, rarely had a reason to go up there, but one afternoon Sasha showed him the space. There was a large, tidy worktable and an industrial sewing machine as imposing as a band saw, so powerful it could sew right through your fingers if you weren't careful. The walls were lined with shelves stacked with folded and labeled projects in progress, bolts of yardage, and dozens of bins filled with fabric, valuable remnants, notions, etc. Sasha explained that his main job was to sew tablecloths for the china department, not mere rectangles of fabric but elaborate quilts and complicated soft sculptures, following specifications laid out by Gavin in cryptic, quasi-architectural scribblings. Gavin called himself a designer, but he couldn't pattern and couldn't sew, and had no practical sense of how to execute anything. He had the tastes of Cecil B. DeMille and the skills of a summer-camp crafter.

"Gavin claims he's good with his hands," said Sasha, "but what he actually means is he's good with *my* hands."

"Why make such a big deal about table settings in the china displays?" Walter asked, as Sasha showed him a work in progress. It was a round table disguised as a gigantic toy drum—five feet in diameter—a drum that might be carried by a nutcracker or tin soldier the size of King Kong. Sasha said Gavin got frantic and uptight because, as he put it, hundreds of thousands of dollars in Christmas sales were at stake, along with a thousand bridal registries, which in California went year-round. *People travel hundreds of miles to see our Christmas displays!* Gavin would exclaim, breathlessly, to goad Sasha.

"You know Macy's is broke, right? They went bankrupt last year?" said Sasha.

"I did hear that . . . after I took the job." Walter frowned.

"Yeah, so, a major part of our job is to spend as much money as we can, in order to make Macy's look as not-broke as possible. Look at this suede . . ." Sasha ran his jadeite fingernails across the top of the toy drum. "It's genuine suede, dyed purple. It's thirty dollars a yard and so narrow I had to triple the yardage in order to cover the tabletop."

"It's kind of . . . beautiful? So soft!" said Walter, while grimly picturing the calf—or calves—that couldn't have imagined this as their fate.

"This is the kind of BS he always pulls. Look at this . . ." Sasha pointed to a seam at the edge of the drum. "He chooses all these insane fabrics . . . He wanted me to sew through two layers of suede, a layer of quilted, padded silk, and taffeta piping—which I made by hand, by the way. No real designer would ask you to do such a thing, because *none of these fabrics work together.*"

"You did an amazing job, though!"

"Well, I have to get it exactly right, or he'll make me rip out the seams and start over."

Walter started to imagine Gavin as an ogre who had, through some borrowed magic, some wily warlock's spell, trapped Sasha in a cinder block dungeon to do his bidding. "I kind of hate to ask"—he winced—"but how much did all this fabric cost, do you think?"

"Oh, I don't know," Sasha wondered aloud, "the suede, the silk, the taffeta, the batting, all this gold rope? Probably more than we make in a week combined . . ."

Then it was Sasha who winced, because a trudging, panting sound that had been rising from the hallway turned out to be Gavin himself, who burst into the room and, without so much as a hello, heaved two large bags labeled "Britex Fabrics" onto the giant purple drum.

"OK," said Gavin, turning out the contents of one bag without looking up. "This is the Southwestern tapestry pattern I was telling you about for the Native American Thanksgiving table. They didn't have any leather fringe, so you'll have to cut that yourself. And here's the gold lamé I chose for the King Arthur–themed table . . ."

Halfway through unpacking the second bag, Gavin looked up and acknowledged the two of them. "Walter," he said, "what the hell are you doing here? Aren't there some panini presses in the basement that need arranging?"

"Uh—" Walter stammered. "Yes, I guess there are . . ."

"Better get down there," said Gavin. "We're not paying you boys to flirt."

Sasha mouthed *Sorry* to Walter as he fled the room, and by the time he pushed through the doors into the bedding department, he could feel anger and humiliation pulsing in his neck, flushing his cheeks and forehead.

That evening Walter and Sasha punched out at the same time and strolled to Powell Street station together.

"What an asshole," said Walter. "Did you ever ask Gavin when his inner child died?"

"Oh, ha—I guess I think his *inner child* is very much alive. You should see him in the crystal displays. He loves Waterford Crystal so much he practically worships it. The Spode and Wedgwood cases are like sacred altars . . . I think he'd fire me if I left a fingerprint on them. Cary says his heart was replaced by bone china."

Walter was searching for a polite way to ask why Sasha hadn't quit long ago when, teasingly, like a magician, Sasha pulled what appeared to be a silk handkerchief from his pocket and handed it to him. The pattern was intricate and dazzling, like blue-tiled starbursts in a mosque.

"It's hand-dyed silk. Fifty bucks a yard. All it needs is a hem."

By the time they got to the train platform, Walter was convinced that Sasha was both a skilled grifter and a wizard with a sewing machine. As it happened, the bins in Sasha's workroom were overflowing with the remnants of Gavin's conspicuous consumption, and once he was certain Gavin had forgotten about some old project, Sasha felt justified in *recycling* some deluxe fabrics he could never have afforded himself. In his sewing room in their apartment, Sasha made many of his own clothes and many of Cary's as well, including the tailored suits that concealed her curves and gave her that dandyish masculine look she wore so well. Sasha had to be careful not to wear anything incriminating to work, but he and Cary had entire outfits made from Gavin's sumptuous castoffs.

The subway train was packed, and they stood close together in the crowd, clinging to straps overhead as they surfed toward the Castro. Walter asked if Sasha had stolen the fabric for the leopard-print coat he was wearing. He hadn't, but Walter was blown away to learn that Sasha had indeed made it himself. It looked utterly professional. Sasha held out his cuff to prove it wasn't real fur, and Walter's heart leapt to his throat as he leaned close to the gamine, petting the soft pile of his cuff. He withdrew his hand as the train slid into Civic Center.

"Where did you learn to do this?"

"My dedushka!" said Sasha. "My grandfather Stravinsky . . . he's the real deal, a bona fide Russian tailor. Had me pinning fabric when I was, like, six. Taught me everything I know. I'm not sure he would approve of my *lifestyle*, but he made damn sure he could be proud of my French seams."

"Where the heck did you grow up, the *shtetl*?"

"Ha! No, in Stockton. He lives in Stockton, of all places."

"Sasha, *you are so talented*!" He was shouting a little, as the train wailed and shot off again. "You should be working for some fashion designer— I don't know—Jean-Paul Gaultier or somebody!"

"What a dream that would be, it would be *so fun* to work for Gaultier or some other crazy, out-there designer. Vivienne Westwood or Rei Kawakubo . . ."

"Why don't you?"

"Oh, I dunno—why don't I uproot my whole life and move to another city, a major fashion center? I'm not sure I could hack it—I can't imagine living anywhere other than San Francisco."

"Why not?"

Sasha laughed dismissively. "Well, for one thing, it would break Cary's heart. Cary swears she could never live anywhere else—I couldn't do that to Cary."

At that Walter dropped the subject, because he could barely find fault with San Francisco, and having found a queer partner in crime, the Clyde-like Bonnie to your bonnie Clyde, seemed like the best possible reason to stay put.

That week, the first in November, the three of them, Walter, Cary, and Sasha, sailed off upon a new friendship at a thrilling, bracing clip. While she worked evenings at the card shop, Cary Menuhin worked half-time at the central library at Civic Center—a college internship that never ended, since her boss had cottoned to her so well. She had two very laid-back bosses, making her a free agent, in a way. Unlike Sasha and Walter, she had no time card to punch. At lunch she would often wander through the Tenderloin to Union Square to meet Sasha someplace, and now she'd meet Walter, too. Cary knew all the cheapest, best places to eat downtown—sometimes she would arrive with sandwiches for each of them: banh mi from her favorite Vietnamese sandwich shop, panini from an espresso bar she liked. They would eat in the square if it was sunny or gambol two blocks up Geary for dirt-cheap pad Thai, or sometimes, if they felt the urge, they would splurge in a restaurant on Maiden Lane.

Walter had known that Cary and Sasha were a couple from the moment he'd first seen them together. There was a kind of force field around and between them, as with every movement, each tacitly acknowledged and responded to the other in voice, in gesture, and even seemingly beneath the skin, in their proprioceptive circuitries. Their body language was eerily harmonious, like watching a theremin player and wondering what infinitesimal worlds were unfolding in the dark matter between any two objects. It was clear that Cary was smitten with Sasha's easy glamour, the same quality that Walter first found so intimidating in Sasha—though he soon felt silly for having been so intimidated. It was equally clear that Sasha adored Cary's offbeat charm, which Walter found so disarming. Cary's was a deep, charismatic charm, as if she were simultaneously very young and very old. Somehow, she was charming in her very soul.

The two had been going out for almost three years and lived together for two of them. Cary loved to mark events and would find any excuse to celebrate. Sasha was tickled when, early that summer, she surprised him by taking him out to commemorate having been together a thousand days. They had a great deal in common: they were the same age, twenty-five, though Cary was two months older. They were both Californians, Sasha from Stockton and Cary from San Bernardino, *the Satanic capital of California*, she called it. Both were Jewish but not observant, although Sasha was only Jewish on one side, the wrong one: his father had married a WASP, a shiksa, whom Sasha strongly resembled.

They were both agnostic on many subjects, the more crucial the subject the less their attitudes inclined toward the hard-and-fast. Sex was a big, amorphous topic, the giant squid in the room. Both would say they were more or less bisexual, but that designation only got you so far if you were deeply skeptical, as they were, about what a man or a woman was in the first place. In the way an agnostic might cop to the existence of a higher being, yet decline to describe its content and contours, the two of them would talk about sexuality, frequently, as an existential given—while all the while admitting they had no idea what it was in the first place. Cary loathed all labels, but sometimes liked to refer to the two of them as *ambivalents* (noun, pl.), which she said was short for *ambassadors of ambivalence*, proselytizers of the value she prized above all others. She loved all the echoes of ambivalence as well: *ambiguity*, of course, but also *ambience*, and *ambidextrousness*, and *ambisexual*, and even *ambivert*, which she said was a mythological beast, half introvert, half extrovert, a unicorn whose horny head longed to go dancing but whose weary hooves would rather stay home, or vice versa.

In time, over weeks and then months, Walter would learn how few people, even people close to them, really believed that Cary and Sasha were a couple. Upon first meeting them, most people assumed that Cary, in her suave suits always paired with a fedora, was a gentlemanly dyke and Sasha, soft-spoken, effeminate, demure, was as gay as they come; ergo, they could not be fucking. Even exceedingly cool queer people—like Fiona, who was bi herself—couldn't quite wrap their head around it. Fiona argued that maybe Cary and Sasha were great friends—best friends—who in getting intimate had made a kind of categorical error: they were playing house and took it all too far. The cruelest theory was voiced by Eliot, who suggested they were playing straight because they couldn't hack being gay. Together, he implied, they were retreating from the oppressive loneliness imposed by the gay dating scene in San Francisco—a sort of backward, partial, failed retreat into straightness.

Walter listened to these theories about his friends' partnership, but listened lightly, trying not to let them take hold. But then, once, Cary's childhood friend Nick spun a theory for him that he thought, regardless of anyone's half-baked ideas about sexuality, could also be true. Nick had it that Cary and Sasha were both performers—Cary deep down in her DNA, and Sasha as a matter of style, a kind of extension of his remarkable poise. And they fell for each other the way band members often do, in a joyous rush of collaboration that caused them to confuse motives and motifs, and tensions and tempos; caused them to forget who caught the melody first and who transformed it, and who laid in the bass and who brought in those bright timbres, and even, once everything was in the mix, whose voice was whose. Falling in love's a scramble, a hash—that was the theory. The night they met, Cary saw Sasha's queer goth band, Singe, perform at a house party. He sang a depressive cover of "Bring on the Dancing Horses," and at once Cary saw the chanteuse smoldering within the gay boy. When she cornered him after the set, her first words to Sasha were: *Start a band with me!*

I don't play an instrument, Sasha warned.

I can tell a natural musician when I hear one, said Cary, like she was the next David Geffen.

One of the things Walter first learned about Cary—what Sasha and many others first learned about Cary—was that she could be extraordinarily persuasive. She had a way of convincing you, without saying so in any explicit manner, that saying *no thanks* to her was like saying *I'm not interested in fun.* Cary, it turned out, was abundantly popular, and not at all in a blinkered, teenage-beauty-queen sort of way. She was popular because she was brave. Cary was constitutionally unafraid to speak to anyone, in any circumstance, and would barrel forward, uncowed, into any situation. She had the enviable superpower of making anyone she met feel at ease speaking to her. Walter couldn't figure out how she did it; it wasn't one surefire trick, or he would have happily copied it, or maybe bottled and sold it.

So, Sasha agreed to start a jazz duo with Cary, and within a year they were living together. A couple years prior, while sifting through a junk shop on Valencia, Cary had unearthed a hollow-body jazz guitar, a rose madder Gretsch with brass hardware and gold purfling, banged up but beautiful enough to reawaken a teenage dream she'd had of becoming Django Reinhardt. She buffed the guitar till it shone, but two years later, she still wasn't Django Reinhardt. Like most people, she loved the dream more than the callus-inducing, tendon-knotting repetition necessary to realize it, and after taking lessons and making some progress, the guitar hung like a trophy in her living room until certain demonic barre chords would deign to give up their secrets. Beside it hung an honest-to-god shrine to Django, a gilt bracket cluttered with candles and fuming frankincense, a framed photo of the guitar god himself (bedroom eyes, drooped cigarette, guitar held high, left hand locked on the neck in a diminished chord)—all a clear appeal to the saint to grant unto her fingers every day greater dexterity. And there they hung, guitar and shrine, until a sudden need to impress Sasha brought the Gretsch down again.

Cary loved to sing. She had a sturdy alto voice that kept in key most of the time, not the voice of a soloist, she'd admit, maybe not a voice anyone might swoon over or want warbling them to sleep, but the voice of a solid backup singer who could pick out a keen harmony. Sasha had a warm, woodwind tenor, which, where his range topped off, slipped into a strong falsetto. When they sang harmony, Cary often took the lower part. For the time being the name of their duo was Bombolone, and they specialized in classic American standards and torch songs, especially ones that could be arranged in recognizable keys with graspable chords. They performed rarely; they had done a few open mics and were always on the lookout for a new venue, but in the meantime they were working on their repertoire.

One of Cary's favorite movies—top five—was the Steve Martin vehicle *Pennies from Heaven*. It came up when the three of them were discussing movie worlds they'd most like to live inside. Walter thought *Pennies from Heaven* was tragic, way too sad to want to live in, but Cary loved the style of it above all. She loved how at any moment any character might burst out into an old Tin Pan Alley song, with a voice misaligned to their gender, and a cheery, hot jazz band swelling out from under a gray mist of phonograph scratches. Sasha pointed out that, for all intents and purposes, Cary did live in the movie *Pennies from Heaven*, since she embodied its style and felt free to burst into song at any time and in any place, whenever she felt the urge.

Cary had an encyclopedic memory for lyrics and a song ready for any occasion. Besides Mona Lisa, whom she'd named so she could serenade her, there were songs for anything she might encounter, in a context as vast as the city or as small as the dresser drawer: *the silk stocking, the cat in the cradle, the bauble and bangle, the street where you live, uptown, downtown,* on *a foggy day,* or *in the still of the night,* from "Manic Monday" to "Gloomy Sunday" . . . it was an endless medley. And although she remembered a wealth of lyrics, many other songs she remembered just well enough to butcher them spectacularly. In truth, she never cared about getting the words right; she'd much rather get them wrong in a way that amused her.

The rose madder Gretsch hung over an emerald velveteen couch in their living room. Cary and Sasha would occasionally perform little concerts after intimate dinners or cocktails with friends—performing by request, although often enough the request was Cary's. Strumming "If I Had You," Walter loved to watch Cary's hands slide up the neck as they left *the whole world behind,* and Sasha's version of "Lush Life" left him speechless. But most of all Walter loved their bare-bones bossa nova rendition of "Fly Me to the Moon" (Sasha shimmied the cabasa), inspired by Miss Julie London, a chesty '50s pinup girl with a voice so breathy you thought she might just expire after every phrase. Sasha insisted that their take was not a parody but a genuine tribute to the *queso profundo* that was Miss Julie's version. Either way, it made Walter's heart flutter in the way artfully distilled camp often did.

The more time Walter spent at Cary and Sasha's place, the more he would come to understand how a home could be a testament to the harmony of a couple, a shrine to their shared experiences and tastes. Their landlord, Barry, was an old gay hippie who lived in the house above them and allowed them to paint the place however they liked. Their complementary tastes were evident in the color scheme. Cary was obsessed with red, and Sasha adored green.

Knowing this, they had to choose a spectrum of unusual shades in order to keep their place from looking like a year-round Christmas superstore. They indulged a love of jewel tones, ruby and emerald, garnet and peridot. The burgundy living room was so dark and warmly enveloping that Cary, to the dismay of some of their guests, called it their *living womb*.

Once, after he'd known them a little while, Walter was at their place while they were readying for an evening out. Cary was practicing chords in the womb, and Sasha invited him back into their bedroom to help him choose between a couple outfits. Their bedroom was an enclosed porch; large windows and a glass-paned door looked out into the garden. It had rained in the last hour, the evening was deep green. Incredible as it was to Walter, Sasha was wearing a plain white tank top and yellow striped boxers; his blond hair was in a loose ponytail at the base of his neck. Still, every once in a while, the gamine returned, and Walter would be dumbstruck, for a moment, by his weird luck, now that they were friends. Sasha wasn't some androgynous idol or some stylish optical illusion; he had a fine mind and a real body, and here it was, slender, pale as a Dickensian orphan, a body with its wan willowy arms holding up different outfits for Walter's approval. He truly was built like a gamine: a slim plank, a narrow-shouldered, uncurving blank canvas any competitive drag queen would kill for. Walter didn't think he could handle staring at Sasha's bare shoulders much longer and looked up at the walls and ceiling, at last taking in the whole room.

"This room is . . . *incredible*," he managed.

"Oh, thank you," said Sasha. "I painted it myself—Cary said to go for it."

Aside from the ceiling and the boxy yellow paper lantern that hung from it, the whole room was a visual love letter to the color green. The base coat was a soothing, soft jade, somehow both cool and warm, the color of a healthy succulent. Laid over this was a whole spectrum of greens, from bright citrus to deep moss. Sasha had drawn the garden into their bedroom, painting sweeps of art deco palm fronds, tree ferns, bamboo stalks with knife-blade leaves. Over the bed the jungle parted to reveal a panorama of hills and, behind them, a distant palace, a pale jade city. The images transformed as they rose up, thinning out, brightening, and floating into an absinthe sky: blossoms became birds, large leaves became billowing hills, hills fleeting clouds, clouds wingspans; soaring birds alit upon high stalks and became blooms again. Was that a hill upon which the jade palace perched, or the crest of a cloud bank? Was the palace in fact an ocean liner, cruising across the sky? It was ambivalent—impossible to say. A large round mirror atop a vanity all but vanished into the greenery; Walter wouldn't have noticed it at all, if it weren't framing Sasha's bony shoulders from behind.

"I based the design on the second-floor ladies' lounge at the Paramount Theatre in Oakland," said Sasha.

"The Paramount?"

"You haven't been to the Paramount?" asked Sasha, who had been deliberating between two blouses. "Oh my god, darling, you'd die! You of all people—it's like dying and going to art deco heaven."

"It's an old movie palace?"

"Uh-huh. It's incredible—massive—I think you could fit the whole Castro inside it—the theater, I mean, not the neighborhood, although *maybe* the neighborhood. And the theme of it is—I'm not sure—*midnight in the deco jungle* or something like that? It's like a night in Tunisia crossed with Tarzan's jungle, all done in lattices and recessed lighting. Oh, sweetie, you'd better have a seat, this could take a while . . ."

"I'm not sure I can even comprehend such a thing," said Walter, perching on the bed.

"We'll make a pilgrimage!" Sasha promised. "But it takes planning . . . it's not always open. It's a concert venue now."

Sasha was no closer to being dressed than when they had started. One potential outfit after another was pulled from the closet and discarded on the chair. Slacks, blouses, dresses, wraps, jumpsuits, and the longer this went on, Walter noticed, the less relevant the distinction between men's and women's clothes seemed to be. Sasha fished a silk muumuu from the closet and pulled it over his head. It was cobalt blue with a pattern of gold and green knots around the neckline. Walter gasped, loud enough that he startled himself.

"Too much?" Sasha turned toward the mirror, then turned back.

"Sasha, you look . . . *gorgeous!*"

"Not too . . . Mrs. Roper? It's so shapeless . . ."

"Sasha, you'd literally look gorgeous in a paper bag."

Sasha stared at Walter for a moment, smiling and perhaps questioning his judgment, before pulling the garment back over his head and discarding it.

"Just choose something, darling," said Cary, appearing in the doorway. "We won't have time to eat before the movie!" She was wearing a tie and suspenders and patterned dress socks, and her shirtsleeves were rolled up from Django-ing. She leapt onto the mountain of pillows stacked on the bed, nearly rolling into Walter's back.

"Isn't this room glorious?" Cary asked, spreading her arms. "Sasha painted it for me. All for me! I snuck him into the Paramount's ladies' lounge and said, *This!*"

"It is glorious," said Walter.

"And this quilt—isn't it the most resplendent thing you've ever seen? Don't you want to be buried in it—I mean, curl up and die and be buried in it like a goddamn pharaoh?"

In fact, it *was* the most beautiful quilt Walter had ever seen; he was afraid to even touch it. It was a patchwork of squares of hundreds of fabrics with gold threads woven throughout, creating myriad illuminated designs.

"I call it our Klimt quilt," said Cary. "Do you know why? Because when we're all swaddled up in it, smooching away, we look just like *The Kiss.*"

"It looks like you stole it from Versailles," said Walter.

Sasha smirked. "Well, let's say if Gavin ever saw it, I'd be instantly fired."

Cary started searching through the mound of pillows, almost frantically, saying, "Darling, where's my favorite pillow you made me? The needlepoint one? I need to show Walter my favorite pillow."

"I think it's buried on this chair," said Sasha.

"Well, then unbury it!" said Cary. "*Please*, I mean. I want to show Wall your handiwork. You don't mind if I call you *Wall*, do you?"

Sasha sifted through the clothes on the chair, reconsidering a few items, and settled upon a floral print silk shirt.

"You did say you hate *Wally*," Cary chattered on, "and *Walt* is, like . . . All anyone can think is Disney, sadly . . ."

"*Wall* isn't too bad. I think I can handle it."

In the course of exhuming the chair, Sasha had discovered an acceptable pair of wide-legged black pants and donned them. "Almost ready," he said, "and here it is!" He tossed a large pillow to Walter, who caught it an inch before his face.

"Do you know it?" Cary said. "It's my favorite quote from *Victor/Victoria*."

Walter ran his fingertip over the little x's embroidered in green satin thread upon the thick weave of the pillow. The letters were framed by a garden lattice, dotted with violets. Something about needlepoint itself was almost unbearable to him. All those patient hours, every movement of the hand memorialized, so much care . . . That was it: the almost unbearable manifestation of such devotion and care. As he traced its ridges, the sentiment printed on the pillow surprised him and yet didn't surprise him at all, and even as he exhaled a little laugh, the simple capaciousness of its meaning made him want, almost, to cry.

I think it's as simple as you're one kind of man, I'm another.

Laura

"WHAT ARE WE LOOKING FOR again?" asked Walter, scanning the crowded bar.

"Bigboi68," said Jeff. "Blond. Said he'd be wearing a Giants T-shirt."

"Bigboi68? That's his name?"

"No, of course not," said Jeff. "His name's Colin. Bigboi's his *handle*."

For Walter the word *handle* conjured an image of Jeff as a skinny, nerdy trucker, barreling down the 5 while picking up tricks on a CB radio.

There was no sign of Bigboi, but the night was still young. They were seated at one of the few squat tables in the back of the Casanova Lounge. The room was deep red, the moody sweep of its cardinal walls broken up by an array of kitschy thrift store paintings. The lounge was lit by hanging lanterns of chunky, colorful resin and those stoplight-red candle holders, glowing magmatic gourds found at every cheap Italian place that ever was, apparently, since the time of the Caesars.

"At least the music's good, thank god!" said Jeff. Since they'd arrived, the DJ set had been a mix of sweet and dour post-punk. At the moment, on the sweet side, it was the Cure's "The Caterpillar."

"Cary would love this place," said Walter, "it's so very red."

"When am I going to finally meet Cary? She keeps coming up."

"Maybe tonight. I invited her and Sasha to meet us here."

"Sasha's her girlfriend?"

"Boyfriend," said Walter, though the word sounded bizarre applied to Sasha. He amended it: "Partner."

"Hold on, Cary and Sasha are straight? Way to keep me out of the loop! This whole time I thought Sasha was a girl."

"Sasha's not a girl. But I think he might be a selkie, or a sorceress or something. You'll understand when you meet them."

"You must be spending a ton of time with them—I could barely get you on the phone."

"I wouldn't say a *ton*," said Walter, sensing resentment creep into Jeff's tone. But it was true, he *was* spending a *ton* of time with Sasha and Cary, it had been a bit intense. He'd seen them almost every day for the last two weeks. He'd been bad about returning Jeff's calls or even checking his machine. More and more, he went to his place only to shower and sleep.

"I bet they'll show up tonight," Walter reassured Jeff. "But meanwhile, we'll keep looking for your Bigboi69—"

"Sixty-eight."

"Well, that's not very sexy."

"I assume it's his birth year . . ."

The Casanova was bustling but still comfortable, a solid turnout for a new, alternative club. The crowd was young and largely queer, but not in a way that could be typified or pinned down; after all, it was a *Mission* crowd. Everyone was glitzed up and dressed down at the same time, like the big-eyed boy at the table next to them, head shorn like Sinéad O'Connor's, wearing a black velvet blazer paired with a ratty white T and a choke chain. There was a cluster of goths—always a heartening sight. Walter had a fear of needles and of permanent or semipermanent choices, and thought that he must be, freakishly, the only person in the room with no piercings or tattoos. Even straitlaced Jeff, whose all-black outfit made him look like a '50s square who had run off to join the beatniks, had recently hopped into the Gauntlet and gotten small spacers in his ears. Walter wondered how long he could hold out before he'd crack under the pressure to conform and go wild—maybe he'd become one of those addicts and pierce his head like a sieve, or get a set of full-body tattoos and wind up looking like a Maori fisherman or *Lydia the En-cyclo-piddia*.

"So . . . you've never seen this guy before, right? Bigboi? Or, I guess, Colin?" Walter asked. "How did you meet him?"

"In a chat room."

"Like, one of those 1-800 numbers in the back of the *BAR*?"

"No, silly, in a *chat room*. CB Simulator. *Online?*"

"Oh, *roger that*," said Walter, still picturing Jeff wielding a CB in the cab of a semi.

Jeff rolled his eyes at Walter—tadpoles darting in his thick lenses. It was unusual for Jeff to be impatient with Walter's technological ignorance. He always claimed it was refreshing that Walter was indifferent to the latest technology; it was worth keeping at least one Luddite friend around for the sake of perspective.

"So, if you meet in a chat room online, how do you know that the person, you know, is who they say they are?" Walter was now genuinely curious.

"Oh, you definitely don't. But that's what we're *here* for. Trust but verify. Also, like any blind date, it's good to meet someplace very public."

"Giants!" said Walter, indicating with his glance a man ordering at the bar with his back to them. The guy turned with his pint and, surveying the bar, scanned right past them. He was massive, built like a rugby player, with a blond crew cut and a neck so thick he looked like he might be a sideshow performer who pulled trains with his teeth. Jeff smiled subtly—it seemed he liked what he saw, but was also enjoying this moment of noticing without being noticed.

"Yeah, that's gotta be him," said Jeff.

"He looks so . . . *corn-fed*." Walter shuddered a little.

"What's that supposed to mean?"

"Nothing! Except that he looks like every other guy from my high school, or like the entire football team in one guy."

"Mmm, I don't know about you, but I'm a *gay guy*, and I like *guys*. The bigger, the better."

"That guy—he really looks like he might be straight, though." Giants T-shirts were common enough that Walter was worried about his friend making a perilous mistake. "Hold on! I thought you didn't like *jocks* or, like, *muscle queens*."

"I like jocks!" Jeff laughed. "I like athletic guys. I said I don't like *technological bodies*."

"Ah." Walter knew that by *technological bodies* Jeff meant those hyper-gym-toned, ultra-fit, zero-body-fat bodies that were in vogue and only possible because of late twentieth-century inventions: Nautilus machines, protein powders, maybe a steroid shot or two, a touch of liposuction and laser depilation. It was one of the ways, Jeff argued, that we were rapidly becoming cyborgs—not that our bodies were machines (not yet), but that our bodies were being shaped by machines. Walter, chronic technophobe, was intrigued by the argument but didn't fully buy it, and he'd pointed out the obvious irony that if Jeff thought everything else could be streamlined by good design, he ought to *love* designer bodies.

Even so, neither of them was a jock, and early on the two had bonded over a shared dislike of ever being topless in a public or semipublic situation. Walter had a tyrannical sweet tooth and the little paunch to show for it, and whenever he imagined the joys of sporting six-pack abs, the next thing he'd remember was pie. As for the gym, he thought he was reasonably fit and couldn't comprehend the need to pay monthly fees to a sweaty mirror chamber where you went to dress in Lycra mesh and lift heavy things to your heart's content. None of it bothered him at all until he found himself in one of those situations where whole throngs of gay men spontaneously got the idea they were Marky Mark and started stripping down to their boxer briefs. Life was full of such rich, unclad opportunities: certain clubs they avoided in SoMa, gay nude beaches, summer street fairs . . . Once, browsing at Rolo, they ran into Eliot and Richard, who were busy investing in fresh jockstraps for an underwear party. When Eliot invited them along, he and Jeff both visibly recoiled.

"I'm gonna go say hi to Colin," said Jeff. "You OK hanging out here?"

"Sure," said Walter. "But, for the record, I still don't understand your taste in guys. In a room full of nice-looking homos, you always seem to go for the one who looks like he'd punch you in the face before he'd say hello."

Jeff shook off this comment. "I told you, I've chatted with him. He's a nice guy! Meanwhile, I have no idea what your taste in men is, since I've never met a single guy you've slept with. Except Eliot, of course."

"Oh god!" said Walter, hiding his face in his palms. "Eliot is *not* my type. By the way, I'll have you know I had sex on Friday night, in fact, with someone who is my type. Or would be, I think, if I had one."

"Oh yeah, who's that?"

"That guy Julian—I mentioned him—Fiona's friend? I invited him to meet me here; he said he might—he might be around the corner at Esta Noche anyway."

"Glad to hear it," said Jeff, "and to hear the ice dam broke on your celibacy."

"I haven't exactly been . . ."

But Jeff had already flitted off to chat up giant Colin, who stood alone against one wall, coolly holding up the wainscoting.

Walter finished his drink and went to smoke outside. It was shortly after ten and misting—not lightly—he pulled the hood up on his jacket. Valencia Street was almost empty—about as quiet as he'd ever seen it. A couple guys from the club were hanging by the parking meter smoking and chatting. As he smoked, he admired the peculiar lavender neon of Blondie's sign across the street—he'd never seen neon that color—the mist around it formed an ultraviolet halo. He thought of chatting with the other smokers, but what he really hoped was to see Julian striding through the mist down Valencia toward him. The truth was he was getting a little desperate to see him again, as soon as possible, and thought about heading to Esta Noche to look for him. On the phone Julian was unsure he'd be there, but swore that if he was, he'd come around the corner to say hi. If Walter went and sought him out, a kind of requisite charade of casualness might collapse. He had already intuited one of the cardinal rules of dating gay men in SF: the biggest turnoff was looking overeager. A sad predicament for certain men, for whom eagerness was their best quality.

The previous Friday Walter and Julian had finally planned to make good on a long-standing promise to get a drink. Julian lived not far from him, with three roommates in an enormous Victorian apartment, above one of the many intensely hip shoe stores that lined Haight Street and proved its primary industry: the shiny vinyl, platform-heeled afterlife of the counterculture. Walter swung by after dinner, and while they were trying to decide where to go, they sat at an Ikea table in the otherwise unfurnished kitchen, which was large and laminate white. Julian brought out a bottle of tequila and some limes—he didn't have any mixer, but he had shot glasses—and he taught Walter to lick the ridge of skin between his thumb and forefinger, salt it with a shaker, suck the salt, do a shot, and bite fearlessly through a lime wedge.

They talked about life in the Haight and places they liked to hang out, and as they talked, Julian pulled an orange from a bowl and methodically sliced it into eighths. He then salted one of the slices with the shaker, casually salting the cutting board and the tabletop as well. Walter was mesmerized by the movement of Julian's lips and mustache as he tugged the rind from the orange slice he was devouring. The scent of atomized orange hung between them.

"What?" asked Julian. "Why are you smiling like that?"

"You salted an orange."

"Ye-ah," he said, in two syllables, the second implying *obviously*. "You never salted an orange? You should try it. It makes it sweeter." Then he laid two more sections on their sides and salted them, indicating with a cocked eyebrow for Walter to try it.

It was a minor shame that Walter had dressed so carefully for a night out, and then they never left the apartment—but not one worth regretting for long, since what followed was absolutely some of the best sex he had ever had. They went directly from the kitchen to the bedroom, leaving half the orange sliced on the cutting board, but taking the taste of it with them. Later, Walter would think of its combination of salt and tang when he was nuzzled up close to Julian's scrotum. Julian's body amazed him—almost everything about it was more compact than his. Walter was gangly and pale, knock-kneed and long-necked and soft-bellied; Julian was smaller, slimmer, darker, dancer sleek. He smelled of the sandalwood oil he rubbed into his hair behind the ears and some other mix of unnamable pheromones that nearly made Walter turn inside out with desire. He had a trim, muscled torso and mulberry-brown nipples, and though he wasn't especially hairy, the black treasure trail that led from his belly button down to his curly tuft of pubes made Walter sigh audibly when he saw it. He was a little thrown off by Julian's foreskin—he'd encountered one only once before. But once he was hard, Julian pulled it back for him, the brown head glistening with pre-cum, and Walter got the hang of it pretty quickly.

All these delights were secondary, in Walter's mind, to the fact that Julian was a wonderful kisser, with his wide, warm mouth, his full lips, his paddle-tongue, and his playfulness, his sense of fun. It was obvious he loved making out; Walter did, too. It said something, he thought, that they made out for an entire half hour—shirtless, pausing for breath, talking and taunting a bit (Walter couldn't resist gnawing at Julian's armpit, but was rebuffed by the bitter assault of antiperspirant)—all before their pants came off. Among gay guys in SF, that alone made them a couple of prudes.

They took their time and went at it twice. The first time, Julian kept the lights on, and they had sex above the bedcover, the harsh overhead light providing its own kind of synthetic high-noon eroticism: there was no ignoring the pimples-and-all truth of the situation. After, Julian wiped a blot of cum from Walter's thigh with a sock from the floor. Only then did they lie under the sheets, talking for a while, before Julian reached for the bong on his bedside table and started rummaging through a drawer for pot to fill it. They smoked a bit, they made out, they went to piss, they finished the orange and ate another. Julian invited him to stay. They smoked some more—the pot was strong, and Walter got so stoned he lost his bearings on time and space. There was not much to look at in Julian's room besides the white walls and molding. Purple-and-blue batik gauze half concealed a window closed against a gray air shaft. Nothing hung on the walls except a poster of that ubiquitous image of Madonna—bracketing her face with her fingers and voguing—styled as the perfect platinum replicant of Marilyn, down to the parted lips, the hint of an overbite. Tacked up beside it was an old pastel postcard of the Corcovado in Rio; the *Redeemer*'s arms spread like jet wings out from under a red rosary, which dangled from the thumbtack, bisecting the Savior into mirrored halves.

The second time they fucked stoned with the lights off, having tried to sleep but being made ferociously horny by spooning nude. They fell into it again, and Walter spent the whole time amazed that he could maintain a hard-on. He could barely recall his name, or how he got wherever he was, or anything else beyond the overwhelming, nearly excruciating warmth of Julian's mouth rhythmically enveloping his cock. Then came the most incredible orgasm of his life—a steam engine bored through and out the back of his skull, leaving it cavernous as the Rainbow Tunnel, and soon his whole being was obliterated, replaced by a runaway train of freight cars with cacophonous pistons, its weighty, calamitous wheels flying from the rails and barreling down through the pot-soaked fen of his brain. On and on it went, blasting everything away, every synapse and sinew, and seeming never to end, so that, amid this joyous, relentless, and complete cancellation, the only semi-lucid thought he formed (slowly, slowly—never fully dawning) was the dopey wonder that he might just be stuck in this orgasm forever. At last, a sigh of relief: he was not.

Afterward, Julian curled off into sleep, but the pot would not relinquish Walter. He was anxious, insomniac, and lay awake thinking about things that didn't do him any good: he wondered that, at twenty-two, he'd never been in love. Maybe he was stunted. He thought ruefully of Eliot, in college, laughing at the carnations he'd brought him, and now the memory came cruelly alive again, the carnations themselves cracking up in Eliot's voice.

Drifting off at last, he thought of the dark-matter Queen Elizabeth who had fallen upon him from the traffic light on Halloween—the cuts on his forehead and palms had taken weeks to heal. He wondered what had happened to her, if she'd broken anything, if she was OK . . . That week he'd looked in the local rags: there was no mention of the incident. But that was the thing in SF, one night you might be the life of the block party, the queen of the night dancing high on a stoplight, and by the next morning, you'd have vanished without a trace.

He wondered, again, if he would ever know how it felt to have sex without the angel of death hanging over him.

After his cigarette, he was wet from the mist. Shoulders up, he slouched around the corner to Esta Noche but didn't go in. He hovered a moment and turned back. On the way, he gave one of his Camels and a light to a panhandler outside the corner bodega, then as he was nearing the Casanova again, he caught the familiar outline of a tall trench coat and a cocked fedora striding toward him from Seventeenth. It was Cary.

"*Amanda Blueshoes!* What the deuce are you doing out here? You'll be soaked!" she said, offering him her arm and leading him into the bar. "I understand the need to moisturize is a constant battle, but this is ridiculous."

The crowd had thinned a little. Cary ordered two large martinis *up* (she liked them dirty, or, as she put it, *filthy*), and they found an open lounge table upon which Cary rested her damp fedora.

"I wanted you to meet Jeff," said Walter, scanning the room and spotting him in a far corner, deep in conversation with his new friend, Bigboi68. "Maybe in a bit."

Cary raised her glass: "Chin-chin!"

"Your health!"

"Gesundheit!" said Cary. Peering over the rim of her glass, registering Walter's confusion, she added, "That's what that means."

"Hmm."

His martini caught the red candlelight and swirled with nearly invisible, icy currents; the gin smooth, deliciously antiseptic.

Cary toasted a second time, declaring, *"I am the king of the di-van!"*

"What is this, two-for-one non sequitur night?"

"No, darling, it's the song! 'Ça plane pour moi'? Plastic Bertrand? The greatest French punk song the Beach Boys ever produced?"

He had been trying to ignore the three blunt chords and shouted French bouncing off the walls, pogoing all around them. "Ugh, this song is so *annoying*, and for some reason I hear it *everywhere*. Did the Beach Boys really produce it?"

"Oh dear," said Cary, head down, giving Walter the top view of her left-hand part, usually perfectly kempt, now zigzagged from her hat. "Did you know they took the definition of *gullible* out of the dictionary and just left the picture of you? People complained it was redundant."

Walter blinked. Over the last week or so, something had shifted a bit with Cary. It was like some threshold had been met, some quota of goodwill over the hours they'd spent together, and now they were able to snipe at each other, playfully getting a little bitchy. It wasn't actual bitchiness; it was always done with a smile, however suppressed. He volleyed: "Are these the same people who want you to update your author photo on the book of the world's oldest jokes?"

"Which I wrote? Because I'm that old?" asked Cary grimly.

"Yes."

"You know," said Cary, "it's not very polite to joke about a lady's age . . ."

"You're no lady," Walter shot back. She winced a little, and he felt like a jerk—maybe this was going too far. Cary never referred to herself as a *lady*, though she used the word in reference to Sasha all the time. And anyway, *lady* seemed like the wrong word to describe someone who so fastidiously styled herself after William Powell.

"Maybe so, but no *gentleman* would ever point that out."

"Sorry!" said Walter, contrite. "Hey, I've got one for you: Who do you think said this? *It's true you catch more flies with honey, but you catch more honeys with vinegar.*"

"Ah! A defense of bitchiness . . . I don't know . . . Quentin Crisp? Eleanor Roosevelt?"

"It was *Dorothy Parker*, of course, stupie! You're the one who asked for *new* Dorothy Parker quotes . . ."

Cary raised her glass with indignation. "*Stupie?* In the course of one minute you've impugned my age, my ladylikeness—if that's a word—my intelligence, and now you're trying to beat me at my own game . . ."

"Sorry!"

"I think you're extremely rude." She smiled. "I really ought to chop your head off with a meat cleaver, or *at least* make you pay for the next round of drinks."

"*That* escalated rapidly." He massaged his trachea with one hand.

"*Ça plane pour moi!*" said Cary. "Anyway, let's not squabble anymore, because we're wasting time and I want to talk about your writing. I have a proposal for you."

The week before, Cary had convinced Walter, with a fair amount of cajoling, that they should share their writing with each other and provide feedback. Walter was pretty convinced the whole thing was a plot to *inspire something* in him, and Cary had to admit it was, and that something was *greatness*. Cary had a sense of scope. So she shared a substantial tome, a big bundle of her poems, song lyrics, limericks, palindromes, pangrams, and aphorisms, and Walter gave her a couple short stories that he thought weren't too fragmentary, revealing, juvenile, or otherwise embarrassing in some unpredictable way. He'd also shared the film treatment he'd written as a special project for his major.

"I haven't gotten through all your poems," said Walter. "You're really . . . Prolific is an understatement, I think."

"Oh, never mind," said Cary. "I want to talk about your film, *Waldo: A Correction*."

"Hardly a film, I mean—it's only a treatment. It's, like, a very in-depth outline."

"Oh, I *loved it*! I love the premise. So, it's a prequel to *Laura*, right?"

"It's more like an alternate version, I guess?" He slurped his martini nervously. "I was in the middle of writing a senior thesis about the villain, Waldo Lydecker, how extremely queer he is, you know. And I thought his motive in the movie makes no sense at all—I mean, the idea that he's in love with Laura, given the fact that everything about him is as queer as a three-dollar bill. So I thought I'd write a version of the story that's not *quite so* homophobic and have Waldo's motives make some sense."

"But in *Laura* . . . the feyness of Waldo, his campiness, is that written into the character? Or was that Clifton Webb's choice, to flame out?"

"Oh yeah, it's in the script. It's in the book, too. There's a whole scene in the book where Waldo is described *mincing* around, pretending to be Laura throwing a cocktail party. So that's when I thought Waldo isn't really in love with Laura—he's jealous and maybe wants to *be* her—but mostly he's sick of her stealing all the men before he gets a shot at them. So, in my version, Shelby's only the latest in a long line of men Waldo had hung his hopes on that Laura comes along and helps herself to. Why should Laura have all the fun? When will Waldo get to roll in the hay with a hot young stud?"

"Clifton Webb was a homo, wasn't he?" asked Cary.

"Yeah, it was more than a Hollywood rumor. An open secret, I guess."

"Depressing, isn't it? That he was so willing to play to stereotype, cashing in on Hollywood's homophobia." Cary frowned briefly. "But, in that case, why make Waldo the killer? I mean, if you're going to rewrite the whole story, you might as well have someone else be the killer."

There it was. Cary had made the subtle shift from praise to feedback and critique. Walter bristled. With his teeth, he pulled a fat olive from a translucent blue cocktail saber and chewed it thoughtfully. "Oh really, like who?"

"I don't know, anyone else . . . Vincent Price, Dana Andrews, maybe Laura herself, the maid . . ."

"Bessie the maid? Why on earth would Bessie want to kill Laura?"

"Because she's a crazed evangelical who deplores Laura's loose lifestyle, of course!"

Walter laughed at this, but all of a sudden Cary became businesslike. "Here's what I think," she said, her tone high conspiratorial. "You and I should write a screenplay together. A film noir. I've been wanting to write one for a long time, and you're the perfect guy to help me."

"What makes you think I'd be any good at that?"

"*Of course you would*, it's your dream job, you just don't know it yet," said Cary. "Do you have any idea what it's like seeing a movie with you?"

"What's that supposed to mean?" He braced for a backhanded compliment.

"It means you're a walking script doctor. You walk out of every movie with a whole roster of trenchant notes you've been working out up here"— she tapped her temple—"and then the next hour and a half or more is: *Here's why that plot was ridiculous,* or *The whole thing should have been rewritten this way,* or *This is how that dialogue should have gone,* and on and on . . . Anyone who didn't know how much you loved movies would assume you hated every last one of them."

He had a chance to stew on this observation, some aspects of which were undeniable, as two old friends of Cary's—slightly older, bearish men who appeared to be a couple—interrupted them. Brief, bubbly introductions led to the obligatory round of catching up, and Walter excused himself to take a leak. There was a line, and when he returned, Cary's friends had gone, and there sat two new double martinis, brimful, though he hadn't finished his first. In the distance, at the front of the bar, he spied Jeff, looking almost un-recognizably short, his profile eclipsed as he Frenched the blond giant.

"To a fruitful collaboration?" Cary asked as they toasted cautiously. "Or anyway, a fruity one."

"OK. What's in it for you? What do you want out of it?"

The answer was so obvious, he should have guessed it first thing. Cary longed to be the gumshoe. She wanted a plum Marlowesque PI role, tailored for her alone. When Walter voiced surprise, saying he didn't know she acted, she scoffed and went on a brief diatribe about how movie actors don't really act so much as rework, for each role, a slightly heightened, fun-house-mirror version of themselves. He was pretty sure such a theory would be highly offensive to trained actors, but he thought she had a point. Then came the second part of Cary's plot, which Walter would never dare contradict: Sasha would play the femme fatale. Give him a little padding and a bias-cut gown, dub him a dame-done-wrong, and write him a torch song to burn through, and his natural, irresistible pout would do the rest.

"Wouldn't Sasha be *fabulous*? A fabulous femme fatale?" Cary asked.

He sat stupefied by what an inspired idea it was. A foregone conclusion for Walter, who had excused his prior dubious behavior toward his friend by concluding that anyone who met Sasha was likely to be immediately smitten, as he had been.

"Where is Sasha tonight?" Walter asked. The question had been nag-ging at him, but Cary had so flooded him with rapid talk that he'd decided to wait until the subject came up.

"He's out tonight—on a date, I believe." Cary announced this almost proudly, like she was prepared to toast the news. And even though he was aware they had an arrangement and a set of guidelines, he wasn't sure how

to take the information. It seemed both inappropriate and irrelevant to ask if
Sasha's date was a man or a woman.

"Aren't you jealous?" he asked.

"Jealous? Pfft." She flicked her long guitarist's fingers. "Why? What for?"

"I thought, you know, you and Sasha are in love . . . and that would make
it hard for you to think of him with someone else."

"We are in love, very much so," Cary assured him. "That's the whole
point. It's because we love and trust each other so much that we don't want to
be possessive. We simply, categorically reject the idea that loving someone
means possessing them."

Something about this idea distressed Walter. He slumped in his lounge
chair.

Cary sighed at him, with a hint of disdain, and went on: "Basically, Sasha
and I agree on two fundamental points. The first is you don't own someone's
genitals. What they want to do with them is up to them."

"Yeah, hard to argue when you put it like that . . ."

"The second is you can't find perfection in one person."

"Per-fec-tion?" Walter asked. He slurred the syllables and the word
warped, like a curse.

"I mean, you can't expect one person to be everything to you. It's not fair
to them, and it's not fair to you."

Part of his brain absorbed this, thinking it was all well and good and
logical. Meanwhile, another part of his brain had soaked up a substantial
amount of gin and had begun to slacken. He knew he was very old-fashioned
and simple-minded, but if you truly were in love . . . Something about the
thought of an open relationship made him queasy. He himself had enough
trouble getting a single date, with just one guy, and now the mossy corner-
stone of monogamy would be chiseled out, and the whole chivalric edifice
of polite, old-school romance would crumble around him. At the moment
he seemed very ill-equipped to gauge his own desires. He thought he was
jonesing for another cigarette, but more than that he wanted Julian to show

up so they could go back to Julian's place and fuck around. He felt envious of the ease with which Jeff met guys—he had been envious of Eliot in the same way—and now maybe he would find he was jealous of Sasha as well. Perhaps some of the anxiety he was busy projecting onto Cary—jealousy on Cary's behalf—had to do with how striking Sasha was to anyone with eyes in their head. Yet Cary was cavalier about it, so assured in her stance that it seemed naive, or at least idealistic. He didn't think Cary was naive.

"What's wrong with you?" asked Cary. "You're pouting like an Olsen twin."

"What if I don't want *perfection*?" he protested. "What if all I want is *one person*?"

"I don't think it's possible to want just one person," said Cary.

Walter blinked at this slowly, with both eyes.

"Don't look at me like I'm crazy," she said. "Hear me out. I think it's possible to *restrict yourself* to one person. I mean, monogamy happens sometimes, I guess . . ."

"Big of you to acknowledge that."

"But desire—that's something else. It's not simply that it's uncontainable—I mean, it is. But it's also, like, relational. Wanting is always wanting more. And what's worse, you always want what someone else wants. Think of poor Waldo! It's not really that he wants Laura or what she has; it's that he wants whatever Laura *wants*. He wants her *wanting*, in a way, and her desires keep eclipsing his. And the great irony is he can't have what he wants by *having* her, and he probably couldn't even have what he wants by *being* her. Because if he were her, he—or she, I guess—in the end would want what someone else wants anyway. Someone else entirely, that is, someone unforeseeable—unimaginable. It's like an endless relay, a daisy chain. Desire is a daisy chain. You see?"

"I literally have no idea what you just said," said Walter, with a morose laugh. "But don't mind me, I'm tired and emotional." This was his favorite euphemism for *drunk*.

"Poor Waldo!" said Cary.

"Poor . . . Hey! Did you just call me Waldo?"

"No, of course not, Waldo, I mean Walter, I was talking about the movie! You look nothing like Clifton Webb, I promise!"

"Not OK!" cried Walter. "Not cool. Not cool at all."

They sat in silence for a moment as the Casanova stirred around them. Walter's mind wandered through the blood orange interior, pondering Cary's drunken homily on desire. He couldn't make head or tail of it. Waldo didn't really want *Laura*, but he wanted *to be her, wanting Shelby*? That much made a kind of sense. But then, if he were her, would she want *someone else*, or *something someone else wanted*?

"Earth to Walter!" Cary was eating an olive. She pinched her blue plastic sword between her fingers and wagged it at him, parrying in midair. "Darling, I think you are very drunk, and we should get some solid food in you!"

"OK." Walter nodded. "Not Sparky's, though—I'm tired of Sparky's . . ."

"No problem. I know a great place that serves crepes at all hours." Cary stood, put on her overcoat, and, discovering a mirror behind her, replaced her fedora and cocked it with care.

Walter sat, stewed. It made no sense, what Cary was saying. At least her theory of desire had the virtue of being extremely confusing and paradoxical, because sex, too, was confusing and paradoxical. But she seemed to be saying that desire was never fully your own, which made no sense at all, none at all, because if desire wasn't your own, what on earth was?

TESTINGTESTINGTESTINGTESTINGTESTINGTESETINGTERSTING

BRAVE NEW WORLD!

         This is my new BROTHER WP1400D
today is Saturday the 13th. .. High Tea with Cary
at the Sheraton Palace, scones, clotted cream afterward
we went to Circuit City and picked out this beaut

    beautiful haunted typewriter that remembers what you type
and can type t a it again!!!

    So sayeth Cary. though I have yet to figure out how. .

also ype typewriter mode and can erase whole worlds! Oerds
words
not

haven't mastered it yet obviuosly but i love the clack

          ilovetheclackilovetheclacklacklackityclack

                              styleisallrhythm
          --so sayheth Ginny Woolf!

OK erase function is going to be KEY. On the righthand is a
minidisk. now that Cary and I have the same BROther WP1400D
we can swap minidisks and share <u>everything</u> orat least all our
writing, that is,)there are limits)

Funnily enough Sasha's sewing machine is also a BROTHER Cary
informs me, and so now drumroll please we each have a BROTHER
and a=ff rom now on all our   everything we type wwill be
like the stiches in Sasha's gorgeous gowns they shall all be
COUSINS

Christmas in Connecticut

THE CHALLENGE WAS TO COMPLETELY transform the first floor of Macy's—the perfume, cosmetics, and jewelry departments—into a winter wonderland, and the entire display team, along with a battalion of seasonal hires, were being paid overtime to make it happen. The cavernous first floor, from its waxed white stone floors to the can lights high in the ceiling, was the least natural place imaginable, a dazzling maze of burnished surfaces of white Carrara marble, chrome, and glass; as divorced from nature as the Death Star. The team had three days—or, rather, three nights after the store closed—to refashion it into the Black Forest. Not anything like the real forest, of course, but a fairy-tale, advent-calendar Black Forest, with towering pine trees lavishly ornamented and glittering with eternally new snow; cuckoos, squirrels, and other woodland creatures; and, generally, every tacky trick in the almanac, including spindly elves in Tyrolean hats and a development of gingerbread cottages. The unveiling of this wonderland, including the much-touted and -anticipated holiday window displays, was slated for Saturday morning, the first blockbuster shopping day before Thanksgiving. The high stakes were drilled into the heads of the team; after all, shoppers would be boating from Sausalito and driving from Merced in order to witness the spectacle.

As it was, almost everyone on the display team had had about as much Christmas as they could take—like kids who ate all the marzipan in one sitting—because they'd been steadily overdecorating all the other departments for weeks. Sasha, who had been unchained from his sewing machine in order to help with the holiday blitzkrieg, declared that if he was handed one more fake pine garland, he was going to hang himself with it. Walter was freed from the basement, along with Clark, who'd been his buddy in the department since the afternoon Walter wowed him with his lobster. For over a week, Walter, Clark, and Sasha worked together—bossed around by Gavin—on the corner window display. The theme was "Christmas in New England," because, as everyone knew, the East Coast invoked a traditional holiday charm that godless, seasonless California couldn't muster.

One night, in the spirit of getting in the spirit, they rented *Christmas in Connecticut* and watched it at Sasha and Cary's. The three of them fit cozily on the couch, beneath the flickering, smoking shrine to Django. It was a boring screwball comedy with nary a screw loose, and not even Barbara Stanwyck, gimlet-eyed queen of the snide quip, could rescue it from its own earnestness. She played a lifestyle columnist, a proto–Martha Stewart type, who was paid to crank out fantasies of domestic bliss with her typewriter, but was in fact a hack, a fraud, and in reality could neither change a diaper nor truss a goose. Naturally, her womanliness is put on trial, in a phony publicity-stunt marriage with a borrowed baby, in a Christmas postcard town where everyone rides around in horse-drawn sleighs, in *1945*. They saw it all through to the dismal earnest end for the sake of Barbara, then uncorked a second bottle of wine, toasted their grandmothers for enduring such an era, and immediately rewatched *Double Indemnity*.

The towering old-growth pines of the Black Forest had three magical nights in which to manifest themselves. On the first night, Wednesday, an enormous moving truck parked itself outside the Stockton Street entrance, minutes after the store closed at six. The display team hauled the timber from the truck, giant pines thick as telephone poles. They had no branches yet, and were unwieldy but light and hollow: fat PVC pipes with cast rubber bark. Sasha said the trunks had been cast from the bark of a real tree and that in fact they were all the same tree, silicone clones. What followed was a rubberized parody of an Amish barn raising. It would take them until midnight to raise the timbers and arrange the forest in midair, atop tall consoles that divided the first floor into a maze of satellite counters. It all had to be done with agonizing slowness and care, erecting the trees on steel bases, fixing them to the ceiling with wires, wheeling ladders and platform lifts around glass cases housing hundreds of thousands of dollars of jewelry and perfumes. At nine o'clock they were given an entire half hour for dinner. Knowing this, Cary came a-knocking on the glass doors of the south entrance. She brought them takeout: pad Thai, egg rolls, papaya salad, and larb. They sat among the bright vitrines of pearl strands and ate from the Styrofoam.

After, Cary wanted to see the Christmas tablecloth Sasha had labored over for several weeks. It was the centerpiece of the holiday china display in the corner window. Gavin wasn't around to police them—he'd pulled seniority and declared he wasn't doing overtime this year. Sasha and Walter snuck Cary into the display, where they viewed the lavish formal table setting by the light of a million bead lights, which it turned out was when Cary hatched her next brilliant scheme.

After three days of overtime everyone was exhausted and getting loopy, including their manager, Cindy. She was a veritable fun-loving Mrs. Claus compared with sour Gavin, who wasn't around to scowl at every choice they made. Someone left the piped Christmas music on, cranking it up so it was inescapable, even blaring from speakers on the sidewalk when Walter took a smoke break. That night was a frenzied rush of decorating, stringing lights and hanging ornaments, rolling out bolts of batting and stapling snowdrifts in place, slotting together plywood gingerbread houses, and posing elves everywhere: cavorting with woodland creatures, leaning from gingerbread shutters, peeking from behind tree trunks in ways that looked (when possible) innocent and nonthreatening.

Last came the blizzard, which arrived in dozens of cardboard boxes. It was stage snow, fluffy paraffin flakes, the kind you see sifted over opera singers in the final act as they die of pneumonia or bleed out after a duel.

They sprinkled snow over every tree branch, every cottage eave, every elf's cap and squirrel's alert tail. They used it to whiteout every wire, seam, and crease, every flaw in the forest. By the end of the night, Walter and Sasha had to admit that, even as an avalanche of alpine clichés had come to rest upon the sales consoles, the team had been utterly thorough, leaving no bough unbedecked, and the whole effect, once lit up, was corny as could be, but somehow still enchanting.

That night, they were in the thick of things as their 9:00 p.m. dinner break approached. Sasha was attending to the three berobed magi who, thoroughly lost on their journey, had appeared by the Clinique counter bearing gift sets of luxury cosmetics. Walter had been keeping an eye out for Cary when he spied her knocking at the south entryway. He waved her toward the employees' entrance and let her in. She was wearing a dark blue cashmere men's overcoat, dilapidated but lovely, and her gray fedora. She was carrying a large woven hamper with a sturdy handle and shoved a grocery bag into Walter's arms.

"I have a surprise for Sasha," she said, with a sly look. "I need your help—follow me." They skirted the jewelry department, avoiding as many coworkers as possible. A cold, weighty clinking in the brown bag he was carrying suggested chilled booze. Cary marched them to the back hallway that led to the window displays and insisted, rather bossily, that Walter turn on all the lights in the windows. He was wary but went along with it.

"You have a half hour starting at nine, right?" she asked.

"This seems like, maybe, not a great idea . . ." said Walter.

"*Wall,*" said Cary, rolling her eyes, "live a little."

Then she marched up the narrow steps into the window display and made her way through another glitzy commodified forest, ducking behind a painted backdrop, toward the New England formal dining set that was Gavin's masterpiece. She set her hamper on the floor at the far end of the long, richly overdecorated table. Walter and Sasha had spent weeks helping Gavin prepare for and execute this diorama; everywhere the space was lit by strands of starlight, woven through boughs and garlands. The forest spilled

over from the contiguous displays, so it was hard to tell what Gavin was trying to represent exactly: A dining set dropped into a tree farm? A ballroom
in Narnia? Sasha had sewn the tablecloth from a thousand dollars' worth of
thick silk tapestry, with a pattern of roving grapevines, deep green leaves,
and burgundy grapes. But as the motif wasn't quite Christmassy enough,
Gavin had Sasha hand-appliqué patches of holly leaves and berries, tucked
into the pattern seamlessly, the whole thing overwrought with invisible
handiwork. At the hems, heavy gold fringe skimmed the floor. Underneath
the ostentatious settings of china, service wear, crystal candleholders, goblets
and tumblers, and glitter-encrusted poinsettias, you'd never guess the table
itself was particleboard atop a team of sawhorses.

Cary had opened her hamper and was bent over, rummaging through it.
"Just give me a few minutes to set up," she said, "then run and get Sasha."

"Cary? What are you doing?"

She didn't answer and didn't look up. Although there were no loud-
speakers in the window displays, the unmistakable strains of "Jingle Bell
Rock" were muffling through from the sales floor and the sidewalk outside.
Walter got a whiff of the scents from Cary's open basket. They smelled herby,
schmaltzy, like an indeterminate holiday roast. *Roast beast.*

"Cary—what on earth?"

"Trust me, OK?" She stood tall and looked him in the eye, smile crooked
and fedora cocked, a queer gangster. "Do me a favor and go and get Sasha.
Give me five minutes."

Walter had to hunt a bit for Sasha, who, it turned out, had gone with
Clark to fetch more snow from storage. That night Sasha was wearing a
jumpsuit he had made, legs so wide it looked like a dress of black rayon with
a pattern of gold and red stopwatches, with fobs that curled like paisleys. His
hair was up in that pristine twist he could pull off so well. Elegant as always,
he looked ready for a night on the town.

Sasha followed Walter and grew apprehensive, as Walter had, when they
snuck through the hallway and up into the window displays.

"Cary. Cary! What the hell?" said Sasha, bracketing his face with his hands, afraid to look directly.

Cary stood at the far end of the table, her smile triumphant. She had lit a dozen candles and laid out dinner for them on the fine china, each place setting framed profusely by silver. The table was set for eight, but there were only four chairs and only three settings had food, giving the whole thing the look of the Mad Hatter's tea party, minus the Dormouse and March Hare. And minus the tea—champagne fizzed in crystal flutes. Something certainly smelled delicious.

"It's what you always wanted!" declared Cary. "Isn't it? I thought— I thought it was!"

"Well, yes, of course, darling," said Sasha. "*Everyone* dreams of losing their job by burning it all down and destroying thousands of dollars of merchandise in the process." But only half of Sasha's expression was exasperation, and the rest, creeping in slowly, was delight. "If Cindy catches us, we are *totally screwed*."

Walter squirmed a bit—the longer they stood there, the more delectable the food smelled, and his appetite was taking over. "If we eat quick, I don't think anyone would know—I don't think anyone would think to look for us here."

It was true, they were sequestered, in a way. One whole wall—the wall of windows—was concealed, taped up with butcher paper. In this shimmering dining grove, awash in ornaments, it was the only place one's eyes could rest. Sasha calmed, but before he sat, Cary swore on her life that afterward she would clean so thoroughly that no one would know they'd been there. They each vowed to cut off the hand that spilled on the million-dollar tablecloth.

Cary, it seemed, could convince anyone of anything, but she was especially adept at convincing people to eat. She served them each a spice-encrusted Cornish hen, on a puree of fennel and celery root, swirled with a jammy something called a *coulis*—none of which Walter had ever encountered before, but *Jesus Christ*, it was tasty, and they were famished, and they carved away at their birds lustily, like medieval courtiers, like King Wenceslas (or someone) tearing a pheasant with a knife. Walter couldn't figure out how, during a cab ride downtown, Cary had managed to keep everything piping hot. He was half afraid she was hiding a hibachi behind her chair.

Cary sat at the head of the table, Walter at the opposite end, and Sasha in the middle. They toasted to a job well done—well, almost done—then a weekend off. Walter sipped the champagne cautiously—he didn't want to return to work drunk. He liked the large bubbles even though Cary assured him it was a mark of cheap champagne; it shouldn't spatter in the glass like soda pop. From behind the wall of butcher paper, Bing Crosby was *dreaming of a white Christmas*—mellowly pining, about to start whistling about it.

"So, what is *Christmas in Connecticut* about this, exactly?" asked Cary.

"Christmas in *New England*, not specifically *Connecticut*," Walter said.

"You don't get New England from this?" asked Sasha.

"Maybe New England via Hollywood, or San Simeon . . ."

Walter let out a facetious wail, and Cary looked concerned, as if he'd dropped something on the cloth and would now have to cut off his hand. Sasha got it right away and explained it was because Walter hadn't seen Hearst Castle yet, and Cary and Sasha had.

"Does it look like this? I'm so desperate to see it," said Walter.

"We'll go soon, darling!" said Sasha. "I promise."

"Road trip!" exclaimed Cary, gnawing a diminutive drumstick.

"I think New England is represented by this hutch," said Walter, gesturing toward a large, faux-rustic cabinet, with an arrangement of Spode china plates picturing the twelve days of Christmas.

"I hadn't noticed that . . . there's so much to look at," said Cary, scanning the grove of trees around them, freighted with decorations like overburdened pack animals. "I've also never felt so Jewish."

"I think New England is depicted through that window, on the backdrop," said Sasha. He pointed toward a valanced windowpane that hung in midair before a painted backdrop you had to strain to see through the alpenglow of Christmas lights and candles. It depicted a winter snowscape: downy banks, clusters of denuded trees, and a tiny horse-drawn sleigh heading over a hill in the distance.

"That's where Barbara Stanwyck is," said Cary. "She's in that sled, shamelessly flirting with that sailor. The minx!"

Walter laughed. "I worked on this window for a whole week, and I never noticed that sleigh."

When he looked back at Cary, she had frozen, staring somewhere over his left shoulder. Sasha turned and, glancing behind Walter, froze as well. His natural pout became a deep frown.

"What the fuck is going on here?" cried an exasperated voice. "What the fuck is this?"

Walter dreaded turning around, but there was nothing to be done.

There was Gavin, standing between two Christmas trees, looking flushed and furious. Internally, Walter panicked, but even as he did, it was impossible to ignore Gavin's resemblance to an irascible Santa Claus, with his reddening cheeks, graying goatee, and a large maroon jacket zipped over his barrel belly. Walter pinched his tongue hard with one incisor to keep from giggling.

"I'm walking up O'Farrell," said Gavin, practically spitting with anger, "and I can tell from the street someone's left the lights on in here, and . . . *Sasha? Walter?*" He tried to throw up his arms in exasperation, but there was simply too much Christmas in the way. "Where the fuck is Cindy?" asked Gavin. "Is someone going to explain to me *what the hell this is?*"

Walter stopped giggling. His hand was over his heart, which might have temporarily stopped. Sasha, who Walter thought couldn't be flustered, looked frightened and at a loss for words.

"*Where's Cindy?* She's gonna *love this* . . ."

Sasha found his voice: "I think Cindy went to get food—she left with Clark."

"You guys are damn lucky she's not here, because . . ." Gavin trailed off while looking at Cary, as if he were noticing her for the first time. "And who the hell is this? Are you a temp?"

Sasha opened his mouth to speak, but before he could, Cary launched a charm offensive.

"Gavin, we've met before! Cary Menuhin . . ." She moved down the table toward him, extending her hand, and when he didn't take it, she backed away, but she never stopped talking, reminding him when they'd met (the previous New Year's Eve), and where (in the produce section of Safeway, by the exotic fruits), and how they had a conversation about kumquats and star fruit. In the course of this bizarrely soothing stream of small talk, Cary invited him, three times, to sit in the upholstered dining chair across from Sasha and join them.

Something about her absolute ease in the situation put Gavin at ease as well, and in the end, his belligerence was no match for her charm. She was performing, Walter noticed, but she wasn't plying feminine wiles; she wasn't widening her hazel eyes or batting her long lashes, softening her voice or being coy. It wasn't a sly seduction; it was an invitation to play, as if they were a bunch of kids playing New England Christmas.

Taken aback, Gavin blinked and began to calm. Walter could hear Gavin's breathing slow down.

"You see, it was all my idea," said Cary. "These two had no idea—*none at all.* But as you know, all these years Sasha has been making these incredible tablecloths for you—gorgeous cloths like this one—and one day he said to me, *I wish I could use one of them, you know, just once?* So I thought I'd—well, you must have had the same thought, many times! You must have thought, *What a shame to spend all these days and weeks designing these incredible tables that no one will ever use . . .*"

Walter winced, because stressing the uselessness of their surroundings called up the frivolousness of their jobs and, if you thought about it too much, the pointlessness of everything they did, which dawned on him several times a day, when he was, say, arranging plastic soup ladles like lilies in a canister or stacking bags of chocolate-covered cherries into an Aztec pyramid. But Gavin wasn't balking, he was listening to Cary, and he listened to her as she led him around the table and pulled the chair out for him, and then he sat, taking it all in with renewed appreciation, maybe even pride. She chattered along, and he listened as she ducked behind the table and emerged a minute later, miraculously having plated a Cornish game hen for him, still steaming a little, still warm.

"How lucky that these were two for one! And how lucky you could join us," she said, placing the bird before him as if this were her own dining room where she entertained regularly.

Gavin was speechless; the four of them sat mute. He lifted a knife, chose a fork among the three in front of him, and held them for a moment. He was about to speak, then drew a breath and harrumphed. He set down his knife and fork. The three friends traded obtuse glances across the table. Walter contemplated the state of his résumé.

Gavin spoke: "You forgot the snow."

He got up from his chair and walked behind a screen, taking care to step over a red-saddled rocking horse and a pile of presents jettying from under a tree. Sasha angrily mouthed something at Cary, which Walter thought might be *I'm going to kill you.* Cary ignored him and filled Gavin's flute with champagne. Suddenly a spotlight snapped on, and a disco ball hanging over the window spun slowly on a horizontal axis, casting bright pixels down upon them. Gavin returned, removed his coat, and hung it on his chair. "That's better," he said, and sat down with a sigh of satisfaction, arranging the opulent tablecloth around his knees. His red plaid shirt fit the theme, clashing festively in the way that everything around them festively clashed. Squarish snowflakes rushed through the curls at the back of his balding head as he cut into the game hen. The rest of them picked at their plates.

With a surgeon's concentration, Gavin dissected an entire thigh from his bird, boned it, and swallowed it in one bite. "This is sensational!" he grunted.

"They're Moroccan spices," said Cary, "my own blend."

"It's wonderful," said Gavin, cutting the meat from the breast, eating attentively, sampling champagne.

Walter and Sasha were dumbfounded, but Cary kept on soliloquizing, saying how glorious the displays looked, including the forest in the jewelry department, and she pointed out some of her favorite objets d'art in the display and said she could see why people traveled from all over the state to get a glimpse. The stream of blandishments seemed to be working on Gavin, who muttered in agreement as he ate, while Walter squirmed in his chair, and Sasha was noticeably queasy, fennel green.

Halfway through his plate of food, Gavin stopped, set his silverware down, and took in the scene. His back was to the window, and everything in his view—except his companions—had been part of his design, his world of fantasy and luxury. Glamour and nostalgia, concocted as a lure for suburbanites. Cary stopped talking, and the silence was filled by Miss Judy Garland solemnly singing "Have Yourself a Merry Little Christmas," and Gavin resumed eating and ruminated contentedly, the tip of his goatee darting about, and Walter thought that, of course, Gavin was the kind of old queen who would be obsessed with Judy Garland. Walter couldn't resist swiping up the last of the sweet coulis with his finger, and as he did so, he regarded Gavin as if he were seeing him for the first time, and some veil of anxiety or expectation had fallen. He saw now that Gavin was just a person and that, despite all evidence to the contrary, he'd been a boy once, and he'd probably collected things, like polished rocks, or Betty Boop dolls, or Mr. Potato Heads or something. He was trying to place the boy Gavin in a decade, but he could never guess anyone's age anyway. Maybe he loved westerns. Maybe Randolph Scott was his first crush, which would be understandable, and he begged his mom to take him to every gunslinging western that came out. And as he sat projecting a whole past onto Gavin, he realized that the man was quietly crying, tears wetting his face as he ate, not brushing them away, as the disco-snow showered down around them.

Walter offered Cary and Sasha a look meant to convey: *Is this silly old queen crying over Judy Garland?* Sasha looked as mystified as he was. It wasn't clear whether Cary had noticed Gavin was crying, but she had noticed that Gavin's glass was empty, and in one movement she reached down and pulled a second bottle of champagne seemingly out of her boot, and peeled the foil from the cork.

"More champagne?" she asked. When he nodded, she popped the cork and added, "I'm afraid it's not very good, it's only Freixenet, after all—"

"I like it!" chimed Walter.

"Darling, no offense, but you would mix 7Up with Franzia and call it sangria."

Sasha laughed at this, but Gavin did not. He was watching the champagne as it rose through the facets of his Baccarat flute, with an intense focus that would make any waiter nervous, but Cary executed the pour without a drip.

Gavin sighed. "It's so nice . . . you young people. Celebrating, I mean." His voice had gone soft.

"What's that, Gavin?" asked Sasha.

"I mean, it's so nice that you can still *celebrate things*. That you *buy champagne*. I haven't bought champagne in . . . a decade? I honestly don't remember how long."

"It's not like we're living large," said Cary. "It's, like, ten-dollar champagne."

"You don't understand—I can't anymore. *I can't do it*," said Gavin, hands folded, eyes cast down. In his lap he held a brocade napkin, but he wouldn't raise it to his face. As though the cloth were too precious to wipe his tears, he used the backs of his hands. "It's just that I've lost too many friends. I've said goodbye too many times. Or worse. Worse, I mean—when I wasn't able to say goodbye. So I don't celebrate anymore. *I can't do it*." He paused, trying to collect himself.

"A couple weeks ago—" Cary started, but Gavin interrupted her.

"No, I mean it," said Gavin, "I'm happy for you, it's good that you haven't been through what I have . . ." He wiped his face again, thoroughly now, and when he pulled his hands away this time, he was trying his best to smile. "Isn't it so lovely in here? All the lovely linens and the exquisite china and silver . . ." He sucked in air and burped a little. "My whole life, I've just loved beautiful things. Beauty is the only thing I've ever cared about. I'm like Tosca: *Vissi d'arte, I've lived for art!* But beauty doesn't save a single life, does it? Beauty never saved one goddamned life."

They were silent. Walter couldn't look Gavin in the eye, so he watched streams of candle wax flow down the tapers, red pooling in the crystal rims.

"I don't know that you can know that," Cary said at length. "I mean, I don't know that any of us can *know that* for sure."

"Believe me," said Gavin, "I know."

Silence reigned again. Walter was startled to see that Sasha was crying, and as he saw his friend lose his customary cool, he thought he might start blubbering, too. Cary frowned, looking admonished. The bright snow flitted relentlessly, never accumulating. Walter felt stupid, and sorry, and a little buzzed, and completely disarmed. He was also relieved. His shoulders relaxed and he slouched in his chair: he and Sasha would not be fired that night. Like a busker on the sidewalk outside, a wistful Dolly Parton was singing "Hard Candy Christmas."

"What's for dessert?" Gavin asked, pushing back a bit from the table. All of a sudden he was upbeat. Tears still dampening his cheeks, he was as cheerful as Walter had ever seen him.

"Crème brûlée!" Cary declared, and Gavin was visibly astonished, even as Sasha and Walter were hardly surprised, when she reached down and pulled from her hamper a blowtorch the size of a small pistol.

Sasha, covered in pocket watches, looked at his thin wristwatch. "Cary, we *really need* to get back to work . . ."

"Oh, don't be a killjoy!" said Gavin, smiling at Cary. "A little crème brûlée couldn't hurt."

The custard was a marvel of creaminess, *tinged with yuzu*, Cary explained. They gobbled it down, and all the while Sasha reassured Gavin that they would clean the dishware spotlessly and reset it with the utmost care. No one would ever know this dinner had taken place. Before he headed home, Gavin stood and thanked Cary for the food, buttoning his jacket, patting his belly, and declaring he hadn't had such a perfect meal in months. The last thing he said to them was: "You're paying for those candles."

It was one in the morning, and they were walking up Market Street. Walter and Sasha walked arm in arm, Cary outpacing them, even with her hamper. For no reason other than camaraderie, Cary had stayed to help them hang ornaments until after midnight, when Cindy declared the job done. Christmas accomplished, enchantment complete. Powell station had closed for the night, and buses were sparse, so they decided to start walking toward the Castro. It was foggy and cool, gray and starless. A bracing night for a walk.

"How in the world did she pull that off?" Walter asked Sasha, knowing Cary was listening.

"The dinner?" Sasha asked.

"No, *Gavin*. How on earth did she win Gavin over? I watched the whole thing and still don't get it. He is the grumpiest person I've ever met."

"Well, you know why I'm with Cary, don't you?"

"I could guess, but I think you should tell me."

"Because she's the most charming man I've ever met."

"Oho!" said Cary. She turned and walked backward for a stretch, the hamper swinging; she looked like she was setting herself up for a pratfall. "And you know why I'm with Sasha, don't you?"

"I never assume *anything* about your motives," said Walter.

"It's because he's the most fascinating, beguiling woman I've ever met!"

Sasha blew Cary a kiss, saying, "Don't trip over yourself, darling."

Cary turned again as they crossed Larkin Street. They approached a flagpole on a small square, a paved triangle so unremarkable that even people who worked there every day probably never noticed that it had a plaque and an official name. Cary set the basket down, raised her arms wide, and declared, "Walter, I've been meaning to show you this! This is it! Right here is where it all happened."

"You've been meaning to show me . . . the world's most boring post office?"

"No, of course not! I'm talking about what's *not* here. You have to see it with your mind's eye."

"Oh, is this where it was?" asked Sasha.

"My mind's eye is blank," said Walter, "and the suspense is killing me."

"This was the site of the Fox Theatre. The one I told you about."

"I thought that was in Oakland?"

"That's the Paramount," said Sasha.

"No, no, there was a Fox Theatre in San Francisco, and it was right here, and it was bigger than the Paramount and more beautiful, some say. It was the greatest cinema palace ever, more glorious than the Castro and the Alhambra and the Vaudeville Victoria combined!"

"I swear you never mentioned it."

"I'm sure I mentioned it, I wouldn't have neglected to mention it."

"She does talk about it a lot," said Sasha.

"What did it look like?" asked Walter.

"I don't know! I've only seen one photo—of the exterior and the marquee. It was from the early sixties, right before they tore it down. But everyone who saw it says it was the most spectacular cinema palace ever built."

The three of them stood for a moment, staring up into the lavender-gray sky above the post office, trying to conjure the contours of a palace like none they'd ever imagined, a lost palace from a golden age they were born too late to see, except in its shadows, its shades, its atemporal silver projections.

"That's what it's about!" said Walter, agitated.

"What what's about?" asked Cary, pulling her fedora from her head and running one hand through her glossy hat hair.

"Our film noir. That's the mystery! *Who killed the Fox Theatre?*"

"Probably no one *killed it*," said Sasha.

"Oh, someone *must* be responsible," said Walter. "It's not here anymore, is it? Someone killed it, out of greed, or malice, or neglect. Maybe it was an evil developer or maybe a malign city council, but someone killed it."

Cary beamed like an insane person.

"Why are you smiling like that?" Walter asked.

"Because I think it's brilliant! It's so brilliant, in fact, that I think I might kiss you full on the mouth." She grinned, and Walter was taken aback. "Sasha won't mind, will you, darling?"

"Of course not, darling, but maybe you should ask Walter if he'd mind?" Sasha stepped toward the curb and waved at a bus driver who was barreling in their direction in an enormous after-hours bus, as luminously fluorescent as a corporate office at midday. "And can we catch this bus first, please? My feet are killing me."

BRAINSTORMINGBRAINSTORMINGBRAINSTORMINGBRAINSTORMINGBRAINSTORMING
    With Cary & Walter

Everything we learned about the FOX THEATER
        (courtesy SFPL)

THE FOX was "the largest, most magnificent
        movie palace ever built!"
            --SF Call Bulletin
                            The RKO Palace? The Faux Theater?
Built in ROCOCO revival style   RKO Silver City Palace?
 (like Versailles: *Not affiliated with 20th C. Fox
Scrolls, seashells...Heaps &   named after Virginia FOX????
 Lashings of gilded gewgaws!)   whoever that is???

It was ENORMOUS: 4,600 seats!!!
several balconies

a Wurlitzer pipe organ fit for a cathedral
with 4,000 pipes!!!!!!!!!!!!!!!!!!!!   Who Killed...?
lining the walls like groves of trees   End of...
                                        Death of...
That's almost one pipe for every seat   Elegy for...
    in the house   Decline
The ENTIRE PALACE WOULD SHAKE   and Fall of...
        (like an e a r t h q u a k e)   Twilight of...
when the Wurlitzer played full blast.   Requiem for...
They held midnight organ concerts   Midnight at...
    to generate revenue   the CINEMA PALACE
        **DEFINITELY include
            creepy midnight organ concert.

                            Rides at Playland:
                            WHIP   SKYROCKET
                            CHUTES DIVING BELL
                            SCOOTER BUMPER CARS
                              TUNNEL O' LOVE

Midnight at the Cinema Palace

A Screenplay

By Cary Menuhin and Walter Simmering

1 CREDITS OVER MONTAGE

Night over the ocean. Far out at sea, no land in sight.
Herrmannesque score: slow, dark, propulsive. The camera
soars over a thick marine layer, tracks the fog toward
land. In the distance: Ocean Beach, glittering carnival
lights of Playland. The Whip, Scooter, Skyrocket, all zap,
spin, and spark. The fog makes land, envelops the Cliff
House, stirs through windmills. Golden Gate Park sinks
in the marine layer. In the Panhandle, fog floods the
eucalyptus. Fog pours over Twin Peaks, through the Castro,
the Mission. Finally, downtown: a miasma, neon-lit.
Crescendo as the titles conclude: "SAN FRANCISCO, 1952."

Shots of a tattered facade. A movie marquee, once
glorious, now dark. Big block letters: "RKO SILVER CITY
PALACE." Crumbling baroque facade. Pigeons fuss in an
ornate grille. Beneath the marquee the entrance is
boarded up.

"Closed for Renovations. GRAND REOPENING: FALL."

A TEENAGED COUPLE approaches the cinema palace. Scrubbed
up, saddle-shoed. She in his varsity jacket, his arm
around her neck. They examine shabby old movie posters. A
surreptitious figure scuttles toward a side entrance, not
wanting to be seen. He carries a bucket and a shovel. He
is FRITZ. FRITZ fumbles with a lock as the TEEN COUPLE
approaches.

                         TEEN BOY
                 Say, mister, any idea when the
                 Palace'll be open for business
                 again?

                           FRITZ
                 Don't bother me, boy, can't you see
                 it says "fall" all over the front?

                         TEEN GIRL
                 Hey, mister, do you know, are
                 they gonna show "Ivanhoe"? I just
                 love Elizabeth Taylor!

                         TEEN BOY
                 Aw, Mitsy, no one wants to see
                 that! Say, can we have a peek
                 inside?

                           FRITZ
                 You kids scram! This is an active
                 construction site. You might fall
                 and break your neck.

FRITZ shoos them away, shuts the door, locking himself
in the Palace. Enormous lobby. Velvety dark. Chandeliers
shed twilight. The silence hisses. Plaster Versailles
with towering columns, capped with scrolls, acanthus.
Majestic staircase soars to the balcony. FRITZ hurries
behind the staircase into the first-floor lounge. Murky
murals and mirrors. Glints of gilt ornament.

                           FRITZ
                  Dr. P! Dr. P! We had visitors!

FRITZ heaves open an ornate door leading to the
auditorium. Glimpses of an opulent interior, rococo
cavern. Against one wall, a tower of scaffolding. High
upon the scaffold is DR. EARNEST PURZELBAUM. He turns at
FRITZ's call.

                      FRITZ (cont'd)
                     [obsequious]
                 I sent them away! Just a couple
                 kids, nothing to worry about... I
                 sent them away, Dr. P.

Woman on the Run

AFTER THANKSGIVING, WALTER AND CARY got to work right away on their screen-play, adopting a routine that, if not especially productive, was certainly peripatetic. On a free afternoon or evening they'd meet at a coffee shop, the Bearded Lady or Jumpin' Java, and drink multiple cappuccinos until their hearts were gunning like diesel engines and Walter thought he might have a heart attack. Then they'd split a streusel cake or something, before determining that the only thing that could calm Walter's pulse was a little booze, so they'd move to the Orbit Room or Paula's and start in on the pints.

All the while they brainstormed and took notes. That is, Walter took notes. Cary had a philosophy that it was better *not* to take notes, because if an idea was any good at all you would remember it, and a couple pints and a martini or two couldn't wash a great idea away, *now could it?* Nonetheless Walter invested in a crisp spiral-bound notebook, and after their frenetic sessions—at home after the hangover had lifted—he would type up notes, inquiries, synopses, and whatever snatches of dialogue they had come up with on his Brother WP1400D. In the coffee shops PowerBooks and ThinkPads were all the rage, but he loved his unhip typewriter: it had a wide banner screen, Martian green and pixelated, with cyan lettering that disappeared if you sat forward or if the angle of the screen was off by a hair. He could type normally or edit line by line; it even had a save function—he could save ten whole pages to print later. Most alluring was the homely, square font, and the comforting clack of the cumbersome keys, and the *tack-tack-tack* of the daisy wheel as it printed, so rapidly the machine shook.

As for the content of the screenplay, they agreed it must be about the mysterious decline and fall of the Fox Theatre. It had to be set in the early '50s, a high-water mark for noir, and the Red Scare should play a big part, specifically queers being implicated in the Red Scare—and then disappearing. They made lists of essential locations: the Fox Theatre; Playland, of course; seedy SoMa bars and flashy North Beach nightclubs. And after that, the arguing began. They debated whether the Fox Theatre should be called the Fox in their film or if it should be some imaginary palace whose history they could tailor to their scenario. Cary proposed the Silver City Palace; Walter loved the sound of it. Then they argued over the title, deliberating the merits of poetic terms like *Twilight* and *Elegy* versus *Fall*, or *Decline and Fall*, or, most bluntly, *Death of*, before settling on *Midnight at the Cinema Palace*.

They had a protracted discussion about who their villain should be and whether there should be one antagonist or a team of them, and if the latter, what the hierarchy of villainy should be. Cary insisted that the main villain should be an evil restaurateur named Ullrich Duxelles (or, alternatively, Ullrich d'Uxelles—she was flexible), a veiled reference to the local star chef Dietrich Ulm, for whom she had sous-chefed at Fleur de Sel. Eighteen brutal months under Dietrich's thumb had scarred her and forced her to abandon the industry. And while Walter was eager to help Cary exact filmic revenge, he figured that if queers were disappearing in large numbers, then they were doubtless being subjected to brainwashing and psychotropic experiments. Some government or major criminal enterprise must be behind it all—an evil entity big enough to have the police in its pocket—the CIA or some megarich organization bigger than the CIA, an international shadow corporation beyond any nation's laws.

It was slow going, yet how was that their fault? At any given place or time there were so many distractions: if they went to Jumpin' Java, likely half a dozen of Cary's best friends would stop by the café, wanting to chat.

Anywhere they went, one or both of them might wind up mooning over a sexy barista or bartender, or be swept away by the voice of Sarah Vaughan on the jukebox at the Orbit Room or the howl of P. J. Harvey stalking them like a she-wolf wherever they traveled. At any moment they might need to rush to the video store to rent another Billy Wilder film for inspiration, but then they would argue over whether to go to Superstar or Metro Video, depending on which dreamy young thing might be on duty that day. (Flirty Matteo with his adorable dreads? Or ultracool Julie with her dark-arts insight into noir?) In short, every single thing that inspired them—the city, the movies, music, coffee, booze, food, flirting with hot boys and girls—simultaneously prevented them from getting a single thing done. Cary was such an inveterate flirt that sometimes she would forget their work and start to flirt with Walter, when the blues came on and the atmosphere at Dalva grew murky and ale-colored and there was no one else around to flirt with. Once he caught her staring at him like a cartoon dog eyes a carmine steak, and he knew it was time to close out and see her safely home to Sasha.

That's how it went: December dissolved like the foam on a pint of Anchor Steam. After obligatory holiday travel, the new year launched and their feverish collaboration continued apace, full of entropic energy, moving fast if not always forward.

One Saturday in January, Walter assumed he and Cary would get together and "write" for a few hours in the afternoon, or at least hang out, but he wasn't sure what was up, as he hadn't heard from her the night before. When he called their apartment late that morning, Sasha answered and explained that Cary was out for the day, maybe overnight.

"Didn't she tell you? Lynnea is in town from Seattle."

"Lynnea?" First he'd heard of her. It was unusual that Sasha answered the phone when he called. Walter had that alienated feeling of hearing his friend's voice disembodied and subtly electromagnetized, thinned through the wires that swagged the hill between them.

"Her ex. Lynnea comes to town every once in a while and gets a fancy suite downtown somewhere. Cary's usually gone for the weekend."

"I see . . ."

There followed an extended pause, because despite all the time they'd spent together, Walter could still get tongue-tied around Sasha. When the three of them hung out it was Cary who kept the conversation bobbing along. But Sasha never talked just to talk; at times he seemed almost spookily comfortable with silence. For several seconds Walter thought the line had gone dead. Already in a mood, he slumped inwardly and was about to say what seemed like the four saddest words in the English language, *I'll let you go*, when Sasha's voice broke through again: "Darling, have you eaten? I'd kill for some good dim sum."

Sasha didn't want to settle for any dim sum. He wanted *the best* dim sum, Ton Kiang. Walter had never been—an oversight Sasha said should be rectified at once. So they waited half an hour for the 24 and another for the 38, on their way out to the Richmond. The weather was miserable, clammy and pallid, sporadically misting. It was one of those days when Walter thought he might start crying, for no reason, at any moment. There was a reason: he was hungover and cranky after overdoing it on a night out in SoMa with Eliot and Richard, who were still in a nauseating honeymoon phase. *When would it end?* To make things worse, he was still moping over Julian, who never called unless he was horny and was always sweet as pie right up until the moment he came, when the lusty afterglow in his dark eyes powered down. In light of his crabbiness, Sasha's cordial, unchatty company felt soothing. Walter was underdressed in a thin windbreaker, and he'd neglected to bring an umbrella. But Sasha'd brought a giant black porter's umbrella for both of them and was chic in a long wool duster and shapely black boots with buttons up the sides. A pair of goggles and keys to the roadster were all Sasha needed to motor off through an Edward Gorey book.

Walter's mood wasn't improved by the ride on a megabus down Geary Street, somehow both cold and muggy, condensation weeping down the windows. They took the last two seats across from each other in the rubber accordion pleats that joined two diesel buses, and the gyrating disk at their feet swung like a teacup ride—sickening—and he imagined they were stuck in a squeeze-box, every bit as loud and mellifluous. They spent another half hour waiting for a table under Sasha's umbrella. By the time they were seated for breakfast, it was two o'clock. Yet Walter's mood had improved, because it was worth it all to wait in the rain in a dome of Sasha's perfume, a jasminey scent mixed with . . . He couldn't place it. So he asked.

"Do you like it? It's Soir de Paris, very old-fashioned," said Sasha. "It was all the rage in the forties apparently. I like it because it has a lot of bergamot in it, like Earl Grey."

"Yes, that's it," said Walter, and stopped short of saying what he was thinking, that Cary was insane if she passed up even the dreariest afternoon with Sasha to spend time with some old flame from Seattle, however fancy her downtown suite.

Ton Kiang was as crowded, loud, and humid as the 38, though pristine and bright as bleached linen, and the steam that enveloped the dim sum carts as they circled the tables was delectable. Throughout their journey, they had been talking about books, one of Sasha's favorite topics after sewing. And being so hungry, they'd inevitably turned to food writing, and from there M. F. K. Fisher was top of the stack. As they talked and ate, a sweet subtext emerged: it became clear that Walter was only saying yes to the dessert dishes: custard tarts, sesame balls, steamed buns, which were, practically speaking, molten candied pork suspended in cake-flour clouds. Noticing the pattern, Sasha chose vegetable siu mai and Chinese broccoli in a shimmering brown sauce.

"I'm beginning to think Cary's right," said Sasha. "You have the palate of a five-year-old."

"That's mean," said Walter. But he couldn't argue. He was busy being transported to another plane of being by a fried sesame ball, which he could hardly believe was real: its perfect roundness, goldenness; the neat seeds allocated like pocks on a golf ball; its crispness as he bit through the thinnest of shells; and then all that hot, gooey sweetness, the curious hollowness, the puff of cloying air from its cavity.

"She always says it admiringly," said Sasha, "or half admiringly."

Walter endeavored to pinch a slick broccoli stem between the tips of his chopsticks. It wagged off; he went at it again.

"You know what I love about M. F. K. Fisher," he said, "is that you might think she was really pretentious, writing about how much she loves oysters and caviar and stuff, but she writes with equal passion about potato chips or . . . disgusting things, like putting ketchup on mashed potatoes."

"Exactly"—Sasha nodded—"or bizarre things, like how the most delicious treat is tangerine sections left to dry all afternoon on a radiator by the window. But you have to be in Strasbourg, or it won't work!"

"Strasbourg, of course! And she makes up words. Like when she wrote about macadamia nuts and said she loved them for their sheer . . ." Walter slowed his approach to get it right: ". . . *macadamianeity*, and I'm thinking, *That's incredible! Are you allowed to make up crazy words like that?*"

"I suppose every word was made up by someone, if you go back far enough . . ."

Their conversation was making Walter feel vague guilt and intense relief in equal measure. Sasha had no idea, none at all, that he himself had introduced Walter to M. F. K. Fisher one sunny afternoon over lunch, and thank god talking about M.F.K. didn't summon for Sasha a repressed memory of Walter, stooped at the end of the Sears lunch counter, ogling like a half-wit. And now here they were at dim sum, *the best* dim sum, he and the gamine. It was a perfect dream; he'd managed to catch and befriend a mirage.

Now Sasha was relating how Cary had introduced him to M.F.K. and how he knew he should probably move in with Cary once he saw her bookshelves.

"At first I thought Cary was a noodge—I mean, a cute one—wanting me to start a band with her. I didn't take her seriously until I saw her bookshelf,

and then I realized she had the two main qualities I look for in a partner."
Then, as if to tease him, instead of coming right out with them, Sasha raised
the teapot and poured the tea, back and forth in intermittent splashes in the
tiny, sturdy cups.

"Which are?"

The teapot sat.

"They have to be an avid reader. I don't trust people who don't love to
read. And they have to know how to tell a *really good story*. Cary, as you
know, can tell one hell of a story."

Now Walter couldn't keep from wondering, as much as he loved reading,
if his bookshelf was wide and intriguing enough for Sasha, if his storytelling
skills were up to snuff . . . and how the entire world would be different—
almost inverted—if everyone thought like Sasha.

"Are you sure you're a gay man?" he asked, then giggled despite himself.
He knew at once it was a dumb question.

"No, not at all." Sasha smiled, elbows on table, cup to lips. "Why do
you ask?"

"Because, you know, gay men's criteria. Sometimes I think anything at
all cerebral doesn't even crack the top ten."

"And Julian?" Sasha asked. "What does Julian like to read?"

This question, which seemed pointed, was a fair one, and not out of the
blue. Sasha, even that morning, had endured plenty of Walter's bellyaching
over Julian. Walter had a crush, to be sure, common as the common cold,
although viruses are real, and crushes are imaginary, like jabberwockies.
Meanwhile Cary and Sasha had sweetly indulged him like a hypochondriac
friend, never telling him to shut up and get over himself, but feeling his forehead and passing the Kleenex and boiling him canned soup. But it was as
if Sasha knew before asking that in Julian's vast Victorian apartment Walter had never spied so much as a single book, not even a coffee table book,
nothing beyond a ruffled *Us Weekly* abandoned on the toilet tank. If he was
serious about Julian, what did that say about what he was willing to give up?

By the time they finished brunch it was late afternoon, and they were far out in the Richmond boondocks, at a loss for what was next. It was still overcast, but the weather had improved a bit, the mist had lifted, and in the west a band of yellow shone on the horizon.

"Come," said Sasha, taking his arm. "Want to see where Playland was?"

Sasha knew very well that Walter was desperate to see where Playland had been. The week before they had watched *Woman on the Run*, basically an extensive travelogue of San Francisco, serviceably shot and lazily disguised as a crime drama. The acting, the plot, the dialogue—all were negligible, but the film showed off the city, and it was from 1950, the moment he and Cary were fixated on. And somehow, even having seen *The Lady from Shanghai* twice, he never realized that there had once been an honest-to-god amusement park at Ocean Beach.

It was exactly no one's idea of a good day for the beach, they realized, with the possible exception of Herman Melville. When they got to the Cliff House it was drizzling, but there they were, so they strolled downhill along the Great Highway toward the park, feeling goth under Sasha's capacious black umbrella. Cars sloshed past, but no one was about. Sasha took Walter's arm and they walked close together, without speaking. The ocean spread out beside them, endless and depthless, leaden, frothing, formidable. The salt spray drifting through Soir de Paris brought with it that undercurrent of death the ocean never fully sheds, of rancid kelp and slick, scaly corpses and god knows what else the gastric depths were metabolizing. When they reached the park they spotted the first windmill, stilled (curious), then strolled on until the blades of the second windmill, also stilled, appeared above the cypresses.

"I'm not exactly sure where Playland was," Sasha said, as they re-treaded their path. "But I've heard it went under when the real estate got too valuable. They built over it. I imagine it was where these condos are up here."

"The eighties-looking ones?"

Sasha nodded, extended his hand, and, realizing it was no longer raining, flapped and folded his umbrella. As they walked northward the sky lightened, and staring across the Great Highway, Walter saw the specter of Playland rise up before them, above the apartment blocks, fully formed, monumental and transparent. He saw it all at once—its volumes and contours—in an isometric daydream, gray and many layered, like the engineering plans he sometimes wondered at last summer at work. The roller coaster from *Woman on the Run* loomed, schematic skeleton of a coastal range. Below it stood the fun house where Orson Welles lost Rita Hayworth in a hall of mirrors. In his mind's eye he took it all in, the strobing facades and cramped back alleys; the raucous rigged games; the cheery concessions, chicken shack, and soda fountain; the boisterous dance hall and milling Ferris wheel. He spied amphibious rides, too: the whitewater chutes, terrifying diving bell, pitch-dark lovers' flume. The fair lit the gloom, crisscrossed by strands of thousands of carnival bulbs. He heard screams and laughter and smelled funnel cakes in the fryer, but the one thing he couldn't imagine were the colors. What appeared to him was a montage of glimpses he'd caught in films and in a file of photographs Cary showed him at the library one afternoon, all in black and white. Maybe he didn't want to picture the colors of Playland, no doubt they were garish, and he loved the moody grayscale of his imaginings, a silver carnival to match their silver city.

"Do you see it?" asked Sasha.

"It's amazing," he said, his voice turned inward and full of wonder, when he realized that Sasha, still holding his arm, had been steering them leftward, toward the beach.

"I wouldn't say *amazing*," said Sasha, who now realized that Walter had neither heard what he'd been saying nor seen what he was referring to. "What are you talking about? I'm talking about the ship."

Playland vanished.

Sasha pointed to the horizon. "It looks like a military ship—an aircraft carrier or something. But what *is* amazing is that it's not foggy this late in the afternoon. I'm surprised we can see so far out."

Walter would have overlooked the ship, a dull dash unzipping the gray sky from the ocean. North of the ship the clouds gaped like the fly of a tent, releasing a distant banner of light, the January sun tucked somewhere just out of sight.

"Speaking of great stories," said Walter, "last week Cary told me this insane story about how the CIA once *poisoned the fog in San Francisco.*"

"Oh, the one with the navy ship?" Sasha nodded. "It changes a little every time. What version did you hear?"

"Well, we were talking about government conspiracies for our screenplay, and she came up with a doozy. It was during the Cold War, and the CIA was experimenting with ways of delivering chemical weapons, I guess, in a real-world setting. So someone had the genius idea to use the fog to deliver poison. They rigged a destroyer with hoses or fans or something, and one evening when the fog was rolling in, they exposed everyone in San Francisco to the teensiest bit of pneumonia. It can't be true, can it?"

"It sounds crazy"—Sasha laughed—"but Cary swears it's true! Did she tell you where she heard it?"

"I thought she made it up."

"Of course she heard it from a *gay ancient mariner* she befriended one night at Twin Peaks. She always says that bar is a trove of local lore . . . and that there's not much an old sailor won't tell you after a couple whiskies."

"It does sound like a conspiracy a hysterical old queen might come up with. Like how the CIA developed HIV to get rid of the gays, at Reagan's orders."

"Yes. But we don't need any conspiracy theories about Reagan, do we?" Sasha said. "His inaction spoke for itself. All he had to do was sit on his hands and not even say the word *AIDS* for six years and watch the queers fall . . ."

Walter shuddered. "So, if the story is true, how come we've never heard about a plague of pneumonia in San Francisco in the fifties?"

"Beats me! To hear Cary tell it, there was one hell of a flu season that year . . ." Sasha shrugged and changed the subject to their next adventure. They *could* explore the ruins of the Sutro Baths, but it was too chilly and wet. Then he sighed, bemoaning the loss, almost ninety years before, of the old Cliff House, the one Adolph Sutro had built. Walter had never heard of it.

"It was unreal," said Sasha. "From the pictures, it looked like a Victorian castle or a grand chateau, much larger than the rock it stood on. I always imagine it's what Manderley looked like, only grander. When it burned down, someone was there with a camera. There are pictures of it on fire and crowds standing on the beach staring. But I always think of mad Mrs. Danvers in her black gown, running through the wings of the burning mansion."

They neared the big, plain concrete box of the modern Cliff House. Coolly, without any fuss or fanfare, Sasha suggested they check out the Musée Mécanique, tucked into the basement, as if he couldn't have guessed that it would blow Walter's mind. It turned out to contain all the remnants of Playland at the Beach; many of its mechanical wonders and oddities had filled the arcade there. Right there to greet them was Laffing Sal, a giant, busty animatronic clown, teetering over them with frankfurter fingers and a bloodcurdling cackle. She'd had the last laugh in *Woman on the Run*, wailing all the while as Ann Sheridan, the wimp, was terrorized riding a roller coaster that wouldn't scare a preteen.

Walter had a strange love of strange machines: not new, slick, efficient machines, but old, scattershot, pointless, wheezing machines; he felt for them, in a way. He loved dioramas, too, and the museum was chock-full of dioramas that were also failing machines. Half of them were on the fritz and looked bedraggled, despite having been sealed behind glass for decades. In the center of the gallery an especially large machine portrayed an entire carnival—swings and freak shows and rifle ranges; barkers, boxers, and caged beasts and all; and all alight, boxing and blinking and freewheeling. They wondered if this was meant to be Playland itself in miniature, and wouldn't it be ingenious if, in a tent in the midst of this carnival, there were a miniature arcade, and within *that* arcade spun another carnival, and within that another, and so on, infinitely, down to electrons orbiting an atom.

The miniature world hypnotized and transported them, and for an hour they shrank inside their adult selves and could only dart around the dank museum, pointing and exclaiming, *Look at the dancers!* square-dancing in the Old Barn, stomping in the Cantina, in Corn Cob Gulch and Cactus Gulch.

Look! How weird!—Suzie dancing the cancan, and vaudevillians wobbling in the Thimble Theatre. *Look—how funny!*—the stuffy upper crust, waltzing through an oceanside ballroom, sailboats asway on the pier . . . And the trapeze lady flying by the band shell, and the aerialists abutting the oil field, and a girl jumping rope in a zoetrope (*or no, it says here "praxinoscope"*). *Watch this*: pump as it might, the fire brigade is already too late to rescue these lovers from their burning home, while the sawmill portends a grisly death for the sawyer . . . And: *Who would smoke El Stinko Cigars?* And: *Doesn't this caged gorilla look furious?* And: *Ten cents to see a live mermaid—very reasonable, no?*

They had their fortunes told by Raja the palmist, and an Egyptian mummy, and a wizard wearing an awful lot of eyeliner, and (Walter's favorite) an enchanted Royal typewriter that advised them to be careful of living too much in the past, which seemed like the museum was scolding its patron base, and one of them wished aloud, and the other wished it, too, that all typewriters could tell fortunes.

In the end, the contraption that enthralled Walter most was a spindly Ferris wheel like a bike tire made of toothpicks. It looked like it would never work, but one quarter in the slot, and the lamps lit and the wheel turned and pairs of painted balsa ladies and gentlemen swung gently in their traps. A sign explained it was made by an inmate serving twenty-seven years at Folsom Prison, and in light of this, the ingenuity of the thing was mind-boggling. Where did he get all those toothpicks, and the glue to hold them, and the knife to cut them? And what did the wardens think he was up to? He couldn't have hidden it under a cot; it must have been sanctioned somehow. And twenty-seven years was endlessly long—what was he in for—homicide? Could hands capable of such delicacy have taken a life? Walter wondered if this (probable) murderer had chosen for his masterpiece the femme backdrop of psychotropic flowers, juniper blue and pea-soup green. Throughout the museum there was an unnerving theme of crime and punishment—a punitive world you could escape through hanging, or beheading, or a slow death in an opium den, or, as it turned out, through toothpicks and glue.

Among some modern video games they found a claw machine. Walter had always had good luck with claw machines, and after two attempts he nabbed from an orgy of colored fleece a lavender thing—a sea lion maybe? or a pale, slender eggplant—with a single, long, spiraling horn emerging from one end.

"What the hell is it?"

"It's a narwhal! I think it's kind of cute. See . . . its eyes are here . . ." Sasha pointed out two black beads whose placement implied a face.

"For you," Walter proffered.

"I'll treasure it always," said Sasha, taking the narwhal, somewhat indelicately, by the horn. It fit snugly in one of the large pockets of his duster.

"Sasha, I have to ask . . . was this your plan all along?"

"You mean, did I lure you out to Ocean Beach so you could win me a narwal?"

"No, I mean the Musée Mécanique. I never knew about it—and you had to know I would love it."

"I had a hunch," said Sasha, taking Walter's hand. "But there's something else I think you'll love even more . . ."

Outside on the terrace stood a freestanding shed, painted yellow with a blue band around the middle—a pale horizon. On its roof was a large drum, and topping that, a pyramid with four faces that turned like a weathervane. Only the sign—"Giant Camera"—clued them in that it was supposed to look like a boxy old camera. In fact, that's exactly what it was, a camera obscura, a thing Walter had read about but never experienced. Inside, it was black, empty, and chill. The ocean hushed as the door sloughed closed behind them. It was extremely dark, and hip-height in the center of the room was a shallow round basin—concave, bluish, and wide—four or five feet in diameter. At first he thought it was a fountain, it seemed to be filled with rushing water. But as they approached he saw it was a projection, a moving image of the ocean lapping the beach outside. And it was turning, because—*now he got it*—a cone of light was descending from the drum above them, and the pyramid, with a lone unblinking eye, was methodically turning, sweeping the landscape, drawing it in. Ocean Beach slid off the edge of the basin and was replaced with a gigantic crag of rock, white (almost) as an iceberg, covered in gulls and whitewashed with their dung. Up they rose in a flock as if startled. The image tumbled clockwise, searching north-northwest over the ocean, periscope scanning for the aircraft carrier they had spied earlier, now vanished. And then—as if it were part of Sasha's plan—the sunset scrolled across the basin, the sun wild and rolling, blazing like a glory hole that might just burn a pit through the enormous retina they stood astride.

"It's a movie!" said Walter, and Sasha, across the basin from him, nodded and leaned forward. Sasha raised one hand, catching a yellow cloud puff in his palm.

Why was it so mesmerizing? It was a mere projection of what they could see directly a few steps outside on the terrace. Something in the mechanism was filtering out frequencies of color, as if the giant eye were slightly colorblind. Everything except the yellow-hot sunset was a soft silver blue. They had seen several peep shows in the museum, and those, too, were primitive movies, for sure. And yet something about them—the awkward brass viewfinders, the faded flip-books, the "naughty" bloomered scenarios—was decidedly not enchanting. The camera-eye now rotated through an otherwise boring passage, scanning the Cliff House's second-story balcony, its row of windows square and evenly spaced like a filmstrip. And then the gray cliffs, and a glimpse of the apartments where Playland once stood, and then the wide beach again, water now brighter and bluer than it had been that afternoon, and the waves washing over the white basin, scalloped at the probing edges and endlessly long, endlessly long . . .

In the end, it was the silly stuffed narwhal that caused a fuss. The next evening Cary called Walter and, making no excuses for her disappearance and offering few details about her weekend adventure with the mysterious Lynnea, wanted to make some plans for the week to come. Walter was happy to chat, but at the moment he felt bored and noncommittal.

Cary must have been on the phone in the kitchen with Sasha nearby (the tap burst on and off as dishes were rinsed), because her next question was obviously not addressed to Walter: "What the heck is this?"

Sasha's answer was faint but clear enough; Cary wasn't covering the receiver. Walter caught the word *narwhal*.

"Where on earth did you get a stuffed narwhal?"

Sasha's voice rose and fell, in and out amid the rushing tap. "*Something something* Musée Mécanique, *something something* Ocean Beach."

"Isn't that funny—I won it in the claw machine!" said Walter, but his excitement seemed to irritate Cary.

"You guys went to the Musée Mécanique without me?"

Muffled in the background, Sasha related their travels to Cary. "*Something something* the Richmond, *something something* Ton Kiang" . . . over this Walter heard Cary's breath pressing in even bursts upon the receiver.

"Sasha, you know—Sasha knows very well—the *Musée Mécanique is literally my favorite place.*"

Walter wouldn't interject again, because he realized then that they were having a spat—the first he'd ever witnessed—and that, in not covering the phone, Cary wanted him to be party to it.

"What the hell?" Cary balked, now addressing both of them. "And you went to *Ton Kiang, too?*"

Now Sasha raised his voice, and fragments of his reply came across loud and clear: "Why do you care? You were off *something something* all day and night with *something something* Lynnea."

Sasha seemed more amused than angry, but Cary sounded genuinely cross: "The Musée Mécanique, Ton Kiang, the camera obscura? *Sashenka,* all of those are better than sex. *Each one of those is better than sex.*"

Sasha rejoined, "*Something something* not very flattering to me, darling."

"*Oh, hell,* you know what I mean. I mean they're all better than sex *with normal people.* I mean *sex with mortals,* darling, not you, of course."

"Nice save," said Walter, but if Cary heard him, she didn't react.

"OK, OK, I'll cop to that," said Cary. "If I do sound the teensiest bit jealous, it's only because you two went on a perfectly awesome date *without me* . . ."

"Don't be silly," Walter began, but Cary was gone . . . somewhere . . . After abandoning the receiver for a few seconds, she returned with a quick "Gotta go!" and hung up on his goodbye.

Walter sat, receiver in hand, wondering how insulted he should feel that Cary had hung up on him. He dropped the droning thing in the cradle.

He wasn't insulted, but something Cary said was sticking in his craw. It wasn't a date he and Sasha had gone on, though if it had been, she was right, it was, or would have been, *a perfectly awesome date*. There was an image he hadn't been able to shake all day . . . and the evening before . . . ever since they'd left the Cliff House to head home. In the dark room, as they'd faced each other across the basin, Sasha had taken his hair down and let it fall at his shoulder. All afternoon it had been knotted at his neck; now it uncurled down his lapel. That small gesture transformed the camera obscura for Walter, from a plywood shack into a fortune teller's tent, and now he saw Sasha as a kind of medium, an oracle, standing before a massive diviner's dish, the ocean in a bowl no less, full of ectoplasm and blooms of phosphorescent algae. Outside the ocean spoke of depths undetectable by sunbeam or sonar, blind albino depths. Gulls griped on their rock, but Sasha remained silent, mum as a sphinx, unaware of what he'd inspired in Walter. Something as cold as a camera, a physics demonstration, had become mystical and prophetic. Luminous, because Sasha was watching it with him.

BRAINSTORMINGBRAWNSTORMINGBRAINSTORMINGBRAWNSTORMINGBRAINS
with Cary & Wall

BACKSTORY: people have been disappearing...
In SF, QUEERS have been disappearing.
Weirder: no one seems to have noticed
The public response: apathy and amnesia
The lost are immediately forgotten...

Context:
 Cold War
 McCarthyism
 Red Scare
 **Lavender
   Scare

Chief of police PARNELL has been ordering
raids on queer bars, performance venues,
private parties...
Rounding up 'creative types'
charging them with obscenity and
  communist organizing
...after that: they disappear

The Vermilion Room:
or: The Carmine Room?
Communist front?
or fruitcake speakeasy?
(basically Cafe du Nord)

VERA SVANIRE: aging film star
& mob wife. started out as a
vaudeville hoofer, used to dance
at the PALACE in the preshow.
   "The Barbary Clara Bow"
      "The Venus of North Beach"

[VERA: Ann Miller type
is Ann Miller still
alive?? CHECK]

MILO BLANKENSHIP:
Vera's dressmaker & gay best friend.
   *Lived together ever since her
   Mobster husband landed in Alcatraz

2 INT. THE VERMILION ROOM, SOMA

Moody subterranean club. Former speakeasy from the '20s.
Packed place, energetic crowd. Natty patrons cluster in
cabals: tables of men, tables of women, and everything
in between. Smoking, drinking. Carefree laughter. Onstage
VERA SVANIRE performs with her band. She shimmies in
sequins and sings "I've Got You Under My Skin." The crowd
eats it up.

Suddenly, a ruckus: boys in blue charge down the
staircase into the bar, surrounding the crowd. Jazz band
stops dead.

                        SERGEANT
                [through a bullhorn]
            Now, now! Everyone remain calm
            and stay where you are... let's
            make this one easy, shall we?

Bedlam!!! Patrons leap up all at once and make a break
for it. Push toward the staircase in droves. The quick
ones make it out. Exits blocked, batons rise; beatings
begin. Tables and chairs are overturned, screams, bursts
of shattered glassware. It's all over in a rapid-fire
montage. Some folks surrender, others fight back and are
dragged away in cuffs. Police vans cart everyone off to the
precinct. The Vermilion Room is a shambles--like a bomb
went off. Left behind, the bartender shakes his head.
Onstage, VERA SVANIRE is left standing alone.

INT. DOWNTOWN POLICE PRECINCT--WELL AFTER MIDNIGHT
Chaos in the lobby as dozens of people are herded and
booked. In the midst of this mayhem, VERA SVANIRE
marches in, chin up, draped in ocelot fur.

                        VERA
            Milo? Milo? Has anyone seen Milo?
            Or the band?
                [to an officer]
            I demand to see Police Chief
            Parnell at once!

EXT. THE POLICE PRECINCT--SOME TIME LATER
VERA SVANIRE and MILO BLANKENSHIP exit and enter a
waiting taxicab.

INT. TAXI
The taxi races off.

                    VERA
          Driver, please take us to the
          Rose Reaves Hotel on Eddy.

                    MILO
               [massaging his wrists]
          Third raid this month! Vera, I've
          simply got to get out of this
          town!

                    VERA
          Do you really think things will
          be better in LA? At least here I
          can protect you. We can protect
          each other.

                    MILO
          Things can't be any worse in LA.
          At least there's plenty of work
          for me down there.

                    VERA
          Don't you dare leave me for that
          vapid, tinseled-up tarpit! I'll
          never forgive you if you do.
          First Vinnie abandons me, and
          now you?

                    MILO
          I'd send money! Lord knows we
          could use it. And Vinnie didn't
          abandon you, he's in prison. I'd
          be at MGM.

                    VERA
          Please explain the difference.

The Elusive Pimpernel

FOR THE MOMENT IT WAS spring, or so the calendar said. In San Francisco, any indications of a seasonal shift were often unobtrusive to the point of illegible. Spring this year was a kind of green inference, something Mother Nature couldn't be bothered to imply herself; it seemed to Walter to be little more than a mood that came over you. Some species bloomed all winter, so there wasn't a sense of rebirth so much as the waxing of something you hadn't realized had waned. And the city *was* greener, cleaner, fresher, because this winter there had been a bona fide monsoon, it poured every day from mid-January through February. Even togged up like the Gorton's fisherman you couldn't leave the house without getting soaked to the bone.

But now that dreariness was behind him. It was a crystalline Saturday in early May, sunny and warming up after a fogged-in morning, and Walter was in a hopeful mood. He was striding through the Tenderloin with a pizza boy's delivery tote strapped to his chest, a bulky triple-decker thing that hung over his shoulder, pinched his neck, and reeked of overcooked lentils—a singularly unappetizing smell. He had no idea what he was carrying, what today's hot lunch was, that is. Usually the Open Hand lunches were high-fat baked pastas and mild enchiladas and things, but regardless the tote always emanated an odor of warm, bilious, regurgitated beans. He'd been delivering for Open Hand every Saturday for over a month.

The hot meal dispatch was on Polk Street. It had taken a while to learn the neighborhood: the first Saturday he delivered lunches it took him four hours between navigating the downtown route and finding individual apartments. When at last he returned to the dispatch, the nervous volunteer coordinator was nearly desperate, thinking he'd been murdered in an alley or had hungrily run off with eighteen tins of baked ziti all to himself. At that point Taylor, the coordinator, was dumbfounded to learn that Walter didn't have a car and had done all the deliveries on foot.

"Most volunteers use a car," Taylor said, miffed. "The meals will have all gone cold."

Walter had no car, so after that they devised a walking route for him that served several blocks close to the dispatch—between Geary and Turk, stretching east to Leavenworth. Even with this shortened route, the demand was such that he had to return to home base halfway through to load up again. It was shortly after noon on this Saturday, and he was still on the first half of his split shift. He was getting to like the Tenderloin, and not perversely, either. It was not because of the *superb nausea* he always felt at some points around the city: some dicey SoMa corners; the lethally under-ventilated mine shafts of some BART stations. (*Superb nausea* was a favorite phrase he remembered from Rimbaud—except for this description of Paris streets, he couldn't remember anything else about the poem.) The Tenderloin had a reputation for being dangerous and seedy, which, as far as he could tell, was undeserved. There were a lot of homeless folks, but most of them didn't want anything from you except maybe a respectful, genuine hello and a few quarters if you had them.

He was walking eastward down Eddy past shabby tourist motels with sun-bleached paint jobs. Downtown these gave way to apartment buildings and residence hotels of dubious repute: lower windows grated, entrances heavily portcullised, the terminal stepladders of fire escapes cranked up like drawbridges. There was scarcely any greenery in this part of the city, but somehow there was a surprising amount of birdsong, and not just the keening of gulls or guttural cooing emitting from hidden niches, but honest-to-god songbird birdsong. And while the May sky seemed to have intensified, the light and the neighborhood alike were still *silver*, a notion he hadn't been able to shake since Cary had described the city that way. Whatever the local patchwork of colors—the pale planes of concrete, the dull alloy gates, the green laurels, the stucco painted battleship gray or buff or blue—the overall effect was silver.

He had his route pretty well memorized, but it changed a little every week, and now he needed to backtrack down Eddy to an apartment building he realized he'd overshot. After so much time scanning them, Walter grew to love the facades of the Tenderloin: the bay windows without a glimpse of the bay; the decorative plaster reliefs in bands beneath the windows or friezes along the rooflines. The deco touches: florals, palms, chevrons; the wandering geometries; the snazzy counterfeits of the ancient and foreign. (Were they meant to be Aztec? Or Egyptian? Mexican baroque? *Who knew?*) A little fumbling and he discovered the address he had overlooked. Like many of the buildings on his route it was a large residence hotel. This one was incognito, but he loved it when they retained their names and their antique signage, hearkening back to some imaginary patrician past (the Senator, the Archers, the Prefect, the Page) or locales both unsung and storied (the homely Hartland, the fair Verona). Like many, this hotel had a twenty-four-hour doorman who sat behind a desk in a glass cube like a box office, waved and smiled and buzzed him in the gate.

There was only one meal to deliver in the building—annoying—but he cheered up when he realized it was on the fifth floor; he would have to take the elevator. Hands down his favorite thing about these old hotels were the antique elevators—most of them so run-down he figured they had to be original—with bike-tire scuffs on their walls and smiling dents clocking every moment of decades of service. This one was a real clunker, with big Bakelite buttons and an outer gate you had to *ka-thunk* in place before the inner door would shudder to a close. An elevator built for two—a skinny two at that—he could barely fit with his carrier, sliding in backward. The ride was desultory, jerking like it might catch on every floor. Pulleys squealed, and the cables fairly sang in a grieving drone: very satisfying.

The fifth floor, and he handed over the last meal of his first shift to a bluish eye peering from a cracked door, a hand with gnawed, maroon-gloss nails reaching around. In a woman's voice, a muttered thanks. But this was unusual; most people, when they heard him knock and call "Open Hand," would open with a hey and a nod or a smile, some asking what's for lunch, some asking about his day, only one or two ever scowling or griping about the wait. In the busier hotels, some residents would hear him calling deliveries and let their doors swing open in anticipation, while a breeze from the window or an oldie from a clock radio would brighten the staleness of the hallway. Often it was this—a hall of expectant doors, watchfully ajar—that convinced him he'd spent his afternoon well.

When he arrived back at the dispatch, he heard loud talk and familiar laughter in the entryway, and there was Cary leaning over the volunteer's desk shooting the breeze with Taylor. She had strolled up Polk after a morning shift at the library. She was wearing a skinny tie and a sharkskin suit and, of course, a fedora to match, and looked for all the world like she'd just bopped over from headlining at Caesars Palace. Taylor was laughing unselfconsciously—Walter had never seen him so chatty and relaxed. He didn't have to ask how they knew each other; he knew they'd never met.

Cary had come to see if Walter was *bored with selfless heroism* for the day (she rolled her eyes extravagantly) and would like to indulge in some selfish hedonism. She wanted him to blow off the rest of the afternoon, ignore the copious sunshine, and go to the movies with her, maybe a double feature. He explained that he still had a dozen meals to deliver before he could do anything else. She pouted and shot an entreating glance at Taylor, and Walter was afraid she was about to ask if he could be excused for the afternoon, like a parent trying to spring their grade-schooler for an early summer vacation.

"It's a beautiful day, come with me!" said Walter. "You can help with my deliveries."

"Most people deliver in pairs," said Taylor. "Teamwork is fun, right?"

"It won't take too long, actually." Walter glanced down his list. "Most of these are in one building—the Archers up on Geary. A couple stops on the way and we'll hit that last."

Cary was game and asked what she could carry. Taylor filled a brown bag with some cans of Ensure for Cary to offer to anyone who might need them. As they strolled up Polk Street, Cary pulled from her breast pocket a torn page of the *Bay Guardian* she had carefully folded around the Kabuki theater listings. She was trying to entice Walter with the offerings. Sasha was in Stockton for the weekend seeing family. They could spend all afternoon and evening at the movies, if they wanted. The only flaw in this plan was that the current offerings at the Kabuki were pretty dismal.

"*Serial Mom*," said Cary, "I know you want to see *Serial Mom*!"

"I do, desperately, but you know we promised Sasha we wouldn't see it without him. He'd murder us."

"Only if we told him. We could see *Four Weddings* again . . ."

"Ugh, no. What did you *like* about that movie? I still haven't forgiven them for killing Mr. Beebe. Four straight weddings, and we only find out that Mr. Beebe was secretly gay with the shy Scottish boy once *he dies of a heart attack*? No, thanks."

"You're telling me you couldn't manage to stare into Hugh Grant's limpid pools for two hours?"

"Not while they're staring into Andie MacDowell's stagnant ones, no."

These negotiations continued as they swung by an apartment building on Larkin. Searching the hallways as they delivered meals, Cary was trying to sell Walter on *Bad Girls*, a movie that asked you to accept Madeleine Stowe as a gunslinging, bank-robbing, sexy outlaw cowgirl. She had almost convinced him that this would be a hoot, when Walter realized that, like perfectly good bologna that had been ruined by the addition of pimento-stuffed olives, someone had snuck Andie MacDowell into this movie as well. He was almost ready to agree to sit through *D2*, the *Mighty Ducks* sequel, as long as Cary promised him that Andie MacDowell wouldn't pop up in a hockey helmet and ruin it.

"What do you have against Andie MacDowell?" Cary asked.

"Nothing," said Walter. "I can't have anything *against* her. She has nothing *going for* her."

"It's true. I know some paper bags who could outact her," said Cary.

By the time they made it to Geary, Cary had given up on the matinee scheme. She resolved that instead they should grab some tacos and go to the Bearded Lady and work on their screenplay, which, as Sasha once pointed out, was racing along with all the speed of blind, arthritic nuns sewing needlepoint embroidery, after hand-spinning the silk. In fact, Walter imagined arthritic nuns were probably much faster and more productive. And he and Cary might have benefited from being confined to a cloister, as for six months the majority of their progress had consisted of ingesting stimulants (coffee, pastries) and depressants (cocktails, Nina Simone) and arguing. They had made *some* progress, developing scenarios and sketching out scenes, testing dialogue on each other. Walter would type up his notes and bring along copies, and they'd mark them up, sometimes with pens, more often with beer stains and dribbles of salsa.

They could argue about anything, from the broadest themes to the smallest ellipsis, but mostly they argued about names. For an entire week they argued about what to call an Irish bartender before giving up in exhaustion and calling him Finn. For some reason, Cary was smitten with the last six letters of the alphabet, the alphabet's clunky remainders, and soon all the characters' names came to look and sound like the final entries in the index of a linguistics textbook. To wit: Ullrich Duxelles (the villainous restaurateur), Lorna Zaftig (the femme fatale), and Vera Svanire (the old vaudevillian whose disappearance sparks the mystery). One character who avoided this unmellifluous fate was Milo Blankenship. He was a lovable old queer who engages the dashing Declan Danner, P.I., to help him find Vera, his missing best friend. And there, almost on scene one, the plot had stalled. Cary thought they weren't getting Milo's voice right, it was *off*. It was weird how unbudgeable Cary could be at times, because when she was inspired, she was unstoppable. If anything, she was too inspired in every direction at once, and at his most overwhelmed, Walter felt like Agnes Gooch trailing Auntie Mame, clutching a clipboard to his frumpy cardigan, trying his best to shorthand a cyclone.

On Polk Street, they made a single delivery at their penultimate stop, and Cary, surprised that she'd managed to give away only a single can of Ensure, thought she might pass off as many as she could to the next panhandler they saw. "What is this stuff?" Cary asked. "It must be awful, judging from the looks on people's faces. They look like I'm offering them a can of leprosy."

As they were exiting the Hotel Prefect, Cary said, "You know, this is the perfect hotel for dyslexics."

"You know, you're a terrible person," said Walter.

"Not at all. I'm a proud dyslexic myself—I think it's the source of all my creativity." When Walter responded with skeptical silence, she added, "Creativity always starts as a kind of mistake, I think. Misreading, mishearing, misremembering—that kind of thing."

"You're being especially obtuse today, Professor Menuhin."

"Call me fat again and I'll chop your head off with a . . . Hold everything!" Cary stopped and grabbed Walter's arm, unduly excited. "Do I get to meet *Lawrence*? Tell me I haven't missed Lawrence!"

Walter blushed a little as he shook his head at Cary—Cary, once again, making too much of something so minor, in this case a set of funny, offhand encounters he had described to her. Lawrence Fonseca was a very sweet older gentleman who liked to stand in his doorway and inveigle Walter into frivolous conversations that went nowhere but never failed to cheer his day. The first couple times Walter delivered to him, he didn't notice anything about the guy, except that his penthouse apartment was up a steep, narrow back staircase, not reachable by the elevator, and was almost impossible to find. The second time they met Lawrence asked his name. The following week when Walter knocked on his door (apartment 00, a digit must have fallen off one end or the other), a fluty, singsong voice came from within: "*Who—is—it?*"

"It's Open Hand!"

Then a cross voice scolded: "I *know* it's Open Hand!"

After a beat, the tenor singsong returned, cooing, "Is it . . . *Waaaaalter?*" Instantly the door flew open and Lawrence was there, his grin so wide it nearly filled the doorframe. He was wearing a summery white linen blouse, white embroidery around the placket, a delicate gold chain around his neck. His feet were bare, and his legs were wrapped in a striped sarong tied in a fringed knot at his hip. A glimpse of tanned thigh. His thin face was lined and tan, and he had a full head of freshly clipped dark hair threaded attractively with gray.

"Walter! As ever you are too kind!" exclaimed Lawrence, as Walter was fetching his meal. Looking down, the man suddenly became self-conscious. "You must excuse my hammertoes!" he cried. "I couldn't find my slippers in my mad dash to the door." He spoke with a slight, unplaceable accent, enunciating clearly, as if whatever accent he'd been born with had been almost trained away. His vowels full, and his U's liquid, he sounded like an American Shakespearian.

Over Saturdays in April, the conversations he'd had in Lawrence's doorway were so trivial that Walter hadn't learned anything at all about the man or his life, and hadn't offered up much about himself, either. But their chats were engaging, and got longer and longer, and at one point Lawrence insisted that Walter call him Larry. Walter figured out that, if he wanted to have a little time to say hi to Larry, he had to plan his route so he'd deliver to him last. For his part, Lawrence never once complained about his lunch arriving late, sometimes quite late in the afternoon.

"You haven't missed Lawrence," Walter assured Cary. "He lives in the penthouse of the Archers, coming up next. I want to show you their fabulous old elevator! But we have deliveries on every floor, so we'll take the stairs first."

The Archers was once a grand old pile, four floors above an empty lobby and a large, unused banquet hall aspirationally labeled "The Archers Ballroom." Outside, its stucco was painted oyster gray with cream-colored plaster corrugations under the windows. There was an enormous old mahogany reception desk in the lobby, but no one ever tended it. They marched in and up the stairs to the second floor, and Cary made the unavoidable observation that the tan shag carpeting, which wound up the staircase and covered the hallways from end to end, fairly reeked. It smelled of varieties of smoke: tobacco and pot, to be sure, and probably more nefarious substances. Only one occupant didn't answer Walter's knock, so when they got to the top floor, his carrier was almost empty. He directed Cary through a dark back hallway leading to steep steps that opened onto the tarred roof deck of the Archers, where they were momentarily blinded by the unfogged afternoon sun. Apartment 00 was a freestanding unit on the roof of the hotel. With its flat roof and flimsy white walls, it looked like an overgrown pool cabana that had lost its resort. A trellis of patterned cinder block protected the entrance.

They knocked. Cary looked confused. "You said it was a penthouse. Aren't penthouses usually *inside* the hotel? This one looks like it might blow away."

They knocked again, waiting a bit longer than usual, and when the door opened, Walter was surprised to find a Black man he'd never seen before, though now he remembered Lawrence alluding to a roommate.

"You must be Walter," said the man, sizing them up in a glance. He was tall, maybe thirtysomething, quite handsome, his dark skin set off against a butter-yellow Lacoste shirt. His smile looked a little disapproving, inverted, his mouth turning down at the corners. "Larry will want to see you—I'll get him."

The man turned his back and disappeared before Walter could ask him not to bother.

"Who's your friend?!" cried Larry moments later, swinging the door wide.

"Lawrence Fonseca, meet Cary Menuhin."

Lawrence braced himself in the doorway and loudly wolf whistled at Cary, and for the first time in their friendship, Walter saw Cary blush. "Look at that suit! You are the most *debonair* thing I've seen in months—maybe years! And here I thought *I* was stylish." He gestured down. He was wearing a pink chenille bathrobe, like an old bedspread with pale green garlands and faded rosettes, and blue velveteen slippers with a counterfeit crest embroidered on the toes. "What did you do, Walter? Drop by central casting on the way here and say, *Gimme your handsomest swain?*"

Cary was smiling helplessly. She had removed her fedora and looked for a second like she might hide her face in it.

Minutes later, Lawrence had invited them in, offered them hot tea, iced tea, popcorn, dried apricots, Vietnamese coffee, Ovaltine, wasabi peas, slices of melon, a place to set down their bags, a seat, a better and cozier seat, a chance to chuck off their shoes, pillows on which to recline . . . all in such rapid succession that they felt too overwhelmed to take in any of it, let alone respond. So they wavered nervously as Lawrence gently pelted them with options. They met Larry's roommate, whose name was Jabez and who sat quietly beside an open window, reading a paperback, as a breeze blew a muslin curtain against his arm. Walter stood on the threshold of a tiny kitchenette that flanked the main room. He had placed the carrier on the kitchen table and was extracting Lawrence's lunch.

"Do you want an extra one?" said Walter. "I have an extra . . ."

Lawrence, standing in the center of the room, turned to his roommate. "Jay, darling, are you hungry?"

"What is it?" asked Jabez, too engrossed in his book to look up.

Walter was about to admit that he had no idea, when Cary offered, "Lentil dahl today! I just had a long talk with Taylor about this month's menus—Oh!" She removed a diminutive can from her bag and offered it to Lawrence. "Would you like twelve cans of Ensure? I can't seem to give these things away."

"Oh, and it's Ensure Plus, the good stuff!" said Lawrence.

"Is it any good?"

"God, no! It's revolting."

"Is it actually Soylent Green?"

He took the can from her. "You know, one of these supplements lists ash as an ingredient. So I would say yes. Doubtless it contains charred human remains."

Lawrence took Cary's bag and proceeded to describe his strategies for consuming the stuff, most of which involved gratuitous amounts of Hershey's syrup. He was describing a cocktail he liked to make with plenty of ice, powdered espresso, chocolate syrup, and an unsparing amount of vodka. As Lawrence and Cary chatted away, Walter placed two sealed entrées on the kitchen table and looked around the place. It was small, one main room, not fancy at all, but very comfortable and clean. The tan carpet—the same rug that reeked in the hallways below—here was unstained and freshly vacuumed. On the eastern wall two windows were open, warm muslin-filtered light filled the room. The breeze that streamed in along with the horn-punctured white noise of Geary Street made the apartment seem like a seaside cabana, the ocean's tides replaced by traffic. There were Danish modern chairs and a love seat, caramel teak and mismatched upholstery, well worn and well loved. An armchair that Lawrence had offered to Walter was occupied by an enormous marmalade cat, one of the biggest felines Walter had seen outside a zoo, who looked comfortably unbudgeable. The walls of the room were crowded, hip-level up, with framed pictures: color photos, black and whites, watercolors, prints—all hung in careful counterpoint. The apartment attested to an entire life, well lived. Walter felt a prying urge to stroll across the room and examine the photographs.

But then his gaze was drawn to a credenza across the room from him, partially blocked by Cary and Lawrence's boisterous conversation. The cabinet was arranged like a shrine to cocktail hour, with glass panels displaying a motley array of novelty glasses and liquors with fancy labels. Above the credenza were two items that caused Walter to hold his breath a little. Framed on the wall hung a large, brightly colored old movie poster for a film Walter had never heard of: *The Elusive Pimpernel*. It was clearly a '50s big-budget period piece: a buccaneer sweeping up into his embrace a courtly dame, a bodiced and bewigged Marie Antoinette type. In front of this lusty couple, standing atop the credenza, was a 16mm film projector, the hub and spokes of its blue steel reel echoing the ribs of madame's large lace fan. A sturdy machine, in mint condition, it gleamed as if polished. Cary and Lawrence were still gabbing away when Walter interrupted them, tugging at her sharkskin shoulder, pointing and saying, "Look at *that*!"

"*The Elusive Pimpernel!*" Cary exclaimed. "Well, that looks like a thrill a minute . . . *Hold on*, is that supposed to be David Niven?"

"It is!" said Lawrence. "Sir David Niven himself. It just doesn't look anything like him."

"I think that's what you call an *uncanny likeness*," said Cary. "Did they use his stunt double for the poster?"

"I've never heard of it," said Walter.

"I would be shocked if you had heard of it. No one has." Lawrence sidled up to the credenza. "It's a rare early poster design. They used the British title. When they released it in the States, they changed it to *The Fighting Pimpernel*. You know. *Más macho, más Hollywood.* But the two are hardly synonyms, are they? *Elusive* and *fighting*, I mean. Chalk and cheese."

Cary nodded. "Apples and orangutans."

"I've always thought, if you're *elusive* enough, you don't really have to *fight*, now do you? I'm surprised you know about David Niven!"

"We're movie buffs," said Walter, examining the high contours of Margaret Leighton's cheekbones, thrust forward shield-like to receive, or deflect, David Niven's kiss.

"Way to understate the case," said Cary. "Saying Walter likes movies is like saying Imelda Marcos has a thing for mules."

"Wonderful! Then you'll be interested in this . . ." Lawrence gestured for them to lean in, and he pointed behind the film projector, to where a signature was scribbled across David Niven's gloved hand. "This is the first film I was in. My mother was cast as Lady Dewhurst, and they needed a little Lord Dewhurst, so she brought me along. I was ten—magical age—and it was such a thrill being on set. The year before, Mum had a small role in *The Red Shoes*, which was my favorite movie, so I was beside myself."

"Larry"—Walter was stunned—"you were in this movie?"

"I was in *this version* . . . and it wasn't much of a performance. No dialogue for me. For the American version, the studio recut it, and Mother and I wound up on the cutting-room floor, as they say. But Michael Powell was fond of my mother, and he signed this poster, dedicating it to me, very sweetly."

"This is incredible," said Cary. "So, you're British? I mean, I'm sorry, I couldn't place your accent."

"Well, I was born in Lisbon. My father was Portuguese. Mum's English. We lived in England until I was ten. Then we moved to Hollywood, shortly after *The Elusive Pimpernel* wrapped. Both my parents were actors, and then, of course, I caught the bug myself—"

"This is too incredible," said Cary. "Maybe someday they'll release a restored British cut, with you and your mom back in it?"

"Oh dear, I doubt it," said Lawrence. "At ninety minutes the thing's already at least half an hour too long!"

"It's true," said a voice from behind them, but when they turned to look,

Jabez was still deep in his book, and neither he nor the marmalade cat betrayed having made the comment.

"I'm so interested in this projector," said Walter, reaching out and nearly touching it.

"It's fabulous," said Cary. "We had one of these in our grade school, for watching movies in the gym. Sex ed and after-school-special kind of stuff."

"Well," said Lawrence, "here we have the two brackets of my long, un-illustrious career: the first movie I was ever almost in, and the ruins of my own ambitions as a filmmaker." He opened the leftmost panel of the credenza, revealing shelves neatly packed with blue-and-gray film canisters. "This is only a fraction of it, of course. The rest is in storage."

Their jaws dropped, and Cary grabbed Walter by the hand, squeezing hard.

"What is it?" asked Larry.

"I think you need to tell us everything about your un-illustrious career," said Cary.

"In that case," said their host, closing the credenza, "you will need to take a seat."

Inviting Walter to sit, Lawrence tipped the armchair forward, and the monstrous cat woke and, paws scrambling in protest, tumbled in a fit of orange onto the carpet. The cushion was furry and still warm from the cat's belly when he sat. Cary perched beside Lawrence on the small love seat. For the better part of an hour, they sat engrossed as Larry regaled them with stories of his life in Hollywood. He had started as a preteen in bit roles in the early '50s, doing walk-ons in B movies, mostly films in which his mother had also been cast. For a while, they were kind of a package deal. Walter and Cary had never heard of most of the movies; virtually none of them had made it to video. Walter went light-headed, however, when Larry assured them that if they rented *Ace in the Hole* and played it at half speed, they could spot him and his mother in a couple of crowd scenes. His mother, Victoria, was paid three times as much for driving to the Arizona location herself and for bringing him along. Lawrence would never forget that trip: the striated buttes of Arizona looked positively Martian to a boy who had grown up in Islington. All this meant that Larry had known Billy Wilder, one of Walter and Cary's great idols, and even been directed by him; never mind that the relationship had been anonymous and conducted through the wide end of a bullhorn.

Meanwhile, if anything they were learning was news to Larry's roommate, he didn't betray the slightest surprise or interest. Jabez sat in his chair by the window, reading with his legs crossed, one foot gently swinging in its espadrille. The paperback that had drawn him so far away was *Bastard out of Carolina*.

Lawrence continued spinning his story: in Hollywood, in classic fashion, his parents' already touch-and-go marriage fell apart completely, and by the '60s, his father, Leonardo, had moved to Spain to extra in a string of spaghetti westerns, in which he was alternately cast as Mexican and Native American, sometimes in the same film. Meanwhile his mother returned to London to work in British TV. But Larry was in his early twenties, sporadically attending USC, his entire education having been piecemeal, and he stayed and played in Hollywood. The longer he studied filmmaking, the more interested he became in directing and the more bored he grew with narrative film. As he put it, he became interested only in the medium's *visionary* properties.

"Film's *visionary properties*?" Cary echoed.

"That is to say, film's *revelatory* properties," said Lawrence. "You understand: the way film, if used the right way, teaches us to see."

Walter leaned in, not quite following. In college, he had barely studied experimental films. His favorite professor, Diane, had been obsessed with Hollywood's Golden Age, and as her acolyte, he replicated her obsession. Walter had never heard anyone talk about films the way Lawrence did now, as visionary or revelatory. Something about film *revealing something beneath the visible*, as subtext is somehow *beneath the verbal*, yet revealed by it. While mulling the implications of this, Walter was on guard, aware of the orange cat whose throne he had usurped. The creature crouched beneath the nearby end table and stared with narrowed citrine eyes at the flesh of his exposed calves. In short order, Cary had steered the conversation away from Larry's philosophy of film to Hollywood gossip. Precisely when Walter was most vulnerable—as Larry was teasing a juicy anecdote about Tab Hunter—the feline lunged, fierce incisors first, and seized Walter's calf like a large, lean drumstick, causing him to cry out and jump from his seat.

"Basilisk!" cried Larry as the cat fled behind the love seat. "You have to forgive Basilisk, he's a terrible misanthrope. But he does seem to take a special disliking to some people. A select crowd. You should be flattered!"

Walter assured them he was fine and sat back down, anxious for Larry to get back to Tab Hunter, even though the pain shooting through his calf was so sharp it was making his left eye wince. As Lawrence finished his anecdote and moved on to an even more hair-raising one about Shaun Cassidy, Basilisk materialized from the other direction, beneath Jabez's chair, and after making some spatial calculations through the tilting of his head, leapt onto Walter's lap. A tense moment as Basilisk gained footing and Walter shifted in his seat, and the heavy beast began to heave like a bellows and purr. His long fur ruffled. His coloring was erratic: his paws and belly and the ridge of his nose were white, and Walter noticed beneath the orange on his flanks generous stipplings of brown and black. Marmalade on burnt toast. Lawrence continued effusively, telling a thrilling but heartbreaking story about his brief connection with dreamy Dirk Bogarde, who was seventeen years his senior. By the bittersweet end of this tale, both Walter and Basilisk had become relaxed, unguarded, and sympathetic, breathing together. He risked petting the creature on the head, and the cat yowled deep in his throat, bit him fiercely on the ball of his thumb, and flew off again, this time toward the kitchen.

"Jesus!" cried Walter, biting his lip to keep from swearing more.

"Basilisk!" Lawrence leapt up, adjusting his robe as he apologized.

"Oh, it's nothing," said Walter, tearing in the corners of his eyes and sucking the edge of his palm, where now there were two raw pink divots. He became self-conscious about openly bleeding in an apartment where he was delivering food to an AIDS patient.

Cary stood. "We'd better get going anyway."

"Oh, my darlings!" said Lawrence. "Tell me your name again?"

"Cary Menuhin."

"Cary, it's been an absolute delight, and I'm sorry our charming conversation has ended in bloodshed and tears!"

"I'm fine, Larry," said Walter, and when Lawrence looked dubious, he reassured him. "I promise."

"You have to bring Cary with you every weekend from now on!"

"Be careful what you wish for," said Cary. "I'm very hard to shake."

A few minutes later, they were waiting for the elevator one floor below.

"Goddamn that fucking cat!" said Walter, bending to massage his calf with his good hand. "Is my leg bleeding?"

"Well, don't swipe at it like that. Now you're just wiping the blood around!"

"Thanks so much for your concern, you're a regular Florence Nightingale."

Cary was abuzz, as if she'd gotten a shot of adrenaline or somehow sneaked a double espresso. The elevator was exceedingly slow, inching up from a mine shaft deep within the earth. Unable to keep still, she hopped from foot to foot.

"What is with you?" asked Walter.

"You totally undersold Larry! Larry is *amazing*," she scolded him. "I think we— I really want to get *writing*. We should get to work as soon as we can—"

"OK, OK, *tacos*, then *writing* . . ." The elevator groaned and banged distantly.

Cary shot down the staircase, exclaiming, "I can't wait anymore!"

He stood for a moment planted on the wretched carpet, then sighed and began following her down. "Cary! Did you get some wild hair up your ass? What the hell?"

Two floors down she slowed, and he caught up to her, and she turned long enough to say, "Don't you understand how momentous this is? Don't you understand what's happened? It's glorious!"

"What's glorious? What's momentous?" he asked.

Cary skipped down the next flight of stairs and the next, her outbursts muffled by the shag stairwell: "We've found our Milo Blankenship, of course! *We've found our Milo!*"

BRAINSTORMINGBARNSTORMINGBEANSTORMINGBURNSTORMINGBSINGBSING
   with C.M. & W.S.

LADIES and GENTLEMEN!
      INTRODUCING
   In her big screen debut:
CARY MENUHIN as Declan Danner

DECLAN DANNER:
P.I. and Intrepid Gumshoe
Hard-Boiled yet Debonair...
*picture the love child of
      Philip Marlowe and
            Nick Charles
            [Yikes!]
   [better looking than both]

Opening monologue/voiceover:
 DECLAN explains he's just
      starting out...
 moonlighting/cutting his teeth
      (day job at the SFPL)

His buddy FINN (Finian? Fitz?)
(bartender at The Barbary Lion)
knows someone (MILO) who needs help
finding someone (VERA)

Who's been secretly poisoning
   the fog? Could it be a
MYSTERIOUS CORPORATE ENTITY?

Good Names for a
MYSTERIOUS CORPORATE ENTITY:
Barbary Land Trust
   (BLT??... not very scary!)
Gold Coast Investment Authority
   (GCIA... slightly scarier)
 Silver City Holding Company
   BEATRICE (as in 'We Are...')
   The Consort
   The Coalition
   The Concern

Jazzy names for Boys in
Vera's Jazz Band:

   Porkpie
   Homburg
   Demuth the Behemoth
   Snaredrum Denny
   Upright Lionel

4 INT. BARBARY LION PUB--NIGHT
Seedy deco cave. Grand old hardwood bar. Downbeat jazz.
Hazy mirrors, hermetic booths. Nearly empty. A few
barflies: grim fixtures.

DECLAN DANNER sits alone in a back booth, his "office."
Sips whisky and soda and smokes. MILO BLANKENSHIP enters,
straining to see in the gloom. MILO approaches the
bartender. FINN serves him, then waves him toward the
back. As MILO approaches, DECLAN nods. MILO sits.

                    MILO
          Mr. ... Danner? I'm Milo
          Blankenship.

                    DECLAN
               [nodding]
          Call me Declan.

DECLAN offers MILO a cigarette from a pack. MILO partakes.
Feeble light seeps from sconces. Match strikes. Smoke
rises.

                    DECLAN
          My buddy Finn here says you could
          use my help... says you're one
          queen short of a deck?

                    MILO
          I do so hope you can help me,
          Mr. Danner. Declan, I mean. And
          please, call me Milo.

                    DECLAN
          All right then, Milo. So, you
          lost your battle-ax, I hear?

                    MILO
               [despairing]
          I lost my compass--I lost my
          North Star!

                    DECLAN
          Domestic squabble, is that
          it? Dame took off and left you
          high and dry? On the hook over
          something steep?

                    MILO
No, it's nothing like that.
Vera's my oldest friend. We lived
together, but it was nothing
salacious. She was like a mother
to me.

                    DECLAN
Vera?

                    MILO
Yes, the very one you're thinking
of. Royalty. San Francisco stage
royalty.

                    DECLAN
I don't follow...

                    MILO
Vera Svanire, of course! Huge
star since vaudeville days.

                    DECLAN
I'm sorry, I--

                    MILO
Oh, for Pete's sake! Where's your
sense of history and civic pride?
"The Venus of North Beach"? She
used to tap her feet off every
night in the preshow at the
Silver City Palace. Mr. Danner,
if you've never heard of Vera
Svanire, I'm not sure that you
can help me...

                    DECLAN
All right, simmer down, sure
I've heard of the "Venus of North
Beach." We weren't on a first-name
basis, is all. I know she was a
mob wife--married to none other
than Vincent "Cinderblock" Svanire!

                    MILO
Oh, she and Vinnie split up years
ago! Amicable... As amicable as

any split between two Italians.
It's true she minded very much
being a mafia wife, but it was the
"wife" part she couldn't get her
head around.

                    DECLAN
And that's where you came in?

                    MILO
Oh, Mr. Danner, if you're any
kind of detective, you'll have
gathered from the moment I
opened my mouth that my interest
in Vera was strictly aesthetic.
Twenty-five years ago I first
did her hair and makeup at the
Palace, and after that no one
else could touch her brows.

                    DECLAN
All right, let's cut to the chase.
When did you last see Vera Svanire?

                    MILO
Just over six months ago. It was
after that rash of police raids
on SoMa joints. You know, brutal
raids at the Lexington, the
Telephone Booth. I was caught in
a raid at the Vermilion Room, and
Vera bailed me out. That was the
last night I saw her, before I
skipped town for LA.

                    DECLAN
          [blowing smoke, raised eyebrows]
What were you all charged with?

                    MILO
Something risible, along the
lines of communist organizing
and conspiracy. What a laugh!

                    DECLAN
The Vermilion Room. Come to

think of it, it does sound like
it might be a front for Reds.

                MILO
Ha! Not for Reds. Maybe for red
velvet cake-eaters. Mr. Danner,
you strike me as someone who can
sort his pinkos from his fruits.

                DECLAN
Sure, if they want to be sorted.

                MILO
Here's the thing, Mr. Danner.
It's not only Vera. After six
months away I can't find anyone
from the Vermilion gang. None of
our buddies. Vera's whole band:
Porkpie, Demuth the Behemoth,
Snaredrum Denny. Can't find a one
of them! That got me thinking.
Something fishy happened at the
station the night of the raid.
It was my third "offense," and I
was facing time, or hefty fines,
or both, and the sergeant made
me a special offer: said he could
make the whole thing go away if I
"volunteered" for an experimental
drug trial of some sort...
something psycho-therapeutic...

                DECLAN
That's fishy, all right. What kind
of drugs are we talking about?

                MILO
Damned if I was going to stick
around and find out! Vera sprang
me just in time. But I can't
help wondering how many of the
Vermilion gang were facing time
and might have taken that offer...
and how many of them are now MIA?

Jules and Jim

THEY WERE AFLOAT. ADRIFT IN a tinny rowboat on an ornamental lake with no egress, floating through a cool summer, near the close of a cruel century, listing toward a new millennium. Walter had given up on rowing, allowing the oars to bob and slice the water, hardware squealing in the ungreased locks. A breeze shuttled them toward a bank of yellow irises.

June. An improbable, cloudless Saturday. The pond, a tepid turtle soup, was so green it might have been dyed to match the palmettos. The lake was ringed in tiers of green: the low, marshy grasses shaded by yellow hawthorns, bright tree ferns, and heavily cross-hatched palms; and above all this, the tall cypresses and Monterey pines, the blue afternoon shining through their rangy canopies as through the metalwork of a crown.

Cary was talking in the back of the boat. Walter had his back to her, but the boat's steel curves caught her chatter, amplifying it like a phonograph bell. She was busy narrating the afternoon, broadcasting to an unseen audience, commenting on their surroundings like a lazy amateur naturalist ill-equipped to host a nature documentary. She would interject such insights as "I'm pretty sure all geese are Canadian, at this point." She called every fish she spied a stickleback because that was the name of another pond nearby.

"Most people don't know there's a lake right smack in the middle of San Francisco," she said. "Several, actually, although the word *lake* is a stretch for most of them."

"You didn't know about Stow Lake until I brought you here," said Sasha.

"True, but I first told you about the buffalos. So we're even Stevens."

Though it was an ideal Saturday, the lake was sparsely attended, and no other visitors had chosen a rowboat: a family of seven had rented two blocky, snub-prowed pedal boats. Having no sense of how to turn them, the parents were trying to get three of their children unstuck from where they'd run aground, by the stone arch that bridged the pond and the small island.

Walter wasn't sure how he'd ended up rowing. Meanwhile, Sasha and Cary had known to bring cushions. Sasha was reclining against a pillow in the bow, his bright white ankles crossed at Walter's feet. He had taken off his sandals, and his toenails were orange as marigold petals. High up, the sun was bright but not hot, and Sasha shaded his head and shoulders with a paper parasol he had bought in Chinatown. It was a stiff, eight-pointed star, painted with black branches and cherry blossoms. He sighed beneath its stellate shade, resting his eyes, his blond braid curling around his neck as his left hand trailed in the water. He wore a thick jadeite bracelet that looked like he had pulled a ripple from the water to wear as a hoop.

"Are you cozy up there, darling?" Cary asked. When Sasha answered with a contented "*Mmm*," she added, "You look as pretty as a picture. You both do!"

They had dressed up for their picnic in the park. Sasha wore a pair of '30s beach pajamas he had sewn in an ultramarine print with cresting waves and flying storks, and big, gibbous lapels, like something Myrna Loy would wear on a boating trip to Catalina. Cary wore a straw panama hat and a soft secondhand linen suit that Sasha had taken in for her. Walter was in pale khakis, a collarless white oxford Cary had approved of, and a mustard-brown kartuz cap borrowed from Sasha. He felt, not unpleasantly, like an extra from *Uncle Vanya*.

The wind shifted, and they drifted away from the banks, out of the shallows. They were sated by the sandwiches and hard cider they'd shared in the

Chinese pagoda after climbing Strawberry Hill. Sasha closed his eyes for a moment and looked like he might fall asleep. Walter turned toward Cary, who helped him raise the oars inside the lip of the boat. Time stilled. They stared in silence as a lone Muscovy duck with a crackled strawberry blotch on its bill crossed their path trailing whorls of blue sky in its wake.

Walter had been thinking a lot about the movie they'd rented the night before, Truffaut's *Jules and Jim*. None of them had seen it, and they didn't know what they were getting into as they sat down excitedly to watch. Over months of intense friendship, they'd developed a habit, not always but often enough, of watching movies hand in hand in hand, even in theaters. The night before, Cary sat in the middle on the emerald couch, holding hands with Sasha and Walter. *Jules and Jim*, they soon found out, is about a love triangle between two best friends who sublimate their desire for each other through their love for a woman, Catherine, played by Jeanne Moreau. Early on, in a scene positively electric with New Wave breeziness, Jules and Jim race after Catherine, who gives chase across a long footbridge. She's dressed as a schoolboy in knickers and has tucked her long hair up into her cap, and she laughs devilishly as she outpaces them. At this point Cary unlaced her fingers from Walter's hand and then from Sasha's, and the three of them witnessed the ensuing psychodrama—chock-full of break-ups and makeups, searing jealousies, and betrayals large and small—each positioned on their own couch cushion, silent and still. When a newborn arrived to square the love triangle, Cary groaned and rubbed her temples, and Sasha went to the kitchen to fetch a bottle of wine, but instead returned with shot glasses and the Stoli that lived in the freezer. If Walter hadn't made a stupid rule for himself about watching every film to the last frame, he would have asked if they wanted to jump ship. At the lurid climax Cary reached for Walter's hand again; it turned out she wanted him to stop biting his nails. Afterward they all exhaled in relief, then hugged good night without a word about the movie. Walking home alone, Walter considered the peculiar appeal of the young Jeanne Moreau. It wasn't a film noir, but she was a femme fatale of sorts: seductive, capricious, demanding, manipulative, childlike.

A dragonfly dodged between Walter and Cary, thin wings glinting like mica, reeling him back to the lake's surface.

"Is a femme fatale just, like, a sexist idea?" he asked, seemingly out of the blue.

"Are you trying to pick a fight?" asked Cary.

"Of course not. But in this one seminar, we read an article that basically said that. You know, like in the movie last night or in *Gilda*, the woman is a beautiful object, a kind of goddess, but in the end, she's a pawn in the men's game."

"I don't think that was the case with Jeanne Moreau last night," said Sasha. "Catherine isn't a pawn, she's very spiny . . . willful. She strings Jules and Jim along the whole time, at every turn."

"Oh, it could have been great, that movie," said Cary. "The whole first half was so fun, and then it degenerated into another boring old battle of the sexes. God, so boring! And all that French-fried BS about the *essence of woman* from the mouths of the male characters. As if they'd just been to a Simone de Beauvoir lecture and gotten the whole thing backward. And all that drama mistaking love with sexual fidelity. So ridiculous—and it could have been so good."

"If they'd only gotten over themselves and gotten along," said Sasha, "it would have been a much shorter film."

"I'm sure it was radical for the early sixties," said Walter. "Plus it was set fifty years earlier."

Some yards away, the three adolescents in their yellow pedal boat, braced by the orange collars of their life preservers, were now drawing a long, twisted arc like an ampersand across the lake, straying far from their parents. They slowly, noisily chased down a family of geese, seeking to harass them.

"I just want *one movie*," Cary said, "where queers can live as queerly as they want without being punished for it or punishing themselves. And one where women aren't humiliated for being sexually adventurous would be nice. Is that so much to ask?"

"So, the femme fatale *is* a kind of sexist idea, I mean, if we're thinking of *Gilda*?" Walter lowered the oars in order to row them out of earshot of the rollicking kids and their parents, who drew ever nearer.

"*Of course it is,*" said Cary. "I mean, *duh*. But that's not why we love them. And that's why, in our movie, we're having Sasha play Lorna, the femme fatale, while I play the hard-nosed detective. The switcheroo."

"All very flattering," said Sasha, "but what makes you so sure I want to play the tragic damsel in your movie?"

"Well, for one thing, *I'm not doing it*. Also, *of course* you want to play the femme fatale, don't pretend you don't, it's as suited to you as your culottes. Anyway, we all know a woman manipulating men using her *feminine wiles* is worn out, so retrograde. But a *man* using feminine wiles would be something entirely different. Possibly revolutionary."

"Is there such a thing as *masculine* wiles?" This sounded weird to Walter even as he asked. "I guess you don't need wiles if you've got brute strength and you call the shots."

"You mean, like us, darling?" Sasha blew him a kiss.

"I think the antidote to that kind of macho BS is what Lawrence said the day I met him," said Cary. "*If you're* elusive *enough, you don't have to* fight." Then she exclaimed, "God, humans are so dumb! We must be the only species in the universe dumb enough to get hung up on some invented nonsense called *gender roles*." Cary became so agitated she gesticulated like a semaphorist signaling the banks. "I mean, take for example this magnificent Canada goose," she said, gesturing toward the strawberry-nosed bird that had doubled back to investigate them. "*He's* not floating around, fretting about the *essence of woman*, now is he?"

"I'm pretty sure that's a duck," said Walter.

"She knows," said Sasha.

"How does she know it's a *drake?*"

"Oh, confound it, that's exactly my point," said Cary. "Goose or duck, gander or drake or hen or whatever, it still doesn't give a damn about the *essence of woman.*" She breathed deep and shook out her arms. "My bubbe always thought all cats were female and all dogs were male because of the German articles. She couldn't shake it, even though she'd spoken English forever. Now, if she thought all cats were girls, did that make her an idiot? No, because she was a genius, especially at backgammon. Sweetest person alive, but at backgammon she'd murder you and laugh the whole time. But the whole German cats thing—it does make you realize that language is part of the problem—part of the racket—the whole masquerade, I mean."

Walter wondered aloud: "Eliot loves to say that all dress is drag, but I don't know if I believe him."

"Well, some dress is more obviously drag than others," said Sasha, sitting upright. "I've always thought . . . you can dress to be invisible, which seems to be what most people do. But I've *never been able* to do that. It always amazes me, it's amazing how much the style of my clothes defines me— I mean somehow defines my sex, rather than the other way around. I'm aware of it *all the time*, and I still don't fully get why it should be that way."

"Now I'm confused." Walter once again gave up on rowing. "Isn't *style* something else? I mean, sex *isn't just style, is it?*"

"It absolutely is," said Cary. "I suspect that's all it is."

"Of course not, that's a crazy thing to say," said Sasha, suddenly irritated.

"If we're talking about clothing, dress, attitude, and all that, then of course we're talking about *style*. That's why I'm really into this idea of *performativity*—"

"Oh god, you're not going to go on about *performativity* again, are you?" said Sasha, stressing the syllables *ti-vi-ty* with disdain. "She reads one Judith Butler chapter in one feminist reading group—nothing against feminist reading groups, of course . . ."

"Yes, I am going to go on about it," said Cary, "because it does make a lot of sense to me, about gender being a kind of performance."

"To me it makes no sense at all," said Sasha. "When I dress for work in the morning, I'm not *performing* anything. When I risk getting the shit kicked out of me by walking through the Outer Mission, I'm not *performing* anything. Do you think I dress like I do because I love being harassed all the time?"

"Sashenka," said Cary, "I understand all that, you know I do, of all people. On the other hand, you love to perform, don't deny it."

Walter sat squirming on the central bench, his tailbone sore from the thin steel. It was rare to see his two friends so worked up.

"I'm *performing* when we're singing together, in front of people," said Sasha, "but it's not *drag* I'm performing, I'm not a *gender clown*."

"I know, I know," said Cary. "You're not a drag queen; I'm not a drag king, either. But I feel like I'm *performing all the time*, and never so much as when I wear clothes like you're wearing now."

"You kind of *are* performing all the time, aren't you, Cary?" Walter interjected.

She ignored him and addressed Sasha. "Tell me honestly, if we switched outfits right now, wouldn't you feel like you were suddenly in a costume?"

"No," said Sasha.

"Well, that's where we're different, I guess, because I absolutely would. If I were wearing that outfit—believe me, my parents would be thrilled to see me dressed so femme, and Mom would assume my *essential womanly* instincts had kicked in at last, and the clock was ticking, and she'd start harassing us about grandchildren . . ."

They were quiet again, on the precipice of a different, heavier conversation. Walter knew a bit of the history here: that Cary never wanted kids, a big bone of contention between Cary and her mother, Joyce, who felt entitled to grandchildren. Cary was an only child and thought, if her mom was so desperate for grandkids, she maybe should have had more kids herself. Joyce said she loved Sasha, and when they started living together her mom began to relax around Cary again, which Cary took to mean: *Thank god her lesbian phase is over.* Cary suspected her mom saw Sasha as a potential—maybe accidental—sperm donor.

The rowboat nosed into a float of lily pads. A stray neon Frisbee sank among them: a UFO lodged in a Monet.

"Sasha," said Walter, trying to lighten the mood, "what if you were dressed, not in a beautiful linen suit like Cary's, but in something super masculine, like dressed as a lumberjack or in a football uniform? Would you feel like you were performing then?"

"Oh god!" cried Cary.

"Are you trying to give me hives?" asked Sasha, glancing down at his forearm. "Because it's working. Anyway, *anyone* would feel like they were performing, dressed as a lumberjack."

"But that gets to my point," said Cary, "all those grunge rockers in flannel plaid—they're *performing something*—a kind of smelly, unwashed masculinity, even if that style is supposed to be rough and authentic, in a way. *It's all style.*"

"What do you think, Walter?" Sasha put him on the spot. "What are you performing?"

Walter hedged a moment, torn. He'd never read Judith Butler, but he had seen *Paris Is Burning* several times. Gesturing at his getup, he said, "I guess . . . I'm serving Russian farmer realness!" He laughed awkwardly.

"Poor Walter," said Cary, "we mustn't go all George and Martha in front of him. Can't we agree to disagree? Or actually, I don't think we disagree. I just haven't done a good enough job explaining that we do agree."

"No, you haven't," said Sasha.

"OK, *big picture*," said Cary, "can we all agree that we're right and the whole world is wrong?"

"About what exactly? Which part?" asked Sasha.

"About *how to live*," said Cary.

"Well, that's obviously true."

"Cosigned and notarized," said Walter. "Meanwhile, my butt hurts."

Cary and Walter switched places, and she gave him her cushion. She wanted to row once more around the island before they turned the boat in. She sat before Sasha, leaning backward into her task. With the two of them facing him, framed by the parasol above and the island behind, and the jade-topped pagoda like a candy dish at Sasha's shoulder, they looked absurdly picturesque. Walter kicked himself for not having brought a camera.

"Tell me about your movie," asked Sasha. "So, I play someone called *Lorna?*"

"Lorna *Zaftig*," said Cary, blindly rowing northwest, heading counter-clockwise around the island. "It means *juicy*."

"I didn't know that!" said Walter. "The juicy part, I mean."

"Ooh," said Sasha, "very flattering, but I'm hardly zaftig! I'll need padding, I guess. And you're the detective, and who does Walter play?"

"Walter plays your brother, Lionel. But he's gone missing, along with a bunch of other queers."

"I won't have any lines," said Walter. "I think I might have been lobotomized."

"My brother's been lobotomized?" Sasha sounded concerned.

"Well, that's part of the mystery," said Cary, talking over her shoulder to Sasha. "*What's happened to Lionel?* We haven't actually worked that part out yet."

"Oh, I do hope you aren't lobotomized, Walter! It will make our scenes together much less fun. And the villain is your old boss Dietrich?"

"He's one of several villains," said Walter.

"So, what's the plot? Your evil ex-boss kidnaps my brother, Walter?"

"No, no," said Cary, "it's kind of a version of the lotus-eaters. Very classical, you know. Ullrich Duxelles makes this delicious, narcotic food . . . he wants people to think only of dining in his five-star restaurants, so they forget about everything in their lives except their next exotic meal. That's the social commentary part. No more politics, no more counterculture. Just triple-crème Brie and Beaujolais nouveau."

"That's kind of already happened, hasn't it?" Sasha frowned. "And now you've convinced Lawrence to play the villain?"

"No, Lawrence will play a good guy, Milo, who has lost someone, too," Cary explained.

"I still have to meet Lawrence."

"You must! As soon as possible. You will *adore* him." Cary was rowing fast now, oar handles high, blades deep in the water. Walter loved the rhythmic splash each time the paddles emerged, dripping ellipses across the water's surface as they lunged forward.

"So you say," said Sasha, "but you keep hiding him from me . . . or me from him. And does Lawrence know you two have cast him in your movie?"

"Uh-huh," said Cary. "Well, let's say he's warming up to the idea. Naturally, we couldn't expect him to agree before he's read the screenplay."

They were nearing the concrete shade of the first of two bridges. North of the island the lake shrank to a shrub-lined channel; a low footbridge pinching its narrowest point.

"Here's a question," said Sasha. "If Lawrence is a film director, more so than an actor, then why not have him direct the movie, rather than play in it? That would make sense, wouldn't it?"

"He can do both!" said Cary.

"And correct me if I'm wrong, but neither of you have seen any of Lawrence's movies, right?" Sasha asked.

Cary and Walter shook their heads, trading looks.

"But he has made a lot, apparently," said Walter, "though almost no one's seen them. They're very avant-garde, I guess."

"But he at least has some idea how to get a movie made, unlike you two. So maybe he could help you with that part?"

Cary, turning to face Sasha, paddled absentmindedly with her left arm, spinning them off course toward the island's bank. "Darling, are you implying that we don't know what we're doing? That we don't have a plan for our screenplay?"

"OK, then, what is your plan?" Sasha folded his parasol as they slipped through a net of shadows cast by cypresses.

"First, we figured, we have to write the best screenplay we can. Aim high. We'll write our dream movie with our dream cast in mind and all our dream locations." Cary continued rowing them in a circle with her left hand, not bothering to correct course.

"OK . . . and then? What happens then?"

"Then we send it to Todd Haynes," she said, "and he *loves it* and says, *I must make this movie at once!*"

"That's your plan?"

"It wouldn't have to be Todd Haynes," said Walter. "It could be Sally Potter, or Rose Troche, or someone . . ."

"Why not Martin Scorsese or Francis Ford Coppola? I hear they're pretty good," said Sasha. "Look, I don't want to be a downer, but I don't understand how you two have already spent a thousand hours writing, over all those cappuccinos and cocktails, and haven't thought at all about what you're going to do with the thing when you're done."

Cary stopped rowing. They slid toward a thicket ablaze with flame-orange nasturtiums and were grounded, stuck.

"We're perfecting our art," said Cary. "Or, if you must have it in commercial terms, we're perfecting our *product*. You can't sell boiled peanuts until you've grown the peanuts and boiled them, you know."

"Magic beans might be a better metaphor," said Sasha.

Cary, noticeably stung, brusquely punted them backward out of the mud. Tall grasses scraped the prow.

"Does Lawrence still have friends in Hollywood?" Sasha asked. "Maybe it would be good to start there?"

"I don't know," said Walter. "He said he lost most of his connections after moving from LA in the eighties. And his partner, Roland, was the only producer he ever had. God, it seems so tragic, I hate to ask about it . . . Roland died a few years ago, after they'd been together almost twenty years."

"It's definitely tragic," said Cary. "But he doesn't mind talking about Roland . . ."

"What did he tell you about Roland?" asked Walter, not sure when such conversations would have happened.

"Oh, you know," said Cary, "a few wild stories from back in the seventies, like how they met in a bathhouse in LA, and how Roland was pretty game about appearing in Larry's films—often nude—and how they were both expats, that sort of thing. Roland also managed the Archers Hotel when he was alive; the apartment was Roland's."

This was information Walter hadn't heard, and now he was concerned that Cary and Lawrence were hanging out a lot, going to champagne brunches and stuff without him.

"I'm doing deliveries tomorrow afternoon, and I'm going to see Larry," said Walter. "You could come meet him then, if you want, Sasha."

"Larry said he'd try to make it to Marlena's tomorrow night," said Cary, "and anyway, Sasha and I have to rehearse with Nick all afternoon tomorrow." She was referring to a gig Bombolone had booked at a bar in Hayes Valley. They had added a new member; that spring Cary convinced her lifelong friend Nick to play bass for them.

As if intuiting Walter's fear of being left out, she went on: "I called Larry earlier this week to invite him personally. Well, you know how he is—turns out it's impossible to get him off the phone. We talked for, like, an hour and a half!"

"Walter, you're coming to see us tomorrow, aren't you?" asked Sasha. "I know it's a tiny place, but I'm actually pretty nervous."

"I know," Cary added excitedly. "It's an actual gig in an actual bar! And it's a whole set! Plus we invited absolutely everyone and their brother Lionel, too."

"I'm excited—of course I'll be there."

Cary had finally gotten her bearings, and they resumed course, but it was slow going, and by the time they approached the stone bridge south of the island she was bored with rowing and wanted to abandon ship, ready to get out right there on the bank and march off. They switched places again, and Sasha rowed them back in silence. Walter was thinking that, since effectively they hadn't gone anywhere at all, the whole point of a boat ride was the pleasure of gliding: leaving behind, if only for a moment, the friction of the pedestrian world. Yet clearly some of that friction had stowed away for the ride.

"Nature's pretty boring, isn't it, when it comes right down to it?" said Cary, fanning herself with her panama hat. "It's like that one thing Goethe said: *Even the most beautiful sunset is boring after fifteen minutes*, or something like that."

"Have we seen any nature today?" asked Sasha.

"Goethe never said that," said Walter.

The Blue Angel

FIONA AND WALTER STARTED DRINKING before dinner. Walter had made spaghetti with meat sauce (Prego and ground beef—what Cary dubbed his *bachelor's Bolognese*), and they sat on the tiny deck outside their living room window. Beyond neighboring gables with green bristles of treetops pressed between them, Cole Valley and the park were nowhere to be seen, tucked under a lint-white coverlet. It was chilly. They wore hoodies, ate fast, chatted nonstop, and polished off a bottle of merlot to keep warm. Newly single, Fiona caught Walter up on the fallout of her fiery nine-month affair with Val, who had recently moved back to New York. Fiona was better off, she knew. Her only real lament was that the sex had been so great—*fully cosmic*, she declared.

By the time Kelly Calypso showed up, they had moved inside, shut the window on the fog, and uncorked a second bottle. Kelly, it turned out, was also single again, and to mark a fresh start, she was thinking about shaving her head, or at least the sides and back, and coaxing the rest into dreads. Fiona warned against doing anything rash in the wake of a breakup—as good as it might feel—and insisted Kelly's hair looked gorgeous. It was currently a deep, chloroplastic green, like a wheatgrass smoothie. The three of them griped about heartbreak and the universal pitfalls of dating, well, anyone—women, men; gay, bi, queer, "straight" (but *straight* always came in scare quotes)—right down to the dregs of a second bottle of cheap red blend.

"Walter, why don't you just go out with Julian?" Fiona asked in all earnestness. She was cocooned in an oversized blue hoodie she'd borrowed from Walter. "You guys always look so cute together!"

"Oh god," said Walter, "he's so dreamy, I had such a crush on him . . . but I had to get over it."

"Wait, why?"

"Uh, he's not interested. I mean, he's not interested *enough*. We're fuck-buddies, I guess you'd call it. Once a month or so we fall back into bed together."

"That sounds perfect," said Kelly, "the ideal relationship!"

"Perfect for him. Once I asked him out on a dinner date and he *laughed*. We were in a cab on the way to his place, and he said, *Let's not ruin this.*"

"Fucker!" cried Fiona.

"Fucker," said Kelly. "Fuck *her*."

"Mmm," said Walter.

It was extra cozy at home on such a foggy night, so it took a little rousing on Walter's part, but Fiona and Kelly had promised to go with him to see Bombolone play at Marlena's. They spilled from the cab on Hayes Street already quite tipsy. Sunday night at Marlena's was hardly a prime time and venue, more like the graveyard slot at a local backwater. What people were calling Hayes Valley had only recently been rescued from under the wreck of the 101 Freeway downed in the Loma Prieta quake. Slowly, boutiques, cafés, even a couple art galleries had sprung and spread like dropseed through an abandoned lot. Even so, that night the bar, narrow as a railroad flat, was crowded with Cary and Sasha's friends. It was sometime after nine, and Bombolone was slated to go on at ten, after a DJ set by some newbie no one had heard of named DJ B'AnderSnatch. As they were fetching drinks, the DJ eased into a set of '50s lounge music so utterly uncool that it defied you to take it as cool (Esquivel, Yma Sumac, Henry Mancini—Walter was tickled to hear "Baby

Elephant Walk" stumble into the playful, grating theme from *Les yeux sans visage*).

They found stools against the wall, and seated on her high stool, Fiona for once was nearly Walter's height. She had shed his hoodie like a chrysalis, and beneath it was a body-hugging black cocktail dress and gumball-bright leggings. Walter, too, had dressed up for the occasion, or at least put on a fancy shirt with his jeans. It was a shirt Sasha had made for him, a beautiful dress shirt he had surprised him with for no reason. The shirt had a pattern of leafing branches in soft spring colors, with leaf-shaped songbirds scattered throughout—subtly—you had to know to look for them. It wasn't really Walter's style (if he had one), but it was eye-catchingly pretty, and he wanted to please Sasha by wearing it.

To match the lounge music, Fiona convinced him to try a mai tai, and a few sips into their drinks, she and Kelly were already talking about porn. Ever since she started working at Good Vibrations, the pro-sex, third-wave feminist sex shop, this was a new topic of interest to Fiona. They were discussing why lesbians liked to rent gay male porn.

"I'm so confused by what you're telling me," said Walter, though he hadn't really been paying attention. He wasn't against porn per se, he liked magazines, but porn movies bothered and bored him from a filmmaking perspective. He was also wondering why he'd never had a rum-based drink that he liked.

"It's hotter than lesbian porn," said Kelly, "like, way hotter."

"Are we talking about *the same* gay male porn?" asked Walter. "Not to sound like a prude, but most of it's so *mechanical*. It's like house music: *uhn-ch, uhn-ch, uhn-ch*—I always feel like I'm watching athletes competing in some endurance sport at a track meet. Not that that isn't hot, in a way . . ."

"OK, have you ever seen lesbian porn? Like, made by lesbians?" Fiona asked.

"Does *Go Fish* count?"

"Definitely not!" said Kelly. "Clipping each other's fingernails and tearing into fresh baked bread *does not count* as porn."

"Lesbian porn is terrible, trust me," Fiona went on, "and straight porn is terrible, and lesbian porn made for straight guys is the worst . . . so all that's left is porn with gay guys!"

"Right," said Kelly, "and one advantage is that there are no women being objectified, and instead you get to enjoy men objectifying each other."

"OK, OK," said Walter, having to shout a bit now over the din, "but it was my understanding that lesbians *aren't attracted to men*."

"Oh, hell!" said Kelly. "It's not that they're *men*, it's that they're hot, sweaty, naked bodies going at each other with abandon. Nothing held back."

"Exactly," Fiona agreed. "It's *energy*, not sex parts. And women in straight porn are all these dead-eyed dolls."

Fiona held forth, and Walter nodded along as if to say, *Oh, I get it now*. But in his head, he was trying to iron flat a Möbius loop that kept popping back up: something that he was meant to find hot that he didn't find especially hot could be found hot by women for whom it was not meant to be hot in the least. *God, sex is weird*. Meanwhile, he was tonguing the roof of his mouth compulsively. The cloying coconut rum in his mai tai made him long for a good ol' G and T, the gay boy's Listerine.

"OK, I'm still confused!" he declared.

"Exactly!" said Fiona. "That's what I've been saying!"

"What's that?"

"I'm saying the best porn is the *most confusing* porn. Not in the sense of *you don't know what you're looking at*, but more like you're never quite sure what you *want*. Like, you're not sure who you want to be, him or her, or top or bottom, or if you want to be that guy or the guy he's fucking. You just want it all."

"Right," said Kelly. "Or maybe, for that moment, you want to be *only* his mouth or her pussy or that giant double-headed dildo and nothing more— not to be objectifying or anything."

Walter felt himself blushing, but then he had a rush of rum-induced lucidity. "You're talking about desire and identification," he said, coughing up old wisdom from film class. "Same question. Who do you want to be versus who do you want to be with? Like, do you want to be Jimmy Stewart and get to kiss Kim Novak, or do you want to be Kim Novak and get to kiss Jimmy Stewart?"

"Uh—are those my only choices?" Fiona wrinkled her nose.

"OK," Kelly offered, "would you rather be Brad Pitt kissing Geena Davis, or Geena Davis kissing Brad Pitt, or both of them kissing Susan Sarandon, in my alternate ending?"

"I was about to pass on both," said Fiona, "until you threw Susan Sarandon in the mix . . ."

"I have to pee!" said Walter, darting off to avoid the question.

It was almost ten. Walter stood in a narrow purple hallway, the oppressive color of which he was convinced was making him drunker. But at least he loved the song the dubious B'AnderSnatch was spinning: Ray Charles's "One Mint Julep," the earthshaking opening fanfare as classic, in its way, as "Also Sprach Zarathustra." The bathroom was locked, but no one else was waiting. He shimmied and bobbed his head to the song's irresistible bebop organ. A skinny, weirdly sexy rat-faced man in a Pretenders T-shirt stumbled down the hallway and, ignoring Walter, tried to pry open the bathroom door, banging away on it before he gave up and marched off crying, "Been in there forever!" Now whoever was in there would think Walter was the asshole who nearly battered the door off its hinges. He would have abandoned the hallway, but he had to pee so badly. All at once the door cracked open and a brilliantined head popped out, declaring, "Wall! That was extremely rude!"

Cary grabbed him by the arm and pulled him into the bathroom, locking the door behind them. The room was tight as a confessional and midnight dark, lit by one bare bulb poking from a socket over the mirror. In such close quarters, he was reminded again how tall she was, how close they were in height. She was wearing a dress shirt and a silk vest embroidered black on

204   Christopher Tradowsky

black, a black bow tie, and sleeve garters, slinky like elastic silver watch-bands. She held a little glass bottle with a lid with a brush; it looked like clear nail polish.

"Jesus, there are so many more people than I expected!" she said, sounding nervous, which wasn't like her at all. "I still have to put on my Django mustache!"

"I have to pee!"

"Well, go ahead!" she said, turning to the mirror and brushing the clear liquid on her upper lip. "I'm not going to stop you."

He turned his back to her and stood above the bowl. The bathroom was stiflingly purple, wretched smelling, and so small that, back-to-back as they were, he could sense their scapulae about to touch.

"I can't do it with you standing here—I'm pee shy!"

"I promise I won't look."

"You'll *hear.*"

"I promise *I won't hear.* I'm busy pressing on my mustache. Here," she said, and unleashed the water full blast from the tap.

Walter unzipped with a resigned burp—more foul coconut—and tried a trick he had developed for dealing with those long, nightmare troughs found in men's rooms in ballparks and leather bars. He concentrated on how drunk he was, feeling himself sway a little, and voided his mind of everything but a warm, woozy buzz, feeling his bladder decompress and listening to anything beyond the sound of his own pungent patter.

He flushed, they swapped places, and as he washed his hands, he was taken aback by what appeared in the mirror over his shoulder. Cary, in the stark light, looked both exactly like herself and completely transformed by the addition of a shapely brown mustache that traced her upper lip, peaking a bit in the middle like a bracket. It didn't look real, but it looked perfect. It should have highlighted the natural goofiness of her looks; instead, against all expectations, it looked distinguished. Here was the matinee dandy he first saw in the Castro Theatre, strutting down the aisle arm in arm with the gamine. He turned to her and stood mute for a moment, wondering who she was. Her slicked hair smelled like cloves.

"Cary, you look amazing!" He held his breath. "You look so . . . *handsome.*"

Cary slapped her hand over her mouth. "Don't make me smile," she said, voice deep, teeth clenched. "The glue's not dry yet!"

To his surprise his recently tucked dick began to twitch and harden in his briefs. He tried not to think of it, but all at once the situation was beyond his control. No way he could admit it—even to himself—but there it went. His dick wasn't to blame, after all, but something in his blood. Strange how his blood could be mutinous, stealthy, circulating on branching paths he knew not of.

The door started rumbling again. Loosely hinged, it banged and jumped in the frame, a flimsy hook jostling in the eye.

"Come on!" came the rat-faced man's voice from behind the door. "Other people gotta use it!"

The little quake stopped as abruptly as it started. For a moment they stood perfectly still. Cary couldn't keep from smiling under her hand, but when she removed it she was poker-faced, the mustache adhering to her upper lip. Still trying not to smile, she raised one eyebrow at him.

"Time to go on," said the dandy throatily. "Give me a kiss for luck?"

A kiss for luck? He laughed and wobbled a little. Of course that was nothing to ask, he had kissed Cary many times . . . on the cheek. He knew her scent, and the soft down of it. But he was drunk enough that he didn't think through the implications of what he said next:

"OK. Do you want to be Jimmy Stewart . . . and get to kiss Kim Novak? Or do you want to be Kim Novak and get to kiss Jimmy Stewart?"

Cary didn't blink. The little purple room was dropping through floors like an elevator.

"What if I want to be Django Reinhardt and get to kiss . . . Amanda Blueshoes?"

Then Cary leaned over—not far, as they were already so close—and kissed him full on the mouth, and he kissed back; it was a chaste but forceful kiss, a silent screen kiss, and her lips were soft and her mustache bristly, and he almost laughed because he thought, *What if, like an old cartoon gag, they pulled away and he was wearing her mustache?* But Walter didn't laugh because Cary didn't laugh, and maybe Cary didn't laugh because Walter didn't laugh. Below his belt, in spite of himself, his blood stood up. And though it lasted a good deal longer than a friendly kiss ought to, still in an instant it was over and she had shot out of the room, down the hall, and left him to face the irascible Pretenders fan, who glared at him in disgust, as if they had been shooting up in the bathroom for the last half hour.

The DJ set came to a maudlin end, with a weepy harmonica version of "Moon River." By that time Bombolone was carefully poised on a makeshift plywood stage atop a pool table. It was just large enough to fit the three of them without an inch of leeway: Sasha standing at a mic, Cary seated with her Gretsch held like a shield, and behind them, their buddy Nick on bass. Nick was straight, endearing, and ordinarily schlubby, but for the occasion he had dressed up in his version of natty nightclub togs. He wore a brown bowler, and he, too, had sleeve garters Cary must have lent him. His bushy steel-wool beard was unruly enough that no matter how dressed up he still looked like a prospector just back from panning for gold in Bodie. Sasha, meanwhile, in honor of the bar's namesake, had pulled out all the stops and dressed as Marlene Dietrich in *Morocco*. Once again Walter marveled at his friend's ability to shapeshift. Sasha looked ravishing in a three-piece tuxedo with a white bow tie and a silk top hat, and under the canted brim he'd carefully curled his hair to mimic Dietrich's platinum cloud. He was pale under the track lights, ruthless as a camera flash. His green eyes narrowed; his mouth a scarlet bow.

The band hadn't had a chance to do a sound check. There was a fair amount of fidgeting with mics and amps as they tried to ward off feedback through curses and the twitching of dials. But then they reached a kind of equilibrium: sound system stabilized, guitars in tune, stage proving sturdy enough to keep them aloft for a good hour. Cary began plucking out a waltz, key of C: gentle but loud enough that the crowd came to attention. After a minute of Cary's vamping, Sasha launched into a new song for them. It was "Falling in Love Again," which Sasha performed doing his best husky, dispassionate, slightly flat Marlene Dietrich imitation. A whoop arose from the audience when he finished the chorus, a premature burst of applause, but Cary and Nick kept playing, and Sasha did his best to waltz in place without falling off the stage. Nick kept the rhythm as Cary tried her hand at some first-guitar finger work, a well-rehearsed impromptu. It was surprising how much sound they produced with only two guitars and Sasha humming along. Then Cary caught the melody and sang an impassioned rendition of *"Ich bin von Kopf bis Fuß auf Liebe eingestellt,"* the entire song in German, just as Marlene sang it in *The Blue Angel.*

When they finished, the audience went haywire, raving as if singing in German while balancing on a pool table were a daredevil trapeze act worthy of Cirque du Soleil. The ruckus was loud enough that Cary tried to say "Thank you . . . We're Bombolone" three times, was drowned out, and finally gave up, smiled, and moved on down the set list. It was a spate of actual and fake German cabaret songs, including "Mack the Knife" and "The Pineapple Song" from *Cabaret.* When Sasha sang "Danke Schoën" (keyed down a couple steps from Wayne Newton), the audience turned out to be amply stocked with *Ferris Bueller* fans, singing along like it was the Gen X "Auld Lang Syne" (flubbed lyrics and all). Between songs Cary would regale the audience with anecdotes from Bombolone's 1929 European tour, assuring the locals that they had received the warmest reception of all here in beautiful Schleswig-Holstein. This, Walter thought, was an extended in-joke meant for him alone, as probably no one else there was thinking of *The Blue Angel,* in which Marlene Dietrich fronted a cabaret act on a tour of nameless German towns.

Walter was taking a cure of gin and tonics, feeling that he'd tried enough new things for one night. While Cary was chatting up the room between songs, and the audience was gently heckling back, Kelly Calypso leaned over to him and said, "Your friend Cary is *hot*."

"Cary?" asked Walter, doing a double take in his head. "*Cary* is hot?"

"Yeah, totally. Sexy."

"Uh," said Walter, confused and wanting to ask, *You know that mustache is fake, right?* But he deflected: "I've always thought Sasha was attractive— I mean, gorgeous, really. Honestly, the first time I saw Sasha, I thought I was going to faint."

Fiona looked at Walter wide-eyed as she sucked at the rim of a second mai tai.

"But Cary," Walter went on, "well, Cary's such a *nerd*—"

"What do you think, Fiona?" asked Kelly. "Who is hotter, Sasha or Cary?"

The bluntness of this question made Walter loathe Kelly for a few seconds as Fiona hesitated.

"Sasha is definitely pretty," said Fiona, "no question. But no, Kelly's right. Cary is hot."

"She's an über-geek! Like, a true dorkasaurus. Singing in *German?*"

"That was sexy," said Kelly. "Kind of toe-curling."

"What the heck?" said Walter. "You know she did that all phonetically. She doesn't speak German; she only likes it because she thinks it sounds ridiculous."

"So what?" said Kelly. "She still sounded sexy."

He was pretty sure the two of them were gaslighting him. *Lesbians prefer gay male porn? German was toe-curling? Sasha was merely pretty? Cary was sexy?* What was this, *fuck with Walter night?*

Now he was annoyed with Kelly and a bit with Fiona, too, and if he thought about it, he was annoyed with the crowd around him, who obviously were there because they adored Sasha and Cary, but in a stupid way, *superficial.* Not like the way he adored them, which was . . . different. Intimate.

Profound, in a way. He *knew* them, he understood—or thought he did—but *goddamn it*, what was up with that kiss? A kiss didn't mean anything, *not here, not now. Not in San Francisco and not anymore.* Everyone kissed everybody, free as water—a joke, a dare. Kisses were party favors, door prizes. *Oh, did you have a nice time tonight? Well, in that case we should make out for a while, nothing to get hung up about, unless you're an idiot born in the wrong century and weaned on cheesy poetry.* What a ridiculous thing to even think about for as long as one more second.

And anyway, in the bathroom—*oh god, how close were they?* Could Cary tell he got hard? And what if she could tell, and what if she told Sasha? What a stupid mess! Maybe it was the mustache—he'd always had a thing for them. No, *how dumb!* It couldn't be that simple: sex wasn't about *trappings*. Hairy legs and husky voices. He wasn't, like, *a mustache-o-sexual*. And what's more—now he really needed to calm down—Cary couldn't be *into* him—it wasn't possible. And one of the main reasons it wasn't possible was that she already had the perfect partner: the boy who could be *anything*, it seemed—man or woman or anything else there was to be—even the reincarnation of Marlene Dietrich rasping "Oh My Lover" like Polly Jean Harvey, sugar all over his voice, the audience eating from his hand—who could possibly want more than that? But then, in spite of his love for Sasha, his friend, his dear close friend, Walter had a troubling thought, one he'd had before, which he tried *not to have*, which made him sad and queasy and excited. *What if Cary were a guy?* Oh man, that would really get messy; then he'd really be done for.

For the rest of the concert, he inched away from Kelly and Fiona and sidled toward the bar, where he got another drink. He tried to pay attention to the performance but was cornered by a friend of Cary's, a theater queen and gym bunny, cute in a scrubbed-up way but too preppy for Walter's taste. The boy's improbable name was John Keats, though he was blasé about it and didn't seem to know how fantastic it was; he'd apparently never read any of Keats's poetry. Walter didn't want to talk over the music, but by way of hitting on him (he guessed), John was relating how much he'd been sacrificing to get in shape, since he'd been cast in a walk-on role—short but pivotal, and totally nude—at Theatre Rhinoceros. Walter thought about asking him to shut up, as Sasha was busy crooning one of his favorite songs, "Autumn Leaves," but actually Walter was wondering *how the hell this guy could not have read Keats's poetry*, since, if he'd been named John Keats, it would have been the first thing he did as soon as he could read.

The concert culminated with another debut: they performed "I'm Not That Kind of Magician," a song Cary had finished writing that week for Sasha to sing in their movie. The song, Cary explained, was about how the character was too much of a glamour-puss to be bothered with any mundane domestic chores. She'd written it for Sasha, but Walter knew it described Cary through and through, a Cary manifesto. Nick kicked them off: it was catchy and bouncy, with a tappy cadence that would have set Fred Astaire off on a tear; he could hear in it echoes of big band brass.

The crowd's enthusiasm had barely waned throughout the concert, even as the cheers and catcalls grew inebriated. When they wrapped it was only eleven, and though the crowd had thinned a little, most of their friends hung around to celebrate. At that point, Walter lost track of Fiona and Kelly entirely, and Cary and Sasha hadn't made it two feet from the stage, assailed by old friends. Walter was stuck at the bar still, getting drunker and talking to John Keats, thinking of excusing himself to the bathroom, but slightly afraid of facing all that suffocating purpleness again. John Keats, not a drop of poet's blood in his veins, kept kvetching about how small the local theater scene was and the annoyances of Actors' Equity. Once he got to the subject of freelancing and unions he might as well have been spewing about corporate finance, for all Walter knew or cared, because at this point the whole evening flooded away, becoming a wash of gin and tonics and rum-coconut belches and "Autumn Leaves" and mustache kisses and double-headed dildos and platinum clouds. *Huge cloudy symbols of a high romance*—all the Keats he could remember, it regurgitated like a burp, and he wasn't convinced it was Keats. He knew it as a crossword clue in a David Lean film. He didn't dare slip off his barstool; the room was adrift, and he didn't trust his footing amid the tide.

Cary did not seek him out after the concert. The last he saw of her, she was leaning against the far wall talking to Kelly Calypso, who had singled her out. They stood under a bright halogen pendant, Kelly's verdigris hair flowing around her blue tattooed shoulders. She looked like a sexy, beguiling siren, and Walter thought, *Yeah,* Cary *probably thinks she's hot, too*, though Cary wasn't a club kid like Kelly—*imagine Cary going out to a rave wearing a vial of cocaine around her neck*—and clearly, between the two of them, neither had any idea what they might be getting into, flirting like that.

And then it was later. Maybe much later. But Walter had no way of knowing. He was too busy trying to face in one direction, sitting upright to keep the birdbath of his brain from spilling over. He sat on the flagstone patio in the garden behind Sasha and Cary's place, on a little cast-iron love seat, stiff-backed, lumpy with iron rosettes. It was very dark, soothingly dark. A cigarette burned in his right hand; he ashed into a low reef of sedums. To his left, Sasha emerged from the bedroom. He was carrying two mugs of tea and handed one to Walter. He told Walter to hold out his hand and dropped two Advil in it, saying, "Take these."

Sasha had changed, washed his face, brushed out his Marlene curls and smoothed his hair back. Sasha again. If it was chilly, Walter couldn't tell. He was warm as mulled wine in a thinly padded bomber jacket. Sasha sat close beside him, bundled in his plush red robe, striped pajama bottoms, slippers. They faced out into the garden as if it were the jungle set of *The King and I* and they were waiting for the second act overture.

It was intensely quiet. The Castro had closed down for the night, the only noise was the shuffling of an intermittent breeze. The garden, which the landlord never bothered to maintain, looked ungainly during the day but sumptuous at night. Behind where they sat, below the kitchen window, a large bed of begonias bloomed, their leaves maroon bat wings, their clustered, pink-stippled flowers waxy and translucent. The sky was pewter—what they could see of it through weaving shoots of bamboo and the fronds of two short, shag-barked palms Cary for some reason called *Wagnerian palms*.

"Wait, where's Cary again?" asked Walter, who was trying to puzzle out the evening's events like a jigsaw whose corners had fallen to the floor. A seamy picture was emerging.

"You *know*," Sasha said, more amused than annoyed. "She went off with your friend with the green hair. She went to her place."

"Ugh, *Kelly Calypso* . . . But is she *coming home?*"

"Wall, I don't think so. And don't stub out your cigarette in those succulents." Sasha handed Walter a ruby glass ashtray that lived on the terrace just for him.

"Oh, of course, sorry."

"Drink your tea, darling, it will sober you up," said Sasha. "Oh, and don't tell Cary I gave you Red Zinger."

"Why not?"

"You know, she's snobby about tea. If she were here she'd force you to drink some of her lapsang souchong."

"Barf! *Smoked tea*, who likes that stuff? I mean, besides her?" He raised his mug, inhaling warm hibiscus. He took a sip, then yelped when he splashed tea on his jacket and it soaked right through. He was fine, he told Sasha, he was fine. Sitting back, he felt the tea form a warm pink star over his heart, and he remembered his songbirds.

"Oh no!" He sat up, unzipping his jacket with one hand and spilling more tea with the other. "My favorite shirt! My special shirt! Sasha—"

"Hold on," said Sasha, taking his mug and helping him shrug off the jacket. He was too drunk to unbutton his own shirt, Sasha had to do it for him.

"Will it stain?"

"Stay here—gimme a minute." Sasha disappeared, and Walter was left sitting shirtless, bomber over his shoulders. He shivered without feeling the chill. His consciousness was lagging; it was only after Sasha left that he realized how sexy it felt to have Sasha undress him partially. He'd been shirtless around his friend only once before, and it was when Sasha had invited him into his tiny sewing room—really a walk-in closet—to tailor the shirt to him. He'd never had a fitted shirt or even thought about a shirt being tailored. Sasha had measured his neck with a tape, and even now in his drunkenness, Walter could feel the warmth of Sasha's fingertips on his clavicle.

When Sasha returned he assured him his songbirds were OK, he'd rinsed the shirt and it wouldn't stain. Soon they were cozy again on their garden bench. Sasha gave him an Alcatraz sweatshirt that a friend, a visiting tourist, had forgotten at their place; it was huge, tacky, toasty.

"Sasha, what the hell is this?" He held up a large mason jar filled with pebbles, potting soil, wood chips, and white mildewing mulch. He had accidentally punted it into the begonias with his heel.

"Oh, you must know about that! That's Cary's Count Dracula jar. I make her keep it out here." Sasha sensed his confusion. "You know that joke Cary always makes that, at this point, she's so completely composed of San Francisco stuff that she can't leave the peninsula or she'll spontaneously combust—like, she'll blow apart on a molecular level?"

Walter shook his head. A slosh in the trough of his brain reminded him why he'd been trying not to move.

"One night we had planned a trip to Chez Panisse, and I said, *How are you going to go to Berkeley without blowing apart?* And she filled that old pickle jar with dirt, saying that, like Dracula, she had to travel with earth from her homeland in order to retain her powers. She carried it to Chez Panisse and back in a leather briefcase. *Earth from her homeland?* She's from San Bernardino!"

Walter set the jar back under the bench. The fungal look of it was nauseating. "Are *you* able to leave San Francisco without combusting?" he asked. "You said once you couldn't imagine living anywhere else."

"I think Cary's right, in a way, being deeply queer as we are—where else

204 Christopher Tradowsky

could we possibly live, and be happy, and feel safe? SF can feel small at times, and sleepy. But *it is* the perfect place to be *ambivalent*."

"I'm only thinking of your future in couture," said Walter, his drunken tongue fumbling over the phrasing, *foo-ture in cu-toor.* "You should be in London sewing Gaultier gowns, you know, for Peter Greenaway films, or something!"

"Oh, believe me, I'd love to sew soupspoons over Helen Mirren's breasts for money, who wouldn't?" Then Sasha began a little soliloquy about how somehow, without realizing it, he felt like he'd gotten married to San Francisco, because committing to Cary meant committing to San Francisco itself. Cary often said she'd never marry anyone because she was married to the city, the city being the only lover she was fully devoted to; everyone else was a sidepiece. As Sasha soliloquized, Walter's attention went fuzzy, noticing how the bamboo shadows in the garden were cast by a single light alone, the bulb that hung in the square paper lantern in Sasha and Cary's bedroom. Through a band of plate glass and a beveled window in the door, Walter wondered at the floating milky-green world Sasha had painted there. The garden grew straight through the glass, the banks of coral bells, the spikes of ginger lilies. The frosty absinthe sky, and the bright lantern shining like a sugar cube, leaking light through the windows. That spring, on a tour, he had seen the ladies' lounge at the Paramount that had inspired Sasha. He liked Sasha's version better: it was more layered and saturated, suffused with emerald undertones.

The Red Zinger was doing its sobering thing. Now Sasha was imagining the delights of other cities—bigger, busier cities—fashion hubs: Paris, London, Milan, New York . . . and Walter was trying to pay attention, though his body was clearly not attentive: he'd slumped down as much as the bench would allow, his mug askew on his thigh, his left tennie worrying the chipped edge of a paver.

"Don't you ever get jealous?" Walter blurted with a boozy urgency. "I mean—sorry!—I think it's only human to get a little jealous. Don't you think?"

"Sure, it's only human. Do you think I should be jealous of Kelly Calypso?"

It seemed he had moved into a grave, emotional phase of his return to sobriety, and he felt the need to confess something, he didn't know why exactly. "Cary kissed me." He covered his eyes with one hand. "Or, I guess, we kissed. Just once, tonight. In the bathroom at Marlena's. It was . . . weird."

Sasha sat up straighter, sipped his tea, and said nothing. When at length Walter removed his hand, there Sasha sat with an amused, perfectly enciphered smile.

"Just once?" asked Sasha. "Just tonight?"

"Uh-huh."

"Hmm. That's awfully slow. For Cary, I mean. Not you."

"Hold on a second." He sat bolt upright. "What's that supposed to mean?"

"Oh, come on, Wall. What with all the time you two spend together? *Working on your screenplay?* Going to the movies, all those afternoons, all those cocktail hours—and how much have you written? Twenty pages? I mean, please tell me *something else* has been going on."

"You mean, all this time you thought we were having an affair?"

"I thought it was *possible* . . ."

The implications of this were too wide-ranging for Walter to get his head around at the moment, but now he felt wide-awake. Sasha seemed not only undisturbed but tickled, even a bit pitying.

"You know Cary has something of a rep, don't you?" Sasha asked. "Usually she gets around. Girls *like* her. Boys too. But ever since she met you last fall, Cary the philanderer has been way more domesticated than usual. Like Barbara Stanwyck, pretending to know how to change a diaper. Meanwhile she's holding the baby upside down."

Walter padded the pockets of his jacket, then his pants, searching for a pack of cigarettes that wasn't there. He cleared his throat and finished his tea in one gulp.

Sasha, in the dark garden well past midnight, was suddenly talkative. By way of explaining how *not jealous* he was of Kelly Calypso or anyone else, Sasha began relating the history of his thinking about monogamy and

206 Christopher Tradowsky

jealousy, and how he realized at some point that you could corner jealousy, stem it, starve it, reason it away. Blow it out, easy as a blue pilot. He didn't say *blue pilot*, Sasha said *pilot*. But Walter was picturing a pilot burning blue, a tiny angel burning blue, then blown out, and a kitchen, like the one behind them, slowly filling with gas.

"You know, I'm not jealous of Cary fucking Kelly, but I have to say you seem a bit jealous yourself."

Walter prayed the bank of begonias behind them would swallow him whole.

"Sashenka, I can't believe I have to say this, but . . . if I were having an affair with Cary . . ." He stalled for a second over such an absurd proposition. ". . . I would have told you. I couldn't have kept that secret. No way. You two are, like, literally the two best friends I've ever had."

"Aw, we love you, too, darling, we do!"

"And anyway, it's ridiculous because Cary was only horsing around, as usual. She was test-driving her mustache. It's not like she's into me."

"Are you sure?" Sasha asked. "You're actually one of her types. Cute, mopey Eeyore, always listening to dream pop and reading rhymed poetry and watching French movies. Always needing to be drawn out of his shell, like a Cancer."

"Oh, thanks!"

"The *sign*, I mean, darling. I knew she had a crush on you when she said, *Walter raises petulance to an art form.*"

There it was: maybe Sasha *was* a bit jealous. A hairline fracture. A crack in his preternatural poise, which, of course, he wore beautifully. Like one of those Japanese raku bowls mended with gold.

"You know, when we're writing together, all we ever do is argue. Argue and drink. That's why we're not getting nowhere—oof, I mean, *getting nowhere fast.*"

"Oh, I know. Like Sam and Diane. For the record, she's the Ted Danson in that scenario. Which makes you the Shelley Long."

"I'm the *Shelley Long*? I think that's the meanest thing you've ever said to me."

"I have to sharpen my femme fatale claws if I'm going to play Lorna, don't I?" Sasha reached over and scratched the scruff of his neck softly, like he was Mona Lisa the cat.

"Mmm, true," Walter purred. "For a femme fatale, you're on the sweet side."

They sat still for a while without speaking. Walter shivered and rested his head on Sasha's shoulder, padded with soft terry cloth. Sasha put his arm around him.

"I'm sorry I called you Shelley Long."

"I'll never forgive you."

Walter was eyeing a cement gnome, very '70s, sun-bleached and paint-scabbed, squatting behind a hosta and piercing the garden's semitropical splendor with a kitschy wink.

"It's very late. We both have work in the morning," said Sasha. "You should stay here."

"I have to brush my teeth."

"We have a stash of clean toothbrushes."

Walter's head had slipped a bit, his ear on Sasha's chest; the tenor rasp of his friend's voice resonated through his robe.

"I think I can fit on the couch," said Walter.

"Cary's not coming home. There's room in the bed."

Minutes later, he felt a bittersweet rash of envy burning him up from within. They were brushing their teeth in the bathroom, Sasha green-googly-eyed in glasses, having taken out his contacts. Of all the things they had done together, this one felt almost unbearably intimate. He turned his back on Sasha for a moment, and there, drying on the curtain rod, was his shirt, branches full of songbirds, orange beaks chirping at him accusingly: *Wall, what are you doing?* Then, as they took turns spitting in the sink, he felt, *Oh, this is what it would be like to have a* real *boyfriend, a life partner, someone you couldn't hide—or hide anything—from.* Then they were in bed together, Sasha on the far side where a high bank of pillows formed steppes beneath the viridian dreamworld of the mural. Walter lay opposite, his head upon Cary's pillows. The lantern hanging from the ceiling was dimly lit; Sasha said he always slept better with a little light. They were tucked in under the gold-threaded quilt, the Klimt quilt that Walter, when he first saw it, thought Sasha must have stolen from Versailles; and if he was honest, he'd always wanted to feel what it was like under its velvety weight.

He closed his eyes. The room spun very slowly. "Sashenka? You guys were wonderful tonight, so amazing. Sorry—I forgot to tell you that."

"Thank you, darling, you did tell me." Sasha's voice was sleepy.

"I told you?"

"Yes, darling, about a dozen times, on the ride home from the bar."

Sasha drifted to sleep, but Walter was haunted by another thought: What if deep down Sasha *was* possessive of Cary, and jealous of Kelly, and maybe even jealous of *him?* And what if underneath it all Cary was possessive, too? What if his being there in bed with Sasha was some kind of play, some gambit on Sasha's part, in a lovers' game? And even though Sasha swore Cary wouldn't give a hoot about his sleeping in their bed, he fixed upon an imaginary melodrama. If Cary suddenly appeared, he wasn't convinced that she'd be thrilled to see him taking her place, lying like Lancelot in her bed, in her queer Camelot, with her gay Guinevere. Would she hit the roof in a rare show of hot temper? Would she cry, *I ought to chop your head off with a meat cleaver*, as she often joked to him, and mean it this time? Or would she shrug, strip to her skivvies, and crawl into bed between the two of them, exactly as Mona Lisa was sliding now, paws tough as little iron fists, moving across the quilt like a sultry bank of smoke?

Mona Lisa pressed into Walter's side and soothed him to sleep, only to rouse him again later by heavily turning on his chest before leaping to the floor. It must have been a couple hours later. A clock ticked somewhere out of sight. The room was cold, and by the frigid light outside, it was around four or five. He had slept fitfully, the inescapable clove scent of Cary's pomade on the pillow infusing his dreams. He stared at the jade palace floating in midair high on the wall above Sasha. For the first time he noticed little glassy portals inset into the swooping, hull-like city walls, more ocean liner than Emerald City. Then he turned on his side and looked at Sasha, who dreamed up skyborne cities, fast asleep on the pillow beside him. *Goddamn it* if he wasn't every bit as gorgeous as the first day he'd seen him, floating above the fray of that noisy diner downtown on a cloud of meringue. And here Walter was, a sham amid their glamour, an interloper in Cary's bed and Sasha's verdant Xanadu, having thought he knew what he wanted, or at least thinking that his wanting had its happy, mundane limits, but now being less and less sure, and only making himself more anxious and insomniac by finally confronting—in the end, was this the question?—*did he want to be Cary and get to kiss Sasha, or did he want to be Sasha and get to kiss Cary?*

If indeed that was the question.

The truth was he had no idea.

BRAINSTORMING with your FAVORITE STORMING BRAINS...
D.J. Reinhardt & Amanda Blueshoes

The CORCOVADO SUPPER CLUB
   is pleased to present
     the magnificent...
       the mysterious...
         the mesmerizing...
             MS. LORNA ZAFTIG!!!

[Introducing Sasha Stravinsky as

   LORNA ZAFTIG

Magician, Muse, and Femme Fatale!]

 Acting on an earlier tip,
DECLAN convinces MILO that they
 should stake out the Corcovado
  in search of VERA'S
              missing bandmates...

At the Corcovado:
  3 Villains share 1 table:

*ULLRICH DUXELLES
    proprietor
    stocky, stern bruiser
    Sydney Greenstreet type

*POLICE CHIEF PARNELL
    rotten cop in DUXELLES' pocket

*DR. JANUS PURZELBAUM
    mysterious, sveltely menacing,
    willowy creep a la Clifton Webb

*The Corcovado:
Rio de Janeiro themed, but
snow white--marble
            and alabaster
Must have:
*telephones on every table!
   (like Cabaret)
      (# by pineapple)

*magic show
   (like This Gun for Hire)

Who the hell is
DR. JANUS PURZELBAUM??
& What does he want??

He runs a Sanatorium:
"Consensus Laboratories,
   a subsidiary of
The Concern, LLC."
   (Unmistakable
former-Nazi Dr. vibes)

11 EXT. THE CORCOVADO SUPPER CLUB ON VAN NESS--JUST
BEFORE 10 P.M.
Sculpted plaster palms arc the entry. A crush of fancy
cars, valets to and fro. Shimmering haute monde emerging.

INT. THE CORCOVADO MAIN FLOOR
DECLAN and MILO are seated at a table for two. Brimming
cocktail stems: Cheers! The lavish interior is all
white. Alabaster palms double as torchieres. Light floods
from their fronds. Onstage: a swing orchestra. "Begin
the Beguine." Couples shuffle and turn. On the walls:
murals of Rio de Janeiro, a lagoon, cockatoos. Patrons
drink champagne, relish large plates of food. DECLAN
takes in the room. One table is raised up, with three
men enthroned. DECLAN recognizes Police Chief PARNELL.
Imperious chrome dome. He squints at the two others.

> DECLAN
> OK, buddy, let's take stock.
> Any of the band members look
> familiar? Anyone who backed Vera
> at the Vermilion?

> MILO
> [Scanning]
> No, not a one that I can tell.
> How odd! I was sure I'd recognize
> someone!

> DECLAN
> All right. How about the two fat
> cats sitting with Police Chief
> Parnell? One of them is Ulli
> Duxelles, I think.

MILO surveys the room and lands on PARNELL. The chief
is hobnobbing with ULLRICH DUXELLES, proprietor, and DR.
PURZELBAUM.

> MILO
> Yes, that mountain of a man is
> Duxelles, the owner.

> DECLAN
> Right, I figured. The big
> shot who's been buying every

                    restaurant in town. Culinary
                    robber baron.

                         MILO
                    Exactly. Word is he and Lorna
                    Zaftig are an item. Something
                    of a "La Belle et la Bete"
                    situation.

Suddenly: Big band fanfare. Dance floor clears. Alone on
the parquet, the white-tuxed EMCEE.

                         EMCEE
                    Ladies and gentlemen, the
                    Corcovado Supper Club is pleased
                    to introduce, once again, <u>the
                    magnificent, the mysterious, the
                    mesmerizing Lorna</u>!

More fanfare. LORNA ZAFTIG floats onto the parquet.
Platinum bombshell. Quicksilver gown, opera gloves. As she
sings, she performs magic, flirting with gents, performing
card tricks, pulling coins from behind their ears.

                         LORNA
                    [Sings. Intro slow and heartfelt.]
               Most men love a magic show
               They're just like little boys,
               They watch with a fanatic glow
               So full of simple joys,
               The end is always tragic though
               When you take away their toys.
               We can play at cooing, but I won't play house,
               You can woo your wooing, but I won't be your spouse,
               It puts me in an awkward position,
               Because I'm not that kind of magician...

Tempo ramps up. LORNA taps along. She handcuffs herself,
then slips the cuffs. Ducks behind one palm tree and pops
out from behind another.

                         LORNA
               I'm a genie, I can pick a lock
               Like Houdini, in a silky frock,
               Necromancy is my stock and trade
               Nothing fancy, but the bills are paid,
               And it's hardly nuclear fission!

```
          I'll pull a shilling from behind your ear,
          Or if you're willing, we can disappear,
          All your wishes are at my command,
          But I won't do the dishes
          Or wear a wedding band,
          Because I'm not that kind of magician!
```

LORNA works the room, flirting. Zeros in on MILO and
DECLAN. She and DECLAN lock eyes. She reaches into the
top hat, pulls out a trophy hen. Puts it back, pulls out
a rabbit. Puts it back, pulls out a turkey feather boa.
Wraps it around DECLAN. DECLAN is immediately smitten. He
breathes in the scent from the boa.

                         MILO
               Like that? Jasmine and
               bergamot... it's <u>Soir de Paris</u>.
               All the rage in Tinseltown.
               Esther Williams swims in it.

LORNA flies across the dance floor, kicks as high as the
slit in her gown will let her. She takes a turn on the
marimba. White gloves flap like cockatiels. DECLAN can't
take his eyes off her.

                         LORNA
          I'll pull a bunny from an old chapeau
          It may be funny, but it brings me dough...
          I'm very limber, on a Ouija board
          Or a marimba, I can strike a chord
          And play you like a musician...
          Try and tame me, but I won't be swayed
          Try and play me, but I can't be played
          Talk of lovin', and you're on your own
          `Cause I can't use an oven,
          And I won't make a home,
          Because I'm not that kind of magician!
```
```

Meshes of the Afternoon

"THAT WAS INCREDIBLE," SAID WALTER. "Can we watch it again? Like, right now?"

"Of course, of course," said Lawrence. "I always think Deren's films don't begin to open up until the third or fourth viewing."

They rewound and began again. *Maya falls asleep in her chintz chair, and the dream starts again, many times over, a succession of Mayas stride up a curved concrete drive, palm-lined, chasing a shadow figure she can never catch. Hooded, spindly, a mirror for a face. The figure moves slowly, draped in black, carrying a large hibiscus flower of white crepe.*

Engrossed in the film, Walter sat beside Larry on the love seat. They watched the small yellow television on a wheeled cart in the corner. Beside it, between muslin columns, late-afternoon light receded through the windows.

Cary had taken over Lawrence's kitchenette and was humming and rummaging around. She had concocted an elaborate dinner menu, and her work was well underway. She'd promised many times to cook for Lawrence; at last the night had come. They were barred from the kitchen until further notice. Walter was waiting for Cary to conscript him to chop onions or mushrooms or something, but so far she'd refused help. Larry, for his part, had promised to finally share a few of his short films with them. They planned a viewing after dinner. He had only a handful of completed films available—that is, in decent 16mm prints he was willing to show.

To pass the time Walter and Larry were drinking coffee and watching

VHS tapes. Larry was exposing Walter to some of his favorite experimental films. The dreaming woman sleeping in an armchair on-screen was Maya Deren, a filmmaker Walter knew by name but whose films he'd never seen— not even available for rent. They were watching what Lawrence called his *passable* bootleg of *Meshes of the Afternoon*. The worn condition of the tape and the fuzzily radiant, pilled picture quality of the TV were far from perfect, yet Walter was utterly absorbed in the interlocking spirals of Deren's parallel world.

Maya walks to the window, you can tell from her gait she's a dancer. Her brown curls are teased out and wild—she's beautiful in a way Hollywood cannot tame. She opens her mouth and pulls a key from her tongue, and as she does so a second Maya enters through the locked door.

"That shot is *so incredible*," said Walter. "I mean, eat your heart out David Lynch."

"Nineteen forty-three," said Lawrence. "People always go on about sur-realism, saying how *bizarre* and *obscure* it is, whereas what always strikes me is how true to life it is—this film especially. It's full of perfectly relatable human emotions. People just don't know what to do with *dread*."

Walter nodded excitedly. "Did you know her?"

"No, I'm afraid I didn't see any of her films until after she died, quite young. But I don't exaggerate when I say this film changed my life."

The mirror-faced shadow once again places the crepe flower upon Maya's pillow.

"Later Deren became obsessed with Haitian dancing and ritual, and voodoo. She was trying to complete a film about Haiti when she died. Rumor has it she was killed by a voodoo curse after crossing a powerful spirit." Lawrence seemed almost delighted by the idea. Walter frowned. There was something tabloid-lurid about the story, yet as they drifted down the stream of enigmatic intercuts ending in the filmmaker presaging her own death, it made a kind of sense.

The film clocked in at fourteen minutes, its pace both languid and brisk, expansive and watchwork tight. As Lawrence searched the credenza for a compilation of Dada and surrealist shorts, Walter ducked into the kitchenette to get them more coffee and see if Cary wanted help yet. She was squatting, eyeing the open oven with suspicion. The stovetop was miniaturized to fit the kitchen, and the oven was accordingly small.

"I think it'll work," said Cary. Her hair was slicked back and her sleeves rolled. She had borrowed a flouncy rickrack-trimmed apron from Lawrence that somehow made her look more butch. "The roasting pan we brought will just fit."

"Oh, thank god," said Walter, relieved that the two baskets and four bags of groceries and utensils they had hauled to Lawrence's on the bus were so far proving sufficient.

A subtle tension had arisen between Walter and Cary since the night of Bombolone's concert at Marlena's two weeks before. As Sasha predicted, Cary hadn't batted an eyelash when she heard that Walter had stayed over in their bed. Walter never asked about her night with Kelly, and Cary didn't offer any information on that front. Anything that might have transpired between them in the bathroom at Marlena's never came up, so Walter figured he was right to dismiss it as a bit of drunken flirting, something queers did compulsively all the time. And ever since he'd seen less of Cary. Robert, who owned Bob's Your Uncle, was in Australia for a month visiting family and had left Cary to mind the card store. She'd closed up every night that week. But when Walter visited her at the store to help her kill time behind the counter, she'd been distant and terse. He began to wonder if Kelly had told her something that set her on edge, though he couldn't remember much of what he'd said to Kelly about Cary that night, except that she was a goofy, nerdy dorkasaurus. Which he would have said to her face, and she'd have thrown it right back at him.

Cary was busy washing a chef's knife, massaging the blade with her thumb to unstick a blot of minced garlic. "When the time comes, I'll need help stirring the risotto."

He suppressed a sigh. As he knew from prior dinner parties, the constant attention risotto required verged on indentured servitude.

"Lawrence says he has another table we can use," Cary went on, "and he said he'll need help setting up the projector. You can help with that."

"Dinner at seven thirty?"

"Yeah—I told Sasha to come at six thirty for cocktails. What time did you tell Jeff?"

"Same. He's always punctual."

He'd already assured Cary of this—it was another sore spot between them. Cary had been cagey when Walter asked if he could invite Jeff to dinner at Lawrence's; Jeff had yet to meet Larry. She said OK, grudgingly, and after some needling on Walter's part she admitted she thought Jeff was *boring* and had *no personality*. Then she backpedaled, insisting that *no, no*, she liked Jeff, and at least he was a good guy and smart, and not an idiot like Eliot.

In the end Walter stirred the mushroom risotto for an entire hour, until Cary deemed it creamy enough. Lawrence napped before emerging from his room dressed for dinner in a cream cable-knit vest and a loose, elegant linen jacket, cuffs rolled. Cary was delighted when she saw him and declared he looked like Rock Hudson heading to the tennis club, which he absolutely did, but Walter gasped at the mention of the first high-profile AIDS death, and Cary looked taken aback. Her smile broke and she stood blinking, ashamed and at a loss for words.

Before she could apologize, Lawrence smiled, accepting the compliment, saying, "You are sweet. You know, I used to get that every once in a while, but not for years now! Of course, Rock was *much* hunkier than me—those shoulders!"

Everyone convened punctually at 6:30. Lawrence mixed cosmopolitans, and Cary served little puff pastry canapés with different fillings; the caramelized leeks and Brie were a hit. Lawrence proposed a toast to new friends (raising his glass to Jeff) and old (turning to Jabez), and then he thrilled Walter and Cary by adding, ". . . and to new projects—a toast to *Midnight at the Cinema Palace!*"

"They let you read it?" asked Sasha, as everyone drank.

"Yeah, I heard no one gets to read it!" said Jeff.

"Well, that's simply because we're still on the first draft and it's only half done," Cary explained, "and we're hoping Lawrence, with all his experience, can help us with it."

"It's wonderful," said Lawrence. "I haven't acted in years, but the character of Milo is delicious—simply delicious. Mind you, this is far from my first rodeo. I can tell when I am being roped into something, but willingly, and with very fine bullion rope, I should say." He beamed at Cary and Walter.

The evening felt eventful, one of those gatherings where the atmosphere is electric with the sense of something happily advancing and, high up, some unseen stars aligning and promising lucky days in store. They drank and chatted as Cary put the finishing touches on dinner. Everyone had dressed for the evening except Jeff, who was dressed up in his way, in a black cotton sweater and black jeans, and with a crisp, fresh buzz cut. Jeff had shown up without his glasses, which surprised Walter; he did a double take when he appeared in the living room. Without his Buddy Holly frames Jeff seemed to have lost some character, his eyes looked smaller, his cheeks flatter, his gaze less glassy and expressive, slightly hardened.

Sasha sat beside Jabez on the love seat; they hadn't met before and hit it off at once, when Sasha asked about the beautiful white embroidered top Jabez was wearing. He said he had bought it from a Hausa embroiderer on a trip back to his childhood home, in Nigeria. It was the first time Walter had realized that Jabez's accent—more pronounced than Larry's, though he wasn't nearly as talkative—was actually a British-Nigerian accent. When the two conversed, Jabez brought out the British slant in Lawrence's speech.

When dinner was almost ready, Lawrence brought up something he had mentioned before—something tantalizing. Despite his attempts to alienate all his Hollywood friends, and despite the ravages of the epidemic on the industry, he did still have one producer friend who was very active in Hollywood. He always visited Benny and his partner in Brentwood at Thanksgiving, a tradition he hadn't missed for fifteen years that had become even more sacrosanct since Roland's death.

"It's gorgeous down there," said Jabez, "they're in a canyon. They have a lap pool. Salt water. Feels like you're in Palm Springs!"

"*Cooler* than Palm Springs," said Lawrence ambivalently. He went on to describe some of his history with Benny, whose full name was Ben Venable, and though it was the story of a long, warm friendship, Lawrence never spoke of his time in Hollywood without flagging, at every turn, his disgust with the whole place. Even so, he made them a generous proposition: he would introduce Walter and Cary to Benny, provided they could complete the screenplay and get it into tip-top shape first. Plenty of time before Thanksgiving. Larry was brutally honest as he warned them: there are never any guarantees in Hollywood. You can work as hard as possible for years on end, giving your all, and it's still more than likely that you'll see your dreams dashed, disassembled, and sold for parts; that you'll be forced to smile as they're warped into something grotesque, unrecognizable, and if you're lucky, unable to be traced back to you.

Lawrence turned gloomy for a moment before Jabez interrupted him with a cajoling laugh. "You always talk as if you're the innocent, wronged party, Larry, but perhaps mention one or two of the bridges you've burned—willfully, I should say."

"Ah, yes, my anarchist filmmaker phase . . ."

"Tell them about—what was that one called? The one that blew up?" said Jabez, laughing through his downturned smile.

"If you insist." Lawrence sighed. "How to explain it? In the seventies I was deep into my *concrete* filmmaking experiments—you know, strictly nonobjective films, no narrative whatsoever. Films *about* vision. And I was taken with the idea of a film that could be seen only once and then would self-destruct. I had a bit of an obsession with a Florentine trecento painter called Taddeo Gaddi who had nearly blinded himself by staring at a solar eclipse, because he wanted to study its unearthly light—perfectly reasonable, I might add. So the film I made, called *Solar Flare*, was a single reel that was all overexposed shots of sunrays and bonfires and coronas—you get the idea—flaring things. Near the very end of each print I put a tiny grommet, hammered it right into the celluloid. It was too small for a projectionist to notice, but I knew it would catch in a projector. In a way, it worked like a charm: the prints caught, melted, then burned up . . . and that's why I have no copies left!"

"And then?" Jabez prompted, eyebrows high. "It also got you banned . . ."

"Well, that was because of Jonas. I hadn't told Roland—my partner and producer, that is—I hadn't yet told him what I'd done with the grommets, and he sent a print of *Solar Flare* to Jonas Mekas, the maven of underground film in New York City, to show in a festival. Well, *of course* Jonas took it for a test-drive at home—it caught fire and blew up his favorite projector, damned near burned down his apartment; so he sent us a bill for the projector and a thorough housecleaning, and a note saying, in no uncertain terms, *you'll never work in this town again!* And he was right, as far as New York was concerned. Roland was furious with me, poor darling. I can hardly blame him, can I?" Larry smiled a little wistfully as he sipped his cosmopolitan.

Following Cary's directions, they moved the party out onto the wide, flat roof of the Archers, where it was a beautiful evening, overcast but temperate and surprisingly clear of fog. The tar-and-gravel rooftop still radiated warmth it had absorbed from the sunny afternoon. To the west, a taller apartment building abutted the Archers, and a large, windowless white wall masked what they might have seen of the sunset. But the building was a corner lot, affording a panorama that swept from downtown over SoMa to Civic Center. To the north, stucco facades scaled Nob Hill like risers. As they ate, the nearest towers caught facets of the sunset, a little bright brass amid the silver. The traffic below, the diesel dragon's roar of megabuses on Geary, and the smell of noodles frying in a Thai place across the street completed the urban ambience. Cary and Walter had carried out two small tables and set them as one large one, with a thick white cloth, cotton napkins, stemware, and candles that Cary would relight regularly, as they blew out in the slightest breeze.

Walter poured the wine. Everyone declared how lovely it all was: the table, the company, the cityscape. Over a prickly endive salad with nectarines, toasted hazelnuts, and goat cheese, their conversations diverged and clipped along. Across from Walter, Jabez was telling Sasha all about the SF Opera, where he'd been working in the box office for a few years and was able to see any opera he wanted almost whenever he wanted.

Larry turned to Walter. "You know, as unpopular as *Solar Flare* was, believe it or not, people liked the sequel even less. Ha ha—I made a second version, a follow-up called *Chromosphere*. Very similar in terms of imagery, but this time, when I showed it, I turned the projector toward the audience; it was a film meant to be projected *onto* the audience, so that no one could see the whole picture, merely irregular flashes—strobes directly to the retina. People hated it!"

"It sounds . . ." Walter searched for the word.

"Aggressive? Annoying? Uncomfortable, to say the least! People accused me of trying to blind them. Which I suppose I was, in a way. But only temporarily!"

"Fabulous!" Cary interrupted. "I think it sounds fabulous!"

Lawrence smiled down the table at her.

"Jeff and I were just talking about blindness," said Cary. "Or actually, that blindness will soon be a thing of the past. Did you guys know that Jeff now has bionic eyes?"

"I don't have *bionic eyes!*" Jeff protested.

"*But you do, Blanche, you do!* He submitted to this *experimental therapy* where they cut his eyes with *lasers*, and now he has twenty-twenty vision. Isn't that amazing? I mean, terrifying, but glorious!"

Everyone expressed their amazement, verging on disbelief.

"I wondered what happened to your glasses," said Walter.

"That sounds incredible," said Sasha. "What I wouldn't give to never wear contacts again."

"I've worn glasses since *first grade*," said Jeff. "I feel like I have a new face!"

"Bionic eyes?" Lawrence laughed. "Please, no! Damned if I haven't seen too much already. Besides, we already have bionic eyes. What do you think cameras are?"

Walter smiled; he could have kissed Larry for saying this. But then the conversation deteriorated into a bloodless but still gruesome discussion of laser surgery. Walter was more than happy to retreat with Cary to the kitchen. They plated the risotto, sprinkling each serving with exotic, twiggy-looking mushrooms and arranging portions of lacquered, magazine-ready roast chicken.

As they were tucking into the main course, Lawrence asked Walter about their screenplay, the first half of which he'd read that week.

"Your screenplay is so interesting . . ."

Walter held his breath. Larry never used generic words like *interesting*.

". . . but one thing I cannot figure out is how you kids got so nostalgic for a time and place you've never seen."

"We've seen it in the movies," said Walter, and winced at having said something so obvious.

"Don't get me wrong, of course I love old Hollywood—and all the things you're alluding to in your script. But I've always been deeply suspicious of *nostalgia*. Even a little nostalgia, I think, can be a dangerous thing."

"Really? *Dangerous?*"

"Why look backward?" Lawrence pressed him. "Why long for a lost world, especially one that was so vicious, so exclusionary? Oh, Wall, don't look so put out, and don't you dare give me some nonsense about a 'more elegant time.' Let me tell you: elegance is ruthless. And when it's compulsory, when it's enforced, it's brutal."

"Larry, are you frightening Walter?" Jabez interrupted. He smiled and refilled Lawrence's wineglass. "This risotto is unbelievably good. Tell us, Walter, what makes it so good? I'll bet you know all of Cary's secrets."

"I don't know half of Cary's secrets," said Walter. "Better ask Sasha."

"The secret is all in the stirring," said Sasha. "And that's Walter's job. Walter's the secret stirrer, aren't you?" Sasha winked across the table. The candle between them nearly blew out; it caught again. Jabez laughed, and he and Sasha resumed their opera talk, while Walter and Larry sat for a moment in silence.

"I'm sorry, have I put you out?" Lawrence asked.

"What's that?"

"Brought you down, I mean. By insisting you're too young to be so nostalgic."

Walter shook his head, unsure what to say. With his tongue he had been worrying a bit of sweet nectarine skin from a gap where it had lodged beside his eyetooth. He noticed Lawrence was eating very little of his meal.

He wondered if he and Cary had misunderstood Lawrence all along. He certainly had pegged him wrong: when they first met, he thought Larry was frivolous. Back then, they would stand in his doorway and talk about literally nothing for fifteen, twenty minutes. But it takes two to have an empty conversation, and now Walter wondered if he'd been the one talking about nothing, because as it turned out Lawrence loved to talk about *so much*.

"The thing is, you asked," said Larry. "You wanted to know about my films, and the main thing you should know is that my films are *empirical*, they are about capturing what I can: the effects of *this* world, *this* present—do you know what I mean?" He fitfully indicated the city around them with his knife and fork. "They're not about some lost paradise, some crumbling Arcadia, or some—I don't know—campy dreamscape, they're about *this world*, which makes itself so terribly hard to love."

As if to belie Lawrence's assertion, the loveliness of the skyline suddenly magnified: the buildings around them began to shine from within, yellow gold in the window frames; the streets glowed warm—practically humming with light. Streetlights, colored neon, marquees snapped on invitingly. A deco tower with a diadem of floodlights sparkled in the middle distance.

"I understand," said Walter. But he didn't, really. Scanning the cityscape, he was stuck on one word; he didn't understand how a film could be *empirical*.

"We'd never thought to have a dinner party on Sarcoma Beach!" said Lawrence. "Parties, yes, of course, we had plenty back in the day, but we never thought to have a proper dinner out here before—I don't know why!"

"Sarcoma Beach?"

"Oh," said Larry, "that's what Roland called it. Some of his gallows humor. He was so naughty. He loved to sunbathe out here and smoke—can you imagine? I used to say, it was like he couldn't get cancer fast enough."

"Sarcoma as in . . ."

"KS, of course, Kaposi sarcoma, those purple—oh, you've seen them." Larry glanced at his bare wrists, astonished, as if he'd lost his watch. "Fortunately, I don't have any to show you! Those horrible purple contusions—large—you've seen them."

Walter nodded. *Of course he had*. And now he was embarrassed that he hadn't remembered the name of the intense-looking lesions he'd seen afflicting so many of Open Hand's clients.

"Oh dear, I am being dreary tonight, aren't I?" said Larry, tilling a bank of risotto with his fork. "The food is absolutely delicious, by the way!" He hadn't touched his roast chicken, which Walter thought was starting to look forlorn.

"You must miss Roland terribly," said Walter.

"I do. Of course I do." Larry looked at Walter, brown eyes unblinking.

"After nearly twenty years—the pain of losing him was so intense as to be hallucinatory, like a drug. Ecstatic even, at times. I don't expect you'd understand that."

Dessert was cabernet-poached pears, walnuts, Moscato, and a large cheese board, because, following one of Cary's favorite aphorisms, *a dinner which ends without cheese is like a beautiful woman with only one eye.* After his conversation with Larry, Roland's ghost haunted Walter for the rest of the evening. There was no dishwasher—he and Sasha washed the dishes by hand—and the whole time Walter thought of Roland, cramped in the tiny kitchenette, cooking and cleaning, making a home and a life. Meanwhile, Cary had the idea that since the night was so beautiful, they should watch Larry's films outside, projected onto the white cement wall of the neighboring building. Lawrence agreed to try it; though the wall was somewhat rough, he thought the texture might add something to the films. So Cary and Jeff helped reposition the tables and carry the projector out as Jabez hunted for extension cords.

They didn't watch movies for long, forty minutes or so. Larry was visibly tired after a long afternoon and evening. The films were short; most lasted five minutes, seven at the longest. Jabez played projectionist, projecting the films as large as he could—about a story tall above them—and little pits and furrows in the cement afflicted the picture in a way Larry thought added a *dimension*; he didn't say more than that, except to make a pun about true *concrete* filmmaking.

The films were vigilantly abstract—mostly shots of architecture, interiors and exteriors, some natural settings—but primarily registering effects of light: reflections, shadow plays, sunbursts; supernovas in grayscale or trippy Kodachrome auras in the color films. As they watched, Walter wondered what *empirical* might mean to Larry and noticed the relentless movement of the camera, probing and piercing, moving *through* and *under* and *behind* whatever it encountered, and finally breaking through, registering things the naked eye could never see. The scale kept shifting, from landscape-vast to microscopically small—the splitting of a cell—in one jump. The world's own velocity no longer mattered: wisteria bloomed in one downward splash, like cliff divers; the full moon popped like a volleyball; lightning probed like a bright, crooked cane. Occasionally a human figure or two would flit through the frame, and Walter's mind would make the leap: *Ah! A narrative.* As if it were a divine rule: Where there's a person, there's a story. And where there're two people—even just one to act and one to watch—there's *definitely* a story. Roland began to haunt the films, sometimes nude and sometimes clothed, smiling like a lover or glowering like an unwilling subject; but even he was treated by the camera as an impediment to vision, something to get over or under or behind, to the real content of the barely visible, the underexposed, the blazing trace, the afterimage.

The last film Lawrence showed was the most colorful. The title card, in Larry's handwritten script, said: *What Roland Saw.* San Francisco played a starring role. The color film stock was bleary at the edges, as if Larry had oiled the lens. Saturated smears framed crisp, shifting imagery: shots of North Beach, Coit Tower. Sunshine over the Pacific's galvanic blue; the Sutro Baths like a Roman ruin; the monumental origami of St. Mary's stiff white wimple. An explosion of bougainvillea and trumpet vine. There were loose threads of dialogue, the tangle of two men's voices saying, *There?—Where, where?— You mean there—No, higher up! Got it?—Think so.* There were shots of the Archers: the facade, the heavy mahogany desk in the lobby. What Walter at first took for beach sand he recognized as the tan carpet in the penthouse. An anomalous shot caught Lawrence, smiling, midafternoon on Sarcoma Beach. The frame blurred, darkened, and cinched to a tunnel. A medicine cabinet flashed, a muslin drape waved, and the rest was dark.

The group sat in fog-cooled silence, the city's restless din rising from below, as Jabez rewound the film and returned it to the canister.

"Tell us about that last one," said Cary.

"Well, it was a collaboration," said Lawrence. "As always, Roland was very game. It was near the end, when he was going blind. His eyesight would fluctuate, going in and out with his fevers. But sometimes it would return, in his left eye only, and he'd gasp—suddenly able to see something with utter vividness—almost always very bright, colorful things. So I said, *Let's carry the camera around with us, and when you see something, let me know. I'll try to capture it.* He enjoyed the project. One of our last outings was going to see it included in a program at SFMOMA. But, of course, he couldn't see a thing by then. Almost nothing, by the end."

The group sat stunned, and before any of them could respond, Larry stood, wrapped himself in a lavender shawl, and said, "It's downright cold! Shall we head inside?"

Jeff headed off to crawl the SoMa bars, and Walter, Cary, and Sasha shared a cab back to the Castro.

"Oh god," said Cary, "was Larry trying to kill us with that last film? When he told us what it was, I felt like he'd kicked me in the gut—and I knew the background, I knew that Roland had gone blind. Even I wasn't prepared for *that*."

"I can't—I'm not sure I can talk about it." Sasha shook his head.

"Bad enough that I almost ruined the evening before it started," said Cary. "Oh, Sashenka, you weren't there yet, but I told Lawrence he looked like *Rock Hudson*. What an idiot! Walter, you should have stopped me! Choked me with a canapé or something."

"How was I supposed to read your mind? Anyway, he took it as a compliment. He didn't seem upset by it, really."

Cary went on to assess the evening as a whole, feeling it had been, for the most part, a success, and went into critiques of her dishes. She wished she'd done something more spectacular for dessert, something baked, richer, maybe a tarte tatin. The cab flew down Van Ness toward Market. The high-serious colonnades of city hall loomed on their left, and as they passed the opera house, Sasha had some news. He was excited because Jabez said they were hiring in the costume shop at the opera. He'd encouraged Sasha to apply, given his construction skills. He would put in a good word for him. The pay would almost certainly be better, and what a relief it would be for Sasha to get out of that airless storeroom and never be beholden to Gavin again. Sasha, clearly taken with Jabez, chatted on about him and what he'd learned of Jabez's early life in Lagos and London.

Walter was preoccupied. He was thinking about a perplexing exchange he'd had with Larry when they were alone that afternoon, watching videos.

"Where's Basilisk?" Walter had asked, looking around. He was extremely wary of Lawrence's cat, a ruthless master of the sneak attack.

"What's that?" asked Larry, trying to locate Stan Brakhage in a stack of VHS tapes.

"Your cat, I mean. Basilisk? Where is he?"

"Oh, darling." Lawrence sounded pitying. "We don't have a cat! We haven't had a cat for a while. We did once, yes—that's right, Basilisk was his name. World-class misanthrope. We had to get rid of him after a point, when Roland was so sick. PWAs can't have cats around—encephalitis in their scat. You must know—you must have heard about that!"

Walter said nothing. He couldn't correct Larry without sounding rude and callous, but it struck him as deeply strange. He had seen Basilisk, not often, but several times during visits with Larry. The cat was a monster: hugely heavy, stealthy, and aggressive. Hard to forget. And now, in the dark cab as it raced up Market Street, Walter stared at the ball of his right thumb, searching for two divots that had been there once, two neat pink marks that had taken over a week to heal from Basilisk's snakelike bite.

A CRANIAL CYCLONE WITH YOURFAVORITE CEREBRALSTORMCHASERS
Cary Simmering and Walter Menuhin (the switcheroo!)

DECLAN DANNER is immediately smitten
the moment he lays eyes on LORNA ZAFTIG
& can you blame him?? She's a bombshell!!!

DECLAN sneaks backstage at the Corcovado
      after LORNA'S magic show.
Outside her dressing room, he's bounced
   by 2 of DUXELLES' goons.

Good film-themed names
for goons & henchmen:

In the back alley, the EMCEE bums
a cigarette from DECLAN & gives him a tip:
LORNA works at Playland most afternoons,
         telling fortunes...

FOLEY   GAFFER
 GRIP   BOOM
 GAUGE   KLIEG
   DUTCH ANGLE
MORTON 'MORTY' TEMP

[Scene between LORNA and DUXELLES in her
dressing room. Jealous & possessive, he
berates her for flirting with other men.
LORNA: 'That's what you hired me for!']

[DECLAN doesn't
 know this yet but:
   There are
 Twin Purzelbaums.
  dunn dunn dunnnn!!
 TWIN PURZELBAUMS??

         MEANWHILE, DOWN AT THE
      DERELICT SILVER CITY PALACE:

   Alone, in near total darkness, a mysterious figure
performs a midnight organ concert on the Mighty Wurlitzer.
   So loud the entire Palace begins to S H A K E!
     The mystery organist is EARNEST PURZELBAUM.

   He is interrupted by his identical twin brother, JANUS.
     EARNEST: "I got it working! Isn't it glorious!?"
     JANUS tells him: "Knock it off! Get back to work!"
   After all: The Palace is doomed. "The Concern doesn't
   want any attention drawn to your activities here..."

14 EXT. PLAYLAND--EVENING

Sunset smothered by fog. As DECLAN DANNER stalks the
midway, strings of lights flash on overhead. Carousel
music, oompah-pah waltz. In the distance Laffing Sal
cackles. At the far end of the park, between the tall
turbines of the Ferris wheel and windmill: a round
canvas tent. The sign: "FORTUNES BY MISS LORNA, THE
PLAYLAND ORACLE." Diagrammed palm. Queen of hearts.
GAFFER and KLIEG smoke by the tent. DECLAN enters to find
LORNA ZAFTIG at a table. She's shuffling cards. Tarnished
twilight. Incense curls. Their eyes lock in recognition.

                    DECLAN
          Pardon me, miss, I'm searching
          for the Playland Oracle.

                    LORNA
               [smiling cautiously]
          You found her. Please have a
          seat. Make yourself comfortable.

DECLAN sits. She hands him the tarot.

                    LORNA (cont'd)
          Shuffle these for me. How can I
          help you?

                    DECLAN
               [shuffling]
          I hope you can help me, miss. My
          name's Danner. Declan Danner.

LORNA nods, not indifferent.

                    DECLAN (cont'd)
          I hear you're what they call a
          "necromancer."

                    LORNA
          Yes...

                    DECLAN
          Meaning you can communicate with
          the dead?

                    LORNA
        Among other talents. Is there
        someone you're hoping to contact?
        Someone dear and departed?

                    DECLAN
        Sure...in a way. I wonder if, with
        your insight, you can tell if
        someone is dead.

                    LORNA
        You don't know if your loved one
        is dead or not?

                    DECLAN
        I don't know that she's dead. I
        only know she's gone.

                    LORNA
        Curious, Mr. Danner.

LORNA takes the cards from him. Lays five on the table.
Cruciform. In the center: the Fool. Blind dumb cluck.
About to walk off a cliff.

                    LORNA
        What is the name of your loved one?

                    DECLAN
        I wouldn't exactly call her...
        Vera. Vera is her name. Or
        was. Maybe you knew her? Local
        luminary. Vera Svanire.

LORNA holds her breath. Smile deadens. She turns her
head and DECLAN matches her glance. Shadows of GAFFER
and KLIEG project onto the tent. Crisp, menacing shadow
play. DECLAN bristles. LORNA shudders, a trapped thing.
She ponders the tarot cards. Puzzled, she examines
DECLAN'S face.

                    LORNA
        You didn't know her. Be straight
        with me. You have no recollection
        of Vera Svanire whatsoever, do you?

                    DECLAN
          Is that what the cards tell you?

                    LORNA
          Your poker face gave it away.
          What are you really after, Mr.
          Danner?

                    DECLAN
          I may not remember her myself,
          but my buddy Blankenship sure
          does. Tabloids do, too. All you
          gotta do is look up: she left a
          comet trail. No one disappears
          like she did.

                    LORNA
               [agitated]
          So, you know someone who
          remembers Vera? I mean, someone
          who is sure she's gone missing?

                    DECLAN
          Sure do. Is that so strange?

                    LORNA
               [whispering]
          It shouldn't be, but it is,
          stranger and stranger. Like so
          many others from the SoMa crowd,
          she's disappeared, and no one
          seems to have noticed. It's like
          everyone's in denial or suffering
          mass amnesia...

                    DECLAN
          So, you've been on Vera's trail, too?

The canvas wags. LORNA stiffens. Shadows of GAFFER and
KLIEG threaten. She lifts one card. Queen of Cups. Throne
of ocean.

                    LORNA
          Vera's one of many, Mr. Danner.
          I'm desperate to find my brother,
          Lionel. Maybe you knew him?

                    Lionel Zaftig. He played upright
                    bass in Vera's band. He's been
                    missing for six months... since
                    the raid on the Vermilion Room.

                              DECLAN
                    Funny how all roads lead back
                    to the Vermilion. Were you there
                    that night, the night of the
                    raid?

LORNA raises one hand: silence. With a nod, she indicates
the goons' shadows bending toward the entrance. LORNA
takes a pen. Scrawls something on one of the cards.

                              LORNA
                    Mr. Danner, I'm afraid our time
                    is up...and...you'd better take
                    the back exit...

LORNA shows DECLAN a flap where he can escape. He gives
her a bill and a hat tip. She presses a tarot card into
his hand.

                              LORNA
                    Be careful out there, Mr. Danner.
                    There are wild buffaloes in the
                    park, you know.

                              DECLAN
                    You be careful, too, Miss Zaftig.
                    The wild ones are less dangerous
                    than the ones in suits, I'd say.

DECLAN flees into the fog and cedars. Passes under
windmills. Beside a streetlamp, he stops to examine the
card she gave him. Fool on a cliff. Written in the sky:
"The Sheraton Palace. 4:00 p.m. this Tuesday. Bring Milo."

Shadows and Fog

CARY AND WALTER WERE ARGUING about Woody Allen again. This time Cary had
started it by whistling "Alabama Song" while they were waiting for the 33 on
Eighteenth Street. It was a Saturday night, chilly and intensely foggy. Cary
was in a funny, upbeat mood and started singing:

> *For ve must find ʒe next visky bar*
> *For if ve don't find ʒe next visky bar*
> *I tell you ve must die, I tell you ve must die . . .*

Walter told a story about how, after seeing *Shadows and Fog*, a strange
woman in the lobby asked him if he had heard *that weird version of a Doors
song* play in the movie. Then Cary annoyed Walter by insisting that, *no*, that
didn't make the woman a dummy, because most Americans know who the
Doors are but have no idea who Kurt Weill is. An old argument reignited
when he declared that *Shadows and Fog* was *so disappointing*—one of Allen's
least inspired—and called it *an empty exercise in style*.

When the bus arrived they took the argument on board with them. They
were on their way to a birthday party Nick was throwing for himself. He
lived somewhere high up the hillside in Twin Peaks—Cary knew how to
find the place, she swore—in something called an *efficiency*, a glass-faced cell
between two concrete slabs, with a stunning view of the city that Cary said

had to be seen to be believed. Sasha, meanwhile, was sick in bed with a migraine or allergies, Cary hadn't specified. So the two met for tacos at Zapata, and then they were off to find the party, Cary toting a bottle of Glenlivet in a beribboned box for Nick and singing about whisky.

Walter marveled at the wonderful thickness of the fog outside the windows, any thicker and they wouldn't be able to see across the street. The bus wobbled and rattled in the back end even more than was customary. They were every bit as settled in their argument as they were in the narrow, molded plastic seats. The argument was never about Allen's early films, which, with a couple exceptions, they both worshipped. It was about where the decline began and whether Allen still had a good movie in him, which Cary insisted he did. Cary had maintained, until recent years, an almost unconditional love for Woody, idol to nebbishes everywhere, without whom, she declared, she might have no sense of humor. Walter thought he must be a megalomaniac, always casting himself as the romantic lead opposite younger and younger love interests, who were somehow spellbound by his sputtered, recycled jokes. He must have thoroughly bought into the idea of his own genius, Walter griped. Cary didn't have a problem with that at all.

The 33 scaled the steepest part of Eighteenth Street and turned left onto Market. They were coming up on the diciest moment of a route Walter knew well: the bus needed to make a horseshoe turn from Market onto Clayton, a narrow side street heading the opposite direction. The turn had to be expertly navigated; if the bus went only a foot or two off course, it would pull from the wires and stall in the middle of the intersection. This happened about a tenth of the time, and it happened now. Turning too fast, the bus skidded, the contraption snapping off the circuit with a rain of sparks. Juice cut, lights out, they careened several yards before stopping dead. The driver rose to fix it, exiting into traffic, cursing all the while. Cary turned to Walter, saying, "Let's go, we can walk from here," and they pushed out the back door and into the intersection, through the fog and the high-beam cones of oncoming cars.

"Where did you say he lives again?" Walter asked, as they walked uphill on Clayton. The narrow street felt narrower in the fog.

"Way up on Graystone, almost to that weird elementary school."

Walter was a pace behind Cary as they strode. Late June and he wished he'd dressed warmer, though he was in a soft tweed blazer and a thin wool scarf; he should have worn a sweater. His new shoes pinched a bit; they were fancy wing tips he'd bought on clearance at work. Cary was in her gray fedora and the navy cashmere overcoat she wore all winter. Clearly in a fine mood, Cary started whistling and then singing softly. It was "All the Things You Are," a Jerome Kern tune she was learning on guitar. (There was a major seventh chord at the end of one phrase that she said, when it resolved, felt exactly like *juicing a lemon*.) Walter began to sing along. He never sang much himself, but Cary sang so often and so unselfconsciously that it inspired him; it made him wonder what the point of being self-conscious was. Meantime, he'd realized his voice wasn't half bad.

Over months they'd developed a game, a wandering game, of rewriting old lyrics as they walked. Some songs practically begged to be parodied. One of their cheesy favorites was "All the Things You Are." The game was simple, improvisational: one of them would sing a line they made up on the spot, and the other would try to rhyme with it. Revise and repeat, until they had a whole new verse, then a whole new song. Their version started:

You are a bundle of attractions,
Which, while magnetic, make me feel tense . . .
You are a jumble of abstractions,
Which, while poetic, don't make a lot of sense . . .

Cary had come up with the second couplet first; she meant it as a biting commentary on the vagueness of the original lyrics, as if Oscar Hammerstein would somehow hear her in the grave and feel admonished. They sang and walked for a couple blocks, not too loud, because the neighborhood was dead quiet. They'd been singing rather than watching where they were going, and in a matter of minutes they were lost and had to turn back. They came across a concrete retaining wall, camouflaged by ivy, fronting a steep staircase that rose, turned on a landing, and zigzagged upward through a green cloister of palmettos, live oaks, fringes of blooming ice plant, and a range of urban chaparral. The fog smelled fresh, fennel-tinged.

"Pemberton!" she declared, pointing to a sign, nearly invisible in the overgrowth. "These are the Pemberton Steps. Follow me . . ."

They climbed up to the next street, narrow as an alley and crowded with parked cars and trash bins, and crossed directly, continuing up the staircase. Walter was winded and had fallen behind Cary by an entire flight, when he stopped, saying, "I love that tree!" Looming over a bed of hostas was a big, tropical-looking thing, superabundant, with clusters of large pale yellow lilies like calliope horns dripping from every branch. In the fog the lilies appeared to glow.

"Oh, those are angels'-trumpets," said Cary. "They freak me out!"

"Why would they freak you out? It's so gorgeous!"

"When I was a kid, the adults always went on about how poisonous they are. Like, if you picked one flower, you'd die instantly. It makes sense they were so adamant, in a way. They're so beautiful you do want to blow them like a trumpet, or eat them, or something."

"Yeah, I can see that."

"I heard the Satanists loved them back in Saint 'Nard"—this was Cary's name for San Bernardino. "Used them in rituals and called them *devil's snare*." Cary turned and continued the hike upward. "Anyway, your turn to start a new verse."

Walter thought for a moment as he moved carefully up the dark steps, then he sang:

You are not all the things you are not,
And all the things you are not aren't you . . .

Cary's laugh was muffled by greenery. It took her a couple seconds to come up with:

You can't be all the things you cannot,
And things that can't be you, you cannot be, too . . .

"This verse is rather existential, isn't it?" said Walter. It always took him longer than it took her, but after a brief pause, he sang:

You could be anything, it seems to me
Except for all the things you cannot be . . .

Cary, a flight above, turned and stared down the staircase at him. She was smiling but sounded annoyed. "I don't like where this is going at all!"

"Are we lost again? Or do you mean the verse?"

"The *verse*. It's very demoralizing, don't you think?"

"Well, of course it's not about *you personally*, is it? I mean, *you* can be anything you want, can't you, Monsieur Reinhardt? Declan Danner, P.I.?"

It was very dim, her whole body a greatcoated shadow. "I adore you," she said.

"I adore you, too," he said, without hesitation.

They stood still for a moment, staring up and down the staircase at each other.

"No, I don't think you understand," she said. "I'm saying I love you."

"I love you, too," he said, again without hesitation. But something in her tone was off. He was so used to her habitual facetiousness that when she turned earnest, it was disarming and even felt a little unfair, like changing the rules mid-play. "You know I do, right? You're, like, my best friend—you and Sasha, of course."

"Oh, goddamn it, Wall." Cary turned and strode quickly up the steps, and he followed as fast as he could, though it was dark and the steps were uneven, crumbling in spots. Cary raced across the next street and up the next flight of stairs. Walter was out of shape, and his new shoes had pinched his heels raw. He called after her to wait up, but she was unflagging. He chased her to the top of the Pemberton Steps, where the greenery thinned, the arcade opening to the sky. In bursts the fog was eerily polluted with light. Emerging on the street, at first he wasn't sure where she'd gone, the narrow road curved up each way amid the deadpan faces of shut garages, rough stuccoed walls, trellises of ivy and morning glory barely stirring. When he caught up with her she was in the middle of the street, shaking her head as she searched for house numbers.

"This isn't right, none of these are apartment buildings anyway." She seemed exasperated. "I can't even find the street name."

"Cary, what the hell?"

"Tell me something, Wall," she said, "how is it possible for someone to be both so thoughtful and *so dense*? Sometimes I feel certain you're the most observant person I've ever met, except about this *one thing*."

This hurt. Walter frowned and turned away from her, turning back after a few steps. "Since I'm so observant, one thing I have noticed is that you've been cold to me lately. For a couple weeks now. I don't know what your deal is."

"Really? You can't think of anything that transpired between us, about two weeks ago, that might have changed things?"

They were standing in the street now. Cary was agitated, gesticulating with her box of scotch. Walter wanted to avoid yelling, if possible. He scanned for illuminated rooms within the nearby houses, for moving silhouettes and other signs of life, but saw none.

"Are you mad because I slept over in your bed with Sasha? Because he swore you wouldn't care. And anyway, I was shitfaced, and nothing happened, as you know."

"God no, I don't care about that at all. I'm talking big picture. Look at how I am with you. Haven't you noticed that I'll find any excuse, no matter how large or small, to spend time with you? Did it somehow elude you that, when we're apart, I'll call you every hour on the hour until you agree to come over or meet me somewhere? Or that I'll show up wherever you are, anytime you call, at the drop of a hat?"

"Yes, of course," said Walter. "I love that—that's, like, our friendship—"

"Usually bringing food, or drinks, or candy, or some other—something—"

"I do it, too. I mean, I find excuses, too . . ."

"Do you wander the streets," Cary asked, "holding hands and singing love songs with any of your other friends?"

"I kind of assumed you did that with all your friends. I thought, you know, it's all part of Caryworld."

"Caryworld? Walter!" she cried, throwing her hands wide. "Isn't it perfectly obvious? If I adored you any more, you'd have to take out a restraining order against me. The real question is how you haven't been hospitalized for third-degree burns from the constant heat of my adoration. You have to have felt it."

"OK, OK," said Walter, raising his hands in self-defense, as if she might be about to cudgel him with the Glenlivet. "I've felt it. I admit I've felt it, too. But I thought, *It's impossible.*"

"Why on earth would it be impossible?"

"So many reasons—where to start? For one thing, you have Sasha . . . and Sasha's literally the perfect boyfriend."

"I'm glad you think so, I agree."

"And, as you always say, you're in love with Sasha. So, what could you possibly want from me—or anyone else, frankly—when you have Sasha at home? I mean, seriously."

"Oh, I don't know! How the hell should I know? All I know is I'm totally smitten with you and with Sasha, too, all at once. *The heart has a logic that logic knows not of.*"

"Now you really sound like Woody Allen. He's used that in at least two movies. I'm sorry, but you can't be in love with two people at once. I don't believe it's possible. Not really."

"You're only saying that because you've never been in love. Meanwhile, it would help if we could find the name of this damn street." She veered past him, and they ambled for a while, searching distractedly for Nick's building. Visibility was so low that it seemed possible it might loom out of the fog at any moment, like an ocean liner about to run them over.

"What's the address again?" Walter asked.

"Oh, I forget," said Cary. "I always know it by sight."

"It's amazing, from up here, ordinarily, you must be able to see all the way downtown. I'll bet you can see Oakland on a clear night—and tonight, nothing. Just embers in the fog."

As they wandered, he became utterly self-conscious and began to shiver in the brisk air. The offhand way she'd said *you've never been in love* was almost cruel, a small betrayal, but as he knew, betrayal was like the mean joke that stings from the truth it reveals. And some part of him wanted to be cruel to her in return, because now he felt that Cary was *greedy*, in the way she wanted to have Sasha for herself, and maybe him on the side as well. Cary was like the kid who'd never learned that she can't have everything she wants and wanted all of it, maybe not in the moment, maybe not all at once, but *all of it*, eventually. He was glad that she'd balked when he'd said *Caryworld*. He'd made it up on the spot, but it was the perfect word, in a way: it captured what it felt like to fall into her orbit. It expressed what, on the one hand, could be so infuriating, and on the other, was exactly what he loved about her and would never wish to change. The truth was he loved her irrepressible appetites, her apparent insatiability, her greedy unwillingness to deny herself any experience.

They had walked up the street as far as they could; it ended in a cul-de-sac. Nick's place was nowhere in sight. So they turned, and strolled back again, and stopped for a moment by a low cement wall that overlooked a vacant hillside lot, overgrown with brush and spindly fennel. Below them golden pin-lights of Eureka Valley endeavored to pierce the fog. By now he was freezing. When nervous, he'd sometimes forget to breathe, his circulation would slow, and he'd go cold and jittery in the arms and legs. He pulled a pack of cigarettes and a lighter from his jacket.

"Oh, please don't smoke *now*," said Cary.

"Why not? I'm freezing!"

"Because we're about to make out, Amanda. Read the signs."

"Are we?" he asked, shaking with nervous laughter. He looked over his shoulder at a sign that said "No Parking Any Time."

"Not that one, doofus!" she said. "Here!" In a few swift movements she had unwrapped the whisky, cracked the cap, and taken a swig. "Have some of this. Liquid courage."

He took the bottle and drank. Scotch wasn't his thing; it tasted like a bog on fire. He handed it back to her.

"I'm gay," he said.

"I'm gay, too."

"OK, but I'm a gay *guy*, meaning I like *guys*."

"I'm a guy, too. In all the ways that are important, that is."

"I would contradict you," Walter said, "but I have to admit, I don't know what those are."

He froze for a minute, his hands on the cold cement. Somehow he'd been backed against the barrier. Too frightened to simply capitulate, too excited to say no, he was paralyzed by the thought that what he said next, *anything* he said next, might break his best friend's heart.

"The truth is, when I moved to San Francisco to find love, you weren't exactly what I had in mind."

Cary removed her fedora, and there was the familiar gingerbready smell of her pomade, her dark hair silky. She narrowed her hazel eyes and smiled. He noticed, not for the first time, that she had surprisingly long canines, which in and of itself was sexy, slightly vampiric. She was handsome; he saw it now so clearly that he couldn't fathom how he hadn't seen it before.

"Is this because you're a size queen?" she asked. "Because if that's the issue, I'll have you know, I have a very large dick."

"Oh, you do, do you?" He laughed ruefully. Now she was using the world's crassest pickup line on him—a drunken lout's Hail Mary—the likes of which he'd expect from some creep during last call at the Midnight Sun.

"Well, I have several, actually. A huge one, and a cute small one if you'd prefer that, and a perfectly midsized one, you know, Goldilocks's porridge. And, of course, a purple dolphin—that one was a gag gift—and a couple others. They're all neatly arranged in my sock drawer, like drill bits."

Halfway through this absurd speech, he was about to stop her and tell her how impossible she was, but then she smiled at him triumphantly, eyeing him like an unrepentant rake, and he remembered that the crassest pickup lines are sometimes the best, because now, in spite of himself, he was imagining her sock drawer and fighting an urge to ask to see it.

By now he'd stopped shivering and felt a bit high, and turned away from her, saying, "God, I wish we could see something of the view from here, it must be so spectacular when it's clear!"

Then, following no logic whatsoever, he imagined he might see farther if he were a little higher up in the cloud cover, if he were standing on top of the wall. It was just low enough for him to get a foot up. He grabbed the pole of the "No Parking" sign and hoisted, forcefully. At the instant he thought he could see the lights of Market Street below, his skull rammed the metal sign. A blunt sword's edge hammered along his part, and he cried out and fell off the barrier—fortunately not over the edge into the chaparral. He landed on his feet, deeply embarrassed, hiding his face and holding his head where it throbbed.

"Jesus Christ!"

"Oh, Walter!" Cary expressed a gamut of emotions at once: brief panic, an inadvertent belly laugh, concern convulsed by giggling. "Why on earth did you do that?"

"I only wanted to see . . ."

He slumped against the wall. They stood and embraced for a long time, his head against her cashmere lapel, with its damp-wool musk. His head throbbed with an indescribable mixture of acute pain and deep comfort. His heart raced. He asked if he'd cut himself, if the cut was bleeding. She pulled back to inspect.

"It's very red, but I don't think it's bleeding, or not much, anyway." She kissed him on the cut, then kissed him once on each temple, saying, "What is it with you and head injuries? Poor klutz. This is like the time I found you wounded on the street and gathered you up and took you home."

And Walter thought, but did not say, that his life hadn't been the same since that moment, last Halloween.

"Do you want more of this?" she asked, offering the scotch. "It ought to warm you up."

He shook his head, and when she leaned in to place the bottle on the wall, he kissed her on the mouth, and she kissed back, and it felt good. It felt incredible and strange in unequal-equal measure, somehow both impossible and inevitable. And then they were making out, just as she'd said they would be, Cary of the self-propagating prophecies. Her kisses were tender, as he knew they would be, her tongue cool, assertive, apricot-sweet. Someone who could be so cutting ought to know how to kiss. It was a while before they stopped to breathe.

Having caught his breath, he said, "You know, you're an impossible person."

"Thank you very much." She nodded graciously.

"Is this a really bad idea? I'm worried that this might be a terrible idea."

"Why would it be a bad idea?"

"Our *friendship*, Cary. It could ruin everything."

"Or it could make everything glorious, perfect, amazing. Exactly right."

"I'm worried about Sasha, too, of course. I love Sasha—I don't want to torpedo our friendship, either. Or your relationship."

She kissed him again. "Don't worry about Sasha. I have a hunch Sasha's going to be cool with it."

"And this *hunch* is based on . . . ?"

She didn't answer at once, but took him by the hand, and they walked back toward the staircase together. Perhaps in an attempt to demonstrate that they hadn't just done irreparable damage to their friendship and their little world, they retraced their path down the Pemberton Steps, with the idea of finding the right street and still making it to Nick's party. It wasn't too late, by any stretch; the party would only be getting started. Walter assured her his head was fine, a little sore. He'd felt dizzy for a minute but was OK now. Cary reassured him about Sasha, saying that part of his being the coolest partner in the world was that he'd be cool about this as well, however they wanted to work things out.

Walter admitted that he'd been jealous when she'd gone home with Kelly. It was a relief to admit it to Cary and to himself; holding it in was making him even more confused. And although he knew jealousy was strictly verboten between Cary and Sasha, he had to admit he wasn't above it, he wasn't immune, and part of him wondered if she'd gone with Kelly to make him jealous.

"Of course not—I didn't imagine I could make you jealous. And anyway, she's your friend, so I thought, *She's Walter-approved.* I thought you'd be happy about it, if anything."

"Kelly is not *Walter-approved*," he said. "I mean, she's cool and all, but she's totally wrong for you."

"She came up after our concert with her gorgeous green tresses and hit on me like I was a rock star. What was I supposed to do? I'm not made of stone, you know."

They came to a dark landing between two flights and paused a moment.

"Cary, where's your fedora?"

"Oh, it fell over the cliff when we were making out. Along with the bottle of Glenlivet, didn't you hear it crash? Twenty-five bucks over the cliff."

"We have to go back and get your fedora! It's, like, your trademark."

"It's long gone, forget it. Plus I have a dozen others at home."

"Yeah, but that one was your favorite, wasn't it?"

"I'm telling you, it's OK. I'll find a new favorite."

The two sat where they were on the stairs. It was cold, and Cary opened her large coat and pulled it around him as best she could. Though they had intended to get back up and find their way to the party, they were somehow anchored to the spot, rocking gently but unable to cast off. And no one came up the stairs, and no one came down, and nearby no house lights flicked on or glared down disapprovingly, so they sat there daftly making out like two teenagers on a lover's leap, for ten minutes, then twenty, then forty. For Walter, what made it deeply weird also made it wonderful: he was necking with his best friend, sure, a boundary had been crossed that couldn't be uncrossed. But this mundane fear was washed away by the revelation, sudden and unmistakable, that it was his first time kissing someone he loved. Meanwhile Cary was one of two people in the world who might understand the welter of sweet, nauseating, irresistible terror she was provoking in him. And lust, too—another paradox: *what a relief lust could be.* As always it was much easier to kiss than to think. And infinitely more fun—as everyone knows—thinking is kissing's pathetic antithesis. So the two of them, arm in arm, were granted a momentary reprieve from thought, from significance, from intent, from care, from cynicism, from San Francisco, from the world. And beside them all the while the angel's-trumpets or devil's snare—whichever it was—shone dimly in the fog.

At last they had to stop again for breath, and Cary said, "Let's go home."

"To your place? What about Sasha?"

"Oh, I've got some news for Sasha—I think he'll be excited to hear."

"Maybe we should go to my place? If Sasha's sick . . ."

Cary stood and buttoned her coat, then held out her hand to him. "Oh, he was lying. He just didn't want to go to the party—he was feeling antisocial."

"What makes you think he'll be *feeling sociable* now?"

Another long silence followed, in which Walter could feel the subtext, the real question, rising up as if through water, rushing toward the placid surface of plain obviousness: *Exactly* how cool *is Sasha going to be with this?*

"Trust me," she said. "It's not too late. Sasha can have a look at your head. It will be like the night you two met! We'll put on some music and pour some wine. Come on, Wall. The night is young, and we are young, and that tree is seriously creeping me out!"

So they tripped their way down to Eureka Street, and when they got to Eighteenth, they nearly raced down the few steep blocks to Cary and Sasha's. A kiss for luck—they made out for a breathless minute under the laurel that shaded the door—and when they came through the foyer there was Sasha, in a corner of the couch in his bright red robe, hair down, reading *Delta of Venus*. When he looked up and saw them smiling hand in hand, he seemed to know what was up—after all, Sasha, like Lorna Zaftig, was more than a little clairvoyant—and he let out a little sigh and placed his book down on the cushion beside him.

Introducing LOTOPHAGINE (TM)
        (Patent Pending)
Developed by <u>Consensus Laboratories</u>
        (Dr. J. Purzelbaum, director)

A proven treatment for:
        -deviance, sexual and otherwise

Primary effects:
        -amnesia, mild euphoria, complacency
        -promotes healthy consumerist urges

Possible side effects:
        -risk of increased hedonism
        -slight risk of total body paralysis

Recipe for LOTOPHAGINE: Start with 5 lbs
angel's trumpet (Brugmansia satanica) blossoms.
Desiccate completely on trays in sunshine or
convection oven. Grind to fine powder.
Mix with 1 gallon H2O and heaping tablespoon
[proprietary reagent]. Strain. Distill. Voila!

A Room with a View

"WELL, HOW WAS THE PARTY?" asked Sasha.

Walter and Cary, shed of their coats and smiling sheepishly, faced their Sashenka in the burgundy living room. It was shortly after 10:00 p.m., Nick's party would still be raging, yet they offered no explanation for why they were home early. The minutes stretched on as, for the first time in their friendship, no one spoke. Candles burned on the console; incense curled from the Django shrine. Silence held sway, seeming inviolable: as ideal as the triangle they had unwittingly formed, each standing equidistant from the others. Cary was giddy, Walter apprehensive, Sasha inscrutable. The energy was high, static, volatile. Walter sensed a kind of alchemical transformation—something in the air had catalyzed. It seemed that something he had always imagined was inert was in fact explosive, like realizing too late—by placing it too close to the gas range—that what he'd thought was gunpowder tea was, in fact, gunpowder.

The paperback Sasha had been reading, tented on the sofa behind him, slid off the cushion, hit the carpet, and softly slapped shut.

As it turns out, it is possible to kiss two people at once, deeply, passionately even. It *seems* improbable: positioning's a bit tricky, it requires some maneuvering and a little forethought, you're less likely to *fall into it*, but it is possible.

That night, the first that Walter stayed with them in their bed, was fun, tender, bumbling, restless, and exceedingly awkward. They tried a variety of approaches: they started out sober, before realizing that a stiff drink or two might help them out. They tried different lighting schemes: direct, indirect, incandescent, candlelit. They shuffled through an assortment of mood music, all of which killed the mood. Things that seemed romantic for two seemed ridiculous for three, and at first, they could barely stop laughing. They moved from the couch to the bedroom after Cary kneed Walter in the thigh, just missing his groin. Later, while lunging across the bed, Walter accidentally elbowed Sasha and nearly gave him a black eye. Walter had had a bit too much to drink and kept having to excuse himself to pee, which meant standing in a buzzed daze at the toilet waiting for his hard-on to calm down. That night, they kept (mostly) covered up, perhaps recognizing how embarrassing it can be to see even one of your best friends naked for the first time, let alone two at once. They tumbled around for hours, and Walter never lost his boxer briefs.

Meanwhile, the rush of contradictory feelings he'd been having since early that evening assailed him throughout the night. At times, he couldn't help wishing he were still alone with Cary on their cool steps; but at times he wished he were alone with Sasha, especially when they first kissed, and it was so blindingly romantic that, *for fuck's sake*, he felt like Lucy Honeychurch in a field of cornflowers, even as Cary stood by watching with directorial interest, like James Ivory setting up the shot. At other times he felt that he *was* alone with each of them, that being with both of them felt, weirdly, like being with one person. More puzzling were the moments where he felt that *they* were alone without *him*, which was bizarre but somehow kind of hot. They took it slow—they didn't go all the way that night. At 2:00 a.m., Walter went out into the garden for a smoke and spent the whole time shaking his head at the cement garden gnome, wondering what the hell he'd done, and if he'd passed some point of no return. Stupid question, it was obvious even to the gnome, whose brains were concrete.

They tried to sleep and barely fit in the bed. A dozen pillows had to be jettisoned for the three of them to stretch out with no wiggle room, and when the cat came and bulwarked herself between Cary's and Walter's legs, there was no getting up. Walter was snuggled up in the middle—pride of place—but hardly slept at all. He was too keyed up, ecstatic, and couldn't keep his eyes closed. And Cary snored, which sort of made sense—she was the loudest of them even when unconscious. It wasn't until the next morning when they woke, bleary before coffee, a little hungover, a little unctuous and crusty and needing to shower, and practically radioactive with pheromones, that there was no more time for stalling. The boxer briefs came off, and they finally had sex. Walter came first—embarrassing—but having had blue balls all night, he could hardly blame himself.

So, it's possible to kiss two people at once, practically, even passionately, but that was only the first in a string of revelations Walter had beginning that night. Many more were to come: other nights, other mornings and after-noons followed, each with its own epiphany. One big revelation: sometimes a woman's libido can outstrip the infamous, much-mythologized appetites of the American male, red-blooded or otherwise. Exhibit A was Cary Menuhin, who, it turned out, despite her mild-mannered matinee idol exterior, was horny *all the time* and whose appetite for sex, like her appetite for life, more than once resulted in both Sasha and Walter crying uncle, sometimes in uni-son. Walter thought that rather than calling herself *bi* or *ambivalent*, Cary might as well identify as a *beast*. (He told her so; she was delighted.) To Wal-ter, the hottest thing about his two friends was how into each other they were. He had gone along with Cary tentatively at first, he was *experimenting*, sure; but Sasha and Cary were *not tentative*, they were all in for each other and now seemed equally into him. They knew what they wanted, and incredibly they both wanted him, and he wanted them both, and the whole thing was too electrifying for him to assume his default posture of moping and fretting. In short, he was happy.

A few times, early on, sex with Cary provoked a minor identity crisis in him, since for years he had defined himself by his insuppressible gayness. If, in the middle of things, he was self-conscious enough to think, *I'm having sex with a woman*, it would freak him out, the thought would deflate him. But Cary's body didn't freak him out; he found it incredible, long and lean and boyish, yes, but curvaceous, too, and he wondered how she managed to camouflage her curves under three-piece suits and things (the answer, of course, was Sasha's tailoring wizardry). Soon after, he found himself wondering if he'd secretly been a *boob man* all along and how he could have overlooked such a thing. Once, post-sex, Sasha mused aloud that Cary had perfect breasts—not too big, not too small—and Cary admitted that some lesbians had told her that, but no guy ever had. She went on to say that they were a pain in her ass and she'd happily trade chests with Sasha in a minute if he wanted.

Sasha, as Walter knew already, was precisely *not zaftig*, despite their efforts to cast him as such. Sasha was thin, but not wiry like some guys—he'd slept with skinny guys before. Sasha was divinely soft, with downy limbs and a hairless chest. Walter had never felt skin so soft. It came as no surprise that Cary was a good deal hairier than Sasha and proud of it. Walter laughed to think of himself as the butchest of the three. His gangly body—a runner's body, though he hadn't run in years—fit with theirs. They weren't muscular or gym toned. Each had their softness and their bursts of ruggedness, too; they shared a kind of nerdy voluptuousness. *We're effete!* Cary would declare. It was one of her favorite words because, as she claimed, *effeteness caused the fall of the Roman Empire.*

Another epiphany, or set of epiphanies: it's too profane to say a hole is a hole—anyway, it's not true—and while two orifices may be created equal, they're not exactly interchangeable, if you're paying attention. Even so, an erogenous zone is an erogenous zone, a hyper-sentient carrefour of nerve endings, and like express lanes on a bridge, any number of them may get you where you're going, it's only a matter of how fast. Frankly, when it came down to it, Walter discovered the difference between rimming and cunnilingus was largely a question of pragmatics, adjusting to minor but significant differences in scale and complexity, sensitivity, and the always *delightfully unstable* ratio of funk to sweetness. All of which is to say that vaginas are not scary, as he had imagined they might be, but rather awesome, even enviable. And all those gay men who squinched their noses and referred to women as *fish* were being misogynists, had no idea what they were talking about, and worst of all, were propagating an insidiously imprecise metaphor.

Without a doubt, underneath their ironic defenses, all three were romantics, but young and horny notwithstanding, so that sex between them would start out as sweet as a minuet at a regency ball and by the end have transformed into a sweaty, lust-fueled relay. Passed like a baton between them, sex could go on for hours. Their sex was playful, impassioned but never too serious, sometimes hilarious, innocent and aimless—full of fits and starts and teasing frustrations and, eventually, release. Cary would play ringleader, like a sex umpire. Every so often she'd call time-out, rising out of a skirmish and proclaiming, *Let's rest for a minute*, or *Let me grab a different toy*, or, simply, *Be right back*. Then Walter and Sasha were left to discover how close they were to or how far beyond the point of no return.

On one unforgettable evening, Cary came to a stop, stood up, and pulling a kimono from the floor, wrapped it around her and headed to the kitchen. Walter had read somewhere that it was possible to get so hard your dick could shatter—like ceramic—if you fell on it or something. His erection felt like one of those. Sasha smiled in sympathy, and they realigned like magnets and proceeded to sixty-nine. In the kitchen, something else was climaxing: between drowsy glimpses of Sasha's milk-pale thighs, Walter heard a rush of popping and, minutes later, smelled the smoldering of molten sugar. Not long after, as they lay talking, sheets strewn, fingers entwined, Cary returned with a tray of fresh caramel corn, first offering it to them, then abandoning it on the dresser because now she was horny again. That night, dinner was caramel corn and a red blend from Chile.

Another time, the three were lying in bed at Cary and Sasha's, having fucked each other cross-eyed. The room smelled potently funky; a nearly visible sex cloud hung in the air above them. They lay in opposite directions—Walter, lying on his back, hung his head off the end of the bed and stared at a corner of the ceiling. It was cream-colored, the only part of the room that wasn't painted some lush green, covered with pillows or clothing, or otherwise overrun with color. Its blankness was soothing. His dick had wilted, and his ass positively glowed with pleasure and pain, when somebody kissed him on the belly. It tickled. From the direction and plushness of the kiss, he knew it was Sasha. Cary, meanwhile, had been holding his left foot by the arch.

"That reminds me," said Walter. "While we were fucking . . . I think I felt the Aristotle illusion." He breathed deeply. "Like, a larger version of it."

"What's that?" came Cary's voice.

"Our legs were mixed up, and I couldn't tell whose legs were whose, and I couldn't tell *which legs I was feeling with* . . . a sort of visual-tactile hallucination . . ."

"What's the Aristotle illusion?" Sasha's voice bounced from the ceiling.

"We learned about it in fifth grade, didn't you?"

He sat up to demonstrate. He told them to cross their middle and index fingers on one hand, forming a little V with their fingertips. Then he said to run their opposite pointer finger along the crook of the V.

"Your crossed fingers feel like they are touching two fingers, not one, while the other finger feels like it's splitting in two—that's what always gets me, I get a strong feeling that my pointer finger is splitting in two."

Sasha tried it. "It's weird, for sure, but that's not exactly what I feel . . ."

"I didn't know there was a name for this!" said Cary, sawing away with her fingers.

"I taught you something!" Walter was triumphant. "I never teach you two anything! Like, there's nothing you don't already know."

"Don't be silly, Wall, you teach me things all the time."

"Me too," said Sasha.

Walter shook his head, disbelieving.

The three sat together for a minute, rubbing their fingers like they might catch fire, entranced for the moment by this ancient grade-school illusion. He wondered daffily if Aristotle had ever taught the fifth grade. Or, presumably in a totally different context, had a threesome.

"This is what sex with you two feels like," said Walter. Sasha laughed, but when Cary frowned, he added, "Only deeply, *deeply erotic.*"

Shortly after the three of them became a thing, Sasha switched jobs, thanks to Jabez, who came through with a connection to the head of costuming at the SF Opera. Sasha showed up to the interview wearing an outfit he'd designed and sewn himself, topped with his faux leopard-print jacket. The costume designer, Peggy, examined the hand-bound buttonholes on the jacket, then asked to see the lining, admired the finished seams, and offered him the job as she handed the coat back. The pay bump was nice, but more than that Sasha was thrilled to be given tasks worthy of his skills: patternmaking and draping and tailoring for human bodies, not tabletops. And Sasha could get the three of them into as many operas as they wanted, weeknights and matinees, on the cheap. Meanwhile, Walter felt stuck at Macy's. By now he was in charge of the basement—gourmet foods and kitchenware—which wasn't much of a responsibility; one can only get so creative with immersion blenders and onion relish. Once in a while, Cindy would let him design a whole window himself. He missed Sasha at work, for sure, but it was for the best. Their relationship had heated up, and they might have started a fun but dangerous habit of fucking in supply closets—which, he was bummed to realize, they could have been up to all along, if he hadn't been so clueless.

Cary still split her time between the library and the card store, but a few weeks after Sasha switched jobs Cary came into some money. It was a small inheritance from her grandparents. Her grandmother, who had outlived her grandfather by many years, had died eighteen months before, but the money had somehow been tied up. It wasn't a ton of money—Cary never said how much exactly—but she was excited, saying it would be a nice boost to help them get somewhere with their movie project. In the meantime, she wanted to celebrate their cozy ménage: she decreed that they should live a bit higher on the hog. She longed to indulge them, to live it up and take in some of the swankier nightlife San Francisco had to offer. She still had lots of friends in restaurants—old battle-scarred comrades from her days in the kitchen at Fleur de Sel. If you left the industry, she explained, you never saw your friends again, no matter where they worked, because without fail six nights a week they were tethered to their stations and were free only after midnight, exhausted, filthy, reeking of sweetbreads, lardon slugs crusting their clogs, too miserable to hang out.

One night, Cary treated them to the latest, hippest restaurant, where an old friend had landed at the sauté station. The Flying Saucer blew Walter's mind; it was the first restaurant he'd been to that he thought must be avant-garde, especially because of the way they blithely ignored most restaurant conventions. It was located on an odd corner on a residential stretch of Guerrero Street, with no other restaurants or stores around. Rumor had it food critics were barred from entry. The interior was eclectic verging on kookie, a candlelit consignment store. None of the chairs and tables matched. A large toy flying saucer hovered over them as they ate; their tabletop was ragged repurposed granite, roughly the shape of Delaware. Patrons were packed in close, and it was almost too loud to talk. Meanwhile, the open kitchen provided a nonstop, Artaudian theater of smoke and steam and profanities. The kitchen never coordinated the dishes but served each entrée as soon as it was ready, so that you were stuck watching your companions eating or wound up being hungrily watched, forcing upon diners the ethical dilemma of *to share or not to share*. There were no menus, but the night's offerings were projected on the wall using a boxy, old overhead projector, providing all the je ne sais quoi of Miss Fern's fifth-grade classroom. Cary was paying and had told them to ignore the prices, but there they were, emblazoned across the wall, and Walter was amazed: *Seventeen-, eighteen-dollar entrées! How could monkfish*—which he didn't even like—*be worth seventeen dollars?* They drank a lot of wine, the cost of which Cary did manage to conceal from them. The entrées were un-canny, architectural—*vertical cuisine*, Cary called it—served in cantilevered layers (cornmeal puck, grilled vegetable stack, charred fillet balanced high like a surfboard or a seesaw), all surrounded by fans of shaved roots, pools of jus, piped opals of aioli, sprinklings of chiffonade and salt flakes.

Walter found himself staring at Sasha's plate, mesmerized by a pink anemone, the gossamer petals of which waved atop a pillar of black rice. He couldn't believe it was edible, and when Sasha offered him some, it dissolved at once on his tongue, a tissue of sea-foam.

"Katsuobushi," said Sasha, "bonito flakes. Dried shaved tuna."

The wine, the katsuobushi—the whole meal dazzled, down to the hand-spun cotton candy served in a martini glass that came with the check. Yet the one element Walter would remember forever was a tomato. He had pulled a little burst balloon, charred and intensely red, from under the fallen tower of his entrée. Halving it with his fork, he put it in his mouth without thinking and was momentarily unable to speak.

Cary caught his eye. "Are you OK, darling? You look like you're going to cry."

"What's the matter?" asked Sasha.

"I'm—I'm fine. I just—I can't believe—*I think* that was a tomato."

"Is it OK?" Cary's brow furrowed with concern.

"It—I don't know—maybe it's all the wine, *but that was one of the most delicious things I have ever eaten. Try it—am I crazy?*"

Cary took a bite. "You're not crazy, it *is* delicious—balsamic roasted. Perfectly cooked—*mmm . . .*" She wrinkled her nose with pleasure.

It was after that night that time began to speed up. Looking back, he would wonder if the Flying Saucer was the beginning of something, a swift-paced life passage, an era in his entanglement with his two best friends. There was something about that meal, or perhaps the restaurant, with its Wonka-like zaniness, was a kind of portal. Or else it was the tang of that tomato—*a ridiculous idea*, nothing of consequence was ever catalyzed by a tomato, no matter how perfectly prepared. But after that evening two things happened at once: time began to blur, and *they* became a *them*. Not merely privately, in their burgundy *living womb*, but publicly. Stepping out together, the three attained a kind of notoriety as *oh, them*, or *those three*, always waltzing around the neighborhood dressed like they were on their way to a supper club, even though it was midafternoon and there were no supper clubs to be found. The confusion people had about Cary and Sasha's relationship—that screwed-up look some folks got when it was clear they were thinking, *How does this work, exactly?*—was somehow resolved by the addition of Walter to the mix, as if he had been the missing piece all along, or maybe he was simply the proxy for everyone else's prurience about Sasha and Cary. *At least someone was getting to the bottom of that situation.* Cary was content to let them talk: "I know some people always thought Sasha and I were a joke," she said, "but now at least we're observing the rule of threes."

One anomalous Saturday, Fiona discovered Walter at home, momentarily detached from his ménage, performing singleton tasks: feeding and cleaning himself, sorting mail and laundry. She persuaded him to accompany her to Crossroads to sell some old clothes and earn a little cash. He didn't have much to sell, but they hadn't hung out in months; it would be fun to catch up. That day the Castro was abuzz with promenading queers, so after the secondhand clothing store they went for juice at Josie's. Fiona's DJ friend Javier worked there afternoons and had concocted a Fiona Special for her alone: carrot, orange, and mango blended with an entire peeled monkey's paw of fresh ginger. Feeling genial, Walter ordered the same. They sat in the garden, which was sunny and unusually crowded, beside a planter of rainbow sherbet heliotrope. One sip of juice and the ginger seared his soft palate, tears sprang to his eyes, and he began to cough.

"Girl, you OK?" asked Fiona.

"I'm fine," said Walter, gulping water. "It's delicious."

"Ginger is good for you! It's great for the digestion."

"I'm sure it is," he said between coughs. "If I can get it down."

Fiona shook her head pityingly. When he'd caught his breath, she reached into her bag and handed him what looked like a bunched rag. "I got you a present!"

"Fiona, you didn't have to . . ." Holding up the worn black jersey, he saw it was a T-shirt. Across the chest, in razor-edged Gothic script, it said "AC/DC."

"Fiona, thank you!" Walter managed, smoothing the shirt on his lap, completely stumped. He traced the jagged slash. "I like the little lightning bolt."

"Ha ha—" Fiona laughed, sucking her nuclear juice through a straw. "You're never going to wear it, are you?"

"I'll totally wear it . . . to bed!" He looked at her, puzzled. "Fiona, you know my favorite singer is Sarah Vaughan, right?"

"Don't I know it. Believe me, I know. But it's not about music, dummy. This is your *welcome to bisexuality* T-shirt! I'm going to be hella insulted if you don't wear it sometime."

He couldn't tell if she was joking or not—obviously she was to some extent. She knew no one in a million years would mistake him for a metalhead. Yet the gift was only half ironic. It was common, with his San Francisco friends, for Walter to find himself sorting through layers of irony, confronting a novel trend or turn of phrase and thinking, *Sure, we all love it, but how much of that love is ironic, and how much is a cool love of irony itself?* Somehow, inevitably, sincerity would creep back in.

"The thing is . . ." he began.

"Oh god, here we go," said Fiona.

"I'm not sure that I am bisexual."

Fiona let that thought float between them for a moment—wavering—a bubble she was hesitant to burst.

"Huh," she said. "I wonder what *your lover* Cary would have to say about that."

"Cary would say I'm *ambivalent*, which isn't like it sounds—to her it's a good thing." Then Walter tried his best to encapsulate Cary's expansive theory of ambivalence. Halfway through his paean to the virtues of never fully deciding anything at all, he saw that Fiona was staring at him with the indulgent look you might offer a five-year-old bent on explaining the vagaries of space travel. He thought he'd better wrap it up. ". . . and that's why," he concluded, "Cary says we're *ambassadors*. She likes to call us *ambassadors of ambivalence*."

"OK, OK, I think I got it," said Fiona, sounding far from convinced. "So . . . if you are *ambassadors of ambivalence* . . . where do you march in the pride parade?"

"I guess . . . we don't?"

"Why not? You should ride on the back of a convertible! Loud and proud! You're ambassadors, aren't you?"

"Yeah, but we're *ambivalent*."

Fiona huffed, blowing up her pixie bangs. "Leave it to you, Walter, to take all the fun out of *bisexuality, literally the most fun thing there is*."

"I'm fun!" Walter began to protest. "I'm having fun—"

Before he could say another word, their conversation was drowned out by thunderous music that sounded like the approach of a small circus. Wandering onto the patio came a band of not one, not two, but *five accordions*, blasting "La vie en rose" at earsplitting volume. Barring the exit, they stood in a crescent formation and played zealously. One woman stood inches from their table, swaying on clogs and singing maniacally, fingers flying over the buttons and keys. Walter loved this song, but it was way too much of a good thing. He leaned sideways into the heliotrope, and Fiona covered one ear with her hand, testily finishing her juice. The band barely paused—a few customers clapped—before they launched into "Istanbul (Not Constantinople)," and Walter and Fiona fled the patio.

He stopped in the bathroom on the way out. Washing up, he began to worry that he'd disappointed Fiona in some way by brushing off her gift and maybe also slighting bisexuality. To appease her, he unbuttoned his shirt and, after confirming that it smelled clean, slipped on the secondhand T. "AC/DC." His effete, clean-shaven mug laughed back at him in the mirror. He fingered the white bolt that flashed down his sternum, the static shock between *alternating* and *direct*. And despite, or maybe because of his ambivalence, the shirt made him feel cool, ironic. Even a bit sexy.

Down Argentine Way

THEY WERE ON THE HUNT for a supper club, a search that would last several months. In truth it was a noir dream they were searching for, a '40s- or '50s-style nightclub, on the level of the Corcovado. But there was nothing like it in town, all the swankiest spots weren't supper clubs—Zuni wasn't it, Masa's wasn't it, nor was Fleur de Sel—but they set off on their intrepid way, through North Beach standbys and SoMa hotspots and boutique hotel renovations downtown. The high-flying Starlight Room atop the Sir Francis Drake had the best view—in theory—though at night the last thing you could see was starlight beyond radiant strata of high-rises, when the air was cloudy as brine. The Redwood Room had the most gorgeous interior, dark wood panels with striations like tiger stripes at midnight, and the actual best view, of some disturbingly good Klimt knockoffs. Often they'd skip dinner and just go for drinks; they were educating themselves about cocktails, graduating from cloying cosmos and chocolate martinis to classics handed down from the Greatest Generation: old-fashioneds, Manhattans, sidecars, Sazeracs . . . A good gimlet is like an invigorating sock in the eye with a lime. A Negroni is an elixir of liquid rosewood, so bitter you suspect it might kill off what remains of your inner child, and which you start out hating but end up craving, like licorice. They tried the Tonga Room, potted Polynesia, where they shared a venomous Scorpion Bowl and danced on a pirate ship while the band played Captain and Tennille on a pontoon in a pool, and every hour on the hour a little monsoon rained down. Cary said it was her life's ambition for Bombolone to play that pontoon boat, as soon as they got a little better and Walter learned to play the marimba. As if to up the ante on the Tonga Room, Caribbean Zone served mai tais and mini shrimp pancakes in the fuselage of a jet plane that, the interior designers did their best to convince you, had crash-landed in a jungle paradise. The small plane was reputedly none other than the Doobie Brothers' touring jet, ambiguously commemorated by a cocktail called *What a Fool Believes.*

They thought they might have struck the supper club jackpot when they heard about the Cypress Club, which, in an auspicious film noir nod, was named after the underground casino in Raymond Chandler's *The Big Sleep.* Word was the interior was stunning, a million-dollar spectacle, funded by Chicago Mob money to boot. When they finally made it in the door, they discovered that the interior was a postmodern take on a potbellied pig, of all things, with walls and serpentine banquettes paneled with sheets of burnished copper, bulging like hogs' bellies. The chandeliers looked like copper teats, big as moonshine stills, depending from a sow's undercarriage. Even the air was copper-colored.

"Philip Marlowe wouldn't be caught dead in a fruity place like this," Walter insisted.

"Sure, but Nick and Nora Charles probably would," said Sasha.

"The team behind Tomorrowland brings you—drumroll please"— Cary drummed the tablecloth—"the world's first steam-engine pig!"

The place was hopping—the hottest reservation in town—and Walter's braised lamb shank was the best he'd had in a city currently besotted with lamb shanks. But the host seemed annoyed to have to give over a four-top to three diners, natty nobodies, and asked twice if their party was complete. The restaurant was on the border of North Beach, which automatically made them tense. It was the neighborhood where Sasha was most likely to get harassed, except for the Marina, of course. (They had a North Beach rule:

Walter always went with Sasha to the bathroom in case of any trouble. And a Marina rule: never go there.) To top it all off, the waiter called Sasha "sir" and Cary "ma'am," which never happened in the Castro or the Mission, and Cary was pissed off by the time they left, and they never went back.

It was then that San Francisco entered the era of Asian fusion, which unfolded between the late-Cryogenic Tapas Explosion and the early Pleistocene Small Plates Epoch. The small plates trend, Walter suspected, was the logical result of restaurateurs discovering that, with a little rebranding, they could charge almost as much for appetizers as for entrées. They followed these fads, which was very easy to do, because in every neighborhood there was a growing echelon of foodies unable to talk about anything else.

At one point, it was the local mania for a wine trend that alerted Walter to how quickly time was speeding along. Cary and Sasha were cooking dinner at their place, and Walter brought the wine. The conversation had turned to a recurring theme: *Why didn't Walter move in with them?* He could tuck his futon and his blue shoes into the shared office/library off the living room and have his own space there. Something kept him tied to his place with Fiona, but he had trouble articulating to his friends that the more time they spent together, the more crucial were the few nights he spent apart from them, in the cozy blandness of his own place.

Sasha stood at the sink draining linguine as Cary held up the wine bottle quizzically. "Wall, where did you find this?"

"Is something wrong?"

"Well, it's Beaujolais nouveau, that's all."

"Yeah, you like Beaujolais nouveau! I thought the label was pretty. It was on sale . . ."

"Well, yes, I guess so, because it's about six months out of season." Cary was amused, she didn't really care, she had popped the cork and was sniffing the bottleneck.

That was his mistake: he'd forgotten that Beaujolais nouveau had a season. What was a season, after all, in California? Although it seemed to be always around, the wine must have had an optimal window—like strawber-ries or brussels sprouts.

"When is it Beaujolais nouveau season again?" he asked.

"Oh, you know, it's those three weeks or so where you walk around and every restaurant has a chalkboard announcing 'Beaujolais nouveau est arrivé!' "

"You're no help."

"November," said Sasha at the stovetop, stirring the pasta into a pan of carbonara.

"Really?" asked Walter. "Has it been six months?"

"It's fine," said Cary, sipping thoughtfully. "The wine is fine. Yummy, actually."

"Hold on, what month is it now?" asked Walter.

"How on earth should I know?" Cary poured the wine.

"It's always Beaujolais nouveau season with you two, darlings," said Sasha, as they sat to eat.

When dining on vertical cuisine wasn't entertainment enough, they would go to the movies, or the opera, or—a new fascination—the theater. The local performance scene was lively, cheap, and scrappy as hell; a year-round game of fringe-festival roulette. Venues popped up literally anywhere: Tenderloin black boxes, Potrero lofts, Bernal backyards. They took in performance art at Josie's Cabaret & Juice Joint, where Lypsinka proved herself the Paganini of lip syncing and Tim Miller (the current bête noire of Jesse Helms, senator from North Mordor) pretended he was having sex with the entire audience at once—a steamy performance that fogged the glasses of every MFA geek in the place. One night they took a taxi way the hell out to an abandoned body shop in Portola, where Kelly Calypso and some thespian friends de-buted an evening of shadow puppetry she'd been planning for years. It ended up being delightful and worth the trip, and the noxious stench of motor oil in the garage only added to the puppets' macabre charm. Meanwhile, the best drag was not the glamour drag at Marlena's or the Elephant Walk, but the gleeful horror drag at the Stud on Tuesdays. There, Arturo Galster once performed in a bodice made of tortillas and a skirt stitched of prosciutto, and (their favorite) Pippi Lovestocking sang Helen Reddy—*Delta Dawn, what's that flower you have on?*—with the severed heads of baby dolls bleeding all over her Ma Ingalls flannel nightgown.

And all the while they danced. In San Francisco, a city that will take any light excuse to erupt into an impromptu block party, they needed no excuses. On any given night, if they were up for it, there was some alternative club where they could dance. On Mondays a Lower Haight club called Filth should have won some prize for strung-out sketchiness; Tuesdays were the Stud, of course; Wednesdays were at Casanova—no dancing, but even the most energetic club kids needed to sit one night out; Thursdays were Sissybar at the Powerhouse; Fridays were the Litterbox at the Cat's Alley, where DJ Javier spun a whiplash-inducing mix of Britpop, post-punk, and indie dance, with sprinklings of funk and Tropicália. They would dance anywhere, on any night, but many of the Folsom bars were too seedy for Cary and Sasha's effete style, especially the ones whose back rooms doubled as de facto sex clubs.

In the middle of this whirlwind of queerness, something exceedingly strange happened. Against all odds, and out of nowhere, *swing dancing* made a comeback. There were inklings that something was afoot when retro jazz bands with names like the Royal Crown Revue and Lavay Smith and Her Red Hot Skillet Lickers started drawing crowds at Club Deluxe and Cafe du Nord. They were blindsided and couldn't figure it out. It would remain a mystery why twentysomething hipsters were all of a sudden setting aside their Sub Pop and Portishead and ping-ponging drum and bass, only to lose their minds over Louis Prima and Keely Smith.

At one point, Fiona, who only liked jazz if it was *acid jazz*, tipped Walter off to a band they might like that was playing at Bimbo's in North Beach the following Saturday. "It's totally your thing," said Fiona, handing Walter an intriguing flyer. The band, called Le Jazz Hot, promised a francophone twist on American swing—not swing per se, but so-called Gypsy jazz.

The moment they set foot in Bimbo's 365 Club, they realized how remiss they'd been in not checking it out before. It was so close—achingly close— to the '50s supper club that Cary had been searching for: a wide ballroom with a checkerboard floor, a well-pounded parquet nicked by the tap shoes of floor shows past; walls ruched in gold and cerise curtains that had absorbed the evaporated sweat of a thousand spotlit musicians; a ceiling ruffled in a fan-palm motif; and to top it all off, it was *mermaid themed*. In fact Bimbo's *had been* the '50s supper club that she'd been dreaming of, but the kitchen had been closed for over two decades, the prime rib and baked potatoes having gone out of fashion with the burlesque shows.

"My heart—I think I might pass out!" Cary said, taking in the ballroom, as a hip crowd poured in, swarming the bar.

"Well, at least don't faint before we see if Dolphina is working tonight," said Sasha.

Dolphina was the notorious "girl in the fishbowl," a model hired to lie in a seductive pose on a chaise in the basement, while a trick of light and mirrors projected her image among the tropical fish in a tank behind the bar. Rumor had it she used to be stark naked, but in the puritanical '90s she wore a fishtail and shell bra, like Ariel. Apparently, if you asked around, everyone knew someone whose aunt or mother had posed as Dolphina back in the day, like New Englanders claiming to have had an ancestor on the *Mayflower*.

They quickly forgot to look for Dolphina, because the crowd itself was so astonishing. Except at the opera, they had never seen an SF crowd so dressed up, but everyone here was their age, dressed top to tail in vintage clothes, like extras in a period film—a very anachronistic one, like *The Hudsucker Proxy*, where you were never sure if it was supposed to be the '30s, '40s, or '50s. The women's outfits were more thorough than the guys'; most were dressed as their grandmothers would have been fifty years before: utility suits with high, belted waists and wide, padded shoulders; A-line skirts and dresses hitting below the knee in big florals and plaids; hair piled high in victory rolls, topped with tams or the odd fascinator. Little touches could make the whole effect both real and unreal: peep-toe heels, white gloves, thin brows almost tweezed away, lips drawn artfully over their bounds with maroon liner. Just when it seemed clear that the decade of consensus was the '40s, some girl would flit by in a poodle skirt and saddle shoes, or a '60s baby doll dress, and break the illusion.

The men dressed more lazily: most had doubtless built their outfits around their favorite chinos and an old blazer. Some tried harder, sporting wide-notched lapels, flared silk ties, pleated trousers, and fedoras. Walter, doing his best, had found a stylish grandpa suit of glen plaid to match a nut-brown porkpie Cary and Sasha had given him. The rockabillies were in their western shirts, lariat trim, mother-of-pearl snaps; random dudes were dressed for a bowling tourney or a midnight luau. Cary outdid them all, in a clover-green cravat and a charcoal pin-striped suit that made her look like she'd come directly from the Saint Valentine's Day Massacre and had tossed her tommy gun in a planter in the lobby.

They ordered Manhattans and snagged a lounge table. When Le Jazz Hot fired up, they were divinely good, surpassing all expectations. Cary gripped the stem of her glass with envy when the lead guitarist started in. He played Gypsy jazz like Django, but not derivatively; he had a flair of his own. She fixed upon his playing with jealous perseveration, her knee bobbing in time, her jaw locked. Walter took her hand, fearing that she might snap the stem of her glass in two. The guitarist was but one star in the band's hot constellation: there was a keyboard player who one minute could tickle the ivories like Rubinstein, and the next strap on an accordion and whip it up into a swoon like Astor Piazzolla; there were trumpets and a trombonist, a killer drummer, a jazz fiddler, and a bohunk bassist who spun the upright like a bobby-soxer. The singers—the guitarist and the female trombonist—slipped so easily between French and English songs that they were surprised to learn the band was not from Paris or even Quebec, but Austin, Texas, of all places.

That evening at Bimbo's was magical, in spite of the fact that they realized they had made two key miscalculations, the first being that three—alas—was exactly the wrong number to take couples dancing; the second being that none of them actually knew how to swing dance. They tried bravely—Cary couldn't follow, she led instinctively but didn't know the moves; Sasha knew how to lead but didn't like to and couldn't show them how; and Walter, except for the simplest two-step, could neither lead nor follow. Meanwhile swing kids whizzed and dipped all around them on the parquet. He tried to follow Cary through a blazingly fast rendition of "Brazil," the pianist nearly pounding the keyboard off the upright. They spent the whole song trying to avoid either stomping each other's toes or being plowed down by other dancers. Then, as they were taking a breather, a postcard-perfect cigarette girl sporting bumper bangs and a snood strolled by their table, and in the course of flirting with Cary, she offered them a promo for dance lessons they could take before Vise Grip played the following week.

"We're doing this," said Cary, pocketing the flyer. "We've got some catching up to do!"

Cary was still flirting with the girl, professing interest in the variety of Altoids on offer, when Walter and Sasha went to dance. It was the middle of a mellow set, the tempo mercifully slow, and Walter did his best to lead, left hand on the small of Sasha's back, just above the silken tie of Sasha's wraparound dress, as he pressed their bellies close and felt the slow sway of the two-step between them. It took him a minute to recognize the song. The singer had abandoned her trombone and, in a smoky mezzo, was singing "Dream a Little Dream of Me" in French. As they danced, Walter experienced a momentary identity crisis when Sasha, very discreetly, told him to check out the legs of a woman dancing beside them.

"They're very nice legs," he whispered. A pale peridot shone in Sasha's ear.

"They are indeed."

Sasha laughed and assured Walter it wasn't what he was thinking. He was admiring her authenticity: rising up the curve of each calf the woman had drawn a straight, crisp black line in eyebrow pencil, the simulation of a seam, a trick their grandmothers had pulled when they couldn't afford stockings.

"Clever," said Walter. "Sweet." He leaned into Sasha's fragrant hair, which was smoothed behind one ear and fell in soft waves across the opposite shoulder. Soir de Paris.

Walter was in love. Sasha in his arms, Cary somewhere near—watchful, orbiting them like a satellite—Le Jazz Hot, the accordion solo taking flight, the dance hall dimness, the blizzard of the mirror ball; and all around them, the lovers in their colorful costumes, each in a world of their own. Somehow it wasn't any one of these elements he was in love with but all of it at once. The intensity of his love for Sasha and Cary did not begin and end with them; it encompassed the room, the street, the city. It traveled with them like a radiant force field wherever they went. He couldn't tell where his love for them left off and his love of life began, it was as confusing as trying to think about where the universe (which we're told is already infinite) might be expanding into. At the same time, he felt a creeping, insidious sadness, a dread common to all young lovers, that it was all so ephemeral, that it could blow away so easily once the dance was done. Swaying with Sasha, he had to fight the urge to ask, *Why me?* He had wondered this often enough, about both Sasha and Cary, about his love for them, as well as theirs for him. And somehow, he knew to leave the question unasked. He knew that *Why me?* was a poisonous question, one that would always leave the asker wanting. Drinking salt water to quench your thirst—because the question begged for a concrete *reason*, and the answer was a mess of *sensation*. Fallible, bodily. Beyond expression—beneath it.

The music transformed, the accordion leading the band down the garden path into a new song, the plaintive strains of which Walter recognized at once: it was the theme from Fellini's *Amarcord*. The melody spun them in a tight circle. It was lovely but so repetitive, mesmerizing and slightly demented, the wailing of a mystic carnival.

"I'm so desperate to go to Italy, aren't you?" Walter asked. "Should we all go on a trip to Rome, or Napoli, or someplace?"

"Of course we should, Wall . . ." Sasha's voice rang a little hollow.

"Are there places you'd rather see first? Maybe Paris or Berlin?"

"It's not that," said Sasha. "With Italy . . . I'm a little worried they'll burn us at the stake, that's all!"

"Burn us at the stake? You're not serious."

"You know why the Italian word for *faggot* is *fennel, finocchio*, don't you?"

"I don't—I didn't know that's what that meant—"

"It's because they used to throw fennel on the fire to cover the stench when they burned the sodomites alive."

Walter frowned.

"We'll go, darling," Sasha assured him, "we'll go, don't worry! I'm sure they haven't burned any queers at the stake in *years*."

"In that case, should we see Paris first?"

Sasha nodded and squeezed him in agreement.

"Should we go kiss Oscar Wilde's grave? I've heard there's this huge stone memorial, and queer pilgrims put on lipstick and kiss it. It's covered with kisses."

"That sounds way better than being burned at the stake," said Sasha.

"Paris it is!"

When they returned to the table, Cary was gone, and in her place was a group of Nob Hill knobs, straight dudes in Hawaiian shirts. They caught up with Cary returning from the ladies' lounge, on her way to the bar. It was Walter's turn to buy a round of Manhattans. The crowd was thick around the bar; he'd have to muscle in as best he could.

"Have you seen Fiona?" Cary asked. "I just saw Fiona—"

The crowd around them was loud, they had to shout.

"Really? *Fiona's here?* She told me about the band, but I didn't think it was her thing."

"Yeah—did she tell you she got *a new job?* She's behind the bar!"

"No, she never said—"

Cary shrugged and, wide-eyed, mimed a drinking gesture, and Walter pushed in toward the bar. When he was near enough he saw what Cary meant: behind a bearded bartender ambushed by hipsters, there was a large aquarium, and there amid the angelfish and miniature kelp was a little fixed rectangle of light where Dolphina had her grotto. He strained to see. It was such a cheap effect: the trick of a child's toy periscope, the mermaid so Lilliputian you could barely make out her features. He blinked a bit before he recognized her. There, in a pinup pose, shoulders bare, arms framing her head, shell bra, fishtail, and all, ocean blue and beaming beneath her jet-black bangs, was Fiona.

Later that week, after work, Walter swung by the apartment to find Fiona standing in the living room surrounded by chaos: half a dozen U-Haul boxes had erupted colorful clutter onto every surface. She was holding a pillar candle in each hand and appeared caught off guard. It was rare that he saw her without makeup, or at least lipstick—it made her look vulnerable.

"Oh god," he said, "you aren't moving out, are you?"

"No, I'm not going anywhere. We do have a new roommate, though." She gestured toward the small dining table by the window. There, in a cage crested with wire curlicues, was a cherry-cheeked white cockatiel, black BB eyes staring. "You remember José, don't you?"

"Sure, from Kelly's mystery boutique on Divis!"

"The store closed with no warning at all. Dude moved to Oaxaca and dumped the whole thing in Kelly's lap. Kelly took all the shadow puppets and a lot of other junk, but I said we'd take some stuff. Her place is even smaller than ours."

Walter sat and helped her unpack the trove of abandoned inventory, mostly veladora candles, crystal-toothed geodes, and papier-mâché Day of the Dead figures. They arranged them on the windowsills and on shelves between their CD and cassette collections.

"I guess you can't have too many candles, can you?" said Fiona. ". . . Maybe you can."

"Feels like I'm at work—if Macy's had a Mexican shrine department," said Walter. "Also, *what the hell, Fiona?* You didn't tell me you were *a mermaid!*"

"What, and ruin the surprise?" She smirked, the cat that caught the cockatiel.

"So tell me, what's it like being a mermaid?"

Fiona shrugged. "Pretty fun. Cold. Kind of boring, to be honest . . . I can't even hear the music down there. I have to bring my own music, or I'd die of boredom." She held up a tall glass candle with a picture of Jesus opening his robe to reveal an engorged heart, licked by flames, pierced by thorns, and gushing thick blood. "God, Catholics are kinky! Maybe I can sell this one at Good Vibes . . ."

They unwrapped tchotchkes and caught up on several weeks' gossip. At the bottom of one box, in a crush of butcher paper, Walter discovered a lone snow globe: large, elliptical, a cheap plastic thing you might find for two bucks at Pier 39. Trapped inside was downtown San Francisco, shrunken and drowned. It was badly made; several major landmarks had broken loose. When he shook it, Coit Tower and the Transamerica Pyramid went flying with the plastic snow.

"Can I have this?" he asked Fiona, shaking it at her.

"Sure, go for it," she said. "Looks like a piece of junk to me."

He stared into it for a long minute as the white pellets swarmed, never landing. The two towers and an unmoored Victorian made soft clicks as they glanced against the globe.

"Dude, are you stoned?" asked Fiona. She'd returned from the fridge and was offering José a romaine leaf through the wire bars.

"No!" said Walter. "Why would you say that?"

"Ah, OK, I get it. It's the free-love stupor."

"What?" asked Walter, giggling exactly like a stoner.

"Wall, you've been sex-stoned for months. Every time I see you. I swear, you don't even know what year it is! Look at this . . ."

From a stack of bills Fiona handed him a blue slip of paper. It was the check he'd left her for this month's rent. He puzzled over it. Fiona and José stared at him, waiting for him to catch on. Had he not paid her enough? No—*there it was*—the date was off. He had written *1994—the wrong year*. He was dumbfounded. *He knew* it was 1995, *he knew the year, for Chrissake*. Yet it seemed he hadn't fully grasped it until this moment. It wasn't newly 1995, either—half the year was gone. He'd gotten the month right, at least—it was June again, somehow.

"Don't worry about it," said Fiona. "So you had a brain fart—happens to everyone. I'm sure they'll still cash it for me."

He let the snow globe settle. The Transamerica tower bobbed torpedo-like on a large air bubble. *What the fuck had happened to 1994?* Panic rose within him: an hour ago they had been seated at the Flying Saucer, and now it was a year later, give or take a month or two. Had that been *a year ago?* Without any seasonal markers, how was he to tell? Every day was another block party, the boys were out eternally strutting in their leathers or muscle Ts, the strawberries were always ripe, the Beaujolais always nouveau.

"Hey!" said Fiona. "Maybe we could teach José to say some stuff? Maybe . . . we could teach him to tell us the date and time?" She leaned down to the cage. "Nineteen ninety-five," she enunciated as José ticked his head toward her. "It's *nine-teen ninety-five*."

It was a come-to-the-sacred-heart-of-Jesus moment, so to speak. Walter was rattled by how quickly the months were racing around him, whizzing like swing kids as he and his two love-stoned partners danced in a slow circle. It was then that he hatched a plan: the next day he started researching gradu-ate programs in film history, phoning schools around the country to request materials. He told himself he was only gathering info, thinking it over. And since he was so casual about it, for now there was no reason to tell Cary and Sasha. He could keep it secret for now, no reason to alarm them.

Of all the clubs where they danced away the days, Walter's absolute favorite was the Sunday-afternoon tea dance at El Rio. Celestial El Rio ("Your Dive," it branded itself), with its Mars Black facade, was viscerally dark on the inside, a wolf's gullet you traveled through only to be reborn on the back patio, a garden sanctuary enclosed on two sides by high walls of carceral cement, half prison yard, half paradise regained. Every Sunday afternoon it booked live salsa bands, and there, couples danced among the spiky yuccas, beneath a tall Mexican fan palm and a white-blooming wax privet. The garden *looked* intensely fragrant, jasmine snailing up its walls and a proud, prolific lemon tree. But no garden scent could penetrate the stink of tequila—El Rio was a riverbed, it ran with Cuervo Gold—and the stench of skunked beer and grilling meat. In the farthest corner, under the carmine sepals of a Callistemon, amid clouds of burning tallow, a man peddled burgers and hot dogs off a grill. Meanwhile, floating above the dance floor, with a smile two feet wide, was a giant painting of Carmen Miranda, big as a billboard, head, shoulders, tutti-frutti turban and all: *una abundancia* of pineapple, grapes, cherries, and limes. Her smile was so strident it looked almost insane, but her hands, framing her face and weighted with drupaceous bracelets, curled as gracefully as the Buddha's: mudras for welcome and protection.

A sunny Sunday afternoon in late August or September at El Rio was an urban Eden, Walter thought, topping his list of quintessential San Francisco experiences. Though people danced in couples at El Rio, the three of them were never at a loss for partners, because *everyone* attended the tea dance eventually. There they would run into everyone they knew: Fiona and Kelly often alighted there; Jeff as well. One Sunday they saw Eliot and Richard, who were still a thing, going strong and living together at Eliot's place nearby in Bernal. Another Sunday Walter ran into Julian, single and sexy as ever, and they danced a few turns around the patio and wound up making out in the dark dive, until a bartender yelled at Julian for sitting on the shuffleboard table and chased them off.

Their very first trip to the club they ran into Jabez and discovered that he could really salsa. He promised to teach them if they came over. So they learned salsa dancing—proper salsa, if just the basic moves—not at El Rio, but on Sarcoma Beach, on the rooftop of the Archers. One evening Jabez brought out a boom box and CDs (Cubana divas Albita and Celia Cruz), and in turn, Jabez and Lawrence took them each firmly in hand and taught them the basic back and forth, dead simple, but requiring a lightness of step and a good swing in the hips to go from plodding to fluidity. Grace is getting the hang of it. When Jabez and Lawrence danced together they moved as one, like an old couple who'd been dancing together for decades, leading and following on impulse—it was mesmerizing to watch.

Meanwhile the specter of Carmen Miranda had inspired them to seek out her films, none of which they'd seen before. The ones they could find were all musicals, zany romps (*That Night in Rio! Four Jills in a Jeep!*), a few of them fun but frivolous, and most of them, frankly, duds. When it came down to it, Carmen Miranda was an unlikely queer icon. Sure, she was camp as camp could be, but Carmen's Hollywood career was pandering to the point of pathos: never the star of her own films, always playing second fiddle to some Wonder bread blonde, forging further and further into self-caricature until there was no path back. In the Mirandaverse, as in Hollywood, all Latino cultures were interchangeable, and she the pink-pancaked face of them all, as if culture itself were elective, another kind of drag. The best of them was *Down Argentine Way*, in which Betty Grable falls head over heels for Argentinean horse racer Don Ameche. While not a good movie, at least it had the catchiest song, "South American Way," though even that was sung in Portuguese, not Spanish, and was a samba, not a tango, so what it had to do with Argentina was anybody's guess.

"It's not a mystery," said Cary, pinpointing Carmen's appeal. "She's the queen of camp, and she's irrepressible and totally game, maybe the most amenable person who ever lived. Like if they asked her to play a Nazi hunter, she would have said, *OK, which turban should I wear?*"

"If only!" said Walter, imagining Carmen hunting Nazis through Buenos Aires, a pistol in her pineapple hat. "That'll be our *next* screenplay."

One perfect Sunday in September, Lawrence and Jabez came along to El Rio. It was technically fall but San Francisco midsummer, as sunny and warm as it ever got, and everyone was decked out in their flimsiest summer best, the mood lively and carefree. The band was especially good, too, a local group called Dos Gardenias, fronted by a diva whose voice was impassioned, heavy as burgundy, and at times so saw-toothed with grief that it would have been unbearable if it weren't so compelling. The band was everything Walter loved about Cuban music: brassy, opulent, super-melodic, hyperactive with percussion, and loud as a fire engine. It was a wonder that the neighbors regularly put up with El Rio's heavenly fracas.

Late that afternoon, Walter and Lawrence sat drinking margaritas on a shady wooden bench across from the dance floor, out of the crush of the crowd, but so close to the barbecue that, when a breeze invaded the garden, they had to duck the smoke. They had a direct view of the dance floor, dense with couples, and the people watching was unbeatable. In there somewhere was Cary— dancing with someone—nowhere to be seen; Sasha and Jabez were dancing where the crowd was thinner, ranging a bit, Sasha spinning at Jabez's cue. Walter tried to talk over the music, telling Lawrence how nice it was to see him out and about, and how good he looked. They had seen each other less often this year, ever since Walter had stopped doing deliveries for Open Hand and started packing groceries in its food bank. Over that summer Lawrence had seemed to grow healthier and, startlingly, younger. Maybe it was that he was more energetic, maybe it was the few extra pounds he'd put on—he looked less gaunt—but somehow, he seemed to have youthened. Larry almost never talked about HIV or his treatments. He'd talk about anything else first, but he attributed the spring in his step to a new drug he'd received from a new trial, *sequin-avir*, which sounded like it had been named by a drag queen. Maybe Larry was mispronouncing it—but the buzz about it was strong and cautiously hopeful.

One song ended abruptly, burning out in brass fanfare. The next was a slow one, much quieter, no trumpets and almost no percussion, just a soft padding on bongos. Walter watched as Jabez and Sasha kept on dancing, slowing to the pulse of the percussionist.

"It's funny, I can't believe I never asked—how did you meet Jabez?" Walter had always assumed it was some kind of British expat thing, as if everyone who'd once lived in London had to know each other.

"Oh, naturally, the same way you meet anyone these days," said Lawrence. "In line for the ATM!"

The banality of this came as a shock. Ever since seeing Larry and Jabez salsa together, Walter had wondered if they had a past or if they were secret lovers, one of those *discreet* gay couples who never touch in front of others, or even mention that they're together.

"Sorry if I'm prying, but were you and Jabez ever . . . involved?"

"Oh, no, no, just good friends. Great friends. He's been like family, really, to me, and Roland as well. Thank god for Jay. He always loved Roland; he moved in to help out when Roland was at his worst. Some nights he would take a turn minding him, helping with the IV, changing the sheets, so I could get a full night's sleep. I'm sure you know, at the time, taking AZT meant you were up several times a night. Like minding a newborn . . ."

Walter nodded. The singer's voice overflowed with longing, and Walter realized the tune was "Siboney," a beautiful Cuban song so famous even he knew about it. He didn't know who or what *Siboney* was, but from what he could make of the lyrics, it was about longing, pining, dying for love.

". . . it's the luck of the draw, really," Larry went on. "Roland and I seroconverted at the same time, all those years ago. There is absolutely no reason why he should have succumbed, while I held on. None. I always imagined I would go first. And if he could have held on until now—who knows? Who knows?" Lawrence almost never spoke this frankly about Roland—his life, yes, but not his illness. A moment later, Larry appeared absent, as if he were thousands of miles away, in Cuba, or Lima, or London. His vacant look broke into a smile. "He would have loved this. Roland. He loved to dance. He'll be thrilled when I tell him we came here. Maybe a little jealous."

"When you . . . tell him?"

"Oh yes! He's very transformed, of course. But I still recognize him when he comes at night to talk. Less frequently of late . . . since I haven't been having night sweats."

"*Si no vienes, me moriré de amor,*" sang the chanteuse. There it was: *If you don't come, I'll die of love.* The song modulated, and there was a long flute solo, and although the jazz flute was sometimes treated as a punch line, it was clear now that what made it embarrassing to some was its intense beauty, the tone almost unbearably pretty and light. It trilled and soared, sounding so birdlike that, in spite of himself, Walter searched for its source—some bright bird—in the branches above them. Kookaburra sits in the bottlebrush tree, wreathed in charcoal smoke. The smoke stung his eyes; he closed them. The song ended, the flute's final trill reverbing from the amps. The crowd applauded; the band began again. When he opened his eyes, Jabez was gone, and Cary had taken his place. She was dancing Sasha slowly into the heart of the crowd.

"Now it's my turn to pry," said Lawrence. "Tell me, what's going on— how's it going with the two of them?"

"Well, it's wonderful," said Walter. "Wonderful, but kind of confusing. At times it's very confusing, to be honest." All that remained of his margarita was ice and a C of salt on the rim. He was nervously tasting sharp pinches of salt and chasing them with melting ice. Salt and cool, salt and cool.

"What's confusing about it?"

Walter laughed. "I mean, for a start, being in love with two people at once? That's messing with my head a bit."

"I don't see the problem." Lawrence blinked editorially.

"Well, honestly, I've never been in love before, that's the first thing. And now, I wouldn't have thought it was possible, but, *for fuck's sake*, here I am in love with a man and a woman at the same time . . ."

"Yes. *And?*"

"*And*, you ask? Well, sometimes—often, in fact—I can't tell which one is which." Another pinch of sharp salt, a chip of cool ice.

Lawrence cocked his head, then concluded: "I still don't see the problem."

"This kind of thing happens to Cary all the time. She's never in love with fewer than two people at any given moment. And Sasha—it's so annoying, but nothing throws Sasha. So I'm the only one who keeps having his mind blown by it. Being in love is *stressful*, isn't it? Am I overreacting? Have you ever been in love with two people at once?"

Lawrence's brown eyes were sympathetic. "Oh yes, of course I have. It's one of those things, I think. Live long enough, live *well* enough, and it will happen. To never have it happen would require cutting yourself off in some vital way. A kind of dumb single-mindedness. A romantic asceticism."

"Sometimes I try to square things in my head, I think, by almost forgetting that they are two people . . . by momentarily mistaking them for one person. Because between the two of them, they're pretty much perfect. But they aren't one person, are they? And it's wrong, and unfair to them, and basically fucked up, to think of them that way . . ."

"Look, Wall," said Lawrence, "no one is handing out prizes for overthinking things. If they were, you'd be laden with medals. Come to think of it, maybe you are right for the academy after all!"

He was alluding to an earlier conversation, when Walter told him he was thinking about graduate school. He'd been considering it all summer and he still wasn't sure, but he asked if Lawrence would write recommendation letters for him and maybe suggest a few programs. Weirdly, Larry became testy when he explained that he was thinking of programs in film history rather than filmmaking. *Didn't he want to be a screenwriter? Wasn't that the obvious path? Wouldn't he much rather be a maker than a scorekeeper, a critic or theorist, or, worse, a historian? Why not make art rather than merely studying it?* They had dropped the subject there, but now Lawrence seemed ready to needle him about it again.

"And what do your two paramours think of you going off to a program, maybe—most likely, actually—in another city?"

"I haven't brought it up with them—I'm kind of scared to. Of course I don't want to leave the Bay Area, but if it comes to that, they'll be fine without me. But don't tell them yet—please! I have to figure out a way to tell them . . ."

"Got it," said Lawrence. "It's not a big deal—hardly worth mentioning—but also potentially explosive."

Walter nodded and smiled.

"Cary still claims you two will finish that screenplay any day now and that she's dying to share the finished product with me and my producer friend. Not long ago, she was saying she wants you two to meet me in LA this Thanksgiving, when I visit Ben Venable. You know she has a whole career in film in mind for the two of you, right?"

"Oh, Cary has a career in mind for everyone and everything," said Walter. "She has a career in mind for me, and for Sasha, and for Bombolone, and for half her other friends, which, as you know, is most of San Francisco. But for the last six months or so our only career has been drinking cocktails."

Lawrence bobbed his head in half agreement. "She does seem rather unfocused. Maybe pathologically so. Regardless, I think you two should finish the damn thing. Make it the best you can. It would be good for both of you—you've got the focus, but she's got the energy."

He wondered then if Larry was being cagey, implying he himself didn't have the energy, that he was phlegmatic.

"I'll make a deal with you," said Lawrence. "I'll write you letters for

282 Christopher Tradowsky

graduate programs, as many as you want, if you promise to finish your screen-play this fall. You two get it done, I'll show it to Ben, we'll see what he says. I can't make promises, of course. But nothing ventured, nothing gained."

"OK, it's a deal—an extremely generous deal—thank you." Walter leaned in, squeezed Lawrence with one arm, then let his arm fall. "Anyway, I still want to know, what do you have against me studying film history? If I want to be a historian, what's wrong with that?"

"It's the secondariness of the thing," Lawrence insisted. "It's not that historians, or critics for that matter, are bad or unnecessary; it's that their work, however creative, is always *secondary*, parasitic in a way. Nothing against parasites—they're just doing their best like the rest of us. But for you, Wall, it's a cop-out. Of all the young people I know, you are too content with catharsis."

"What's that supposed to mean?" Walter smarted. "And what a weird thing for a filmmaker to say!"

"Why should it be?"

"Because films are catharsis, that's *all they are*. That's what every film is about."

"Not so. My films are *not about catharsis*." Larry suddenly seemed cross.

"That's not even possible. I don't understand how that's possible."

"It's very simple. My films do not *represent* experiences, they *are* experiences."

Walter frowned, stumped. This was one of those puzzling things that Lawrence sometimes came out with, like about film's *visionary properties* or its *empiricism*. It was a trick Larry had of curtailing an argument by saying something almost totally opaque. It was effective, or at least it worked on him, which was why he found it so irritating. Larry was absent-mindedly shaking the ice in his cup along with the music. Walter asked if he'd like another margarita.

"Look, darling, you know I love you, but I did not come here to play the gay sage and explain film to you, or help you decide your career path, or even to soothe your dreadful anxiety over having *two perfect lovers*. I came to dance, a lot! Preferably with a young stud. So, for crying out loud, are you going to ask me to dance? Ask me to dance, or get out of the way! I'm in my prime, you know."

Walter stood and held out his hand.

"You're leading," said Lawrence, and Walter led him across the patio, away from the panting barbecue, onto the sunspotted dance floor beneath Carmen's enveloping gaze, and deep into all that frenetic, euphoric loudness.

Aria

FREDDIE MERCURY WAS MAKING HIMSELF comfortable on one side of the king platform bed. He had a tumbler aglow with vodka cranberry in his left hand,
and it brimmed perilously over a snowy duvet with an elaborate, unreadable
monogram at the center. Across the wide room, Debbie Harry stood before a
lowboy dresser, staring at the enormous black-and-white photograph framed
above it.

"Do you think this is Ivan?" asked Debbie. "I haven't met him out of
costume."

The picture was a formal nude of a very beautiful, sleekly muscular
young man—a depilated dancer's body—his face half in shadow. It was unclear if his skin was very dark or if it was an effect of the picture's careful
underexposure. The man was not quite nude; he wore a flimsy ballerina's
crinoline around his waist, which concealed nothing, but framed his thighs in
bright white bursts as, with one hand, he raised it to expose a large, flagrantly
relaxed dick and low-hanging balls.

"Sure, it's Ivan," said Freddie Mercury. "You can tell by the intense hotness. Don't you think?" Debbie nodded in agreement as Freddie went on: "I
think he must be one of those guys whose hotness radiates off him no matter
what he's wearing—or how ridiculous the costume. Anyway, I'm annoyed
with Ivan at the moment."

"It seems kind of arrogant to hang an erotic nude of yourself in your house, doesn't it? And such a massive one? The picture, I mean." Debbie was trying not to fixate on the large dick, arranged dead center in the photo, which hung centered on the large wall. Ivan's cock was the room's vanishing point.

"Where else would you hang an erotic nude of yourself? Someone else's house? And it is their *bedroom*," said Freddie, sipping his drink and leaning back against the pillows banking the headboard.

"Why are you annoyed with Ivan?" Debbie asked. "Do you begrudge him his gorgeous mansion and his effortless hotness?"

"Of course not! Don't be silly. Downstairs, he got all pedantic about my costume. Said I was doing eighties Freddie Mercury." He ran his free hand over the six silver buckles that jangled unfastened on the front of his yellow jacket. He looked like an unserious soldier, a majorette or a gay nutcracker, an effect amplified by the red stripes running down the outer seams of his white pants and by his wide mustache, black as a dime-store comb. "I guess they're very strict about this being a seventies party. Who's more seventies than Freddie Mercury, I ask you?"

"I don't know. Barbra Streisand?" This answer was prompted by the disco rising up the stairwell from the party downstairs, the strident Barbra-Donna diva-off "No More Tears (Enough Is Enough)."

Freddie sifted his cocktail through his mustache. "This house is a little ridiculous, don't you think? It's so tasteful, it's almost excruciating."

They looked around: the spacious room was painted flint gray with the faintest purple tinge, as if the designer aimed to evoke all the charms of the inside of a galvanized toolbox. A large green-gray painting of a spatchcocked cityscape hung over the bed: either a genuine Diebenkorn or a very good approximation.

"We shouldn't be up here," said Debbie. "It's really rude of us."

"Oh, BS. A house this ostentatious *begs* you to explore it. I think Mitchell and Ivan would be insulted if we didn't."

Debbie walked to one of the vertical ribbon windows that flanked the bed. It faced south over the Fillmore toward Japantown. "I think this is the fanciest house I've ever been in. All this room for two people? What did you say they did? Ivan is the arm candy, but Mitchell is the CFO of what again?"

"I dunno—Pottery Barrel or Cratery Barn, one of those. Get a load of this!" Freddie had put his drink down and was holding an enormous veiny pink crystal, milky like quartz, carved into a dildo. He held it up for Debbie to see the smoothly scored frenulum, an elegant, inverted Y, like *rén*, the Chinese character for *man*. "Do you think it's salt?"

"Please don't lick it—please don't—" Debbie protested, too late.

"It's not salt," said Freddie, wrinkling his nose. "It must be rose quartz."

"Yuck—you have to know where that's been! Where did you find it?"

"Right here—check this out!" He stood the phallus on a sturdy white base and thumbed a switch on a cord. Pink light beamed up through fissures in the shaft. "Do I have to take back what I said about excruciating tastefulness?"

"Do you know how Ramon Novarro died?"

"No," said Freddie. "The silent film star?"

"Yeah, famous closeted heartthrob. He was beaten to death with a huge onyx dildo he kept beside his bed. A couple of hustlers murdered him."

"Holy pantalones! That is horrifying!"

"The dildo was a gift from Rudolph Valentino. You know, one heart-throb to another . . ." Debbie perched wistfully on the end of the bed.

A roar like whitewater rapids erupted from the master bath, after which a pocket door slid open with magnificent smoothness, and there stood David Bowie, backlit. *Aladdin Sane*–era Bowie, in a red-and-blue-striped jumper, shiny vinyl, with a metallic collar and gold space-age epaulets. His red hair stood on end, and the legendary red-and-blue lightning bolt shimmered across his face.

"Every time I see you it takes my breath away," said Debbie.

"Why thank you, darling," said David. "You two *must* see this bathroom—it has to be seen to be believed!"

The bathroom was larger than many kitchens in SF. It was white except for the slate tiles that covered the floor and a walk-in shower that could have fit another bathroom within it. Debbie checked her lipstick in the mirror over a marble his-and-his vanity. Freddie and David were busy admiring an enormous freestanding hammered-copper bathtub framed by two ribbon windows running floor to ceiling.

"I think they used this in one of the Indiana Jones movies, didn't they?" asked Freddie. "Slap a gold eagle on it and it's a dead ringer for the Ark of the Covenant." He turned and scolded Debbie: "Wall, don't you dare pull that wig off!"

"I won't—I'm adjusting it. God, it itches! I really don't think I look like Debbie Harry anyway."

It wasn't Sasha's fault; the costume was perfect: the white satin spaghetti-strap shift right off the *Parallel Lines* cover (of course Sasha just *had it around*), the white sandals, the platinum wig. Walter wasn't comfortable in drag—his embarrassingly white shoulders were too broad for the dress, he didn't like pretending to have boobs, the socks in his bra were lumpy and malformed, and he hated the powdery smell of the foundation covering his stubble. But then he leaned toward the mirror and admired the streaks of peacock blue that Sasha had lovingly painted over his eyes, brightening the purplish recesses where the deep sockets met his nose. The iridescent streaks, the dark mascara and eyeliner, the whole effect, nearly turned his gray eyes blue. He smiled. He had to admit, pressing his lips together, he loved his bright fuck-me-red lipstick, which made his mouth larger and made him feel glamorous, something he'd never felt before.

Behind him in the mirror Freddie was making the moves on David, who was backed against the copper tub.

"Don't kiss me! If you ruin my makeup, I'll be furious! Why are you *always so horny?*"

"Can you blame me?" Freddie pawed at the zipper on David's jumpsuit. "It's not my fault you two are so goddamn hot. Anyway, I can kiss around your lightning bolt." He kissed David on the neck, moving his way up behind the ear.

"Oh god," said David as Freddie went for his buckle. "Do you know how hard it is to zip this back up?"

Walter stopped admiring himself the moment he realized what was happening behind him, and what Freddie had tucked precariously under his arm. He swung toward them.

"What do you think you're doing with *that*?"

"Oh, you mean *this*?" Freddie raised his arm and held out the pink phallus like it was a prize zucchini. He left David half unzipped by the tub and, crossing toward the vanity, caught the door handle and slid the door closed. "Debbie doesn't mind if I mess up her makeup—do you, Debbie?"

"*Put that down*. There's a *huge* party downstairs . . ."

"That's two stories down," said Freddie. "No one will hear us. Here." Freddie set the phallus on the counter between the sinks. "There you go. I guess nobody really wants crystal fragments in their coochie anyway."

Freddie kissed Debbie passionately, breakers crashing, a real *From Here to Eternity* beach kiss.

"This is a terrible idea," Debbie muttered, scooching up onto the counter and trying to avoid slipping into the sink, while they barely unlocked lips.

David came up close beside them now, his jumper unzipped to the navel, his chest hairless except for a little warm blond down. "My two rabbits," said David tenderly, kissing Debbie's shoulder. "Lemme double-check the door is locked . . ."

David apparently did a bad job of it, because seven minutes later the door slid back open and there was Cher in full Pocahontas getup: eagle feathers tied into her flat-ironed hair, a cascade of chunky turquoise and silver down her décolletage. Her midriff was exposed above a zigzag-patterned skirt that draped to the floor and slit to the thigh; her tanned, muscled abdomen was familiar from the large nude photo that hung in the bedroom behind her.

Who can know what Cher might be thinking at any given moment, but this is what she found in her master bath: David Bowie leaning against her hammered-copper bathtub, his space suit undone to the crotch, and Freddie Mercury and Debbie Harry, in various states of dishabille, jumbled up on the sheepskin rug before him. And each as happy as three prize terriers in file in Alta Plaza Park, noses planted in each other's privates, having the time of their lives. When they saw her, they froze in place.

For a moment, nobody moved. Cher looked surprised but unfazed. She giggled and, in a voice notably higher than her famous contralto, said, "Well, aren't you guys sweet?" Then she cocked her head and, walking over to the counter, picked up the crystal phallus. "Now what is this doing here? This shouldn't be here!" She shook her head. "Hold on a sec . . ." The ménage waited as she strode through the bedroom and placed the crystal on its base, then walked back, her cork heels gently drumming the hardwood as she went. Upon her return they were scrambling to cover up, and Freddie spoke for them: "Ivan, we are so, so sorry! It's all—"

"Oh god, don't apologize." Cher laughed nervously, batting her hand at them, then stuck out the tip of her tongue, blowing raspberries. Turning again, it appeared she might be leaving, but instead she slid the door closed, and with the elegance of a dancer, tan leg bursting from her slit, bent down and began untying the leather laces that strapped her shoe to her ankle. She looked up, smiling graciously, and asked, "You don't mind if I join in?"

"Not at all!" said Freddie, after a beat.

"No," said David, looking astonished behind his lightning bolt.

"Uh—no?" said Debbie, stifling a nervous laugh.

In another minute Cher stood barefoot before them. "Where are my manners?" she asked. "Does anyone want some coke?"

"No!" said Freddie and David in unison.

"We're good!" said David.

"No, but thanks so much for offering," said Debbie.

Cher apparently didn't lock the door, either, because some ten minutes later it slid open again, and there stood Sonny Bono with his chestnut pageboy, bell-bottoms, and fringed suede vest, a novelty sheriff's star pinned over his heart. His frown was framed by the droop of his handlebar mustache. Cher didn't notice him at first. She was busy making out with David Bowie and getting a hand job through the slit in her skirt.

"What the fuck, Ivan?" Sonny seemed furious, but as the quartet unknotted itself, apologizing, zipping up, and tucking in, it became clear that Sonny had barely registered what they were doing and was angry about something else entirely. He seemed to be ranting about the cranberry cocktail he was holding in his hand.

"What the fuck is the matter, Mitchell?" said Cher. "What are you freaking out about?"

"Look at this, just look at this!" Sonny led Cher to the bedside table. He pointed to the surface, beside the glowing pink phallus, where someone had carelessly left their drink. A rheumy butterscotch ring had eaten deep into the maple finish. "It's ruined!"

"So? What's the big deal?" Cher was exasperated. "So we get it refinished!"

"It's a *Noguchi*," said Sonny, livid. "You can't just *get it refinished*."

Thirteen minutes later the three disgraced rockers were hoofing down Fillmore Street, trying to hail a cab and having no luck at all. Walter thought that maybe no one in Pacific Heights needed cabs. Probably they called them from their mansions, or they had the maid call them, or had the maid alert their driver. He dodged into the street, arm raised, whenever he saw a lit sign.

Already two had whizzed by. He wondered if removing his wig would help, if it would make him look more or less like a strung-out hooker.

Sasha was trudging fast downhill in his bright red space boots, eager to get far away from the scene of their impropriety. Cary raced to keep up with him.

"I've never been so embarrassed!" Sasha yelled, at intervals crying with anger and laughing in exasperation.

"It's OK, darling, it's OK," Cary repeated every twenty feet.

They stopped on the sidewalk in front of a large furniture boutique. There was no room for furniture in the panoramic display windows, however; they were full to bursting with hundreds of Chinese silk lanterns of all sizes, lit and floating, a teeming flood of red blood cells. The sidewalk glowed red.

"We weren't even supposed to be there! *You know* I hate crashing parties."

"We weren't crashing! Lawrence invited us . . ."

"It's definitely crashing if the friend who invited you never intended to show up. And don't start with me about *making connections*. Mingling with the A-gays. Seeing if you can find support for a screenplay you can't even finish writing."

Walter hung back from the spat, keeping an eye on the half dozen cars inching down the hill toward them. For the moment Cary was too cowed to argue.

"Mitchell isn't going to *invest in your movie project*," said Sasha. "He's going to send you a five-thousand-dollar bill for his Noguchi table."

"I wouldn't be so sure about that," said Cary. "Mitchell likes me."

"Mitchell literally doesn't know you from . . . Freddie Mercury."

Walter didn't dare interrupt. Like Sasha, he felt humiliated by the incident. Yet now he couldn't help noticing how wonderfully '70s the setting looked, awash in red light as they were: a scene from a Scorsese film—sadly lost—in which David Bowie and Freddie Mercury have a public lovers' spat on a sidewalk in a soundstage Chinatown.

Cary, as proof that Mitchell liked her, pulled a business card from her wallet and presented it to Sasha.

"When did he give this to you?"

"On the way down the stairs."

"As we were being escorted out? That's crazy!"

Cary shook her head: "We had a little conversation about the bathroom. I told him the heated floors were a really nice touch. Then he gave me this card and told me to call him, said it was his private line."

"Gross! Cary? Gross!"

"You guys?" Walter called. A checkered cab had wheeled around the corner and halted under his raised arm.

"Well, I'm not going to *call him*," said Cary, tossing the card in a trash bin as she moved toward the taxi. "I'm not planning to prostitute myself with some old guy who looks like Sonny Bono. I don't care how rich he is."

Cary scooched in first. Before they followed, Walter and Sasha had a silent exchange. Sasha shook his head wearily. Lipstick gone, the once-crisp lightning bolt was smeared upward across his forehead and temple. Walter overflowed with compassion for Sasha; it was the first time he'd seen him really lose his cool, and he never wanted to see it again. By his left ear Sasha's wig had gone askew, and a little mesh at his sideburn was curling up with such pathos that it made Walter want to whisk him home, and put him to bed, and wrap him in his arms, and love him forever.

The cab ride back to the Castro was intense. Squeezed in the middle, palpable tension radiated from either side of him. He wondered if he should beat a swift retreat to his own corner, ask the cabbie to make a second stop at his place. But that wouldn't help the nagging feeling that he was, perhaps, the secret source of their domestic strife. Things between them had been strained for weeks; it was a tension he could trace back to the Saturday of the blackout.

In a string of ideal autumn afternoons, it had been yet another cloudless Saturday when there was not a thing amiss in the world, and Walter had been strolling through the Upper Haight, window-shopping, enjoying a day off and an afternoon alone. But something was amiss somewhere . . . someone was about to lose their job at a PG&E substation nearby. All at once the sidewalks were filled with frustrated consumers, spilling from the stores, having been told they couldn't buy anything. The power had gone out and everything was down—lights, cash registers, security sensors. People blinked on the sidewalk, like lab mice expelled from a dark maze, looking upward as if the source of the outage might be cosmological—an eclipse or an alien visitation—and mystified at what was to become of an afternoon when no money could change hands. Walter would never find out what had caused it; that was the day he learned the term *rolling blackout*. He felt a surreptitious delight in seeing the tourist traps grind to a halt. On the sidewalk a large family was fighting over what to do now that they'd been ejected from a gauzy imported clothing store called Dharma.

There was a vital energy in the air—the kind provoked by a sudden, compulsory collapse of routine—snow day energy. For Walter, the blackout would have been of no consequence at all, if, walking eastward toward Masonic Avenue, he hadn't raised his eyes above the storefronts and noticed residents throwing open the sashes of second- and third-story windows, peering out to see what was up. From a bay window above one of the myriad shoe stores, a young man was waving at him and calling him by name. It was Julian, dark-haired and dark-eyed Julian, leaning from the shadowy window and laughing, his face lit with schoolboyish glee. Walter wasn't sure what he wanted, until he realized Julian was beckoning him: "Come up, Walter! Come on up!"

Walter laughed, too, because it felt like something from an Italian operetta, the lithe young lover leaning from a window into the *piazzetta*, calling, *Vieni, vieni!* to a passing paramour. How could he possibly resist? He climbed the stairs to meet Julian—handsome, vibrant, horny Julian—and they honored the blackout in the traditional way couples have honored blackouts, ever since that industrial fall from grace when the world was, maybe regrettably, electrified. Julian's roommates were out, and he led Walter down the long hallway to a sunroom in the back of the apartment. There they fucked around—first on the couch, then on the carpet, naked and awash in greenish light from the windows and the intense smell of a blue gum eucalyptus, whose weeping mesh of sickles shielded them from the eyes of neighbors—Walter hoped. They worked up a sweat and ended with a shower. They were making out under a dark deluge when the lights blazed back on, the spell broken. Julian had to rush back down the block to work.

His blackout tryst with Julian wasn't a big deal, he told Cary and Sasha about it—it was too fun not to share the story: *How I spent my rolling blackout.* Cary and Sasha would never object on principle. According to them Walter should feel entirely free to fuck around with Julian, or anyone else for that matter. The whole thing would have been of no consequence whatsoever if it hadn't happened that, several days later, Cary and Walter were squeezing in a little early-evening sixty-nine, when Cary raised her head from his crotch, unstraddled his sex-addled smile, and said, "Darling! You have crabs."

"I do?" he asked. "Really, I do?"

She led him into the bathroom and, sitting on the edge of the tub, extracted from his pubes a living speck, a tiny wriggling asterisk. He was astounded that she was able to pick it out, the signal of the single tick, through all that noise of wiry hair, but there it was, wriggling on the tip of her finger. It was no big deal, she assured him, flushing it down the bowl, everyone got crabs sooner or later. They'd had them before. But they both knew these crabs were the gift of Julian, as otherwise none of them had strayed outside their trio recently. Even this wouldn't have mattered, except that now they had to wash every piece of laundry they owned. They began as soon as Sasha got home from work and after Walter's inaugural expedition—a queer rite of passage—to Walgreens for Kwell.

Walter and Sasha spent that night at the laundromat while Cary made dinner. They had to wash so much because, truth be told, they'd gotten piggy and stopped using the dresser in favor of the armchair, and stopped using the hamper in favor of the bedroom floor, where much of their underwear and clothing wound up in a crumpled potpourri, or closer to a mulch, smelling . . . not good, but comfortingly funky, kind of autumnal. Doing all the laundry at once was a pain, but then there were items that couldn't be machine washed: the handmade outfits, the dozen silk and needlepoint pillows, the sumptuous Klimt quilt. These had to be bundled tight in trash bags for two weeks, until the lice had suffocated.

Something about the whole incident seemed to suffocate Sasha's libido over those same two weeks, which got to Walter, the guilt dampening his libido, too, until at last even Cary was affected. Their sex life suffered right up through the night of their curtailed foursome with Cher. Through it all, something finally dawned on Walter about Sasha and Cary's dynamic. The ineluctable truth was Cary was a slob. She loved to cook but never washed a pot; she loved to dress in fitted suits but, strangely, didn't care if they looked rumpled or smelled a bit ripe. After all, what was cologne for? Her tastes were those of a sophisticate, her hygienic impulses those of an adolescent boy. Under her debonair facade she was funky, and Walter had thought, more than once, that the whole arrangement probably wouldn't have worked for him if there hadn't been something about her pheromones, a sweet musk he found irresistible.

When it had been the two of them alone, Sasha and Cary managed to strike a balance that, though precarious, was for the most part equal: Cary would do the shopping and cooking, Sasha would do the cleaning up. Cary respected Sasha's need for general order and refrained from leaving the exploded detritus of her creative whims in the middle of freshly tidied rooms. Walter disturbed this order. Once they became a trio, there were too many meals to cook for too many mouths, too much sex to be had and innumerable outfits to shed in order to have it. There was no order—diversion was the order. In short, there was too much fun to be had, none of which involved cleaning. The apartment became an opulent disaster, the air cloyed by perfumed candles Cary brought home from the card store. Living so haphazardly weighed greatly upon Sasha, but it didn't bother Cary at all; she was happy as a magpie in her nest of glitzy scraps and paste gems. And Walter, as usual, was slow on the uptake, too sated in their luxuriant sty to sense trouble brewing there.

That evening in the laundromat, kaleidoscopes of their lives whirling in the dryers around them, Plexiglas portals steaming, Walter and Sasha found themselves folding a mountain of underwear, most of it Cary's boxers.

Walter laughed despite himself and shook his head. "I'm so sorry, I know this is all my fault. But I also think . . . Cary's a genius, in a way."

"I doubt she'd argue that point with you," said Sasha. "But I get it. You mean, because right now she has her two partners folding all her underwear for her?"

"It's very intimate, isn't it?" Walter grazed the slightly ridged weave of a pair of boxers with one thumb. "Folding your lover's underwear, I mean?"

Sasha rolled his eyes and sighed. "Yeah. The job is yours if you want it. Frankly, I've lost count of the number of times I've hand-washed a piece of clothing that I made for Cary that she left in a heap on the floor."

As it happened, domestic chores were one of the few places where boring, old gender roles tripped Cary and Sasha up in an inverted, ironic way. If pressed about housework, Cary would have one of two responses. Taking the low road, she'd admit that she was lazy and didn't care about cleaning up, and argue that anyway she didn't mind living amid chaos. There's something homey about one's own mess, after all. Claiming the high ground, she would decry the sexism of hundreds, nay thousands of years of Western culture, all that uncompensated domestic labor on the part of women, as women were traded between men like broodmares and pack animals, the weight of which history sought to pressure her into becoming someone's housewife. And she simply wouldn't do it. She was *not that kind of magician*.

Invariably the first argument made Sasha angry at Cary's selfishness, but the second worked on him. It weighed and wore on a fracture, a fault line down the middle of their union. So that these two, for whom skepticism about gender was a deep article of faith, neither of whom saw themselves as essentially male or female, when it came to cleaning the stovetop or vacuuming behind the couch, suddenly looked like a throwback from a '50s sitcom: Cary the crass, swaggering man of the house; Sasha the deferential housewife, too polite to henpeck. Walter, meanwhile, could only see them as perfectly matched—the very model of life beyond conformity. He'd overlooked this dynamic entirely, including the way his own mass weighed upon the fault line, until the night he was folding a pile of Cary's underwear and musing on the intimacy of the gesture. Sasha eyed him like he might gag him with a pair of rolled-up boxers to shut him up. Then came the least enchanting, least fun conversation he'd ever had with Sasha, in which Walter vowed—cheerfully, since it had only just occurred to him—to help out more around the apartment. Sasha said he'd be delighted to show him where he kept the toilet bowl cleaner, since Cary couldn't tell him.

That fall, domestic concerns were scuttled further as Cary was off on a new project. For a year she'd been promising Kelly Calypso that Bombolone would collaborate with her on an evening of shadow puppetry. The show they cooked up was a program of murder ballads called *Miss Otis Regrets* after Cole Porter's parody of the genre. Kelly and friends would work the puppets, and Bombolone would accompany, with Cary and Sasha narrating and singing live. Impulsively, with little more than a month to rehearse, Kelly booked performance slots at Cafe du Nord in late October, convinced it would be the perfect Halloween show.

After that, there was no time to waste. Virtually every night Cary and Sasha rehearsed murder ballads in the *living womb*. Bombolone even added a member, Kelly's friend Caleb, a bashful bank teller and straight stoner, who grew mushrooms in an equipment shed in his backyard and proved equally adept on the banjo and the fiddle. It was weird for Walter, hearing Sasha and Cary sing songs of murderous revenge between lovers, between parents and offspring, between sisters. They were songs of seething envy and possessiveness, as far from his friends' enlightened ideals as he could imagine. Walter wasn't exactly jealous of Kelly—or so he told himself—but it was hard not to feel left out. It wasn't the first time she'd captured Cary's attention, only this time she was monopolizing both Cary's and Sasha's time.

Meanwhile, their screenplay, which had been back-burnered for months at a time, was nearly done—an unexpected twist considering how sporadically they had worked on it. The plot was fully plotted, the dialogue hashed out. While Cary was preoccupied, Walter sifted through piles of notes and half drafts, and managed to type up a complete version. It was amazing how focused he could be if he wasn't being summoned to cocktail hour every evening. One Saturday afternoon he walked to Kinko's and spent an hour of triumphant boredom xeroxing their screenplay and having the copies bound: one for himself, one each for Sasha, Cary, and Lawrence. With great ceremony he packed up a fifth copy with a cordial letter and mailed it off to Lawrence's friend Ben, the producer in LA. Lawrence promised that they could rendezvous with Ben in Los Angeles after Thanksgiving—he'd made the same promise the year before, but they'd blown that chance. Still, Cary was adamant that the three of them would make it this year: "It's the big break we've been waiting for!" she declared. They'd make an adventure of it, take the scenic route down California 1 and show Walter Hearst Castle, maybe stopping in breathtaking Big Sur and kitschy Solvang, that inexplicable Danish Brigadoon.

November came around again, as it tended to, though clearly no one asked for it. Walter slipped right back into spending every evening with Cary and Sasha, but before long he realized that Cary was in a snit about something. She pretended nothing was wrong but was becoming increasingly terse. She'd never figured out that, loquacious as she was, if she suddenly went quiet her friends assumed the worst. When Walter pressed her, she came out with it:

looking through screenplay drafts on a diskette he had shared with her, she had found an application letter addressed to NYU. Cary asked when he was planning to tell them about grad school, and then Walter's scheme came out and, with it, all his anxieties about his future and theirs. It was a hard sell to argue that he was still only thinking about it, what with the applications completed, the fees paid, and rec letters sent. Lawrence had known for months. Likewise, it was hard to argue how much he wanted to stay with them when he hadn't applied to a single school in the area. The closest school where he might wind up was in LA.

Sasha found out about it that evening when he came home from work to find Cary and Walter fighting in the kitchen, keeping it civil but barely. Sasha had a bag of groceries in hand, and before he could set them down, he had irritated Cary by taking Walter's side, saying he thought it was a wonderful idea. When Walter explained he was pursuing programs in film history, Sasha said it made all the sense in the world.

"How can you be so cheerful?" Cary accused Sasha. "You do realize what this means. You realize, Walter's planning on *leaving us*."

"That's not it at all!" Walter yelped.

"Don't be so dramatic," said Sasha, organizing groceries in the fridge. "He's not *leaving us*; he hasn't even gotten into a program yet. And grad school could be great for him . . . *grad school is a good thing!*"

"No, it's not," said Cary. "Everyone agrees that grad school is terrible, *especially* our friends in grad school. You go in overflowing with curiosity and hope, and emerge disillusioned and up to your eyeballs in debt, and an awful pedant on top of it all . . ."

Walter shook his head and laughed, but Cary went on.

". . . and for whom, exactly, is it a good thing? *For whom?* You waltz off to get a fancy degree, and meanwhile I have to give up my best friend? Sounds like the fuzzy end of the lollipop to me!"

"I thought *I* was your best friend," said Sasha, brandishing a bag of bok choy.

"No, you're my *favorite person*. Walter is my best friend, but far from my favorite person right now."

They were silent for a moment, until Cary realized that the two of them wouldn't stop staring lasers at her until she explained herself.

"It's very simple," she said, addressing Sasha. "Walter's *my* best friend, and you're *his* best friend, and I'm *your* best friend, so it balances out. But when it comes to favorite people, the current flows the other direction: you're *my* favorite person, and Walter's *your* favorite person, and I'm *his* favorite person."

"Ha!" Walter guffawed loudly. "What the . . . ? You can't be serious . . ."

She couldn't be serious, of course. But in a bizarre way, it made sense. This much he understood: True friendship means responsibility. Favoritism is reckless.

"What an elaborate scheme—how on earth did you come up with that?" asked Sasha, letting his hair down as he ambled toward the hallway.

"If you think about it, it's true. The three of us—we're bound together by these two opposing currents . . . like electromagnets."

"You have the oddest ways of saying I love you." Sasha's voice trailed behind him into the bedroom.

They reached a détente, which largely rested on an assumption Cary made that, worst-case scenario, Walter would move to LA for a couple years. He was certain to get into one of the programs there, she averred, and would choose UCLA or USC over anywhere on the East Coast or, perish the thought, the Midwest. Since this scenario cheered Cary up, Walter went along with it without mentioning complicating factors, including that the film historian he wanted most to work with was in Chicago. The topic was tabled until he heard back from programs. Yet every few days Cary would make another jab about Walter *abandoning her*, or her and Sasha, or her and Sasha and Lawrence, and at exactly the worst time, when they'd finished their screenplay and were in a good position for Larry to help them out. Never mind that Sasha told her many times to knock it off. Never mind that Lawrence had recommended him to grad programs or that living in Los Angeles—if it came to that—might prove an advantage if anything ever became of their screenplay.

Though Cary assumed that Walter would move to LA, she couldn't help trashing the city, which Walter wasn't able to defend, as he'd never been there. Once when they were grabbing dinner at Zapata, Cary threatened that Walter wouldn't be able to get his beloved super burritos in LA. Sasha declared this a bald-faced lie.

"Don't listen to her," said Sasha. "The Mexican food there is awesome."

"It's not the same," said Cary. "It's not as fresh. It's not as good."

Walter was frowning into his spicy burrito, searching for an elusive vein of sour cream that must have been rolled into the heel. Cary had the right idea. If she wanted to extort him into staying, Mexican food was the way to do it.

"If you move to LA, darling," Sasha said, "I'll visit you there all the time."

"I won't," said Cary. Like most San Franciscans who grew up in SoCal, Cary made a big show of how much she loathed LA. She dismissed it as the polar opposite of San Francisco's smart, foggy heaven: a smoggy hell of airheads, avarice, and sprawl. "You both know I'll combust if I drive south of the Cow Palace. You two have fun down there."

"Don't be silly," said Sasha. "I'll pack your Dracula jar myself."

They were going to LA the week of Thanksgiving, and even as she kvetched about it, Cary organized an elaborate holiday road trip. She borrowed Nick's Vanagon and booked hotels for the trip. She wouldn't let Walter help plan because she wanted much of it to be a surprise, though she couldn't suppress her excitement about the hotel where they'd be spending Thanksgiving. Walter was *gonna die* when he saw it.

The drive down the Pacific Coast Highway was breathtaking—quite literally—both because the coastline presented the most spectacular landscape Walter had ever seen and because the price of the view was a rollercoaster ride on a narrow highway that clung to cliffs ranging from vaguely treacherous to heart-stoppingly sheer. Whoever planned the highway obviously had cloven hooves: a bunch of mountain goats or probably Lucifer himself. And Cary wasn't the most focused driver. Sitting in the back, Walter felt himself turning green and cracked the window to keep from being sick. He lay on the camel-colored vinyl seat, closed his eyes, and pretended he was rocking in a train carriage.

Going over their weekend plans, they realized that none of them had talked to Lawrence in several weeks. Neither Cary nor Walter had managed to get him on the phone, and each assumed the other had been in touch.

"It's odd, his not answering, considering he almost never goes out," said Cary. "Don't you see him every weekend, on your delivery?"

"Cary," said Walter, "you know I haven't delivered for Open Hand in months. Didn't you coordinate with them for Friday at Ben's place?"

"Larry gave me Ben's info weeks ago—maybe a month ago. I have his number. I'm supposed to call them when we get to LA on Friday morning."

Piecing it together, they figured that Walter had been the last to see Larry, a full month before, when he'd stopped by to drop off their screenplay.

"But you two must have seen him . . . Didn't he come to your show at Cafe du Nord?"

"He was supposed to but missed it," said Sasha.

"Actually, that's when I last talked to him," said Cary. "He called to apologize for missing the show. Said he'd been under the weather. Flu or something. But he was in good spirits . . . on the mend."

"Strange . . ." Walter muttered, eyes closed, rubbing his temples to ward off carsickness.

"We'll call from the hotel tonight," said Cary.

They stopped to picnic on a cliff overlooking a secret, inaccessible beach between two bluffs. Below them a waterfall sprang seemingly out of the rock itself and tumbled in a windblown stream a hundred feet or so onto the beach. After lunch Sasha drove and Walter sat shotgun. Breathing in the sea air, his nausea passed. All that afternoon, the drive was inhumanly beautiful: a parade of natural beauty in such abundance it was impossible to grasp as it raced by. Late November and the coastal range was April green, the sky a radiant cobalt, vibrating and almost limitless, only a thin white rim of haze where sky met horizon. There, as in an airplane, one saw (or imagined) Earth's curvature. They were on a planet, after all. A planet! And all afternoon the rays of a titanic neighboring star—called a *yellow dwarf* by intelligent mites—combed the green chaparral and dazzled the serpent skin of the Pacific. As they traveled south, the range became less grandiose, the hills lower, more rolling, paler, thatched by arid grasses.

Cary was antsy in the back seat. She chattered sunnily and kept kneeling forward between them, fiddling with the radio. She was snapping cassettes frenetically in and out of the slot, searching for decent music in a crate of old tapes. Toward evening they passed a sign for San Simeon, and Sasha pointed to the top of a distant hillside, saying, "There it is!"

Walter had to squint to see anything. "It looks so tiny from here—like a toy," he said.

Hearst Castle hovered, a glowing limestone strip above a forest of live oak and sycamore. Both forest and castle looked out of place—none of the surrounding hilltops had forests, or castles for that matter. What they could see of it looked like Mission Dolores: two white stone pinnacles like bell towers, between them a terra-cotta roof, tassels of tall palms wagging above it all.

"We have to keep going to San Luis Obispo," said Cary. "Sorry, we're not staying in Hearst Castle tonight." She'd been fast-forwarding through a mixtape and settled on a song she liked. The ravishing opening strains of the orchestra were familiar: it was Pavarotti singing "Nessun dorma."

"This is rather dramatic," said Sasha.

"Let me get this straight—*we're not* staying at Hearst Castle tonight?" Walter asked. "Well, that's total BS."

"No, no." Cary laughed. "We're staying someplace even better. This music is a clue."

"What the hell? Better than Hearst Castle? *Turandot* is a clue? Are we sleeping in Grauman's Chinese Theatre?"

"No, stupie, we're staying at the Madonna Inn—you know, the *Aria* hotel!"

The Aria *hotel*. Right away he knew what she meant. It was, like Graceland or Dollywood, a place whose legend he'd heard of but that he couldn't quite believe was real. The Madonna Inn was used as a set in one segment of *Aria*, a not-very-good anthology film from the '80s that was basically a string of music videos for famous arias. Walter and Cary both loved the soundtrack, but the movie was lame in the way anthology films usually were. The hotel, meanwhile, was joyously, eye-poppingly, mind-bendingly kitsch, so much so that it managed to make a great aria, Verdi's "La donna é mobile," sound as tacky as a commercial for pink Chablis.

"Was there even a story to that part of the movie?" Walter asked. "I can't remember. Something about Beverly D'Angelo—poor Beverly D'Angelo—and an Elvis impersonator?"

"You know, it was a sex farce. Husband and wife just happen to cheat on each other on the same night at the same hotel. They both film kinky sex tapes with their partners, and later they get the tapes mixed up. It's like a sleazy 'Gift of the Magi.'"

"Sounds awful!" said Sasha.

"The movie made the Madonna Inn look trashy, but it's not," said Cary.

"It's like a charming Swiss chalet. Only on steroids. And built on volcanic caves. It's more outsider art than sex hotel."

"Are we required to make a sex tape?" asked Walter.

"Sex tape totally optional."

An hour later they were settling into their lavish suite. Cary sat in an armchair fiddling with a princess phone, a filigreed brass brick stuck with colored rhinestones. She cradled the headset as it distantly rang and rang. Walter and Sasha explored the suite. Cary had requested a room that combined the hotel's two themes, rustic cave and Swiss chalet. On the ground floor were suites constructed of granite boulders—darker and rougher, but otherwise a lot like Fred Flintstone's house. A postcard on the dresser explained that their room was built around a forty-one-ton boulder that served as a hearth. This weighty Paleolithic theme was balanced by the Swiss chalet motif that characterized the rest of the hotel, an ultra-frilly matchstick mansion of white- and pink-painted timber. It seemed the decorator, Phyllis Madonna, had derived her notion of Swiss culture solely from Heidi movies and Little Debbie Swiss Rolls.

Cary was leaving a rambling message on Lawrence's machine as Walter ducked into what he thought was a stone grotto but turned out to be a walk-in fireplace, with a brass screen and gilded tongs and pokers, clearly there for show, since it was a gas fixture with cement logs.

No luck reaching Lawrence, Cary called home to check her machine. Walter wandered into the bathroom. Half the room was rustic boulders that gleamed like they'd been polished with floor wax. Sasha was standing clothed in the shower, itself a sizable cave, a dark stone yoni.

"Stand back and watch this," said Sasha, turning a brass fixture, which squealed as water gushed from a crag high up in the wall. Opposite the waterfall was a wide stone bench. "Not a sex hotel *maybe*, but this shower was built for sex."

"Jesus, are you supposed to shower in here or go spelunking?" Walter asked.

"A *kind* of spelunking, I guess—"

"Ready for champagne?" Cary called from the next room. She appeared in the doorway peeling pink foil from the neck of a bottle still dripping from the ice bucket. "It's pink!"

"Of course it's pink!" said Walter. "Everything good is pink, isn't it?"

"And no two pinks are the same, are they?" asked Sasha.

"And they're all here!" said Cary.

The half of the suite that wasn't varnished boulders was painted, upholstered, tufted, or draped in pink. Phyllis must have had one hell of a time matching all the shades: at some point she'd given up. The mauve rafters clashed with the bubble-gum walls, the tea-rose bedding, and the maroon and cerise upholstery, all of which clashed with the cabbage roses on the carpet, their petals fleshy and lurid. Everything that wasn't rough stone or gooey pink was gold-leafed, including the rococo couch, the expansive amoebic mirror above it, and the two chandeliers that hung over the king bed, its headboard like a monolithic remainder from Stonehenge. It was all so over-the-top that it kind of worked, though Walter suspected that was only because the lights were so dim. One good, strong shaft of sunlight through the casement window and they might all be blinded.

"Looking at the carpet makes me feel dirty," said Sasha.

"*Dirty* dirty, or dirty salacious?" asked Cary.

"Both, really, but more the latter."

"I'll drink to that!" said Cary, handing them flutes of pink bubbly.

That night they didn't leave the hotel room. They lit the fire with a button, which helped with the damp speleological smell. They got drunk on pink champagne and had sex in the cave with the waterfall. The context seemed to demand it. After all, how often would they happen across a shower that fit three? By turns it was erotic and awkward: hot and cinematic while getting it on under the warm torrent, chilly and jagged when pressed against the walls or the stone bench. The slipping hazard seemed considerable, so they moved to the bed to finish the job. Cary, in her birthday suit, had taken a pink bath towel and twisted it on her head like a turban, and was rifling through a suitcase looking for a harness.

"Who's getting fucked?" she asked.

"Darling, I think we're all getting fucked." In one movement, Sasha slid backward across the bed, kicking the rose coverlet to the floor. His pale body gleamed in the gold light of the gas fire, and he was half hard, which Walter always found so sexy—it made his own dick twitch. Tumescence is catching.

Nude and still dripping, Walter toweled his belly with one hand. With the other he massaged his back just above his butt. "One of those rocks almost pierced my back. I think the shower might have given me a spinal epidural!"

"Oh dear, lemme see . . ." said Cary. From her crotch bounced an alert silicon number, a particular favorite she'd named Jimmy. She examined Walter where it hurt, pressing her thumbs into the small of his back.

"That feels good."

"I don't see anything but your adorable dimples, which you've always had." She pressed a wet kiss onto his shoulder and whacked his thigh twice with the dildo. "I love your dimples. Now get in bed."

"Yes, sir, bossy!" said Walter, taking her down with him by the harness.

At four in the morning he awoke, overheated. The bed felt too big. Cary was snoring, and Sasha was gone—the two must be related. A pallid pink light filtered in under the curtains. He went to take a leak and, dark as it was, divined Sasha's outline blanketed on the couch. It wasn't that uncommon, at home, for Sasha to retreat to the couch when Cary was snoring; in fact it was getting more common. Walter felt somewhat guilty that he could usually sleep through the ruckus. He slipped back into bed and prodded Cary until she turned on her side. She was quiet as he spooned her, but now he was wide-awake. The room was a mausoleum, slightly clammy and so silent that from across the room he could hear Sasha's breathing.

He wondered, not for the first time, if Sasha hadn't been a little distant from him, from them, and for a while now, maybe months. He fixated on a moment at lunch, when Sasha was staring down upon the secret waterfall in its enchanting cove and looked miserable. When he'd asked how he was, Sasha shook his head and winced, covering his eyes with sunglasses. And then that night, in the middle of sex, how strange to hear a trace of weariness in Sasha's voice when he'd replied to Cary: *I think we're all getting fucked.*

Citizen Kane

THE NEXT MORNING THE SUGAR in the cheap champagne had done its worst, and they were crabby and hungover, and the banana walnut pancakes and roofing-tar coffee at San Luis Obispo's finest diner did little to improve their moods. They each had headaches, but Cary hid hers best. She was dressed jauntily for the trip to the castle, in a bowling shirt and her white woven panama hat; she called it *septuagenarian chic*, like Don Ameche in *Cocoon*. Sasha, meantime, was butching it up, which for him meant a floral oxford, a short linen jacket, and jeans. Walter had seen him in jeans only a couple times before; he never wore them unless he had to go to Oakland or the Marina or someplace he was worried about getting harassed. He knew that Sasha would be happier—they would all be happier—if he could have worn his Myrna Loy beach pajamas to tour Hearst Castle, in which case the ghost of Marion Davies could've eaten her heart out. In the end, Sasha would be out of sorts and sulky all afternoon, barely speaking a word to either him or Cary, and Walter would attribute it to the hangover and the provincial dress code.

Afterward Walter would wonder if it was his own failing that something as magnificent as Hearst Castle could be such a letdown. It must have been his bad attitude. After all, the Casa Grande was everything it was cracked up to be: a display of wealth, opulence, and museum-worthy decorative arts unlike anything he'd ever seen. Wanting to see as much as they could, they signed up for not one but two hour-long tours, the first of the private suites in the upper stories, the second of the entertaining rooms on the lower floors, both of which ended with a visit to the Roman pool in the basement. Eleanor, their docent, was a doughty Hearst partisan in her mid-sixties with a pewter Prince Valiant cut and sturdy nurse's shoes. She knew her stuff and relished burnishing the Hearst mythology—Walter wondered if she wasn't a lineal descendant with some skin in the game. She also seemed slightly jaded, like she might have preferred to be home with her grandkids for the holiday weekend. She omitted large chunks of backstory that might explain what they were seeing, then sighed deeply when anyone asked a question like, *Wait, how did a seventeenth-century coffered ceiling from Spain wind up in SoCal?* The answer was always the same: *He bought it.*

They started in one pinnacle and worked their way down. In one tower they visited a secluded guest room, where Gothic traceries in the windows performed a kind of alchemy, dissolving the ruthless coastal sunshine into radiant fanned crescents. Walter would have liked to climb onto the mahogany bedstead with a good book and lie there all day, reading and watching the light sift and dim. Hearst's private library was likewise enchanting, an entire Gothic chapel of hand-carved hardwood they had somehow hoisted up several stories and fixed in midair.

By the time they toured the lower floors, Hearst's MO seemed patent: go to a European town struggling to rebuild after World War I, offer to help by paying cash for half their chateau and grounds or the local church, then cheerfully cart off their cultural patrimony on an ocean liner. Eleanor took no issue with these operations. She was obsessed with numbers. Large, round numbers, that is, that betrayed the antiquity of things: that ceiling was 400 years old, the tapestries, too; these choir stalls were 500 and 600 years old, respectively; that marble was a 300-year-old copy of a 2,000-year-old original; and on and on, roll-calling the centuries, filed in layers like so many striations in a canyon.

The longer the tour went on, the harder it was to ignore that the castle was a Frankenstein's monster of old sanctuaries, cut up like cadavers, cemented together, and electrified. Like the bolts and stitches in Boris Karloff's head, it was easy to see where the pieces of the jigsaw almost fit but didn't quite, where the styles of far-flung eras clashed. He should have known—this was something *Citizen Kane* got right. Kane's Florida Xanadu barely held together visually: in one shot Orson Welles would stroll out of a Gothic cloister through an obscure annex of the Louvre and into the Taj Mahal, and one fluid, unblinking tracking shot held it all together. Hearst's palace made *slightly* more sense, but as in the movie, it became obvious when the marble was painted plaster. Then there were the vast concrete spaces where money and time ran out. On the outside, the back end of the Casa Grande was cast cement. Devoid of gewgaws, it looked industrial, like an old brewery or a college science building.

The room Walter loved best was the Roman pool on the lowest level, in part because, while imitating a Roman bath, it was wholly original to the building. No major portion of the room was revealed to be a kleptomaniac's trophy scalped from another site. Instead, the pool—big as a ballroom—was a love letter to the color blue. All the brightest variegations—ultramarine, lapis, turquoise, sky—scintillated from mosaics that adorned every surface, ceiling to drain. Accenting the blue, the pool, the pillars, and every architectural detail were traced with gold tiles. Grotesques of medieval whales, two-tailed sirens, shimmering starfish, and sailboats that were somehow also sea monsters were hemmed in by bands of sea green and gold meanders. There were coffers of stars on the ceiling and sunbursts in the depths of the pool. Holding Cary's hand, Walter was dumbfounded by the beauty of the room, and wondered why blues and greens didn't clash in the same way pinks and reds did.

"Can you swim in it?" asked an excited boy who looked about twelve.

"Oh no, oh no!" said Eleanor. "Well, some employees have been able to enjoy it on special occasions. It's very cold! But as for visitors . . . the tiles are fragile, and then there's the liability . . ."

"The *liability*," Cary whispered as they were led from the room. "Was there ever such a killjoy as liability?"

Walter nodded. "You read my mind: tragic that the two pools are the best part of the whole castle—and no one can swim in them."

"Except Eleanor, of course."

On the second tour there were many more spoils to admire. Near the end, they were in a grand reception room huddled around a massive fireplace lifted from a French chateau. The group was small; aside from the three of them there was one family of four, tourists from Vancouver, with two teenaged daughters who might have been identical twins, they were certainly identically bored. Clearly, on the afternoon before Thanksgiving, Americans with any decent sense of family values were at home thawing turkeys and baking pies. Eleanor implied as much by her impatient tone. Still, she dutifully rattled off all the Hollywood royalty who had hobnobbed in this very room.

Sasha was wandering the far end of the gallery, staring up at the tapestries with a maker's eye. They were fading, their colors slowly draining from hunter green and rose gold into pale straw. Everyone on the tour seemed a bit depressed—it couldn't just be Walter's hangover—the afternoon itself was yawning. He wondered about the ornate choir stalls that lined the walls of the room and the thousands of choir members and clerics who might have sung and worshipped in them over hundreds of years. He wasn't religious at all, but he felt that some of their devoutness must still be there, steeped in the grain. There was something unseemly about it, taking someone's church as a backdrop for your flapper bacchanalia. He wondered if there weren't some former choir boys, in their eighties now, who would still like their old sanctuary back.

By the time they returned to the Roman pool it was late afternoon. Nearing sunset, the light had shifted and the room dimmed, and all the blues were sinking into a rich ultramarine range. Someone had turned on the marble torchieres that lined the pool, and they glowed warmly, doubled in the glassy surface. Their oblong globes were veined with gray, like sun-filled storm clouds. By now Eleanor was ready to pack it in. Half the tour had heard this part of her spiel before, and she was speeding them along the side of the pool with her back to them, rapidly lecturing the walls. Her voice was loud but almost inaudible, her speech shattered by echoes.

"Any questions?" Eleanor confronted the group. Clearly she didn't want questions.

There was a hesitant silence, then a shaking of heads. Amid this silence came the faintest little plash, a negligible sound, like the jump of a tiny bass. The group turned to look behind them where Cary, who had been lagging behind, stood beside the pool, and floating on the placid surface, a couple feet from her, was her panama hat.

"Oh, crap!" said Cary. "Oh, shoot!"

"Oh no," said Sasha, "don't tell me—"

"Don't move!" said Eleanor. "Nobody go anywhere! I'll grab the hook . . ." She huffed loudly and dodged behind a pier.

Cary knelt down and reached for the hat. "I'm sure I can reach it—it's so close!" The white straw hat, upright, innocent as a toy boat, drifted farther out on the pool.

"Cary? Cary!" Sasha's voice was steely.

Cary waved Walter over, saying, "I can totally reach it. Give me your hand—help me balance."

"Cary," Sasha cried, "don't even think about—"

With one hand Walter gripped Cary's wrist, and she gripped his. It was a bad idea, he knew, yet she couldn't be dissuaded. He tried to hold her steady. She leaned out and he leaned back, and for a second it seemed to be working—her fingertips flicked the brim of the hat, and it bobbed along teasingly. It all happened so fast—he felt Sasha's hand on his back and heard Eleanor's voice echo. The weight of Cary's body tugged at his shoulder. The pressure of her right foot pressed against his, not an anchor but a fulcrum, not to steady herself but to unbalance him. She won the tug-of-war, and they went in headfirst—for an instant conjoined at the hips—legs last, splaying like a cartwheel. They split the water with a deafening splash, and he was propelled missile-like into the deep pool. The freezing water gripped him, his skin bracing, his clothes dragging his limbs. *Goddamn Cary.* Hearing muddled screams, he twisted underwater and, peering up through chlorine sting, saw warbled bodies waving from the poolside. On either side of them stone lamps glowed like gibbous moons. To his left, Cary's legs kicked away in the direction of her hat. Before him another terrific splash broke the surface, as Eleanor came plummeting in a sheath of silver bubbles feetfirst into the pool, with not a moment to spare to save one or both of them from drowning.

Eleanor hadn't lied, the water was very cold. Walter and Cary were reminded of this as they were forced to drip-dry on the windy hilltop while Eleanor hunted down blankets, then as they soaked through the blankets on the bus ride down to the parking lot, then as the blankets were brusquely rescinded and they were driven shivering back to the hotel by Sasha, who wasn't speaking to them and whose anger compounded the chill.

Several times on the trip back Cary protested that it was an accident, until Sasha, angrier than Walter had ever seen him, cried out in exasperation: "Do not fucking bullshit me, Cary."

Sasha dropped them off at the hotel, saying he needed to be alone. He wanted to drive to Pismo Beach nearby. It was dark already, but Sasha didn't seem to care. Walking to their suite, Cary made a crack about how giving them the silent treatment, then vamoosing to drive around by himself, was the butchest stunt Sasha had ever pulled.

They warmed up in the shower, then switched on the fire and sat on the bed, searching through a binder of laminated ads for dinner options other than the steak house in the hotel, where they had Thanksgiving reservations the following afternoon.

"I don't think I can eat anything," Walter said, feeling dread in the pit of his stomach. "I'm actually really worried about Sasha. I think he's really mad at us . . ."

"He's not mad at *you* at all," said Cary. "He's furious with me, though." She gave him a look, half pleading, half amused, and her hazel eyes sparked. "I mean, *you're* not mad at me, are you?"

She went to kiss him on the cheek. He pulled back.

"You're not *really mad*, are you?"

He shook his head. "It was a dumb thing to do." He was cross, or at least deeply annoyed. He couldn't figure out what the hell was going on with Sasha. If Sasha had laughed off the whole incident, he might have been able to as well.

"Yeah, but . . . a kind of awesomely dumb thing to do, right?"

She was squeezing his hand and stole a kiss behind his ear, along the hairline, where it tingled the most. When she kissed him there his toes would curl without fail. The puppetry of the nervous system—he was a marionette whose wires were all coiled up inside him.

"Just think—for the rest of your life you can brag that you got to swim in the forbidden pool at Hearst Castle! Honestly, what would you do without me?"

"Well, I wouldn't be banned from Hearst Castle for life, for one thing."

"Oh, hell, they'll never remember us. I'm sure they don't have a gallery of outlaws hanging in the box office."

"I feel certain they will *always* remember you."

He felt sick to his stomach, and they decided to nap until Sasha got back. It was dark and still in their rococo cave, the only light from pink-gold flickers the fire projected onto the wall above the television, the only sound the sigh and riffle of the gas fixture. He fell asleep in Cary's arms and slept soundly

316 Christopher Tradowsky

for who knows how long. He slept long enough to migrate across the bed from Cary, not noticing that she'd gotten up when the door handle turned. Half awake, he heard hushed voices from the far end of the suite, but was incapable of rousing. What woke him at last was a soft sound that tensed his entire body with dread. It was the sound of someone gasping a little, struggling to breathe. It was the sound of sobbing.

He found them sitting, each with their legs curled up defensively, on either end of the wide, gilded couch. A small lamp on the table beside Sasha shed an oval of tawny light in which the cherry-maroon upholstery looked gruesome, like dried entrails. He sat across from them on a crag projecting from the hearth. Sasha hid his eyes behind one hand; Cary was sobbing into the sleeve of her silk pajamas.

"He's leaving us!" cried Cary. "He's dumping us!"

For a split second Walter mistook who Cary was addressing and who *he* was. He thought Cary was back to griping about him possibly moving. Then it hit him what she meant.

"No! No, no, no, no—" Walter repeated as his heart raced, and his vision blurred with tears, and now he was the one trying to catch his breath.

Without looking up, Sasha began softly, "It doesn't have to be such a big—"

"It is a fucking big deal, Sasha!" Cary yelled. "You're only the love of my fucking life!" She shivered and her body shook as she sobbed, and Walter felt the shuddering of her body in his own chest, felt himself heave with tears as she cried. "Tell him what you told me," Cary spat, wiping snot from her nose with her sleeve.

Sasha sighed, summoned his poise, and said, "When we get back to the city, I'm planning on moving out."

"Great fucking timing, huh?" Cary cried. She squirmed in place and pulled a pillow from behind her back, gripping it like a shield over her chest. "Do you know what else he said? He said he wants *off the Cary-go-round*."

This made Walter laugh and shrug, even as he fought back tears. Very softly he mouthed, *Caryworld*.

"Caryworld," Sasha echoed tenderly.

Cary's face was pressed into the pillow, her head shuddering. If she'd heard them, she said nothing.

Then time itself seemed to warp with grief—the minutes were endless, but the hours flew by as they talked, and fought, and fought, and talked. Anything any one of them said was followed by twenty minutes of silent misery. No one budged from where they sat. The stone where Walter had perched ground at his tailbone through his briefs.

At some point in the midst of this purgatory, Sasha said, "I've just felt like a third wheel . . . for a long time now." He was crying and wiping his tears backward across his temple, compulsively smoothing his hair behind his ears.

Walter laughed miserably; he couldn't believe his ears. "Sasha, *I'm the third wheel*, it's so obvious. I've *always been* the third wheel." A vision flashed before him, of the two of them harmonious without him, or rather *before him*, on the night he first saw them together, dressed like starlets at the Castro. He shook his head vigorously. "The two of you cannot break up—I can't even comprehend it. You two—I said it before—you two are fucking Nick and Nora! And I'm *Asta*."

"Sasha, no way you're the third wheel!" said Cary, her smile abject. "You're the biggest, most important wheel of all. You're the big wheel on the penny-farthing!"

"I'm fucking serious, Cary."

"I'm serious, too!"

"Have you ever felt like the third wheel?" Sasha asked. When Cary appeared stumped, he said, "It's a serious question."

"What do you mean? Do you mean, like, in life?"

"I mean, I've felt like the third wheel. I do right now. And Walter says *he's* felt like the third wheel. So I'm asking if the two of us have ever made *you* feel like the third wheel."

"Whatever!" said Cary. "You're the big wheel, and Walter's the axel or the linchpin, or probably you're the linchpin, too. Whatever! You two are the whole bicycle, and I'm the handlebars, or better, I'm the stupid plastic tassels on the handlebars. My point is metaphors are idiotic. All of them. At some point they all fall apart."

"This is all my fault," said Walter. "I should have buzzed off a long time ago. The two of you would be just fine." As soon as he said it, he realized he was begging to be contradicted.

"It's way more complicated—" Sasha began, but Cary cut him off, saying maybe Walter had a point. Maybe it was Walter who had put ideas in Sasha's head about leaving, since he was so excited to fuck off to grad school. And now Sasha was inspired to get out while the getting's good.

"Cary! You're being *so possessive*," said Sasha, wielding the dreaded p-word, a kind of curse, possessiveness being their number one taboo. "It's *obvious* that Walter should . . ."

At last Walter was spurred to defend himself. If he didn't speak, he was going to wail. "I don't see why this is so hard for you to understand, Cary. I don't want to leave you two, I don't. I love you both . . . to distraction. You are *both* my best friend. You are *both* my favorite person . . . but . . ." He paused to catch his breath. ". . . the grad school thing—I have to *do something*. I'm trying to do something *serious* with my life."

Cary sniffed, her eyes bloodshot, her face pink as the rouged wall behind her.

"Yes, Cary, I'm sure it sounds dumb to you, but I need to find a *career*. Two years of my life, and what do I have to show for it? Really? Two years at a shitty job that can't ever go anywhere, unless my life's goal is to wind up like Gavin. And meanwhile, all we do is fuck around and drink and eat—I've gained fifteen pounds at least. I'm scared to check. Oh, and I'm pretty sure I'm an alcoholic now, thank you very much. And meanwhile, I'm, like, racking up a ton of debt, because I took out a second credit card, like an idiot."

"But—wait a minute—I've been paying for everything," said Cary.

"Of course you haven't been paying for *everything*, Cary. You're not actually my sugar daddy—"

"So—hold on," said Cary. "You're worried about debt, and your solution is to go to grad school and rack up more of it? And what about our screenplay? What about our movie?"

"Fuck our movie, Cary. Our movie is a fucking pipe dream." He stifled more tears. He felt mean, petty, ruthless, and yet helpless. "No one's gonna give us a dime for our screenplay."

Cary shook her head. "Why would you say that? Why should it be any more of a pipe dream than *grad school*? We *made something together*, Walter. We built a world together—"

"For god's sake, give him a break," Sasha broke in. "The only reason you're mad about his *possibly* leaving is that he's choosing for himself. It's the first time in eighteen months that he's not letting you lead him by the nose. In fact, he's still letting you lead; he's just *thinking* about making a move on his own, and you can't stand it. He'll probably cave and stay."

It was rare for Sasha to be so blunt. The dart sank deep. He knew Sasha was right, that he was too willing to be led. And now Sasha's claim that he felt like the third wheel suddenly made sense—that his own willingness to go along with Cary's whims had made Sasha feel sidelined. His playing the up-for-anything sidekick had forced Sasha to play the scolding spouse.

Exhausted and heartbroken, he repeated a refrain he'd been using to assuage Cary for weeks: "I probably won't even get in anywhere."

He needed to smoke outside and slipped on shorts and a hoodie. It was after two in the morning. They had skipped dinner; his stomach was in knots and he thought he might never want to eat again. Nothing would be resolved that night. When he returned to the room, the lights were out and the fire was dialed low. Sasha was bundled on the couch; Cary had retreated to the bed. He brushed his teeth and fumblingly hugged Sasha good night, whispering,

"Love you," and getting no response, and his heart broke all over again on the few steps to the bed. Cary, pressing her head into his shoulder, sobbed herself to sleep.

Early that morning, Walter dreamed he was standing in the tower of Hearst Castle, peering at the landscape through leaded glass. The sky was filled with snow, whirling snow that swarmed the air but never landed, not on the dry hills, not on the brittle oak forest, not on the concrete castle. It was fake—of course it was—spores of flaked asbestos and mica, like they used in old movies. Fireproof, evanescent, toxic to inhale. The snow hissed softly, a gas-fire hiss. He tried not to breathe in, but couldn't hold his breath for long. Beyond the swarm of flakes there were no clouds, only clear sky: winter blue, intensely bright. The sun gleamed emptily as if there were no substance to it, as if it were a mere reflection—a glare upon a glass globe.

The next afternoon their Thanksgiving meal felt like a wake held in a Valentine's Day–themed amusement park. The restaurant's decor matched that of their suite, but on a grander scale and demonstrating less restraint. The same carpet of carnivorous-looking cabbage roses stretched throughout the dining room, the same riotous palette of pinks and reds. They were seated in a large round booth, high-backed and upholstered in shocking pink vinyl, which clashed with the coral tablecloth, the ruby stemware, and the scarlet flocked wallpaper. Even the slice of cake that sat half eaten before Walter fit the theme, crusted with curls of white chocolate dyed shell pink.

The three of them sat bleary-eyed and discomfited, and hardly spoke a word throughout the meal. The food itself seemed depressed: tepid slices of turkey breast, taupe stuffing, mashed potatoes and milk-white gravy. Walter was surprised the chef had passed up a chance to dye the mashed potatoes pink. His favorite dish was the garnet disk of canned cranberry jelly served on a gold-rimmed saucer. None of them wanted dessert, but the *signature pink champagne cake* came with the prix fixe.

He sat in the middle of the round booth, between his friends, feeling trapped. Sasha, he knew, was sad but resolved, sure that he was making the right decision. Cary had cheered up somewhat that morning—she and Walter had taken a drive to check out Pismo Beach for themselves, hoping to run into Bugs Bunny. No such luck. They'd waded in the surf and wandered under the pier, trying to envision a life together without Sasha, and for a couple hours the gloom lifted between them. Back at the hotel, things were tense again as they argued over whether to bother with their dinner reservation. In the end it was their only option.

The enormous restaurant was virtually empty. The only other patrons were the family of tourists from Vancouver who had witnessed Cary and Walter's antics in the Roman pool the afternoon before. The family regarded them from a nearby booth, the father giving a little wave. Walter felt freshly embarrassed, recalling the soaking-wet bus ride they took together, and seeing them made Sasha visibly cross again. Cary, meanwhile, had reached an angry phase herself. She was mad at Sasha for breaking up with them now and ruining the elaborate weekend she'd planned. She was angry at Walter for apparently giving up on their screenplay the day before they were going to talk with an actual honest-to-god film producer about it. She was ready to drive straight back to SF and declared she would have if they hadn't promised to meet Lawrence and company the next afternoon.

Walter had never felt so confused and heartsick. He couldn't tell if he was more heartbroken for himself, losing Sasha, or for his two best friends, losing each other. It was that damned Aristotle illusion again. He was looking upward abstractly, only half taking in his surroundings, when he realized he was staring into a gigantic tree, or a caricature of a tree. Around a stone pillar someone had crafted a canopy in gilded metalwork. It was the definition of overwrought, its sprawling branches fixed with fairy lights and leaves like wide brass spades. Dozens of electric candles sprung from gold magnolias, and a flock of solid-gold cupids dangled heavily from cables, bellies round as melons.

The server swung by their table; she was dolled up in an alpine dirndl— in pink, of course. "Is one of you Cary Menuhin?" Her glance darted between them.

Cary nodded.

"There's a phone call for you—you can take it at the front desk. We didn't want to bother you, but he said it's urgent."

"At last—this'll be Lawrence!" said Cary, sliding from the booth and dashing off.

"I feel like I've been eating this cake for a year and a half," said Walter, breaking the silence between him and Sasha.

It was the first time they'd been alone together all day, and the sheer volume of things he longed to say kept him from saying anything at all. If he thought it would do any good, he would have said, *Don't leave, please don't leave. Don't leave Cary, don't leave us, don't leave me* . . . Instead, he was talking about cake.

"There's a strange flavor in the frosting. It tastes kind of . . . chemical?"

Sasha looked queasy. "I have less than no appetite."

Walter glanced up into the thicket of gold branches on the ceiling. "I wonder if this frosting contains Lotophagine. I'll bet it does."

"Lotophagine?"

"It's from our movie. It's a drug concocted by the one villain, Dr. Purzelbaum—part of his evil plan for social engineering. It's mildly hallucinogenic, but it also makes you forget your troubles, your trauma, your past. Dr. Purzelbaum uses it to poison things—he poisons the food first, then the fog . . ."

"Lotophagine—like the lotus-eaters?"

Walter nodded. "Basically, you forget everything bad that's happened, and then all you want to do is play. It makes you live in the moment—it turns you into a compulsive consumer."

"That sounds like Cary," said Sasha, smirking a bit. As far as Walter knew, this was his first smile in twenty-four hours or more.

"You mean it sounds like something she would make up."

"No, I mean a drug—mildly hallucinogenic—that makes you forget all your troubles so that all you want to do is play? That sounds like Cary."

"Oh!" said Walter. "Oh. I guess it does. But . . . that's why we love her, right?"

"Right." Sasha shook his head. "Right."

Cary was taking her sweet time with the phone call, and the longer she was gone, the tenser the silence grew between them. From hidden speakers somewhere Frank Sinatra was snapping and swinging through "Fly Me to the Moon," a cheesy song Walter had always liked, but for some reason, at the moment, it made him want to die. He gulped wine from a garish red goblet.

"I want you to know," Sasha said, "I never thought of you as a third wheel. I understand feeling like a third wheel—the anxiety of it—but I never thought of you that way." Sasha fidgeted with his fork, his fingers thin and graceful. "The truth is, by the time you showed up, I was questioning our relationship—Cary was, too, I know. We'd been in a slump. And you showed up and Cary was so excited. You know how she gets . . . how infectious it can be."

Walter squirmed in the tight booth. In his lap he'd been twisting his napkin; he had to stop for fear of shredding it. He was surprised to find himself crying again. He stared at Sasha's hands because he couldn't raise his head to look him in the eye. "So . . . I wasn't the third wheel, OK. But . . . what was I? The jump start? The roadside assistance?"

"What's with the vehicular metaphors? I mean, if you must put it that way . . . you were *way more* than a jump start. Maybe an extra gas tank? Or . . . a burst of rocket fuel?" Sasha laughed gently. "Does that make you feel better?"

Somehow the idea of being rocket fuel wasn't any more comforting than being a third wheel. He knew the only thing that would give him comfort was if Sasha took it all back, said it was all a terrible mistake, that he'd stay with them, and that everything would be exactly as it was. Something Sasha said the night before was still ringing in his head: that while he still *loved them both*, that was *beside the point*. It was incomprehensible to Walter how loving them could be beside the point. It seemed like the only point that mattered.

He summoned the courage to look Sasha full in the face. "How are we ever going to make it through this weekend? Cary made all these plans—we're supposed to go to Disneyland on Sunday, for Chrissake."

"'The Happiest Place on Earth,'" said Sasha, glancing around the room. "Look at it this way—it'll be a nice change of pace from this dump."

Cary never returned to the table. They waited for twenty minutes, during which the waitress was also missing in action, and when she appeared at last, she said she hadn't seen their friend. They swung by the front desk on the way back to their room. No sign of Cary. The Vanagon was still parked by the main chalet—she hadn't taken off on a joy ride.

They found Cary back in the suite, huddled in the corner of the couch where she'd sat the night before. For a moment it seemed like she'd regressed, her face was once again raw with tears. It was Jabez who'd called; he was still in San Francisco. He called to say that Lawrence had died that morning, of an acute fever, in the IC unit at the UCSF Medical Center, where he had been for the last ten days.

DECLAN DANNER has rescued LORNA ZAFTIG
from the clutches of nefarious
Dr. JANUS PURZELBAUM!

After the shoot-out at the sanatorium,
DECLAN, LORNA, & MILO head for the
Silver City Palace, dragging
DR. PURZELBAUM along at gunpoint.
    They arrive just in time for the
        midnight organ concert

    ***Climax in the auditorium of the
        Silver City Palace!***

Finally, our heroes discover what
EARNEST PURZELBAUM has been up to
all along. He was supposed to be
burying the bodies
(i.e. the braindead victims of
his twin brother's lab experiments)
in the basement of the palace.

Instead EARNEST has been "restoring"
the palace & reanimating the victims,
including VERA SVANIRE and her
entire jazz band. He's turned them into
    a Frankenorchestra by wiring them
        up to the Mighty Wurlitzer

EARNEST sees the cinema palace as one
giant machine, an enormous automaton
with the Mighty Wurlitzer
        as its command center,
            because obviously:
                A BRAIN is an ORGAN
                & an ORGAN is a BRAIN!

In a climactic speech,
EARNEST PURZELBAUM
reveals his scientific
innovation:

an 'ingeniously simple'
process he calls
        esemplastic
            siliconization.

The human circulatory
system is drained
& replaced with a
gelatinous silicon
(stable & pliable)
leaving neural pathways
& motor functions
        intact...

After that, the basic
motor functions, nerves
& musculature, can be
triggered & controlled
by electrical pulses,
with relative ease...

INT. RKO SILVER CITY PALACE
EARNEST PURZELBAUM onstage in a spotlight, wearing a
smock. He eyes his brother, JANUS, being held at gunpoint
by DECLAN and LORNA, accompanied by MILO.

                    EARNEST
          Fritz, it's time! Sooner than I
          thought, but it's finally time!
          Fritz, get the lights!

                    FRITZ
          The stage lights, Dr. P? All the
          lights?

                    EARNEST
          All the lights, Fritz! The grand
          reopening of the cinema palace
          is nigh! Let's set the place
          ablaze!

Backstage FRITZ stands at a large circuit board of
double-pull switches. Down the row he goes. Chandeliers,
sconces, spots--all burst with light. The facade of the
RKO Silver City Palace is suddenly illuminated. Towering
neon letters, half shattered, read "KO SI VER CIT." Fifty
thousand bulbs blink and dazzle.

EARNEST is blinded by high beams. He cowers behind
his raised arm. Behind him onstage is an entire jazz
orchestra: drums, percussion, brass and clarinets,
strings. Musicians mute and deathly still, like
mannequins. Wires sprout from their skulls. Braided
cords snake down their backs. At their feet, a black
carpet of wires and circuits. Standing center stage at a
microphone, smiling like a waxwork, is VERA SVANIRE.

                    MILO
               [crying in anguish]
          You monster! I'm going to be
          sick... What have you done to my
          Vera?!

                    EARNEST
          My friend, you should be thanking
          me! You will thank me in a
          minute. You see, I was tasked

with burying Vera in a cement
crypt, in the catacombs beneath
the Palace. And instead, as
you see, I have preserved and
reanimated her. Watch, she can
sing and tap dance as if she
were twenty years old again!
The Venus of North Beach--
reborn from the breakers! And
the Silver City--this grand old
cinema palace--will rise again,
magnificent, outshining all its
past glory! Fritz! Fire up the
Mighty Wurlitzer!

Backstage, FRITZ gleefully raises the last and largest
switch. EARNEST leaps from the stage into the pit and
mounts the organ bench. Subterranean bellows begin to
drone. Slowly the massive instrument, laden with pedals
and keyboards, rises from the pit like the hull of a
ghost ship from the abyss.

                    EARNEST
          Did you know, this organ has four
          thousand pipes in the walls all
          around you? Imagine the task of
          rewiring it all!

EARNEST pads pedals and fiddles with keys. The orchestra
springs to life: strings pluck and saw, trumpets rise,
drums rumble, cymbals splash. As Earnest plays, so does
the orchestra. Precisely, mechanically. A music box, large
as life. As he pulls out the stops, the volume swells
like a tide.

VERA tap dances in place, waist fixed, propped up and
bolted to a frame. Beaded fringe flashes, legs flop like a
marionette's. A windup songbird, she sings "I've Got You
Under My Skin."

                    EARNEST
                  [shouting]
          Let's pull out all the stops for
          this chorus, shall we? We might
          never get the chance again!

EARNEST maniacally pulls out every stop on the
Wurlitzer. The orchestra blares, a deafening caterwaul
of four thousand pipes. The stage begins to quake.
Proscenium rumbles and shakes. Plaster ruptures and
sheers, tumbling in clumps.

JANUS, DECLAN, and LORNA cower under the oppressive
noise. MILO rushes the stage.

                    MILO
          Vera! Darling Vera!

                    DECLAN
          Milo, she's gone!

MILO struggles desperately to unplug Vera, tearing
at her wires. VERA keeps hoofing and singing. On the
proscenium arch, gilt encrustations crack; lime chunks
hail down.

                    LORNA
          Milo! Come back--Vera's gone!

EXT. RKO SILVER CITY PALACE--NIGHT
The palace shakes to its foundations. On the facade, lit
bulbs pop, shooting sparks. A meteor shower as the last
of the neon shatters.

INT. RKO SILVER CITY PALACE
The ceiling vibrates like a drum. Chandeliers shudder
and sway. With a supersonic crack, the highest balcony
collapses onto the loge beneath it.

                    DECLAN
               [to LORNA]
          We'd better get outta here--this
          place is gonna blow!

                    LORNA
               [toward the stage]
          Milo!

Onstage, MILO has rescued VERA. She lies limp in his
arms, eyes waxy and wide. He removes her wig. Lovingly,
he pulls the last of the electrical nodes from her

head. Around him loose wires spark, catch flame. DECLAN grabs LORNA and pulls her toward the side exit. A column collapses, blocking their path, as JANUS escapes through the exit.

EARNEST plays on, ecstatic, while the orchestra melts and the Palace burns. Ceiling vaults yield to the sky. Smoke churns dragon-like out into the night. DECLAN and LORNA flee under the groaning, swaying balconies, through the dark hallway as it crumbles. Racing through the grand foyer, a thousand splendors collapse, tumbling down around them.

EXT. RKO SILVER CITY PALACE--NIGHT
DECLAN and LORNA, hand in hand, dash from the imploding Palace. They flee down Market Street. Beneath the death throes of the Mighty Wurlitzer, the sound of approaching sirens. Fire trucks race to the scene. As half the Palace caves in, the music snuffs out. Firemen unleash their deluge. Arcs of gushing water are lit by fire as the grand old palace burns and burns and burns and burns.

Solar Flare

WALTER STOOD SMOKING ON SARCOMA Beach, his back to the Tenderloin. It was shortly before noon on a Saturday in January, and the sky above the Archers Hotel was a radiant gray teeming with light, a screen still illuminated after the film's run out. He was staring at the compact structure where Lawrence had lived for so long, which Larry had always referred to grandiosely as the Archers' penthouse. He was thinking how strange it can be to get a good long look at something you thought you knew well—an object, an interior, your home—and realize its actual contours are not the contours you'd imagined all along. Larry's penthouse now seemed insubstantial, a Sheetrocked shed. The flat roof over the entryway, the screen of patterned breeze blocks, and the mute, monotonous whiteness of it all conspired to make it look much larger than it was.

He'd been crying and had lit the cigarette hoping the buzz would spur him back to his senses, remind him to breathe, dry his tears, numb him a bit. It was a miscalculation: he felt nauseated and short of breath. At any moment he could start blubbering again. He needed to blow his nose.

The apartment door clicked and yawned inward, and Jabez emerged. Walter wiped his eyes with his jacket sleeve. They hugged briefly. He offered Jay a cigarette and a light.

"Thanks," said Jabez. "Thanks for coming to help today."

For a while they smoked in silence, leaning against the brick parapet that lined the roof. Two pigeons alighted on the roof nearby. One carried something in its beak—a French fry or scrap of bread. The second was missing a foot and hopped along behind the other on one coral talon, hoping its companion might share.

Walter was there to help prepare for a memorial service—not really a service, neither a wake nor a funeral—the invitations called it a *celebration* of Lawrence Fonseca's life and career. There had been no funeral, though he and Sasha and Cary had returned to SF the day after Thanksgiving in anticipation of one. But Lawrence loathed funerals. According to Jabez, the night before he died, he dictated what should happen next, insisting that he be cremated before anyone saw his body. Then, in a fever, on a smoothed-out, grease-spattered bag from his final meal of Chinese takeout, he had scrawled exacting instructions for his own celebration. It should be after the holidays—sometime in the new year, when more people would be free and feeling hopeful. He wrote out the guest list and an ideal menu of refreshments, assuming they could find someone to foot the bill. Most important, the list contained a full program: two hours of short films to be screened, the ones he deemed his best. On separate scraps of paper he had designated which of his possessions would go to particular friends. Walter was moved to learn that he had shown up on this list, that Larry wanted him to have the wonderfully garish poster for *The Elusive Pimpernel* that Michael Powell had signed for him. It was enormous; Walter was already stressed out about how on earth he would get it back to his place.

"How are you holding up?" Walter asked.

"Oh, as well as can be expected," said Jabez. "Of course, I miss him all the time."

Walter nodded.

"I've been trying to get all his stuff sorted. *There's a lot of it!* I'm happy to be able to keep the flat. But it's felt like a mausoleum of late."

"Any way I can help—literally, anything I can do—let me know."

"It's not only Larry's stuff. There's a ton of Roland's junk that Larry couldn't stand to part with. There are two storage units in the basement I'm afraid to even unlock."

Wordlessly, they finished their cigarettes. Jabez was very easy to be quiet with. A man of few words, for sure, but it seemed to Walter that Jay never cared to fill up silence with talk, a rare quality among gay men. Sasha had that quality as well; Walter envied it. Larry didn't have it. Cary certainly didn't.

He wasn't at all sure how to dress for a celebration that was explicitly *not a funeral*. He'd chosen black chinos and the fitted shirt Sasha had made him with the pattern of songbirds. The shirt itself made him sad now; he'd worn it in part as a signal to Sasha, whom he hadn't seen in weeks, that he missed him. Jabez was dressed for a celebration. He wore a beautiful batik shirt of tangerine, lime green, and sky blue, all edged in black. The pattern reminded Walter of a photo he'd seen of migrant monarchs swarming fir trees in Mexico.

"Jay . . ." Walter began, unsure how to ask what he wanted to know without either sounding accusing or losing his cool and breaking down in tears again. He cut to the chase: "Jay, at the end, when he was in the hospital, why didn't you call us? Cary and I, we left a bunch of messages. Why didn't you leave a message telling us what was going on?" His voice began to crack with grief. "Really, I would have loved to see him again—to say goodbye."

"You know, you're quite a pair, you and Cary." Jabez frowned.

"If you'd only let us know, we never would have left town that week. We would have *been there* . . ."

"So somehow it's my fault that you didn't know Larry was as sick as he was?"

Walter bowed his head, stubbed his cigarette. The two pigeons had been joined by others, and the little flock squabbled, the leader with its French fry giving chase across the tar and gravel.

"When I last spent time with him, he was feeling so much better! He *looked* better. He told me he'd been taking a new drug—something with *sequins* in the name?"

"Saquinavir?" Jabez grimaced. "When did he tell you that?"

"September, I think." The flash of Carmen Miranda's smile. "I'm sure it was September."

Jabez shook his head. "You understand he had dementia by the end? He was never part of that trial—everyone was buzzing about it, of course."

Acute pain gripped Walter above his abdomen, assailing him for his ignorance, his negligence.

Jabez shrugged. Orange monarch wings tensed and relaxed with his shoulders. "You and Cary talk as if you were Larry's last and only friends—like he died friendless and alone without you. Not the case. I was there—*a lot of us* were there. He said goodbye to everyone he wanted to say goodbye to. And a few he didn't. I can tell you that much."

Walter was crying again, a little, thinking once more how insane it was that someone could exist one day and not the next. It seemed impossible, a mistake. A bug in the creator's coding, an obvious flaw in the design.

"I didn't know," Walter said. *"I should have known."*

The Tenderloin hustled along below, engines idling, horns rebuking. The pigeons were gone, except the one-legged bird. It hopped along the roof-line and dove into the street.

Jabez changed topics. "Look, on the phone, I said that Larry wanted you to have that big movie poster, *The Elusive Pimpernel*?"

"Yeah?"

"I should warn you—you've got a custody battle on your hands." Jabez smiled his inverted smile, a warm, teasing look in his eyes. "Come inside . . . there's someone I think you should meet."

The apartment felt stuffy, January light straining through muslin drawn over the windows. There were half-filled cardboard boxes placed around the room, on the floor, the coffee table, the love seat. Walter's eyes went at once to the bare north wall: the dozens of framed photos and small paintings, tokens of Lawrence and Roland's life together, had been taken down; pale rectangular ghosts hung where the pictures had. The one picture remaining was the largest, *The Elusive Pimpernel*, still centered above the credenza.

"This is Walter. He's come to help us set up," Jabez said, switching on the overhead light. It was unclear who he was talking to, until Walter heard a small sound—a half cough, a throat clearing. He turned, and framed in the hallway was a short, slight, older woman with arresting blue eyes and wispy ash-blond hair in a sensible bob. She held out her hand and Walter took it; it was alarmingly small but firm.

"How nice to meet you, Walter. I'm Victoria Fonseca." Her English accent was thick and, to Walter's ear, posh, a little stagy. Larry hardly spoke of his mother, beyond alluding to her disapproval of many or most of his life choices.

"Likewise," said Walter, sounding starstruck.

But he wasn't starstruck, he was haunted: he was shaking hands with a woman he'd assumed was long dead. He could see Lawrence in her, in her cheekbones and brows, in the undeniable charm of her smile. She was tiny and had maybe the narrowest shoulders he had ever seen. She wore a white linen top with an elaborate lace collar. Despite her smallness, there was something about her bearing—the way she stood, the style of her—she was unmistakably her son's mother.

"You're just in time to help us sort photos," said Victoria. "We need to choose which to take downstairs and display during the funeral. Pardon— the *celebration*." She stood near the credenza, indicating a collection of framed snapshots arranged upon it in a loose grid. "For now, we're boxing the ones we don't want to take downstairs. Maybe Lawrence's friends will want some of these? I don't know half the people in them . . ."

Walter scanned the photos, which he'd examined before when he'd gotten the chance. Lawrence had pointed out some of the locales. There were lots of vacation shots: green peaks in the Azores, blue-tiled Lima, medieval towns in Europe, North Africa. There were posed snaps and candid shots: Roland and friends at brunches and flea markets, strolling near the Russian River, in the redwoods, or amid carpets of pink-blooming ice plant, somewhere south along the coast. Lawrence was missing from many of the shots, except for his eye, his ever-present framing sensibility. There were plenty of shots with Jabez and plenty of people Walter didn't know, but mostly images of Roland, whose tanned head and closemouthed smile were constant throughout. Half the people in the photos were Roland.

"I think it's an easy choice," said Jabez. "Let's take all the shots that have Larry in them downstairs—there aren't that many. We'll pack up the rest."

"Where's the projector?" Walter asked, noting the absence of Lawrence's prized possession, which he'd always kept displayed on the credenza.

"It's downstairs in the banquet hall," said Jabez. "Folks from the PFA have already descended."

Walter shook his head—*had he missed something?*

"Pacific Film Archive. There's some confusion about whether his films will go to them."

"I should say!" Victoria coughed.

"Anyway," Jabez went on, "they're insisting that a professional projectionist run the show today. None of us will be touching the films. Not anymore, if they have their way."

"We shall see about that," said Victoria. "A takeaway bag is hardly a binding legal document, now is it? Or perhaps it is in America."

She moved closer to Walter and spoke quietly, as if confiding in him, as she extended one hand toward the frame of *The Elusive Pimpernel*. "To the point, young man, this poster was given to me by Michael Powell himself—it certainly would have been inappropriate for a director to give such a gift to a ten-year-old boy. Still, more appropriate than presenting it to a married woman, I suppose, if you take my meaning."

Walter nodded.

"You see, I'm afraid I can't allow you to have it. It's too dear to me, no matter what Lawrence said. My poor darling. We all know how delirious he was near the end . . ."

"I understand," Walter said, and the woman smiled, taking his hand and patting it in thanks. He examined the gallery of photos laid out before them. Among them was an especially dashing headshot of Lawrence—it must have been from the '70s, he guessed, from the wavy mid-length hairstyle and the mustache. He'd never seen it before.

"Maybe I could have one of these pictures of Lawrence? After today, I mean, if no one lays claim to it?" He looked around for Jabez, hoping for his approval as well, but Jay had vanished. They were alone, and Victoria was still clutching his hand.

"You see, Mrs. Fonseca"—he was getting choked up again—"I loved Larry. I loved your son . . ." He thought it might be an important thing to say to a grieving mother, to assure her that her son was loved. But Victoria frowned sourly, dropped his hand, and stepped away. Now he assumed she thought he was confessing to an affair with a man twice his age, that he was confirming her fears that her son was a deviant, or worse, a chicken hawk, a pervert. A pederast deserving of his fate.

"I don't mean . . ." he started, but she had disappeared into the kitchenette. He thought he heard her mutter, *Thank you very much*, but her voice was vinegary.

Jabez emerged from the hallway. "Don't worry, Walter! Lawrence left you something else you're sure to love . . ." He was carrying a large, unwieldy piece of plastic luggage. "And I, for one, am not going to fight you for it!" He set the boxy thing down, and Walter saw that it had a cage door on the front; it was a crate . . . for an animal.

"Now the trick—bear with me a minute—" Jay zipped back down the hallway, cooing, "C'mere, you," and emerged with his chest swathed in thick marmalade fur. "The trick will be to get the old bugger into the carrier. You know, he's a famous curmudgeon."

"You're giving me *Basilisk*?"

"Larry said *you said* you'd love to take care of him!"

A pair of citrine slits stared out from the fur with disdain.

"What? I had no idea you still had him—I thought Larry had given him away? Honestly, I wasn't sure he even existed!"

"Oh, he exists," said Jabez. "We tried to give him away—several times—to neighbors. It never stuck; he always snuck back. We'd leave the window open, and there he'd be."

Walter felt like he was seeing a ghost: a fat, fanged poltergeist he'd be taking home to live with him after the party.

"Don't worry about offending Vicki," Jay said a little later, as they rode the elevator down to the lobby. "She basically means well. But there are reasons Larry would go for years without talking to her."

"He barely mentioned her to me."

"She has a tendency to swoop in, and when she does, she wants things done *just so*, her way, which is rarely how Larry envisions them." Jabez frowned. "*Envisioned them*, I mean."

"Is she driving you crazy, a little?"

"Thank god she isn't staying with me, that's all I can say."

The Archers' ballroom was a large banquet hall adjoining the lobby. It stood unused most of the year and smelled strongly of dust, of neglect. There were no windows to throw open and no fresh air to be had outside—exhaust from Geary Street permeated the lobby. A projectionist was busy fussing with Lawrence's projector, placed atop a rolling cart stacked with film canisters. Shuffling about, the man had kicked up a dust storm, which roiled in the projection beam as he tested the lamp. The ballroom's decor was a half-hearted callback to a Gilded Age salon, with contours of decorative trim, cobwebs in the crown molding, and cut-glass fixtures with half their drop crystals missing, half their bulbs burnt out. The room was painted a dingy yellow, greenish like old beeswax. The floor was worn hardwood, thank goodness, not the tan shag that stank so badly in the hallways. Walter went to find a broom.

Soon Cary showed up to help as well, sharp as ever in her sharkskin suit. It was the suit she was wearing the day she had met Larry, when he'd called her *the most debonair thing* he'd ever seen. They pushed the banquet tables flush with the walls, decked them with cloths, and arranged folding chairs in rows. The projectionist, whose name was Lucas, had unfurled a portable screen, a large stiff sail. He was taking the projector, a bona fide antique, for a test run by screening *What Roland Saw*, a film that Walter had been anxious to see again, the one about Roland going blind before he died. Walter turned away from it; he couldn't bear to watch it at the moment.

Jabez chose one table as a kind of shrine and busied himself setting up pictures of Lawrence and other memorabilia: framed certificates and awards from film festivals; his infant shoes, cast in bronze, carried all the way from London by Victoria. A florist appeared with a bannered wreath ("In Memoriam"—Walter thought, *Who ordered that? Someone who hadn't heard this was a party*) and several large bouquets—silver plant, tuberose, and Casablanca lilies—their pervasive sweet smell brightening the room. Victoria arrived in the ballroom with Larry's ashes stored in a modest cedar box, which, she was quick to inform whoever would listen, she had not chosen and thought was too plain. Walter was surprised the urn was so small—all the vibrancy Lawrence exuded in life was now trapped in a beveled box smaller than a shoebox. Jay set the urn in the center of the arrangement, beside the dashing headshot of Lawrence from the '70s. Walter stared at the picture, entranced by Larry's sideburns and his ingenuous, Hollywood-hopeful smile. He must have been in his thirties, but he looked so young—you could almost see the child peering through the eyes of the man. He wondered what might have happened if he'd been born two decades earlier, if he'd met Larry in LA in the '70s, if they would have been great friends, or maybe hated each other (*no, of course they could never*), or might have had a brief wild fling, or fallen in love. The fantasy ended, like all such fantasies about the golden age of disco and bathhouses, with him wondering if he'd be dead now, too, like Roland and Lawrence, or dying, like so many others.

Late that afternoon, as the celebration began, Jabez slipped a CD of romantic Cuban classics into a boom box, and when he heard the strains of "Siboney," Walter knew that what was coming might be nearly unbearable.

"Are you OK?" Cary asked, standing with him, her arm around his waist.

"I'm OK," he said. "I've never been to a funeral before, or a memorial, or a wake or anything! I've never had anyone close to me die."

"Makes you very lucky," said Cary. "Thank god Lawrence didn't go for the whole open-casket visitation thing. Man, those are grim."

"Is it bizarre to be serving food? Who can eat under these circumstances?"

They were standing near the buffet, which was surprisingly lavish, considering he'd brought Lawrence free lunches every week for most of their friendship. Jabez had found a café on Church Street that was able to fulfill Lawrence's exacting menu. It was a traditional English high tea: finger sandwiches (cucumber, watercress, gravlax, and—Lawrence had stipulated—*canned* asparagus); crumbly scones with raspberry jam, marmalade, clotted cream; dark chocolate strawberries; and poured fondant petits fours. There was a station for tea and coffee, and a single waiter, whose only job was to pour prosecco. It would have been delightful if it weren't so crushingly sad.

People arrived in a steady stream, chatting and noshing as if it were any other Saturday-evening fundraiser or art opening. Within half an hour the ballroom was crowded, and yet, as far as Walter could tell, only a few people appeared mournful. Many were laughing and catching up, including Cary, who had gone to fetch drinks and wound up having an animated chat with an older man in a very expensive-looking business suit, whom Walter didn't

recognize. Glancing around, Walter wondered if Larry's friend Ben the producer had traveled from LA for the memorial, since they'd never met—their
meeting having been permanently postponed by Lawrence's death. It seemed
crass to pry and ask Jabez for an introduction now. Through the crowd he
could see Jabez's back—his brilliant cotton shirt—he was hugging someone,
someone was hugging him. From across the room he recognized the lithe
hands grasping Jay's shoulders. It was Sasha. His heart leapt—once—then
sank sharply.

With little ceremony, Sasha had moved out of the apartment on Eureka
in early December. They were still in touch—he wasn't even that far away—
a friend of theirs in the Lower Haight had needed a new roommate as soon
as possible. But the brusque ordinariness with which Sasha moved felt cruel.
A few extremely painful days of packing and moving boxes, and that was it.
The mundane end of a glorious era. Cary cried for a solid day. Since then
they hadn't seen Sasha—it had been several weeks. And now here was their
Sashenka, looking lovely and solemn and half a world away as he comforted
Jay. His hair was swept up into that *Vertigo* swirl. One beauty secret Walter
had learned about the gamine: Cary was always the one who'd fixed Sasha's
hair like that, it was too hard to do oneself. Cary was great at styling hair,
though she didn't like to advertise it, it was such a fussy, femme talent. He
wondered who'd done Sasha's hair that day.

Walter stood holding a single dipped strawberry on a cocktail napkin. It
looked repulsive to him, the chocolate sweaty with condensation. A woman
next to him was telling her companion, as a weird sort of flirtation, that she
couldn't stand strawberries because the seeds on the flesh got stuck in her
teeth. Cary broke away from the gaggle of gay men that had formed around
her and circled back to Walter, passing him sparkling wine in a plastic flute.

"Who *are* all these people?" asked Walter, sniffing the prosecco.

"I assume they saw the ad in the *Weekly*."

"There was an ad? For Larry's *funeral*?"

"*Celebration*. Didn't I mention it?"

Walter shook his head.

"I told you. There was an item in the arts section. Once the Berkeley Art Museum got involved, they wanted to promote the event. *An evening of experimental film by a local master.*"

"The Berkeley Art Museum? What do they have to do with anything?"

"They run the film archive . . . they're cosponsors?" Cary indicated the buffet with her arm. "They paid for all this food? I swear I told you this."

"No, you didn't."

"I did, darling. You've just been checked out for the last two months."

Walter bit his tongue. Cary had her back to Sasha. She must not have seen him from across the room, or they would be having a different conversation.

"Who was that you were talking to over there? In the suit. He looks like a senator."

"That was Mitchell, of course."

Walter blinked, half afraid that Cary would tell him the guy was an ex.

"You've met—when we saw him last he was dressed as Sonny Bono, remember? He interrupted the orgy we were having with his wife—uh, husband."

"Oh god, keep it down, we're at a funeral for crying out loud!"

"*Celebration*, and don't shush me."

He could feel a pointless argument coming on, as if the situation weren't painful enough. It was a relief when Lucas from the film archive began speaking over the crowd, directing their attention to the projector. It was hard to hear—folks just kept on chatting. Lucas was saying how wonderful it was to see so many people in attendance, even on such a sad occasion. He was excited to share some truly innovative short films with them. Walter tried to follow his speech but was distracted by his appearance, his bad Caesar cut, his corduroy blazer, his pabulum complexion. A cliché of a cloistered scholar. Suddenly all Cary's jokes about how sad grad students are and what academia does to people—break their spirits and drain their personalities—seemed horribly on point.

"We'll start the screening in a moment," said Lucas. "But first, Victoria Fonseca would like to say a few words."

Victoria, who had been standing to one side, now took center stage. "Hello." She coughed. "Hello—most of you won't know me—I am Victoria, Lawrence's mother."

She was so petite, her voice so quiet, and yet as she spoke she appeared to grow larger, to fill the room, or perhaps the ballroom narrowed, shrinking around her to an intimate scale, as she bound them with her starlet's spell.

"In speaking to you, I am defying my son's wishes." She raised one hand as if in benediction. "Lawrence said *no speeches*—he didn't want speeches. Even so, I'm his mum. And he didn't say *no stories*. So I'll tell you a story. This was back in the day—goodness, forty years ago or more—he must have been twelve, I'd say. We had moved to Hollywood, and Lawrence's father was forever away on location. Often it was just the two of us, mother and son. It felt very cozy. Well, one time we drove out to the middle of nowhere to work as extras in a Kirk Douglas film—drove all the way to Gallup, New Mexico, on the storied Route 66. It was all so arid, so alien, for a couple of Brits—we thought we were on the moon!"

Victoria paused for a moment. She seemed far away, transported to the scene she was describing. "We were eating sandwiches in a drugstore in Gallup, and Lawrence turned to me and said, *Why did you bring me here?* And I asked, *Do you mean to New Mexico?* He said, *No, to America!* And I said, *So we can be movie stars, darling! Wouldn't you like us to be movie stars?* And he said, *I don't see the advantage.*" Victoria expelled a ringing laugh. "I mentioned—he was *twelve*. I told him the advantage was movie stars get to live forever. *Didn't he want to live forever?* And he said—ha ha—he said, *That sounds very tedious!*"

She blinked back tears. "Well, I suppose my son has been spared the *tedium* of living forever. So shall we all. Movie stars or no!"

A pause, full of tentative finality, as she folded her hands at her waist. A breath in and out, and then: "Many of you may know . . . it was no secret that Lawrence and I rarely saw eye to eye. But I must say that, in the end, if I could have traded my life for his, I would have. In an instant."

The room was silent. No one spoke or moved for a little eternity. There were tears then, the spontaneous tears of people who had all of a sudden realized the cocktail party was a wake after all. Victoria turned to Lucas and said, "Shall we watch some movies?"

Once the lights were dimmed and the program began, Walter had the impression that they were on a ship, sitting in rows on a funeral barge, the screen a single sail, and Lucas the helmsman, their Charon. The daydream was provoked by the many images of windblown things in the first film, called *Vortices*, which Walter hadn't seen before. There was no story—he knew not to expect one. A mysterious young man with an '80s haircut frolicked by the seaside, Lands' End by the look of it. There were cresting waves and wind-whipped cypresses, stirring banks of calla lilies, and the boy smoking among them, blowing smoke out to sea and kisses to the cameraman.

Beside him, Cary was distracted, and Walter knew why. They hadn't had time to say hello to Sasha before everyone sat for the screening. They'd waved to him from across the room. A few rows up on the other side of the projector, Sasha was sitting beside Jabez. It was obvious that Cary was unnerved by seeing him; she could barely sit still and kept holding her breath, wheezing like an asthmatic as she massaged her sternum. Walter took her hand in hopes of calming her. As the program went on, he noticed that Lawrence, as cinematographer, liked to fake out the viewer, homing in on things that seem solid but proved ephemeral, and vice versa: not a glass bulb but a soap bubble; not a sugar cube but a marble block. Things revealed themselves by how they shattered or dissolved. At one point, the screen itself seemed to come unstretched and flap freely like a luminous flag, then the frame pulled back: it was a dress shirt on a clothesline.

It was a lot of abstract film, much of it black and white, much of it silent or

344 Christopher Tradowsky

with minimal, incidental sound. Yet the audience sat engrossed, their reactions hushed. No one spoke above a whisper in the few minutes it took Lucas to rethread the projector. Walter wondered if they were transported by the films the way he was or if there was something about the solemnity of the context— they were communing with a dead man's visions—that kept them riveted, in suspense, as if reviewing the evidence of what he'd seen in life might somehow resurrect the man. That was the theme of *What Roland Saw*: the proposition that witnessing a red bougainvillea, just as Roland had seen it—and not even the bougainvillea per se, but that blazing scarlet shade—might resurrect the man for an instant. The dead see again, through the eyes of the living, as Aristotle thinks again, through us, when we read his thoughts. Knowing what was coming at the flash of the title card, Walter felt prepared to see *What Roland Saw* and watched it analytically, despite the pangs he felt when the camera caught glimpses of Larry or when he heard his friend's voice off-screen asking, *Where, where?* Beside him Cary was now a wreck and excused herself once the film ended, rushing from the room. He thought she'd be right back, but when she missed one whole film, then another, he went to search for her.

Easing the door closed behind him, he found himself alone in the dusky lobby. He looked for her in the bathroom—nothing. He searched the sidewalk; the sun was setting and the evening colorful. Up and down Geary, storefronts began to glow inwardly; signs of commerce buzzed to life. It was silly to search for her outside—she didn't smoke. It seemed unlikely that she'd wandered off somewhere, she wouldn't have taken off. Back in the lobby, he thought she might have gone up to the roof, and was about to head up the stairs, when he heard sniffling coming from the corner opposite. Retracing his steps to the enormous reception desk that lined one wall, he searched behind it and found Cary sitting curled against the wall in its mahogany shadow, her head buried in her arms. He knelt beside her and felt her back shuddering as he embraced her.

"I couldn't handle that movie the first time around," she muttered into her knees.

"I know," said Walter, kissing the glossy hair on the back of her head, inhaling her warm pomade. "I know."

Some minutes passed. The traffic noise rattling down Geary was muffled but relentless. They were entirely alone; not a soul passed through the lobby.

"How did we not know?" Cary asked, lifting her head and drying her eyes.

"That Larry was so sick?"

She shook her head, then bowed it again. The seconds dragged torturously. "That Sasha was so unhappy. It was only three months ago, when we were doing the show with Kelly. Everything was great then!"

She pulled back from his embrace; he sat at a slight remove. The dark corner was suffocatingly close. The stiff brush of the carpet under his palms made his skin crawl.

"We've been over this," he said quietly. "It's hard for me to see Sasha, too."

"I think he's dating Jabez!" she cried, her voice despairing.

"Cary, they're just sitting together."

"They're *holding hands*—did you see they're holding hands?"

"They're *friends*. It's a funeral, for Chrissake!"

"You wouldn't think they're just friends if you saw when Sasha showed up—the way they greeted each other."

"I did see, actually. *They hugged. Big deal.*"

Cary tightened her arms around her knees, and the tears came again. He could never stand to see her cry and summoned his strength to keep from joining her. Their dumb argument seemed more absurd when he realized he was staring into the shadows at a three-hole punch atop a heap of old office supplies on a grungy shelf. At least the discarded office supplies made him feel less like they were sitting in a coffin.

"I knew it would end this way!" Cary spat. "I knew he would leave me for a *real man*."

His heart raced—her words made him instantly angry—but he wasn't sure why. It wasn't that she was making him question Sasha; he felt sure that

Sasha and Jabez weren't fucking. And aside from the quick turnaround, it wouldn't matter if they were. Meanwhile, if Sasha had left Cary for a *real man*, that wouldn't explain why Sasha had left *him*. *Or would it?* None of this made Walter irate; it was something deeper, a more fundamental betrayal in what she'd said. A betrayal not of any one of them alone but of their world-view, of what had made them *them*.

"Goddamn it, Cary, Sasha didn't leave because you're not man enough, or even because you're not woman enough, or because you're not *anything* enough."

"Then why——?"

"I don't know! Probably because he was sick of folding your underwear!"

"That's a stupid reason to leave——"

"Is it? I don't know! I don't know why he left, either. But I do know that you don't get to turn my world upside down and say, *All the old rules about how to live don't matter*—especially rules about what makes a *real* man or a *real* woman, or what it means to be gay or bi or *ambivalent* or whatever—and then take it all back and say, *Never mind, psych! I guess the rules do apply after all.*"

She sniffed and bobbed her head in half agreement. His dressing down seemed to cheer her up briefly. Through the shadows he could see she was narrowing her eyes at him.

"And you!" She shook her head. "You're going to leave me, too!"

"I am not—and can we please not fight about this now? I am not planning on leaving you."

"You're moving to Chicago, I can feel it in my bones. I knew it as soon as that guy called you—that professor you want to work with."

He sighed. In truth, it was a call he wouldn't have told her about, if she hadn't been sitting in his living room with him when it came. "He called me *back*, is all—he was answering my questions about scholarships and stuff. I told you, I haven't been accepted yet."

"You're getting in, Wall, and *you're going*." She wiped her tears diligently, with a kind of finality. "And what's more? I'm OK with it. It's the program you want, and I'm not getting in the way of that. Surprise, I'm not a total selfish asshole after all."

"I've never thought that, *never*. And *if* I do get in, *if* I move to Chicago, you can come with me! Wouldn't that be fun? Sharing some crappy grad housing in Hyde Park?"

"Are you insane?"

"You can bring your mason jar from the garden so you won't blow apart when you leave San Francisco."

She frowned. "That's just it—I'm not leaving San Francisco—I *will* *never* leave San Francisco. You know that as well as anyone."

"OK, OK. I get all that." He was feeling claustrophobic, anxious for this miserable argument to end so they could return to the comparatively upbeat funeral that was happening in the next room. "Even if I leave, we don't have to break up—I'll come back . . ."

"If you move, I'm moving on, we're splitting up. That's that. I love you, Wall. But I will never wait around for *some man*, I will never do that. And I hope you never will, either."

He was out of words. Momentarily cried out, too exhausted to argue, he sat back, rubbing his chin like he'd been sucker punched and marveling at how everything always seemed to come to a head at once. They embraced then, a deep, desperate embrace, nothing held back, a hug that felt momentous. When at last they pulled away, Cary said, "I miss Milo."

"You miss Milo Blankenship?"

"Yes, that's what I said."

"You understand . . . Milo isn't real. We made him up!"

"He's real to me! Exceedingly real, more real than many people we know and purport to like. And now, he'll never come to life, because we've lost Larry. Only Larry could have played him, just like only Sasha could have played Lorna. We've lost Larry and we've lost Sasha, which means we've lost Lorna, too. We made a little world together, you and me. And I loved it. *I loved the world we made.*"

"I did, too. I loved it, too. But we never had any idea what to do with it, did we?"

"You know . . ." A spark flashed anew in Cary's eye.

"What? What is it?" Walter asked. "Oh god, you're not horny *now*, are you? Not here!"

"No, doofus! Get your mind out of the gutter. In that room—that very room over there—is a big-time Hollywood producer named Benjamin Venable. You sent him our script back in October, didn't you?"

"I did . . ."

"So now, all we have to do is go find him."

"How do you know he's in there?"

"Jay told me. He said he would introduce us. We'll wait until the screening is over, then we'll pounce!"

"If you say so, darling."

He kissed her on the forehead, on the tip of her nose, on her mouth. At the moment he was too worn out even for his own skepticism. Along with the script he had sent Ben Venable his phone number and address. If he'd read the script or passed it off to an assistant, they hadn't been inspired to reach out.

"Can we please get out of this gross corner?" Walter asked. "I can hardly breathe back here—I feel like we're in that Poe story about premature burial."

In the hours, days, and even years to come, Walter would be left to wonder if he could have prevented the calamity that would follow. If he and Cary had returned to the ballroom a *little* earlier—even ten minutes earlier—could he have warned them what was about to happen? If he'd been sitting in the audience, waiting in the yellow dimness for Lucas to cue up the next film, he could have caught the title card when it blinked before them, scrawled in Lawrence's inimitable hand. He could have recognized the title, *Solar*

Flare, right away as *that film*, the one Larry had sabotaged, which made him infamous in some circles and had gotten his films barred from festivals in New York. As it was, he was not in the room, so he was not there when Lucas, blamelessly following the set list, picked up the next canister in the pile. He was not there when the spools spun to life and the black compass wound down, *5 . . . 4 . . . 3 . . . 2*, and the titles came rapid-fire. Though he'd never seen the movie, he might have recognized the imagery Lawrence had described to him once as *flaring things*: sunspots, bonfires, and blinding coronas . . .

But he was not in the room. And as it happened, it was late in the program, and the event had gone long, and the prosecco was strong, and once *Solar Flare* was set in motion Lucas slumped in his chair and started snoozing, at exactly the wrong time. No one could blame him; he wasn't the only one dozing off. As reports had it, the movie itself, though formally ingenious, was otherwise intensely boring, full of long sequences that were so overexposed they were pure white, appearing blank. What could be seen of the film was on fire: fearsome eclipses, angel-blue flames, hellish spitting magma. So it was hardly surprising when the screen itself started blistering, a black-ringed orange bubble forming at its center, then inflating to fill the frame, which warped and burst and seethed. As it happened, no one noticed when the film caught. No one noticed a thing until the smoke rose from the projector, the strip snapped, and sparks from the lamp raced up the celluloid like a fuse. By the time someone screamed—too stupefied to yell *fire*—the take-up reel was shedding sparks like a Catherine wheel. Gasping, people leapt from their seats. Someone thought to unplug the projector, but by that time the machine itself was burning robustly from within, like a well-fueled hibachi. Flames shed from the projector onto the dozen spools that Lucas had left loosely stacked around it. The assembled would discover, in a few terrifying moments, just how badly the Archers flouted the fire codes: no extinguishers, no sprinklers, no emergency exits, and doors that opened inward, so that those in a panic to flee began pressing helplessly against the doors.

It was the pounding at the doors, the scuffling and screaming, that drew Walter and Cary back into the room; they had to shove inward against the press of the crowd. The doors sprung wide, and the mourners fled, leaving a wreckage of chairs and coats behind them. In the center of the room raged a column of fire where the projector had been, smoke blanketing the ceiling. A heroic cater-waiter ran toward the inferno with a champagne bucket full of ice, tripped, and fell headlong into the cart, knocking it off-balance. In a fireball it tumbled onto a pile of chairs. At last someone's hand found an alarm and pulled it. Unable to believe his eyes, Walter was among the last to escape the ballroom. He ran to the shrine of photos to see what he might salvage. The perfume of Casablanca lilies mingled with the suffocating smoke. Cary followed and berated him, dragging him from the room by the cuffs. The denizens of the Archers Hotel, their surprise at the fire alarm evident in their haphazard clothing, were slowly descending the staircase and crossing the lobby, annoyed and disbelieving, until they caught sight of the ballroom, bright orange and raging like a magnificent hearth.

By the time the fire trucks arrived, closing off the block and blasting their torrents into the lobby, smoke and flames were billowing from the second-story windows. The sun had set, and all around the burning hotel the Tenderloin was awakening, ready to turn on and tart up for a Saturday night. On the sidewalk, police corralled the crowds, and while most of the attendees from Larry's memorial had scattered, Walter, Cary, and Sasha were standing where they had been directed to stand, behind a police line kitty-corner from the hotel. The tenants who had been home when the fire broke out milled anxiously around them. Walter and Cary were pressing Sasha for information, trying to determine what had gone wrong, but Sasha was in a panic and unable to give any certain answers.

"You guys, I'm telling you, I don't know—I was watching the movie! I didn't notice anything until it was too late!"

Walter was staring up at a window that had blown out in the corner unit on the second floor. Sheets of fire were whipping against the tall carnation-red sign reading "The Archers Hotel," its old-time saloon font outlined in still-lit neon. He scolded himself for finding it beautiful, for eyeing a rising column of smoke and thinking, *Huge cloudy symbols of a high romance.*

"What film was being shown, do you remember?" he asked.

"You want to know what film you missed? What difference does it make?" Sasha threw up his hands. "I'm really worried about Jabez right now."

"Wait—what's wrong with Jay?" asked Cary.

"He ran upstairs to the apartment—I tried to stop him—"

"What the hell? When was that?"

"After the fire started—he pulled the alarm and ran upstairs. He said he absolutely needed some things—his papers, his passport—he said he'd come right back down—"

"Holy crap, that's awful!" said Walter.

"And now no one is coming down through that fire—"

"There's a fire escape, isn't there?" Cary asked. "I don't see one, but there has to be a fire escape in the alley, doesn't there?"

Sasha told them to wait there and, pressing his way through the crowd, ran to search for Jabez in the alley.

"Whatcha got there?" asked Cary, glancing down at the cedar box Walter was clutching with both arms.

"It's Larry's ashes," Walter replied, a little snidely. He was surprised, even a little indignant, that no one else had thought to grab them while escaping the burning banquet hall.

"No! I'm talking about *this*," Cary said, grabbing a framed photograph from where he had tucked it under one arm. She held it out, and the glossy, youthful Lawrence smiled up at them. "He was a dreamboat back in the day, wasn't he? I can see why you nabbed this one. Look at those delicious muttonchops!"

"Can you please be serious for *one second*? I am literally holding the man's ashes."

She frowned, admonished, but continued to moon at the photo of Lawrence.

"Oh, thank you! Oh, thank goodness you thought to grab the urn!" Victoria had appeared beside them. In her tiny white hands she gripped a leather purse, as if afraid it might be ripped from her at any moment. She had no coat and looked cold in her linen blouse. Walter and Cary offered her their jackets, but she refused them. An awkward silence passed between them despite the chaos of the scene, pierced by sirens and police dispatches on bullhorns.

Walter held the cedar box out to Victoria, saying, "Would you like to take them? Uh . . . I mean, *him*?"

She squeezed her bag closer. "Walter, would you be such a dear and hold it for me?" She glanced around, unsure where to go or what to do next, then raised her chin, resolved. "I wonder—would you be so kind as to walk me to my hotel? Would you carry my Lawrence for me?" She patted the box with one hand.

"Of course we will!" said Cary, a little too cheerfully.

"It's a few short blocks up that way," said Victoria. "I'm at the Monaco."

"Oh, the Monaco is lovely! The bar is lovely!" said Cary, ignoring Walter, who was elbowing her.

Soon Sasha reappeared, Jabez in tow. "Found him!" he proclaimed, clearly relieved. Sasha held up a small Naugahyde suitcase covered in Day-Glo Pucci swirls. "He stopped to pack, of course!" Sasha rolled his eyes.

Jabez stepped up to join them. In his right hand the cat carrier swung with evident weight. "I brought you something," he said to Walter.

"I have a cat!" Walter said, turning to Cary.

"You have a cat? This is unexpected!"

"I'm as surprised as you are."

Cary bent down to peek at Basilisk through the grille. "Hello, you monster!"

She took the crate from Jabez. Jay had been talking to the police—there was nothing to be done until the fire was well and truly out. Sasha invited him to stay over that night at his place. For the moment, they were at loose ends, so the four of them decided to escort Victoria back to her hotel.

"I suppose the party is over." Victoria sighed, shaking her head at the site of the Archers, still expelling an abundance of smoke from the charred second story, though no flames were visible. "Lawrence always did love a dramatic exit!"

It was a curious funeral procession as they walked uphill toward downtown, and the sidewalks became cleaner, the apartment towers taller, thinner, and more elegant. Jabez led the way, chatting with Sasha and Victoria. Basilisk was so heavy that Cary and Walter dragged behind a bit, the irate feline squirming and yowling all the way.

Walter's heart was heavy with the profound awareness that he was carrying all that was left of his friend. *How deeply weird the term* remains *is*, he thought, *both literal and inapt. And how horrifying the industry term* cremains, *like an off-brand coffee creamer.* At the moment he felt selfish; he didn't really want to give the ashes back to Victoria. In his grease-spattered will Larry had not specified what he wanted done with them, but letting Victoria return them to a London suburb seemed wrong—profane, in a way. Larry must have wanted *something else* done with them, something more significant. But what? He was hoping Victoria would at least let him keep the headshot—maybe she wouldn't notice it under his arm.

Both he and Cary were manic by now, buzzing from what had transpired. Going over the order of events and what they'd gleaned from others, they wondered aloud if they'd have been able to prevent the whole disaster, if only they'd been in the room.

"Cary, do you think—it seems so crazy—but do you think Lawrence *planned* for things to end this way?"

Cary was laughing—completely inappropriately, he thought. "How should I know? But I'm certain he would think it went *better* than he could have planned." Trying to stifle her laughter, she smiled from ear to ear.

"What could you possibly find amusing about this situation?"

"I'm sorry, I'm sorry! It's just that the irony is too perfect!"

"What on earth are you talking about?" He stopped stock-still. "Why are you giggling, you lunatic?"

"It's kind of beautiful, I think. The irony is that we were all running for our lives from a burning building, and *you* stopped to rescue the ashes of the arsonist."

That spring, Walter and Fiona's place was crowded, chock-full of life and Día de los Muertos tableaus. Basilisk came home with him; they hoisted the cockatiel's cage as close as possible to the ceiling. Leaping from vantage to vantage, stretching as he might, the marmalade monster could not reach the birdcage. With feline cool he'd recline on the bookshelf and initiate hours-long staring contests with José, who squawked occasionally but betrayed no fear, whose fermata eyes never blinked.

Fiona was single at the moment and spending more time than ever at home. Meanwhile Cary practically moved in with them, spending every night at their place. Her own apartment was much larger, but sleeping in the bedroom that Sasha had painted without Sasha, without his bank of pillows and his purloined quilt and his culottes in the closet, was too painful for Cary to bear. As Walter could have predicted, pressed into close quarters, Cary and Fiona became fast friends. Fiona taught Cary to play poker. There followed a string of nights when they stayed awake drinking and playing heads-up amid a pantheon of burning Mexican saints until two or three in the morning, well past pumpkin time for Walter. Their increasing closeness—and Fiona's beauty—made Walter nervous. One morning, as he scrubbed purple dregs from the wineglasses they'd left out, he begged Cary not to sleep with Fiona.

She laughed him off at first and then got angry, swearing that of course she wouldn't do *something so messy*. After all, *Fiona was Kelly's best friend*. He hated feeling jealous, but in truth, it was Fiona's common sense he trusted to prevail in that situation. Cary loved him, he knew, but she disdained all boundaries—even so-called healthy ones—and the mundane tyranny of common sense as well.

Basilisk was hostile toward Walter, but over a month or so they forged a relationship based on tentative mutual respect, tempered by deep suspicion. The cat was warmer toward Fiona; she'd bribe him with scraps of tilapia and other unctuous tidbits. Cary was the only one he'd let pet him. When she entered the room, the beast would roll over and expose his white belly as if he'd been possessed by a spaniel. The apartment was clearly too cramped for Basilisk's lifestyle. If they left the window open, he would disappear over the eaves, sometimes for an entire day or overnight, returning only when Walter left offerings of soft food on the sill.

The cat had lived with them for over a month before Walter finally found the note.

One blustery March morning Walter managed, with great effort and a little bloodshed, to trap Basilisk in his carrier and haul him downhill to the Haight for a physical. They were waiting in the exam room for the vet, and in the antiseptic chamber the cat had staked out the opposite corner and was attempting to turn Walter to stone with his citrine glare. Under a ragged towel bunched inside the carrier he found a folded sheet of stationery. Pulling it out, he was surprised to discover it was addressed to him. Ballpoint ink, a familiar hand. He returned Basilisk's suspicious gaze, unfolded the note, and read:

Walter,

Forgive Lawrence if he told you I was gone, he did not know, he could not know! I come and go as I please, I was never his either to keep or to send away. Apartment buildings are porous, after all. The Archers is an armature, the city's a sieve. What you saw in me, he never knew! But you're so clever you recognized at once that I am no one's house cat, no, not a cat at all, but Ammit the Devourer. Five thousand years old, an ancient incubus, a psychopomp (look it up), he who lies hungrily in wait.

For Larry I waited and waited, and waited again, upon his bedspread at night or on the pebbles of Sarcoma Beach, and when at last I saw he was at his frailest I leapt from the sill and devoured his soul. Now Lawrence lives within me. He walks where I walk and sees what I see. He struggles from within to control me (ever the director—ha!). But he cannot, because I am an immortal demigod, and he is a poor, weak shade.

Walter, mark my words. There is no other life, after or otherwise. There are no other realms, no underworld, no limbo, and certainly no nirvana. Do not search for other worlds, do not long for them. If you long for immortality, I'm it! I'm your best bet.

From now on you must care for me—for us. That is imperative. If you fail, I will pounce. I will kill you with cat-scratch fever and eat your soul, as I did to Lawrence, and Roland, and ten thousand men before them.

Don't try me.
Basilisk

28 EXT. OCEAN, FAR OUT AT SEA--EVENING
Camera hovers over a thick marine layer. Fog sweeps
toward Ocean Beach. The rickety towers and spinning
contraptions of Playland. Midway lights. Sweethearts
stroll. Lovers at the soda fountain; lovers at the
ring toss, entering the fun house, the mirror maze.
Everywhere, the carousel's strident song. Everywhere,
the cackling of Laffing Sal. Camera sweeps the midway,
past the carnival pavilions, seedy sideshow tents. Beyond
them: chain link. Beyond that: cypresses.

EXT. GOLDEN GATE PARK--EVENING
A short way down a juniper path. One of two enormous
windmills turns in the fog. Beneath it, parked on a
gravel access road, a boxy white van marked "Silver City
Engineering. A Division of The Concern, LLC." Two figures
in hats and coveralls exit the van. They unload steel
cylinders, big as torpedoes, into the windmill. Label on
one canister: "CAUTION: CONTENTS UNDER PRESSURE. GASEOUS
LOTOPHAGINE, 100 lbs."

Blades of the windmill spin, slicing the fog. From tubes
that line the blades, streams of white gas pour forth.
Gas merges with the fog, carried off with it, gray into
gray, swept away through the park.

Evening fog floods the park, the avenues. Fog overtakes
the light rail, the N train sliding eastward from the
Sunset. Thick fog chills the Richmond, the Fillmore,
Japantown, overcoming the tourists, the shoppers with
their happy hauls. Rushing over Twin Peaks, fog sweeps
through the Castro, the Mission. Fog wreaths Coit Tower
and blankets Union Square.

EXT. DOWNTOWN--EVENING
The workday ends. It's cocktail hour. Sidewalks teem with
workers, freed for the evening. They trot in overcoats
toward the watering holes of Market Street, SoMa, North
Beach.

Weary, relieved greetings: handshakes, hugs, pecks on
cheeks. Coats shed, tables claimed, bottles uncorked,
cocktails streamed into coupes. Laughter and cheers:
"Salud!" "Prost!" "Chin-chin!" A happy noise: the clamor
of glasses clinking, jazz combos firing up. Talk and talk,
laughter and banter and nattering, and everywhere the
roaring white noise of blissful amnesia.

                      THE END

Grand Hotel

SASHA MOVED INTO A GORGEOUS old deco tower on Buchanan Street in the Upper Market, a stone's throw from the Mint. It was from the '20s, twelve stories tall and white as salt, an elegant pillar, like Lot's wife gazing back over the Castro. Spread beneath each window bay were bas reliefs in triptych: the leaves of philodendrons like shields in a coat of arms, fiddleheads and trumpet bells, and scrolls upon scrolls, abstract cochlea and plaster palmiers. The same motifs erupted all around the grand entrance, where the columns flanking the doors were encrusted—like the Gaylord's downtown—with strata of scrolls (paired like parentheticals). Columns with a thousand ears, bent and attentive to the city's cries and rumors.

Behind these columns, day and night, a doorman tipped his black derby and eased the glass doors open with buff gloves, and inside all was champagne light and ebony trim, the elevator filigreed brass and glossy, hardwood marquetry. From the windows of Sasha's tenth-floor apartment, where they talked until sunrise, you could see for miles upon miles, even in the predawn dark, north to Vallejo and south to Hayward, and east beyond the bay to the sunrise shooting gold smelt over the peak of Mount Diablo.

But of course, there never was such a vantage on Mount Diablo, because there is no deco tower so tall, not in the Upper Market. Sasha's building was not a grand old hotel but a serviceable apartment block. Beige and blank-faced, it was raised in the '40s and only six stories tall, though the hill it perched on made it appear loftier. Sasha had a bay window, into which he pushed his mattress for the best reading light. On a clear day you could glimpse the Oakland hills—a blue-gray smudge—and a band of water south of the bridge, as bridge and bay shone dully like aluminum. All the embellishments were in Walter's head, in his memory: the elaborate reliefs, the fastidious doorman, the champagne hallways, and heaven's elevator . . . He imagined it all in retrospect, tacking on a few more ornaments each time he recalled the one evening he visited Sasha there and stayed the night, which turned out to be the last time they made love.

Grand Hotel was playing at the Castro, and Cary happened to be out of town: she'd packed up her Count Dracula jar and motored off for a family visit down south. Walter hadn't seen Sasha in six weeks or more. Sasha and Cary weren't speaking at the moment. Cary was still too sore, not because of the breakup, she insisted, but because Sasha had quit Bombolone and wouldn't think of coming back. She was sure the band was dead without their lead singer; no one could replace Sasha. And though Cary swore up and down she didn't mind if Walter spent time with Sasha, the sunny, antagonistic way she would interrogate him afterward told a different story. In the end it was easier to let things slide.

That Friday he called Sasha's new number, convinced that they could not miss Greta Garbo at the Castro in her most celebrated role (a double bill with *Queen Christina*), and they planned to meet at the theater the following night. It had been long enough since they'd seen each other that, approaching the marquee and spying Sasha at the ticket booth (leopard-print coat, receiving tickets from a visored, elderly agent like a white toad in a terrarium), Walter experienced that jolt you sometimes feel seeing a loved one again after a hiatus, that selfish inner voice that pleads, *Please don't have changed, or if change is inevitable, please don't have changed too much, and only in ways that I can comprehend and love.* An embrace from Sasha, a ticket traded for a kiss, and his anxiety dissolved completely.

The movie felt a bit dusty, fuddy-duddy, or maybe it was John Barrymore, whose residual silent-era eyeliner highlighted his middle age—a little hard to accept as a sly, spry jewel thief and heartthrob. And Garbo proved the quintessential example of a star who couldn't really act, but acted unconvincingly in a hugely magnetic way, the serene mask of her face a silver screen within a screen, an invitation for ever more projection. By the time she uttered the most famous phrase to pass her lips, *I want to be alone*, Walter and Sasha were holding hands again, like they always used to at the movies, and Walter squeezed tightly as if to say, *There it is!* He knew then that he'd have to concoct a convincingly boring lie; he wouldn't be able to tell Cary what he'd done that Saturday night. They skipped out on *Queen Christina* and went to the Orbit Room for cocktails. And blame it on fate—the jukebox roulette spun out "Embraceable You," Ella Fitzgerald vying for the Guinness World Record for most romantic version of the most romantic song—they wound up back at Sasha's place.

The sex was deeply bittersweet. What started out (Walter hoped) as a new beginning, as it intensified, felt more and more like saying goodbye, very slowly, over and over. Not at all like breakup sex, infused with patent awfulness, but post-breakup sex: hopeful, electrifying, confusing, hopeless, elegiac. Valedictorian sex. Afterward they dozed on the bed beneath the window. Preferring to sleep with a little light, Sasha opened the curtains to let in the sulfurous haze of the city. Luminous pollution elided the starlight. They slept. Just after 3:30, marked by the insistent blinking colon on the clock radio, Walter went to take a leak and, returning, realized he was wide-awake. His drowsiness had been driven off by utter confusion over how he could so desperately miss someone who was at that moment lying in bed beside him.

Sasha had set up the entire studio as his workroom. Near the foot of the bed stood a sewing table, his Brother sewing machine, an ironing board, and a new dressmaker's mannequin with a wooden knob where its head should be. In the dark, the walls of the room appeared haunted by spirits, like a medium's tent, the shadow realm of the Playland Oracle. Low on closet space, Sasha had hung his outfits from the picture rail, displayed elbow to elbow and hip to hip, like in a vintage shop. Even in the dark Walter recognized them: the beach pajamas Sasha had worn to Stow Lake, the wide-legged slacks he wore to work, the red robe he often bundled up in at Eureka Street. Something was missing, he knew what it was . . . Walter patted the new feather duvet that covered them. When he moved out, Sasha had taken the Klimt quilt with him. Here, it was nowhere to be seen.

His restlessness must have roused Sasha, who turned toward him. Propping his head up on his elbow, he murmured, "I see you can't sleep, either."

"I miss you, Sasha." Walter was crying. He tried to hide it, but it was in his voice.

"I know, darling." Sasha sighed. "I miss you, too." An interminable pause. "It doesn't matter, though. It's better this way."

Sasha was deep in shadow, his expression unreadable. Walter shivered a bit, though it wasn't cold, and sucked in breath. "Do you remember what you said to us that night at the Madonna Inn? You said, *I love you, but that's beside the point.*"

"It's true. I still feel that way."

"What does that mean? I don't understand it *at all*."

Sasha flipped onto his belly, propping his chin with his pillow, his face pale in the cool gloom of window light.

"Let me ask you something. Are you going to tell Cary you saw me tonight? Are you going to tell her we slept together?"

Walter stalled before answering, but he wasn't deliberating. He knew. "No. God, no. It's so ironic—I think you're the one person in the world she doesn't want me to sleep with. In the whole world, you're the single person who can make her jealous."

A low, knowing laugh from Sasha. "And why's that?"

Sasha peered bay-ward. Walter stared at his lover's profile, the flat cheeks, the worried mouth, chin buried pensively in the pillow.

"Because she still loves you, because she wants you back—*we* want you back, Sashenka. We bicker all the time since you left, we're petty and short with each other. Cary's convinced I'm going to up and leave for Chicago and that'll be the end of us."

"You did get into Chicago, though."

"I did."

Now Walter turned, following Sasha's sight line, gazing down over clusters of duplexes on Pearl Street and Elgin Park, toward the flat-topped warehouses of SoMa. Across the bay, the fog was lit from within by strands of golden mercury lights, where dockworkers at Oakland harbor must have been grinding away on the graveyard shift. *Commerce never sleeps.*

"We were both blindsided when you left—we racked our brains and couldn't figure out why you'd rather be alone than with us. At the movie tonight, I thought, *Sasha's just like Garbo.* A sphinx. A gorgeous riddle. It's like you left us, saying, *I want to be alone.*"

Sasha sat upright, agitated, his face and torso limpid in the meager light. "Don't you see? That's exactly the point. I am not fucking Greta Garbo, am I? And I'm not Veronica Lake or whoever else Cary always wished I was. I'm flattered by the comparisons, believe me, but at some point . . ." Sasha pushed his hair behind his ears. "At some point I think Cary stopped seeing me clearly."

Walter sat up now, facing Sasha and mirroring his stance, his back to the window.

"It's like the whole Lorna Zaftig thing." Sasha shook his head. "She said you two wrote Lorna for me, and I said, *I can't act.* And she said, *That's OK, Veronica Lake couldn't act, either, you just have to be yourself.* And I'm thinking, *Who do you think that is?* I said, *I'm not zaftig*—and she said, *Movie magic will take care of that!* One day she called me your *muse,* and I thought, *Give me a fucking break.* Sure, it's flattering to be someone's muse, but when your muse turns around and tells you to wash your own damn underwear, the spell is kind of broken, isn't it? It turns out I'm *not that kind of magician,* either."

"I'm so sorry, Sashenka . . . ," Walter said, reaching for him in the shadows, but Sasha stayed put, just beyond reach.

"Oh, hell, *whatever*. I was never going to be able to bring Lorna to life for you or for Cary. I'm not actually a character in your noir fantasy world."

"We just—I swear—*we adored you*. That's all." He shook his head, thinking of his complicity in what Sasha was describing. Sasha was not accusing *him*. Sasha said, *Cary stopped seeing me clearly*. But now Walter wondered if *he'd ever seen Sasha clearly*, considering he'd always thought of him as a kind of idol: a starlet, a magician, a gamine. Untouchable, in a way. The whole time they were together, he felt amazed by his luck—undeserving of someone so obviously stupendous. But it never occurred to him how unfair they were being to Sasha, that Sasha deserved something deeper than adoration. Adoring someone to distraction wasn't knowing them deeply or loving them too intensely. How stupid of him, what an obvious mistake—to offer someone worship when it turned out they wanted—they wanted— And now he was mortified to realize the truth of the matter, that *he had no idea what Sasha wanted*.

"Sasha," he asked excitedly, as if he'd solved the riddle of the Sphinx, and it was so obvious: *"What is it you want?"*

"How the hell should I know?" said Sasha, shrugging, palms up and empty. "All I know is Cary was too keen to answer that question for me. She always purported to know exactly what I wanted, including, let's face it, *you*. I'm sorry, but in all honesty, I don't know what would have brought us together if it hadn't been for Cary."

The windowpane inches behind Walter's back was cold, he sensed its thinness; a chill zipped up his spine. It hurt to hear it, but Sasha spoke the truth. He could have worked at Macy's for years without screwing up the courage to speak to Sasha. He owed so much to Cary's kismetic force.

"Lotophagine," he said at length.

"Lotophagine, *maybe*. But it's deeper than that. Believe me, I will love Cary until the day I die. But Cary's someone whose personality is *so strong*—her tastes and desires and opinions are so strong—and she's so extravagant, that I began to fear her personality was eclipsing mine—like I was losing myself to her . . ."

Walter frowned. "You make her sound kind of insidious . . ."

Then Sasha leaned forward and grabbed him by both hands, pulling him nearer, the duvet bunching between their knees. Sasha's expression was bright through the predawn dark. For a brief flash, he looked inspired. "Think about this: What if I said to you, *I'm moving to Paris. Let's run away together—move to Paris with me!* What's the first thing you'd say?"

It was a thrilling, electrifying question. He hesitated long enough that Sasha added, "Be honest."

Part of him wanted to kiss Sasha full on the mouth and say, *When do we leave?* Instead, he bent and kissed Sasha on one hand, awkwardly, at the knuckles. "The first thing I would say is *What about Cary?*"

Sasha took back his hand, massaging it where the fumbled kiss had landed. "Exactly. You can't imagine the two of us being together without her, for the same reason you won't tell her about tonight."

"Yes, because it would break her heart."

"For a while, yes, maybe . . ."

"And I couldn't do that to her . . ."

"She's not fragile. She won't break."

". . . because *I love her.*"

"Because you're *still under her spell.*"

"Yes. Of course. What's the difference?"

They talked longer, not an argument but a discussion, animated and inconclusive and exhausting, until it was nearly dawn, and feeling the night was spent and there was no chance of catching up on sleep, Sasha boiled water for tea. As assam steeped in the pot they fell asleep atop the duvet and slept an hour while the sun appeared, and the room warmed, and the tea became bitter and undrinkable. Walter rose and dressed, and as Sasha slept, he kissed him goodbye on the temple—lightly, not wanting to wake him—and let himself out. It wasn't yet seven.

What's the difference? he wondered as he entered the elevator, all brass and marquetry, ornate as a sun god's chariot. Pressing the starred knob for the lobby, he dropped swiftly from the tenth floor and exited through the grand foyer, all champagne walls and ebony trim. *What's the difference?* he asked the doorman, who tipped his derby and smiled indulgently. And the enormous columns with their thousand ears heard his question but gave no answer.

Walter never told Cary about the night he and Sasha saw *Grand Hotel*, thinking he was sparing her and protecting their relationship. But he might as well have, because what he'd learned from Sasha that night—*finally, and beyond a doubt*—was that *they* were a thing of the past, that there was no returning to the way things had been between the three of them.

It doesn't matter. It's better this way. He couldn't be with Sasha without Cary. And now it seemed that, all along, the three of them had been volatile, an unstable molecule, a little too much heat and their fragile equilibrium was blown, repelling Sasha and leaving him and Cary sluggish.

So often he marveled at how many of Cary's prophecies came to pass. Many of them were self-fulfilling, of course, but in some instances the universe seemed to be bending inexorably to her biases. He had gotten into the University of Chicago, as she'd predicted. In the end he couldn't resist going; the school, the program, the aid package—they were far and away the best deal he got. It spelled the end of their relationship, just as she'd said it would. She wouldn't move, she wouldn't do long distance, even if he flew back as often as he could. They came to an excruciating impasse and broke up in early summer, two months before Walter planned to move in August. At length it was simply too painful to stay together, knowing the end was looming, so they broke up in hopes of salvaging their friendship, only to discover that friendship, for the time being, was too painful as well.

No doubt it's written somewhere—some ancient codex or ledger of comparative heartbreak—that early summer is unquestionably the most painful time for a breakup. End a love affair in early June, and all you will see, all summer long, is the rest of humanity pairing off, flirting shamelessly on sidewalks and subway platforms, strolling in lockstep, pair-bonded at street fairs, clogging botanical gardens with wedding parties, packing picnics and driving off to secluded greens and secret beaches, to celebrate—and consummate—new love.

Never, ever break up in June. Break up in January.

From: "Cary Menuhin" <bombolone@hotmail.com>
To: "Walter Simmering" <wsimmering@uchicago.edu>
Subject: Re: Fall Break
Date: Mon, 16 Sept 1996 12:29:55 PDT

Dearest Amanda,

Imagine my shock and disorientation upon receiving electronic mail from Walter Simmering, notorious Luddite and technophobe! What's next? If you call me from a cellular telephone my heart will stop dead, and it'll be all your fault. Incidentally this is only my second missive from this account. "Brave new world!" as you'd say.

Gothic revival architecture with corn motifs . . . the Midway Plaisance . . . chili cheese dogs in the business school . . . Hyde Park certainly sounds like heaven, for someone. OF COURSE "History of Silent Film" is your favorite class, that is so you, the most Simmering thing you could have Waltered. So Simmering it's boiling. We're all rocketing toward the new millennium, and you're stuck in the belle epoque, flying to the moon with Georges Melies.

Please do come visit for the *Miss Otis Regrets* revival! We've begun regular rehearsals with Calypso and Co. All's well, although god, puppeteers are oddballs. They're all freaks and extroverts, like actors, only they're cripplingly shy: *Everyone watch as I invisibly pull all the strings!* Kelly's the exception, of course, pure extrovert that she is.

I'm still heartbroken that S. won't join us, believe me I tried, I begged, but my powers of persuasion failed me. On the bright side, Kelly was able to book us at the Stage Door downtown. A real goddamn venue, six hundred seats and an old vaudeville theater to boot! You know I'm thrilled about that. It would be so good to have you here to help celebrate. Stay with me. We may be crowded out by boxes at that point, but we'll make it work. I'm still blindsided and unprepared for the move, I admit. But having you here ought to cheer me up.

Your doting,
C.M.

P.S. Aside to Basilisk: If Walter gets too mopey and depressed, please bite him firmly on the ass, right where butt cheek meets thigh. That usually does the trick.

Midnight at the Cinema Palace

THERE WAS SOMETHING WRONG WITH the sky. The color was off—by a shade or two. Walter lay back in the grass on the slope, and from where he was lying could see nothing but sky and the shadow-bluff of Sasha's shoulder looming beside him.

"I feel like I'm staring through a filter," he said. "A pale yellow filter. The light is too gold." The sky was cloudless, but high above them, two jet trails had been drawn, stuttered like chalk marks, and were expanding, diffusing. In color they, too, were off slightly. Chalk yellow.

"It's smoke in the air from the wildfire," said Sasha. "North of Sacramento. Yesterday I swore I saw falling ash."

"Really? Yikes! It's warm, too, isn't it? For late October? This must be what LA is like."

Walter sat up, too fast, and the rush of sensations that comprised Dolores Park lunged at him: the height of the hill they sat upon, the large palms that studded the park and lined Dolores, the birdsong he liked to imagine came from escaped parrots. To their right, above a palm tree round as a planet, shone the weighty gold Beaux-Arts dome of a church; to their left, beyond the tennis courts, the domed bell tower of Mission High, Spanish baroque, tan and teeming. In the distance between, the downtown skyline, jagged as a broken comb, appeared hazy, eerily yellowed. It was midmorning, still early on a Sunday, yet the park was scattered with people. Some had slept there—and slept still—bundled up on cardboard or in the cool arid grass. Club kids circled like pigeons, still tweaking from a long night out. Then came the morning wanderers, like them, with coffee.

"How was the show last night?" asked Sasha. "I'm sure they managed just fine without me."

"It was wonderful, I was so impressed. Cary, Kelly, Nick . . . they really got it together on this one. I'm sad you weren't in it, though. It would have been better with you." This sounded like flattery but was true. Cary had done her best—she gave it her all when performing songs herself—but when Nick pinch-hit on the duets, it was clear his musical gifts were in his fingers alone. "Cary's worked hard on her playing. I think she's improved a lot."

"She might just get to be Django Reinhardt after all someday," said Sasha. "I don't put anything past her. Is she furious that I skipped opening weekend?"

"Yes," said Walter. "Silly question. Of course she is."

Sasha combed the grass with one hand, beheading and strewing white clover blossoms. "Whatever—it's fine. I'll catch it next weekend. And you went with Fiona? How's Fiona?"

"Glam as ever! It was great to see her. She's still at Good Vibes—still selling toys and breaking hearts. Too bad she couldn't be a full-time mermaid, she killed at that job."

"Who knew being a mermaid doesn't pay?" said Sasha. "I was always surprised she could hold still long enough for that gig. She's a perpetual motion machine."

"She hasn't slowed down a bit! She wanted us all to go to a warehouse party last night after the show. Even Kelly had to beg off. Imagine, Kelly Calypso, too tired for a rave? Something's changed there."

Sasha laughed and eyed his watch. "Speaking of sleepyheads . . . shall we see if Cary's awake yet?"

"Doubtful, but let's see . . ."

They stood and shuffled down the slope, then cut over to the sidewalk that curved down along the light-rail tracks to Eighteenth Street. Walter talked more about *Miss Otis Regrets*. The solid turnout meant the show might break even. If they made a little money, Cary and Kelly were thinking of extending the run.

"I'm very impressed they booked the Stage Door," said Sasha, "and nearly filled it! I'm happy for them. I hope it lasts."

"I think Cary'll make it last—I don't put anything past her, either, as you know."

Sasha was as dressed down as Walter had ever seen him, in jeans and a shapeless gray top, almost a smock. The outfit might have disturbed Walter if he hadn't known what was in store for them, that they planned to help Cary with painting. Anyway, it hardly mattered what Sasha was wearing, because he looked gorgeous as ever: graceful, vibrantly at ease, green eyes lively as they strolled and chatted. His hair was pulled into a loose ponytail at the back of the neck, like Catherine Deneuve's in *The Umbrellas of Cherbourg*. Walter had an old urge to reach for Sasha's hand as they walked, but they each had coffee—and they hadn't seen each other in months—it felt awkward.

They neared Eighteenth and Church and turned toward the Castro, and a rank stench of urine and trash accosted them as they passed an enormous garbage bin parked on the street, piled with the scooped innards of an entire house. Half a block later they were enveloped in jasmine. Pink-tipped tendrils wove through a galvanized gate, exhaling sweetness.

Sasha shared his big news: he was traveling to Paris and London in early spring. He'd convinced Jabez to go with him, since Jabez knew both cities well and Sasha had never been.

"The truth is," Sasha admitted, a little sheepishly, "I'm scouting out places to move."

"You're thinking of moving? To *Paris*? Or *London*?"

"Well, not forever. Maybe for a few years? We'll see. I'm not sure how it would work. I've been longing for something new, thinking of getting into fashion, into designing. Not sure if I'll need to go to school—I already have the construction skills and experience—I know how to pattern and stuff, obviously. That's half the battle, I think. The other half is connections, which I'm not going to make here . . ."

"Hold on—when is this happening?"

"Spring—we'll be in Paris for fashion week—*isn't that amazing?*"

"That is amazing," said Walter, feeling envious yet excited for Sasha. "It's *so hard* for me to think of you living somewhere other than San Francisco! Or rather, it's impossible for me to imagine San Francisco without you." He caught himself pouting, then shook it off. "SF will be depleted without you."

"Well, that's the thing," Sasha went on. "I feel like I've been timid, thinking about where I could travel . . . where I could live. I've always thought, *I can't help being me.* The way I am, I'm always going to stick out, even dangerously so. But if I assume that this city is the *only place* I can be happy and comfortable in my own skin, without seeing something of the world . . . I'm cutting myself off in advance, aren't I?"

Walter nodded. Getting into fashion was a no-brainer for Sasha, it was brilliant and obvious and necessary. Now he fervently wished that the Chunnel extended to Chicago.

"Of course, it's the kind of move that Cary would never sanction. *Paris and London?* They don't have anything on San Francisco, do they? You saw how she was about your move."

"It's true"—Walter laughed—"she's still mad."

The night before, after the show, he and Cary had met up with Jeff at the Pilsner, got roaring drunk, and closed the place down. Back on Eureka Street they shared Cary's bed, which she'd wedged between bookshelves in what had been her office. She could no longer sleep in the back room by the garden, sleeping alone in Sasha's jungle paradise was more than she could take. Though he was crashing with her, they had made a choice not to fuck around, since they were trying their best to stay friends and have some boundaries.

But then—boundaries be damned—they climbed under the covers, and soon they were spooning. Cary crushed him from behind in a bear hug. Ten minutes later she was snoring loudly in a little oblivion, eons away, while he lay awake, trying to decipher titles on spines in the dark.

"Do you know what she said to me last night?" He laughed. "We were falling asleep, and right before she dropped off, she said, *I will never forgive you for leaving.*"

"Oh god!" Sasha shook his head. "She probably means it, too!"

"I'm sure she does!"

They stopped for a minute to admire a pair of pristine Victorians on the south side of the street, walled off from the sidewalk, three stories tall, steep switchbacked staircases rising to their porticos. One of these conjoined twins was painted in shades of taupe, the other in garish pinks and oranges, cobalt flash glass in the windows. It seemed impossible to admire the aesthetic of one without condemning that of the other. They stood proud in their mirrored aesthetic worlds.

Walter thought, *Those neighbors hate each other.*

"Speaking of things I'll never live down," he said as they moved on, "Cary's still in a snit about our screenplay. Apparently it's my fault we never did anything with it, since I was the one who left for grad school. I think she imagines we'd be writing screenplays for Martin Scorsese by now."

"Typical, right? There are just a couple practical steps missing in her thought process."

"The thing is, I spend ten minutes with her, and suddenly I'm convinced that she's right about everything. There probably isn't any city, in the US at least, where I'm likely to be happier. It's been six weeks, and so far I can't forgive Chicago for not being San Francisco. Maybe, like she says, our screenplay *is great*, maybe writing for movies *is our destiny.* She always wanted us to dream as big as possible. It was always: *Let's start our movie with an aerial shot flying in from the ocean! Let's have a nightclub made of alabaster! Let's have an entire cinema palace collapse and burn to the ground! The production team can work out the details.* Production team? No one was going to invest that kind of money in the dreams of two gay nobodies."

"I get it—she starts dreaming big, and it's intoxicating."

Walter sighed. "Thinking about our screenplay now makes me sad."

"Why should it? You should be proud of it, I think!"

"The truth is, even though it took us *forever* to write, we were *so into it.* And it became real to me, that version of San Francisco; it started to have a life of its own. Declan, Lorna, Milo . . . for a while they became more real to me than some people I've known. Cary said the same. It's like this whole dimension that might have been, that no one will ever know about. Its fate is to live in a drawer, gathering dust."

"But, Wall, don't you think that's the fate of most art? To sit gathering dust somewhere? If you think about it . . ."

"Ugh, that is grim! I'm not sure I like where this is going . . ."

"If you think about it," said Sasha, "in the history of the world, the vast majority of artworks were probably seen or appreciated briefly, if ever, before they were thrown out, or lost, or destroyed. Most artists are anonymous. Most art is lost. Don't you think?"

"Are you trying to cheer me up? If so, you're doing a terrible job."

Past Sanchez Street, the sidewalks crowded. The neighborhood was up and about, the brunch set out in droves, hungover and frisky, off to cruise each other while waiting in line for an hour at the Patio or Luna Piena. Around Noe Street, perennial Sunday garage sales junked the sidewalks with tables and shelves, molded patio chairs, boom boxes, roller caddies, the cracked plastic husks of modern domesticity and planned obsolescence. One sprawling sale sucked them into its force field, and they browsed for a while. Sasha examined Depression glass while Walter picked through several crates of dollar apiece VHS tapes, mostly bad '80s movies and some porn. Still, he couldn't help sifting for overlooked gems.

"I meant to tell you," said Walter, "it's so exciting—there's a film of Lawrence's in Chicago. It's at the Video Data Bank—on VHS, which, you know, Larry hated video. No idea if the copy is any good, I haven't had a chance to see it. But if it's good, if there's enough there, I might be able to build a thesis around it."

"That *is* exciting," said Sasha. "Any chance they have more of his works? Jabez says there's some dispute over the films they found at the Archers."

"It's such a mess! You know, after the fire, I'm not sure how many of his films still exist, or what state they're in, or if there's enough to do anything with them. On the other hand, I'm glad the whole damn building didn't burn down!"

Months before, Jabez had related to him the saga of the fire's aftermath, how most of the fire damage had been contained to the ballroom, the lobby, and the second floor. The cavalry had arrived in time: the hotel wouldn't need to be razed. The basement storage units, however, were flooded. Jabez spun a hair-raising tale of how he and the super had unlocked Lawrence and Roland's storage units to find a dripping, sooty pulp of cardboard boxes, ruptured and gutting their contents: ruined books and clothes, keepsakes mummified in newsprint. Buried among these were boxes of films in various formats (Super 8, 16mm, 35mm, VHS) in various states of disorder and decay. Some had no canisters and had unspooled into celluloid rats' nests. Some were visibly molding. The whole wet mess of it had gone to the Berkeley archive for them to sort out, if they could. The story made Walter's skin crawl, although Jabez helped answer a question that had been nagging at him. Lawrence couldn't have intended to set fire to the Archers specifically. In his will, the hotel ballroom had been one venue among many, low down on the list of places he'd suggested for his memorial service. Topping the list was Dolby Labs.

Walter held up a well-worn copy of *Steel Magnolias*. "Worth a dollar?"
Sasha shrugged.

"And then there's Lawrence's mom," he went on, putting the tape back. "Let's say, Victoria's a bit crazy. And a little intractable. She wants what's left of those films with her in London—Lord knows what she wants to do with them, stuff a mattress? She's disputing Larry's will, which, I get it. It's written in pencil on a brown paper bag. So whether his films will stay at the archive is up in the air."

"It would be wonderful, though, if there's enough of Lawrence's work left for you to study, wouldn't it?"

"Oh yeah—it feels like a rescue mission. I've been calling around everywhere, because Jay said that Roland, being the practical one, would send prints out to film festivals and usually tell the organizers to keep them. Or he'd send duplicates or videos directly to archives. It was Roland who sent that video to Chicago, thank god."

"I'm so sad that we never met him," said Sasha. "Roland sounded so amazing. Anyone who could have captured Lawrence's heart, you know?"

They strolled on toward Castro Street, having resisted the grubby, sun-bleached wares of the sidewalk sale and those of several others. Through its eerie autumnal filter the yellow day was mockingly beautiful, as if admonishing them for imagining there might be another city in the world worth living in.

"Promise me something," said Walter, "when you go to Paris—"

"You want a *Venus de Milo* beer koozie from the Louvre?"

"No! Do they have those? No! Sashenka, promise me you'll go to that famous cemetery outside the city and kiss Oscar Wilde's grave for me."

Sasha took his hand, squeezed it, and held fast, pulling him forward. "I promise! I'll put on a whole tube of lipstick and kiss it a thousand times."

At Castro they ducked into Cliff's Variety to pick up a few things Cary had said she still needed: Spackle, sandpaper, a couple drop cloths. It was only as they were checking out that Walter was struck by the awfulness of the task ahead of them—a task he had offered to help with because of its awfulness.

"This fucking sucks. Why couldn't the new owners let her stay in the apartment? Aren't there tenants' rights laws or something?"

"You've heard the stories," Sasha said, "about how you're allowed to evict someone if you say you're moving a family member into the unit? They say landlords are evicting people so their so-called granny or second cousin twice removed can move in for one month. Then they move them right out again and double the rent!"

"You guys said Barry was a sweet old gay hippie. He wouldn't have sold the place to assholes like that, would he?"

"Apparently he did," said Sasha.

At Diamond Street they stopped in Cala Foods to get sandwich stuff for lunch. Deli meat, cheese, soft sliced bread, and sweet pickles. Despite her significant culinary chops, that summer Cary had reverted to bachelor mode, keeping virtually nothing in the house but canned soup and Tostitos. As they neared the apartment, Sasha admitted he was nervous to see the state of the place after Cary had lived alone for the better part of a year.

"I get it, but so much of her stuff is packed up in moving boxes now—it looks pretty tidy." Walter laughed with nervous frustration. "I'm sorry, but even if she has to move out, I still don't understand why Cary has to repaint the whole apartment herself."

"We put a pretty hefty deposit on the place—and I'd like my half back, too, you know. I'm not *just* here out of the kindness of my heart."

"Yes you are, Sashenka."

As they turned onto Eureka, Walter felt a wave of intense sadness at the task before them. Dread darkened Sasha's green eyes.

"I'm glad you're here for this," said Sasha, squeezing his hand again.

"I'm glad I'm here to help, too." He squeezed back. "I mean, this might be the last thing in the world I want to do right now! I might prefer getting a root canal. But I'm glad I'm here."

They found Cary in the kitchen. On the counter by the sink were half-packed U-Haul boxes, blooming bubble wrap that caught the sunlight. She was drinking coffee and strumming through "Miss Otis Regrets" on the Gretsch, which sounded cold and tinny un-amped. She was awake and upbeat, unduly excited that they had brought her sandwich fixings and painting tarps. She wore a tank top and some ocher-colored work pants held up by suspenders.

"You look like you're off to paint murals in Coit Tower for the WPA," said Sasha.

"*Exactly* the look I was going for." Cary winked.

They started in the burgundy living room, shoving the furniture and boxes into the center and draping it all in old sheets, like a kid's fort. Cary had started spackling; there were rough plaster stars on the widest wall where she'd displayed her guitar beside the Django shrine. Above, soot blackened the ceiling from all the votives burned there over the years.

There were only two rollers, so Walter and Cary took them to tackle opposite walls, as Sasha did some sanding and detail work with a brush. Cary laid down a tray and began to pour paint into it, viscous and synthetic smelling, catching drips with a brush. Dipping a fresh roller into the tray, she rolled back and forth, blue fleece soaking in white latex.

"It's definitely going to take two coats," said Cary, standing back from her work. The thick bands of paint were drying to a hideous purple beige. "Maybe three."

"Why do people love white walls so much?" Walter asked, rolling paint petulantly. He laid it on too thick, and the roller stalled and slipped, the paint streaking and dripping. He began again, more methodically, watching as the white roller swiftly drained every ounce of life and character from their once *living womb*.

"I'd better do some sanding in the back room," said Sasha. "That'll take several coats as well."

Alone together, Cary and Walter barely talked as they worked. Mona Lisa was perched imperially on a plinth of white-draped boxes, like an

Egyptian goddess who had subjugated and enjoined them to paint her tomb. Squinting, she monitored Cary's progress.

"How's Basilisk?" Cary no doubt felt the weight of Mona Lisa's gaze on her back.

"Belligerent as ever, I'm glad to report. He hates that I won't let him outside to explore Hyde Park. He bites me every chance he gets and scratches if I try to pet him. He's definitely waiting for me to die so he can eat my head. It's going great!"

"Belligerent Basilisk. Cat after my own heart," said Cary, dropping onto the couch beside Mona Lisa and gathering the creature up on her shoulder like a stole. "It was prescient of Larry, wasn't it? I mean, that he knew how much you needed that cat."

"Prescient, or diabolical?"

"Same difference."

They finished two coats in the living room and went to help Sasha. The back room, where they'd spent so many nights together, was now empty except for a kitchen chair and two tarps spread across the floor. Sasha stood on the chair, sanding away at a cloud bank in the absinthe sky. Under his touch the mural was softly dissolving, reverting to plaster.

"I shouldn't have painted this so thickly in the first place," said Sasha. "And in oil, what was I thinking?" He moved the chair over a foot or so, stood upon it again, and began sanding away at the portals of the jade-colored ocean liner that Walter had spent hours wondering over, imagining the passengers, the intrigues playing out inside the suites, as it eternally sailed the skies over their dream jungle, and yet never moved.

Beside him, Cary swallowed hard, then coughed. "OK, then," she said, and set down her paint tray and raised her roller.

Walter couldn't bear to watch. "I need a cigarette," he said, backing away, letting himself out into the garden.

The garden was no retreat, however, from the upheaval being wrought inside. Somehow, while staying with Cary, he hadn't noticed that the new owners had already begun overhauling the garden. As he smoked on the stiff-backed bench with its tough iron rosettes, he realized it was one of the only elements of the garden still in place. Looking around, nearly everything else had been or was in the process of being dug up. The little forest of bamboo and budding camellias were cut down and piled up like so much brush destined for the burn pile. A large bucket, its handle clasped by the cartoon hand of a red rubberized glove, stood heaped with wilting uprooted hostas. The two fern-fronded Waggie palms had been dug up, their roots wrapped carefully in burlap. They leaned exhausted against the neighboring fence. The massive pink begonia that grew beneath the kitchen window had disappeared entirely—as far as he could remember, it had never stopped blooming.

There was evidence of new designs being set in motion: a pallet stacked with bags stuffed to bursting with gravel and mulch; short sheets of rolled steel, rusted red orange; piles of shale blocks, iridescent blue. Beside him stood a tower of old flagstones, newly exhumed, soil encrusted. Lying on top of them, as if on a Viking pyre, was the painted cement gnome that used to huddle among the hostas. Now retired, relegated to a stiff bedrest, he winked at the sky. It seemed senseless that this overgrown, barely tended garden, which had responded so robustly to neglect, should be sacrificed to someone's grand design.

It was bright in the garden, and the windows were almost opaque with brilliant reflections, though not quite brilliant enough to blind him to what was taking place inside. He could see through shadowy patches into the room where Cary and Sasha chatted as they worked. The door was ajar, and he caught fragments of their talk, amid the occasional shriek of traffic from Eighteenth Street nearby. He cowered on the bench and sucked in smoke as they took rollers and began blotting out Sasha's green Xanadu with wide white stripes. It was sickening—and they just kept painting, ruthlessly—he didn't know how they could do it. Especially Sasha, who stood on the chair stretching high into the corner, blotting out swaths of pale green sky with a single swift movement of the roller. It was a matter of minutes before their dreamworld would be fully whitewashed, all its verdant flora snuffed out in a few rash strokes. He went lightheaded, his heart racing, and he dropped his head into his hands, eyes shut tight to stave off tears.

Raising his head again, he thought he must be dreaming. Over the garden walls, out of the pale yellow blue, came flakes of ghostly gray, floating light as poplar blossoms. For a moment the sky teemed with a squall of ash—spiraling atomically—innumerable, yet so sparse he might have imagined it.

Sasha had said there were wildfires—where exactly? Near Sacramento? If so, the ash had made a long journey for something so ephemeral. Was it ash from a nearby burn pile? Maybe Mount Diablo was erupting over Stockton—anything seemed possible. Was it errant ash from the Archers Hotel, touring for months before reaching this garden? Or ash from another realm—from the Silver City Palace? The cigarette he was holding had blown out—could it be ash from his own hand? It hadn't been real, *how ridiculous*. It must have been in his eyes—floaters—mere shadows in the vitreous of his eyes.

The room was white. Had they thought to take photos? It didn't matter. Pictures or no pictures, he knew soon he would doubt if Sasha's mural had ever existed.

It was then he knew that he would leave this garden, this apartment, the city and people he loved best, only to spend years in utter disbelief that everything he'd experienced here could have been real; that he had lived an ecstatic year or two; that he had felt such intense joy and, simultaneously, the dread of its loss. It was awful, the ephemerality of it all, confined to feeble memory, as every moment lived eventually, relentlessly, assumed the guise of a dream.

His friends would be OK, of course, no matter what. Sasha and Cary, they were shapeshifters. And shapeshifters have futures like galaxies: too bright and far-flung to observe directly, too numerous to count.

I will never forgive you for leaving.

Cary was right, in a way. He was the one who'd fucked it all up by leaving. And he'd left, he saw now, because he'd rather freeze joy in time, in memory, than endure its uncertain transformation. So he'd confine himself to a dusty carrel or an unlit archive, and there he'd stay, searching through notebooks, through celluloid scraps, for proof that any of it had happened at all, in anything like the way he remembered. He'd be the one scrambling to piece it all back together, staving off oblivion with scribbling, with words, archiving shadows for posterity. He would be the fool forever running from the burning palace, carrying the ashes of the arsonist.

Acknowledgments

I AM FOREVER GRATEFUL TO my writers group—Gregory Hewett, Emily Oliver, and Bonnie Nadzam—who read draft upon endless draft and responded, not with tears of exasperation, but with unfailing warmth, encouragement, and incisive critique. I am indebted to friends who read early versions and provided crucial feedback, including Jonathan Kauffman, Lon Troyer, Miles Ott, Cade McCall, and Maria Vendetti. My memory needed regular prodding: thank you to Kim Tradowsky Porter, J. Carlos Perez, Steffan Schlarb, Pete Howells, Megan Vossler, and Amey Mathews for sharing recollections of a receding time and place.

On the topic of noir: in addition to the films celebrated in the novel, I was inspired by the innovative and ingenious queer noir of San Francisco playwright Sean Owens. Thank you to Kathryn Wood for the femme fatale lessons, which were truly lessons in life. Please accept this dissertation in partial fulfillment of degree requirements. I found inspiration as well in the beguiling noir poetry of James Cihlar, the biggest Barbara Stanwyck fan I know.

I am grateful to the Lambda Literary Foundation and to Chuck Forester for establishing the life-changing J. Michael Samuel Prize.

Thank you to my agent, Kent Wolf, for his cool head and wise counsel. Many thanks to Olivia Taylor Smith and Brittany Adames for the affection they showed my bevy of queer characters. Thank you to the team at Simon & Schuster for the care they took with this book.

Thank you to my parents for supporting—or cheerfully tolerating—every creative project I've ever attempted, even the most harebrained, and to my siblings for their lifelong love and support. Finally, boundless love to my husband, Ross Elfline, best friend and better half, there for me through every hairpin turn in this *cockeyed caravan*. I am inspired, every day, by your courage and resilience.

About the Author

CHRISTOPHER TRADOWSKY is a writer, artist, and art historian. He was awarded the J. Michael Samuel Prize from Lambda Literary in 2023 and the BLOOM Literary Journal Prize for fiction in 2013. He earned a PhD in art history from UCLA. He teaches undergraduate art history and mentors in the creative writing MFA program at Augsburg University in Minneapolis. He lives in St. Paul with his husband. *Midnight at the Cinema Palace* is his debut novel.